After a career in the
Brenda Clarke begar
children had left sch
has written about tw
of which were publi:
maiden name of Bre

Brenda Clarke lives with her husband in
Keynsham, Bristol.

Also by Brenda Clarke

AN EQUAL CHANCE

and published by Corgi Books

Sisters and Lovers

Brenda Clarke

CORGI BOOKS

SISTERS AND LOVERS

A CORGI BOOK 0 552 13556 9

Originally published in Great Britain by
Bantam Press a division of Transworld Publishers Ltd

PRINTING HISTORY
Bantam Press edition published 1990
Corgi edition published 1991

This book is set in 10/11 pt Cheltenham Book Medium
by Colset Private Limited, Singapore.

Corgi Books are published by Transworld Publishers Ltd.,
61–63 Uxbridge Road, Ealing, London W5 5SA, in Australia by
Transworld Publishers (Australia) Pty. Ltd., 15–23 Helles
Avenue, Moorebank, NSW 2170, and in New Zealand by
Transworld Publishers (N.Z.) Ltd., Cnr. Moselle and Waipareira
Avenues, Henderson, Auckland.

Made and printed in Great Britain by
Cox & Wyman Ltd, Reading, Berks.

PART ONE

1960–1

1

WHEN SHE PUSHED OPEN the kitchen door, there were the customary smells of damp washing and boiled potatoes which Joanna associated with Monday evenings. Whether coming in from the cold of winter or the heat of summer, it was always the same: piles of unironed clothes in untidy heaps; the remains of Sunday's joint sliced on to the blue-and-white meat-dish which had once belonged to Grandma Harding; a saucepan of potatoes boiled almost dry on the stove; her mother nowhere to be seen.

Joanna opened the door leading into the hall and shouted: 'Mum! I'm home!'

Jean Marshall clattered downstairs, her soft brown hair escaping in wisps from the pony-tail at the back of her head. Her grey eyes wore their perpetually worried expression, as though she found domestic life a trial, which she did.

'Where's Terry?' she asked, and Joanna experienced the familiar prickle of irritation.

'It's her games night. She's playing hockey. She told you this morning. I heard her.'

'Did she?' Jean put up a hand and pushed a strand of hair away from her eyes. 'Now you mention it, I believe she said something.'

Joanna explained patiently: 'She's in the school eleven, and there are a couple of big matches coming up before we break for the Easter holidays. She can't cut practice.' She nodded towards the kitchen. 'I think the potato-saucepan has nearly run dry.'

7

As her mother gave a despairing moan and dived through the open doorway, Joanna went on upstairs, humming the current number one hit, 'My Old Man's a Dustman', under her breath. On the first-floor landing she paused for a moment, then moved towards the room overlooking the back garden of the old Victorian house, which had been Grandfather Harding's for the past four years, ever since he had come to live with them following Grandma Harding's death at the comparatively early age of fifty-five.

Joanna tapped on the door and went in.

'I'm home, Gramps.'

Reginald Harding looked up from the book he was reading and smiled.

'Hello, love. Had a good day at school?'

Joanna nodded, crossed to her grandfather's chair and stooped to kiss him.

'Not bad.' She always said that, regardless of the truth. She dumped her bulging satchel on the floor by the chest of drawers and perched on the arm of his chair. 'What are you reading?'

Reginald flicked the book shut to reveal the title *Cider with Rosie* and the name Laurie Lee.

'You should read it,' he suggested. 'It's beautiful. It's about the author's childhood in a Cotswold village.'

'I'll borrow it before you take it back to the library.' Joanna giggled. 'Perhaps *I'll* write a book one day. "*A Bath Childhood*, by Joanna Marshall." How does that sound?'

Her grandfather laughed and shook his head. 'It doesn't have the same ring to it. Besides, there have been too many books written about Bath: histories, architectural studies, novels.' He glanced at his favourite granddaughter's face, paler than usual beneath the heavy fringe of brown hair. The thickly lashed blue eyes had half-moons of tiredness underneath them. 'Much homework?' he asked sympathetically.

Joanna grunted. 'It's O-levels year,' she said, offering no further explanation.

Reginald Harding had no need of one. Until his retirement, six weeks earlier, at the age of sixty, he had been one of Her Majesty's Inspectors for Schools, a position he had held for the past ten years after an adult lifetime spent in teaching.

'Never mind,' he consoled her. 'You're not going to find it such hard going as your twin.'

Joanna sighed, slipping off the arm of his chair and picking up her satchel.

'I'm not so sure that's true, Gramps.'

All the girls had called him that since they were little and had been taken to dinner every Sunday at their Harding grandparents' home overlooking Henrietta Park. Reginald Harding had never objected to the title, although he had always been a very young-looking man for his age. He still looked nowhere near his sixty years: a small clean-shaven man, as neat and precise in his habits as his daughter Jean was disorganized and untidy. Bernard Marshall was often overheard to remark wistfully that his father-in-law's room was the only one in the house where you could find anything. This was not strictly true. The twins' bedroom was equally spick and span. Joanna had inherited her grandfather's love of order.

She went on: 'Terry's one of those people who seem able to absorb great chunks of knowledge without actually trying. She doesn't do half the studying I do, but her end-of term results are always heaps better than mine. She never does any revision, either, until the last minute. It's just not fair.' But Joanna grinned as she spoke. She loved her sister Theresa more than anyone else on earth.

Reginald Harding reflected that, for identical twins, the two girls were remarkably dissimilar in character; living contradiction of one of his pet theories that people who looked alike *were* alike. Theresa, the elder of the two by half an hour, was a thoroughgoing extrovert. Joanna was much quieter: a listener, not a talker, always ready to lend an ear or a hand wherever it was needed. Other people's problems never bored her, as they did her twin. She knew

9

more about Reginald's early life than all her three sisters put together, and had an instinctive sympathy for the difficulties of advancing age.

'How's the hip?' she asked now, one hand on the door-knob. 'I don't imagine this April weather does it much good.'

Her grandfather smiled gratefully at her. Jean never remembered to enquire.

'It hasn't been too bad today. I managed a walk in Victoria Park this afternoon without too much pain. I like to watch the children playing on the swings. By the way, did your mother tell you your Aunt Dora's coming to stay for Easter? She's *resting*, or whatever they call it, between jobs, and Jean foolishly gave her an invitation.' Reginald laughed. Any mention of his younger daughter always seemed to amuse him.

Joanna grimaced. 'Dad'll be furious. He can't stand Aunt Dora at the best of times, but especially not during the holidays.' She mimicked her father's voice. ' "I work damned hard during the term, Jean. Teaching maths to a lot of snotty-nosed kids is hardly a bed of roses. I feel I have every right to expect a little peace and quiet during my vacation!" Besides,' Joanna went on, gratified by her grandfather's roar of laughter, 'where's Aunt Dora going to sleep? Davey's home in four days' time, so she can't have *her* room. I suppose she'll have to sleep on the couch in the study. That'll make Dad crosser than ever. He's planning to work on that new maths text-book he's writing over Easter. Oh, well!' Joanna said resignedly. 'It looks as if we're in for a lively time.' She raised expressive eyes to the ceiling and went out. A moment later, she popped her head back in again. 'At least one person will be glad to see Aunt Dora. Freddie!'

As Joanna reached the top of the second flight of stairs, her younger sister, fourteen-year-old Freda, was just emerging from the small back bedroom which she had all to herself. Unlike the twins, she had never had to share, but it was still

10

a sore point with her that she was not allowed to have the big front bedroom, above her parents' first-floor room.

'It's not fair', she would argue hotly with her mother, 'that Davey should have it. She's not here all term, but I'm here all the time! If I'm going to be an actress like Aunt Dora – and I am! – nothing you and Dad can say will make me change my mind – then I need the space to rehearse. I need a big mirror, like the one in the front bedroom, to watch myself when I'm acting. To see what I'm doing right, or wrong.'

Jean Marshall recognized the justice of her youngest daughter's argument and was secretly in agreement with it, but her counter-argument was always the same and – to herself at least – equally valid.

'You know your father couldn't stand the noise with you stomping about overhead, spouting lines and playing that dreadful record-player at all hours of the day and night. If he hears another chorus of "Living Doll" at full belt, I don't think he'll be answerable for his actions.'

So Freda would retire, defeated, with *sotto voce* animadversions about people who didn't like Cliff Richard having no soul, and Jean would be left in peace until the next time.

Joanna paused in the act of humping her satchel into the room she shared with Theresa.

'Hi, Freddie! Did you know that Aunt Dora's coming for Easter? Gramps has just told me.'

'Great!' Freda moderated her first enthusiasm. 'Where's she going to sleep?'

'The couch in the study, I imagine. Davey'll be home, so she can't go in there.'

'Oh, good!' Freda was relieved. 'She won't have to share our bathroom.'

The girls had their own bathroom on the top floor, installed two years previously at – as their father was never tired of reminding them – considerable expense. The truth was that after his father-in-law had come to live with them, and with four daughters constantly washing

11

their hair, taking showers and doing their make-up, Bernard had found one bathroom totally inadequate and himself forever locked out.

'That reminds me,' Joanna said, 'you forgot to clean round the bath after you'd finished last night. I had to do it, as usual.'

'Sorry!' Freda apologized airily. 'I had a lot on my mind. The drama group has asked me to play Ellean in their summer production of *The Second Mrs Tanqueray.*'

'You're a bit young for that, aren't you?'

Freda smiled pityingly at her sister. 'I can pass for at least eighteen on stage. And I'm one of the best actresses they've got. You should come and see me some time.'

Without waiting for Joanna's reply, she swept regally down both flights of stairs to the kitchen, where a harassed Jean was still trying to salvage something from the wreck of the burned potatoes.

'Oh, not again, Mum!' Freda forgot whatever role she had been playing in her mind and became instantly practical. She glanced at the kitchen clock. 'Is there time to do any more?'

Jean shook her head. 'Your father'll be in any minute, and you know he likes his meal as soon as he gets home. And, anyway, I can't spare the time. Anthony Douglas is coming for his lesson at six, and I haven't even looked at what I'm doing with him this evening.'

Before the war and her marriage to Bernard Marshall, Jean had been a biology teacher at one of the Bristol schools. The family of four little girls who had arrived at regular intervals between February 1943 and January 1946 had compelled her to abandon her career. In recent years, however, she had begun to take evening pupils who needed extra biology tuition, and it was with an overwhelming sense of relief that she had turned from the inimical world of cooking, shopping and endless washing-up, which somehow she had never quite mastered, to the far less alien one of chromosomes and enzymes. She imparted her knowledge to reluctant young minds with an enthusiasm for her subject which often inspired in them an interest not previously felt.

In the case of Anthony Douglas this was unnecessary. He intended, with a single-mindedness which his extremely rich, but self-made and largely uneducated, parents found unnerving, to become a doctor. As biology was the weakest of his A-level subjects, mainly because he did not get on with his teacher at the exclusive and very expensive day-school he attended near Bath, a friend of his mother had recommended Jean Marshall, and he had started coming to Nightingale Close two nights a week, just after Christmas.

Freda had mashed and scraped as much of the potato as she could salvage into an oven-proof dish, and was now busy grating Cheddar cheese over the top. At the sound of Anthony Douglas's name, she glanced up and grinned.

'I'd forgotten he's coming tonight. That explains why Terry was cursing this morning about having to stay late for hockey practice. She wants to get properly tarted up before he arrives.'

Her mother frowned. 'I do wish you wouldn't use those vulgar expressions, Freddie.' She added anxiously: 'Are they still going out together?'

'Now and then. Mind you, I think Terry makes most of the running. She's definitely nuts about him. I don't know that *he's* so smitten, really. Of course, they've got a common interest, with him wanting to be a doctor and her determined to be a nurse.' Freda held out the dish to her mother. 'Pop that in the oven to heat through and melt the cheese. That bit of "mousetrap" is so strong, no one will notice the potatoes are burned. Give me the saucepan and I'll put it in soak.'

She was engaged with this mundane task when Theresa came through the back door in her usual tempestuous fashion. 'Terry the tearaway' her father had christened her when she was small; but habits so endearing in the toddler had proved less fascinating in the teenager. Her parents and sisters complained that her boundless energy

13

exhausted them; that she had only to be in the same room to make them feel tired. Theresa laughed good-naturedly at their criticisms: only Joanna knew that under the seeming indifference her twin was sensitive to other people's opinions.

'I know I make a lot of noise,' she would confide unhappily, 'but I can't help it, Jo. I'm restless. I hate sitting still. Knitting and sewing don't interest me. I've never been any good at them; I'm all thumbs. And if I see something, or think of something, I have to tell people straightaway. I can't bottle things up, like you and Davey.'

And that was perfectly true, Joanna thought now, as she slipped into the kitchen to find out how supper was progressing, just in time to hear Theresa's excited description, with appropriate actions, of the three goals she had scored during the practice hockey match. Her twin's voice and flailing arms seemed to fill the kitchen.

Fifteen minutes later, Bernard Marshall's five-year-old Ford Prefect turned into Nightingale Close, a cul-de-sac of tall Victorian houses erected towards the end of the previous century. It looked faintly romantic under the pale spring sky, and provided a small oasis of peace and tranquillity after the concentration of evening traffic building up along both the main routes between Bath and Bristol. As Bernard manoeuvred the Ford into the driveway of number four and got out to open the garage doors, a bright red Aston Martin sports-car came to a halt outside the house. The young man, still wearing school flannels and blazer, who swung himself nonchalantly over its side never failed to irritate Bernard Marshall.

'Hi, there!' Anthony Douglas smiled his winning smile and nodded towards his car. 'Like it? My parents gave it to me for my eighteenth birthday, last month.'

Bernard frowned, hitching his heavily framed glasses higher up the bridge of his nose. He did not approve of young people still at school receiving such expensive presents. Nor did he approve of the amassing of large fortunes out of the manufacture of pickles and sauce. Or the manufacture of anything, if it came to that. Bernard believed in socialism and the fair distribution of wealth.

'Is this a social call?' he demanded, passing no comment on the sleek and gleaming monster parked outside his gate. 'Do you want me to tell Theresa that you're here?'

'No, no! It's Monday, remember? Bio lesson with Mrs M.'

'Ah! Yes!' Bernard regarded the younger man with open hostility, his temper not improved by this reminder that it was the evening of the cold remains of the Sunday joint and, if Jean ran true to form, burned mashed potatoes. (How, in God's name, did anyone burn mashed potatoes?) He had had a particularly trying afternoon, attempting to reconcile the fourth form to the mysteries of Pythagoras' theorem, and vented his spleen on Anthony Douglas.

'That's some kind of Newspeak, is it?'

'Sorry?' The classically handsome face, with its straight nose and clear blue eyes, assumed a puzzled expression. ' 'Fraid I don't understand.'

'This verbal shorthand you use ... Orwell's *Nineteen Eighty-Four*.'

'Ah! Quite!' Clearly, neither the author's name nor the title meant anything to Anthony. He was, however, fully aware that Bernard did not like him, and was astute enough to guess the reason why. He mentally kicked himself for bringing the car. Unlike his father, Anthony had no wish to parade his family's wealth. He had merely succumbed to a very natural wish to impress Theresa, of whom he was mildly fond.

Warily, he followed Bernard Marshall into the house.

2

FOREST MOOR SCHOOL FOR GIRLS, unlike its rivals, Cheltenham Ladies' College and Roedean, was of comparatively recent date, having first opened its doors shortly before the outbreak of war, in the spring of 1939.

In the twenty-one years of its existence, however, it had gained a reputation quite as formidable as that of its competitors, both for academic and for sporting achievements, and places were as hard to come by as finding snow in the Sahara. Among those anxious to enter their daughters at some future date were oil-rich sheikhs from the Middle East, members of the British aristocracy, American millionaires; all of whom would learn, in due course, that money and privilege, by themselves, were simply not enough. Unless a girl had outstanding ability either in the classroom or on the playing-field, she would never be admitted to Forest Moor. If, on the other hand, she displayed talent in one or both of these areas, but her parents were unable to afford the extortionate fees demanded, an annual grant and generous allowances would be offered. 'The Robin Hood principle,' one disappointed parent had scathingly called it.

The Board of Governors, however, were perfectly happy with this state of affairs, and knew that the system of rigid selection was the basis of the school's spectacular examination results, and made it the cradle of so many sporting champions. Forest Moor was well able to support its scholarship pupils from the money poured into its coffers by the wealthy.

The school also had one other great asset: its headmistress, Anthea Marshall. Although still under thirty in 1939, she had been chosen from an impressive list of candidates – a few with better academic qualifications than hers – because the panel of selectors had recognized a quality of dedication in her, lacking, to a greater or lesser degree, in all the rest. They had realized that Anthea Marshall was totally committed to the ideas and ideals they wanted Forest Moor to represent; the belief that talent, whatever form it took, must be nurtured and encouraged in specialized surroundings, not left to be dissipated among the common herd.

The selectors had also recognized in Anthea a woman undistracted by anything or anybody outside her chosen profession. She was a born teacher, had no men friends, stated categorically that she was not interested in marriage, and was patently prepared to devote herself to Forest Moor for as long as she was needed. She had obtained a First Class Honours degree at Girton in Saxon and Medieval History, a subject which, as the panel of selectors saw it, had no relevance to modern times. Miss Marshall, the chairman pointed out, was unlikely to feel any sudden urge to go into politics or write long letters on the state of the economy to *The Times*.

Subsequent governors of the school had had no reason to disagree with that original assessment. During the war, the position of headmistress of Forest Moor had been considered of sufficient importance to be classified as Reserved; and apart from the bombing of Southampton, four miles distant, during the winter of 1940–1, life inside the school walls had continued almost undisturbed. It had also weathered the postwar Labour government, together with its brave new world; and now, with the Conservatives back in power for the past nine years, and looking set to continue well into the future under the benevolent guidance of 'Super Mac', there seemed no reason why Forest Moor should not continue to be among the top five or six girls' schools in the country.

17

There was only one slight cause for concern among the more forward-looking of the Board of Governors, as this Easter of 1960 approached. Anthea Marshall was about to celebrate her fiftieth birthday. Not old, by modern standards, and she would doubtless continue in harness for as long as she possibly could. It was not unreasonable to suppose that she would still be running Forest Moor well into the 1970s. But when she did eventually retire where were the Governors to find a similarly dedicated successor, a woman prepared to devote her entire life to the best interests of the school and to maintain the system virtually unchanged?

If certain members of the Board were losing sleep over the question, Anthea most certainly was not. Had they consulted her about the problem, she would have told them not to worry. She already had her successor in her eye: a girl being moulded and trained to step into Anthea's shoes when she at last felt the need to quit; a seventeen-year-old pupil at the school, who would sit her A levels the following year and pass them with flying colours. A girl who was destined for Oxford. Anthea's niece, Davina.

'You know you're not allowed to go into Southampton without supervision. Why did you break the rules?'

Davina, standing on the other side of the big leather-topped desk in the headmistress's study, cleared her throat nervously. In two days' time, when the school broke up for the Easter holidays, she and Anthea would travel home to Bath together, aunt and niece. During the next few weeks, Davina would be in and out of Anthea's Royal Crescent flat with the ease of someone who knew herself to be always welcome. But, for the moment, they were still head-mistress and pupil, and Davina was as nervous as any first-former when confronted with her aunt's displeasure.

'Well?' Anthea's blue eyes, so like her brother Bernard's, gazed sternly across the top of the desk. Davina did her best to avoid their look of accusation.

She glanced desperately around the study, although she knew every inch of its book-lined walls by heart. There was the marble mantelpiece – a feature of all the old eighteenth-century Forest Moor House rooms – with its carved swags of vines and ivy; underfoot, the familiar red, blue and ochre pattern of the Axminster carpet. There were two good reproductions on the cream-painted walls: a Tissot, 'The Gallery of HMS *Calcutta* (Portsmouth), 1876', and 'The Road to Sydenham' by Camille Pissaro.

On an inlaid marquetry table near the window was a small collection of framed photographs, pride of place being given to one of Anthea herself at her graduation ceremony, wearing cap and gown. Another, taken six years later, was of a young Bernard, similarly attired and looking, Davina always thought, insufferably pleased with himself. He featured again in a studio portrait of him and Jean taken shortly after their wedding day, in August 1940 – Bernard, on this occasion, looking uncomfortable in a badly fitting army uniform. Standing a little apart from the others was a photograph of a young air-force officer in a plain wooden frame, the white surround mottled with brown spots where the damp had, at some time, got to it. On the solitary occasion when Davina had plucked up sufficient courage to ask her aunt who he was, Anthea had replied discouragingly: 'A friend. Our paths crossed briefly during the war.' Further enquiries made at home elicited no more information. Neither Bernard nor Jean would own to any knowledge of him.

Looking at the photograph now, Davina wondered why her aunt should have kept it all these years, if it had no sentimental value for her.

Anthea's voice broke in on her wandering thoughts.

'Was it a boy? Did you go into Southampton to meet some young man? That's the usual reason, I find, for the sixth-formers breaking bounds.'

Davina lowered her eyes once more and studied the pattern of the carpet.

'Yes, Miss Marshall.'

'Look at me when I'm addressing you, Davina! That's better. Who is this boy and how did you meet him?'

'He's Irina Malenovsky's cousin. He came here with Irina's mother and step-father on Open Day, just after Christmas. He wrote to me last week to say he'd be in Southampton today on business, and would I see him? I wrote back and said "yes". I thought' – Davina's eyes slid away from her aunt's and concentrated on the view of open parkland and new school buildings outside the window – 'I thought it might be fun.'

'And was it?'

Davina could see two girls, in the school's dark green and white uniform, walking along the tree-lined path from the new science laboratory, donated and magnificently equipped by Texan oil millionaire Robert Cutler III, in recognition of what Forest Moor had achieved for his daughter, Luanne. She stared at the couple for a moment or two until they disappeared from sight, then switched her gaze back to her aunt.

'No,' she said flatly. 'It was very boring.'

It was Anthea's turn to lower her eyes, to hide the relief that they must be showing.

'Did this young man make a pass at you? I believe that's the popular expression.'

Sensing the lessening of tension in the atmosphere, Davina realized it would pay her to be completely honest.

'Yes, he did, but I didn't like it.'

'He kissed you? Where was this?'

'In the Civic Centre Art Gallery. We went there because it was warm.'

Anthea raised well-marked eyebrows. The thin mouth, carefully made up like the rest of the strong, almost masculine face, broke into a smile.

'How very unsophisticated! I should have expected Irina Malenovsky's cousin to have a car. One of those large flashy American things with fins.'

Davina giggled. 'He has. A car, I mean; but it's a Daimler. Very staid and awfully middle-aged. He wanted me to go for a drive with him, but I said "no", so we went in the art gallery instead. I don't think he was very pleased. Afterwards, he took me to tea at the Dolphin. Then he suggested he brought me back to school, but I wouldn't let him. I was tired of him by that time.' Davina spoke contemptuously. 'All he talked about was polo and his conquests of other women.'

Anthea leaned forward, linking her hands together on the desk. Somewhere, deep in the old house, a bell was ringing for the evening homework session in the main hall, from which sixth-formers were exempt. They had their own private bed-sitting-rooms for study.

'Sit down, Davina,' she said quietly. And when her niece had drawn up one of the straight-backed chairs which stood ranged against the walls she went on: 'I've been meaning to talk to you for some while, but I've kept putting it off because I'm not sure if you're ready yet for what I want to say to you. However, I don't think it can be delayed much longer, and with the Easter holidays coming up you'll have plenty of time to think about it.'

Anthea paused for a moment to consider the young face on the other side of the desk, and was amazed, as she so often was, by the strength of her love for this child. She had always been fond of Bernard, the brother six years her junior, and after their parents died, when she was twenty-five and he just starting out at university, at the age of nineteen, she had been, in some sort, a mother to him, always ready to offer advice or more practical help if it was needed. But she had never felt more than a mild affection for him, and after his marriage to fellow-teacher Jean Harding they had drifted apart. Anthea did not care for her sister-in-law, and as for her three younger nieces, she thought of them as pleasant enough girls, polite, deferential, but it wouldn't worry her if she never saw any of them again.

But Davina was different. From her earliest years, the child had touched a chord in Anthea Marshall's heart. She was so much brighter than her sisters and she liked learning

21

for its own sake. She had a natural ability to absorb and classify information, and although she was good at every subject she tackled, and brilliant at some, history was her great love. It had made for an even stronger bond between aunt and niece; and, long before she had left the infants' school, Davina was spending days of every holiday in Anthea's company, sleeping at the Royal Crescent flat so as to be ready for some new expedition the following morning to Glastonbury or Wells, to Malmesbury or Tewkesbury. They had explored deep into the heart of Somerset and Wiltshire and Gloucestershire, unravelling historical threads and delving into the past. Later, during the long summer vacations, Anthea took Davina abroad, to Paris and Rome, Delphi and Cairo. Fellow-holidaymakers often mistook them for mother and daughter, a misconception which neither of them bothered to correct unless it became imperative to do so.

And when Davina was ready for grammar school it was Anthea who had insisted on her sitting the entrance examination for Forest Moor.

'Don't worry about the fees,' she had told her brother and sister-in-law. 'I shall be paying.'

Neither of them had protested, although it would have been all the same if they had: she would have won that battle. She had always intended that Davina should be indebted to no one but herself for her education, and the major start in life that it would give her. If Bernard and Jean had tried to thwart her plans, she would have fought them tooth and nail. But they had not. She had always known in her heart of hearts that it would be an easy victory. They would never stop her seeing as much as she wanted of Davina.

She smiled at her niece to show that this afternoon's rather foolish and unworthy little escapade was forgiven if not forgotten. Girls would be girls, and there was bound to be some kicking over of the traces, although in Davina's case she would prefer it not to happen too often. Which was why she had made the decision to speak to the child now. It was time she understood and accepted her vocation.

'One day', Anthea said, speaking slowly and giving weight to every word, 'I want to see you sitting here, in this room, behind this desk, headmistress of Forest Moor. It won't be yet, and it will take some doing, but if anyone can achieve it you can.' She saw by the girl's startled expression that the idea was new to her; something Davina had never even considered. Anthea congratulated herself that she had not spoken a moment too soon. She went on: 'But it is a goal which will need single-minded dedication and a long preparation. A levels next year, with top grades to get you into Oxford. An Honours degree in Medieval History. Then a long hard slog, gaining experience, teaching in other schools. You must know the job from the bottom up to make a good headmistress. And a couple of books with your name on the covers would be of inestimable value to impress the Governors when, in twelve or fifteen years' time, I step down from this job and the post becomes vacant.' Anthea drew a deep breath, noting the girl's eyes, huge grey pools in an almost colourless face. 'But, as I said just now, it will take enormous dedication. There can be no distractions like boyfriends or marriage or a family. I detect so much of myself in you that I don't think you'll find these deprivations any hardship. *I* never have.' She indicated the room with a sweep of her arm. 'This school, my girls, the results we achieve are my home, my family, my friends. Don't say anything now! Just go away and think about it for a while. But I'm sure you'll find in the end that it's what *you* want, too.'

'Irina! Are you awake?'

Irina Malenovsky sat up in bed, startled to see Davina standing in the doorway of her room, a ghostly figure in the white cotton nightdress which the Forest Moor authorities considered appropriate night-time wear for spring and summer. Sixth-formers, with their many privileges, could choose what they liked, and it seemed typical, somehow, of Davina that she should keep strictly to regulation dress. Irina glanced at the illuminated dial of her bedside clock and saw that it was half-past two in the morning.

'What's the matter?' she hissed. 'Aren't you feeling very well?'

'I'm OK. I just couldn't sleep.' Davina came forward and sat on the edge of her friend's bed, shivering a little with cold. 'Rina, how important do you think marriage and children are?'

'You wake me up in the middle of the night to ask me this?' Irina was pardonably annoyed, and, as always when that happened, the mid-European accent, which defied specific identification, became more pronounced.

'It's important that I find out.' Davina reached for the other girl's dressing-gown and huddled into its folds of pale pink silk. 'I thought you might have some idea.'

'You're the one to know about families,' Irina pointed out, snuggling down again beneath the bedclothes. 'You're the one with all those sisters and a grandfather living at home. Even at school, you can't get away from family. Who else do you know who has an aunt for a head-mistress? Me, I'm just a nomad, wandering around Europe after my father and his fancy woman. I guess, in the end, it depends upon the person. Some people need marriage and all that goes with it. Some don't.'

3

'Darlings! How lovely to see you all! Girls! Come and kiss your Aunt Dora this instant and don't let me have any nonsense about being too old!'

Dora Whitlock had arrived in Bath thirty minutes earlier, and had taken a taxi from the station to Nightingale Close. It had been no surprise that there was nobody there to meet her. She knew Jean to be notoriously absent-minded and guessed correctly that she had forgotten to brief anyone concerning the time of her sister's arrival. Not that it worried Dora. Since her last divorce – and, indeed, for many years before it – she had been accustomed to fending for herself. None of her three husbands, including her first, Ralph Whitlock, to whom she had been married the longest, had been more than vaguely supportive, all of them resentful of the long separations when Dora was away on tour. Her own fault, she supposed, for marrying each time outside the profession; but she consoled herself with the reflection that if she had married a fellow-actor there would have been other hazards. Jealousy was a powerful factor in breaking up show-business marriages, and Dora had been moderately successful in her way. She had been in a fair share of West End productions and, even when on the road, had travelled, more often than not, in distinguished company. And she did enough television work nowadays to be recognized every once in a while, even if most people could not recall her name.

'I know you,' the man in the opposite corner of the compartment had said to her, as the train pulled out of

Paddington station. 'I've seen you on the box. You're . . . er . . . you're . . . er . . . well, anyway, you were the mother-in-law in that play on BBC last week. I thought you were bloody good.'

Dora had accepted the tribute with becoming modesty and, in return, had entertained her companion with racy, if largely apocryphal, stories from the Green Room until they arrived at Bath Spa. Regretfully, the gentleman had then been forced to say his goodbyes, as he was going on to Cardiff on business. Dora had smiled with relief and, after a quick look round to make sure that neither Jean nor one of her nieces was there to greet her, had headed down the stairs and outside to the taxi rank. Her brother-in-law she had not even contemplated seeing. She and Bernard avoided one another's company as much as possible.

The moment she was indoors, the whole house was filled with her presence. Her voice, trained to project to the back seats of any theatre in Britain, travelled up the stairs to the first-floor landing and penetrated even the closed door of Bernard's study. Yesterday, the Bristol schools had broken up for the Easter holiday, and he had hoped to put in at least two days' work on the maths text-book he was writing before his sister-in-law arrived on Good Friday. Now here she was, and it was only Wednesday. He knew, without being told, that Jean had muddled her dates again. It amazed him that she never confused either the day or the time of a single evening lesson; but, then, teaching was what Jean liked doing. She had always resented being forced to give up her career so soon.

Dora's case, her coat and several bags were strewn around the hall by the time Joanna reached the bottom of the stairs. Theresa and Freda had got there ahead of her, and all three were chattering nineteen to the dozen.

'Careful, Freddie darling, you'll crush my hat!' Dora, laughingly protesting, was smothered in Freda's enthusiastic embrace. 'Terry, watch where you're stepping! That carrier's full of Easter eggs from Harrods. Jo, my sweetheart, come and give your Aunty Do a kiss!'

26

Later, when they were all sitting round the big oval table in the dining-room, having lunch, she remarked: 'It's odd, you know, Jean, how all your girls have names which can be shortened to boys'. I expect a psychologist would have some explanation for it.' She raised her eyebrows. 'Where's Davey?'

'She comes home this evening,' Bernard answered shortly.

Jean added: 'She'll be here at tea-time. She stayed on a couple of extra days at Forest Moor so that she could travel back with Anthea.'

Dora raised her eyes from her plate and the portion of steak-and-kidney pie which she had been warily regarding, and frowned.

'You both ought to keep your eye on that relationship. It seems damned unhealthy to me. Sorry, Bernard. I realize Anthea's your sister, but the theatre teaches you that a lot of queer things go on in real life. That woman's obsessed by Davina. Anyone would think she was the child's mother. You really should try to lessen her influence.'

Joanna caught her grandfather's eye and grimaced. She wished Aunt Dora weren't quite so outspoken. The well-meant interference only infuriated her father, and she saw Bernard hitch his glasses up his nose, always a sure sign of irritation in him.

'I wish you'd mind your own business, Dora! How I bring up any of my daughters is not your concern.'

Dora flushed painfully, and Jean stepped quickly into the breach.

'How long are you resting for this time, my dear?'

Her sister turned to her gratefully and even risked a forkful of home-made pie. When she had emptied her mouth, she said: 'I've the half-promise of a part in a new BBC series. My agent rang me before I left home.' She smiled across the table at Freda, her self-confidence restored. 'Are you going to watch "An Age of Kings"? First episode's on the twenty-eight of this month. Shakespeare made easy. All the historical plays from *Richard II* to

Richard III chopped up into one-hour bite-sized chunks. Worth watching, though. Chock-a-block with some very fine actors. Keep an eye out for the gorgeous hunk of manhood playing Hotspur. Name of Sean Connery.'

The awkward moment was past. Freda and her aunt were immediately deep in conversation about the present state of the British theatre, acting prospects in general and the current programme being staged by the Bristol Old Vic. Reginald Harding, an avid theatregoer for all of his adult life, contributed various and often irrelevant memories of his own.

'I remember Leslie Howard coming to the Little in thirty-seven, I think it was, to put on a play he'd written himself. What was it called now? *Alias Mrs Jones*! That was it. Peggy Thorpe Bates and Lockwood West were members of the company in those days. Pity the Council never rebuilt the old Prince's Theatre after it was bombed. I used to enjoy going there to see all the touring companies, all the stars. Ivor Novello, Harry Lauder, Evelyn Laye . . .'

Joanna looked at her father and winked. Bernard raised long-suffering eyes to heaven.

Theresa was hurrying with her food.

'Mum, can I skip pudding? Anthony's calling for me. He's taking me for a drive.'

Jean looked vague. 'I suppose so,' she said. She continued with more animation: 'Remind him that I'm still expecting him for his extra tuition. I know it's the school holidays, but he needs that coaching if he's going to get a decent grade in biology.' She added as an afterthought: 'You might as well bring him back to supper.'

Bernard asked sharply: 'You haven't forgotten that Larry Walden is coming this evening, have you?'

Jean was reproachful. 'No, I haven't. But with nine of us sitting down to supper already a tenth isn't going to make much difference. It's liver and bacon. I'm sure I can make that go round.'

Lawrence Walden was junior English master at the same

28

school where Bernard taught mathematics, and in spite of the fact that he was fourteen years younger than Bernard, being not quite thirty, the two men had struck up a friendship.

Lawrence had first visited the house in Nightingale Close two years ago, shortly after the break-up of his marriage and all the trauma of an acrimonious divorce. The only child of elderly parents, who, in their turn, had been only children, he had never before encountered the clamour and confusion of a bustling family life. If his ex-wife, Emmy, had had any relations other than the uncle and aunt who had brought her up, she had certainly never visited them in all the six years of their married life, and they had had no children of their own.

It was the aura of loneliness, which hung about Lawrence Walden like a cloak, that had first attracted Bernard Marshall's pity. Later, the pity had turned to liking, after the pair of them had discovered a mutual interest in politics. They were both dedicated socialists and peace campaigners, and two years previously had been on the first Aldermaston march together. It had been the divergent nature of their politics, as much as anything else, which had alienated the Waldens from one another, and it had been a great pleasure to Lawrence to find himself among a group of people who, from its most senior member to its youngest, automatically assumed that anyone with a conscience voted Labour.

But, in spite of all this, Lawrence Walden was still a man who liked his own company, and neither this sense of empathy nor the desolation of his flat in Clifton Wood would have made him so frequent a visitor in Nightingale Close had it not been for Joanna.

He had been in love with her for over a year now: an emotion which appalled him on account of her age. She had been barely fourteen years old at the time of their first meeting, and there had been nothing about her which made her outstanding. Indeed, she was overshadowed by both her twin's natural exuberance and Freda's

29

histrionics, and by her elder sister's beauty whenever Davina was at home. So it had been with a feeling of total disbelief that Lawrence had suddenly realized how much the anticipation of seeing Joanna had come to mean to him. When he thought of Nightingale Close now, he pictured only her; hers was the first face that came into his mind when he woke up in the morning, the last before he went to sleep at night.

To begin with, after his discovery, he had tried to keep away, turning down invitations to Nightingale Close and even trying to avoid visiting Bath itself, in case he ran into her – always a possibility in so small a town. But Bernard was plainly hurt by these unaccountable refusals, and Lawrence persuaded himself that it would be churlish, as well as foolish, to reject a friendship which meant so much to both men because of his feelings for Joanna. So long as he gave no hint of those feelings to anyone, there was no harm done. He could continue to visit Nightingale Close. He would get over his infatuation for Joanna in time, he told himself, and probably the best way to do that was to see more of her. Self-imposed absence would only strengthen his affection.

Only it hadn't worked out like that. He knew he was still as much in love with her as ever, when he found himself seated next to her at the supper-table that Wednesday evening before Easter. Amid all the noise and chatter, she was quietly self-contained, laughing and answering when spoken to, but too shy and too serious to contribute much to the general flow of conversation. That, as always, when she was present, was dominated by Theresa, particularly animated tonight in the company of her new young man. He was an extremely handsome youth, whom Lawrence had not met before, but who, he gathered, was one of Jean's pupils. Theresa, with a careless familiarity which hinted at an underlying insecurity, called him 'Tone'; the rest of the family referred to him as Anthony.

Lawrence knew all the others seated round the table, even Jean's younger sister, Dora Whitlock, whom he had

30

met on several previous occasions, and who was also familiar to him as an actress. She, her father and Freda were discussing Arnold Wesker's play *Roots* due for a revival at the Royal Court in June, with Joan Plowright in the lead; Bernard was holding forth on why Labour had lost the Brighouse and Spenborough by-election the previous month; Jean was doling out portions of greasy-looking liver and bacon; and Theresa was giggling and whispering with Anthony Douglas, who seemed faintly bored by the whole proceedings. Joanna was watching them all with a smile of amused detachment. The chair between Jean and Anthony Douglas remained empty.

'Davey's late,' her grandfather remarked presently, during a lull in the conversation.

'Probably gone up to Royal Crescent with Anthea,' Jean replied, untroubled. 'She'll be here soon. I expect Thea will send her home in a taxi.'

Joanna noted the frown which puckered Dora Whitlock's brows, and said quickly, to forestall any further airing of her aunt's unwelcome views: 'I think I can hear a car outside now.' The front-door bell rang, and she got hurriedly to her feet. 'What did I tell you? I'll let her in.'

Joanna left the room as she spoke, and through the half-open door the others could hear the murmur of voices and the thud of cases being lifted into the hall. Davina called good-night to the taxi driver as he ran down the steps and banged the garden gate shut behind him. The front door closed with its customary rattle, because one of the panels of stained glass was loose. The next moment, Joanna returned, followed by her older sister.

Davina was still wearing the school uniform in which she had travelled from Forest Moor, but this was no affair of gymslip and blazer. The dark green suit over the impeccably laundered white poplin blouse was as becoming as anything that she might have chosen for herself, and the tan nylon stockings, allowed to sixth-formers, ended in smart brown court shoes with medium-high heels. The one item which did proclaim the schoolgirl, the green beret

31

adorned with the school badge, she had removed in the taxi and left with her cases in the hall. Her hair, the soft mid-brown hair which all the girls inherited from their mother, swung in a shining curtain across her face; and the grey eyes, also Jean's, were cool and remote as she surveyed the unusually large supper-party. A faint flush of embarrassment tinged the unblemished, almost transparent skin.

Anthony Douglas, raising his eyes in casual curiosity from his plate, sat as though turned to stone, his mouth slightly and ludicrously open. He thought he had never seen a more stunning girl. Davina was like her sisters; there was a strong similarity between all of the delicate oval faces, framed by the straight brown hair, but the formation and distribution of features had not produced identical results. Freda's nose was slightly tip-tilted, which, together with her too round chin, gave her a permanently pert expression. Even the twins were easily distinguishable now that they had grown up, and not simply because they were different in character. They both had their father's blue eyes, but Joanna's were more widely spaced and the lashes thicker than Theresa's, although Theresa's eyebrows were more heavily marked. Davina, however, had inherited the best features of both parents, and the result was a beauty which was beginning to turn men's heads in her direction. The fact that she seemed totally unaware of their interest only added to her attraction.

Until that moment, Anthony Douglas had looked upon girls as creatures whose sole function in life was to admire him. He honoured them with his company for a week or two – perhaps longer if they were very lucky – and then dropped them. He was no more callous than any other handsome, spoiled only child of rich parents, who had been overindulged from the moment he was born, and in spite of this fact there was a real core of sweetness and good humour to his nature. Nevertheless, even his best friends were forced to admit that he was conceited. But from the first second of setting eyes on her he knew that for him Davina Marshall was different.

'Sorry I'm so late.' Davina stood, poised for immediate flight, her nervous smile embracing everyone around the table. She bent and politely kissed her mother's cheek, causing Lawrence Walden to note, as he had done on previous occasions, the apparent lack of warmth between Jean Marshall and her eldest daughter.

'Been with Thea, I suppose,' Bernard said indulgently. 'What time did your train get in?'

'Four o'clock. Hello, Aunt Dora! Hello, Gramps!' Her voice suddenly warmed with genuine affection as she moved round the table to give her grandfather a hug, at the same time ruffling Freda's hair as she passed her. 'Hi, Pig Face!'

Freda would have taken instant exception to this form of greeting from anyone else, but she merely grinned at Davina and blew her a kiss.

'Aunt Dora's staying for Easter,' she volunteered.

'How nice.' Davina's tone was unenthusiastic as she turned to acknowledge Lawrence Walden's presence with a smile and a handshake. 'Hello, Terry,' she added to her sister.

'Davey darling!' Theresa surged to her feet, enveloping Davina in a bear-like hug. 'How long holiday have you got? Four weeks?' And without waiting for an answer she went on: 'Tony, let me introduce you to my other sister, Davina. Davey to her friends. The one who's away at boarding school. Davey love, this is Anthony Douglas.'

4

THEY HAD BEEN to the Embassy cinema in Bristol, to see a British film, *The Mouse That Roared*, and a Hollywood version of *Lorna Doone*, then driven back to Bath in the Aston Martin, in time for tea at the Old Red House in New Bond Street. Afterwards, they went for a walk in Sydney Gardens.

Easter was over, and the house in Nightingale Close had grown quieter with Dora's departure. Bernard resumed sole mastery over his study and became better-tempered as a result. Jean stopped making desperate culinary experiments which invariably flopped, and settled down happily to arranging her summer schedule of evening pupils. The twins found life less wearing without their aunt's vociferous presence, and only Freda and Reginald Harding genuinely missed Dora and her theatrical anecdotes.

Davina, however, was scarcely aware that Dora had gone. Normally, it was she, more than other members of the family, who objected to her aunt's rather raffish persona. She considered Dora vulgar and never hesitated to say so.

'All those "darlings" and "sweeties"! And I'm sure half the stories she tells aren't really true. She just does it to shock. It's so horribly common!'

Her sisters laughed at her and branded her a snob, but Davina was impervious to their jibes. She had no time for her mother's sister and didn't care who knew it.

But this time Dora's visit had passed almost unnoticed

by her. Davina had been too wrapped up in Anthony Douglas to have time to spare for anyone else. She was confused and preoccupied by her totally unexpected feelings for him. From the moment of their first meeting, that evening of her arrival home from school, there had been mutual attraction between them. When he had asked her out, Davina had hesitated, not because she did not want to go, but because it was generally accepted in the family that he was Theresa's boyfriend. But when she had offered it as an excuse Anthony had been indignant.

'Sure, I like Terry. She's a great girl, and we've been out together a few times. She's good fun, but that's all. She knows she's as free as I am to date anyone she chooses. There's nothing serious between us.'

Davina wondered uneasily if her sister saw the matter in quite the same light, but realized that on Anthony's side, at least, he was telling the truth. So why shouldn't she go out with him if she wanted to? Joanna's reproaches on behalf of her twin only made Davina more determined.

'It's mean,' Joanna had said angrily. 'You know how fond Terry is of him.'

'I can't help it if Anthony doesn't feel the same way.' Davina was always so calmly reasonable that her sisters usually ended any argument with her in a state of frustration. 'It's not my fault if he prefers me.'

But even as she spoke Davina knew that, had she been in Theresa's shoes, she would have fought tooth and nail to retain the affections of Anthony Douglas. At the same time, this excess of emotion scared her. Her life was mapped out for her: she would become a teacher and, eventually, headmistress of Forest Moor. Any other course would be a betrayal of Anthea, who had given her so much and whom she loved far more than her own mother. And in many ways it was what she wanted for herself. She had never been very interested in boys, and had always felt excluded from the dormitory and common-room gossip of the other girls, before she had graduated to a private room of her own. The stories of their sexual adventures during the holidays, and their prurient giggling over Tim Bates, the gardener's husky young assistant, had left her cold. There was nothing she felt she could relate to. She supposed she didn't like men. Her one attempt at a date with Irina Malenovsky's cousin had convinced her that this was so. As she had told her aunt, she had found him boring, and his attempts to kiss and fondle her repellent.

Now, suddenly, here was Anthony Douglas and she was in the grip of a welter of desires and emotions that she would have deemed impossible a week or so earlier.

They leaned on the stone parapet and stared down at the railway track which had been cut through what had once been Bath's answer to Vauxhall Gardens.

'It's difficult to imagine', Davina said, as the London-bound train thundered into the tunnel beneath them, 'all those eighteenth-century beaux and belles, drinking punch and eating wafer-thin slices of ham, and watching firework displays from the booths they'd rented for the season.'

'I wouldn't know about things like that,' Anthony said, one of his arms creeping round her waist. 'History has never been my subject.' His lips brushed against her cheek.

'Don't,' she whispered.

'Why not?' He sounded both hurt and resentful. 'Don't you like me, Davina?' He insisted on giving her her full name. Everyone else used the abbreviation, and it made him feel she was more personally his. He had never experienced that longing for ownership before, and it disturbed him. '*Don't* you like me?'

'Yes, of course I do.' She put up a hand which trembled slightly to push the curtain of hair out of her eyes. 'It's just that I'm not sure if I want . . . well, that sort of thing.'

'What sort of thing?' he asked, pretending not to understand her.

'That!' Davina exclaimed irritably, pushing his hand away from her left breast which he was kneading through the thin cashmere sweater she was wearing.

She was looking particularly attractive this evening. With the navy blue sweater she wore a red bell-shaped skirt over a stiffened petticoat, and a wide elasticated belt cinched in her waist. A navy-and-red striped scarf was tucked into the sweater's neck, and she had borrowed a pair of Jean's gold hoop ear-rings. But she still wore nylons and her brown school shoes in place of the ankle-socks and low-heeled pumps of her more fashion-conscious contemporaries.

Anthony was used to this form of courtship. It was an accepted fact of life, the continual sparring between the sexes. Nice girls didn't 'go the whole way' before marriage, but that never prevented even nice boys from trying. What was known as 'heavy petting' was something they had all learned early, from American films, but the Permissive Society was still a long way off. Boys usually accepted the limits imposed by girls without too many recriminations; but, for some reason which he could not fathom, Anthony, who normally played the game according to the rules, and who knew just how far he could go without giving offence, felt exasperated by Davina's rejection. He wanted her, all of her, now, at once, with a desperation he had never before encountered. He tightened his painful grip on her breast and propelled her round to face him, clamping his mouth roughly on hers.

She struggled violently, pushing with her hands against his chest. A man out walking his dog regarded them with avid curiosity.

Eventually, Davina managed to break free, panting and dishevelled. The navy-and-red striped scarf had torn loose from her neck and lay trampled on the ground. Furiously, she stooped to retrieve it.

'Don't you ever dare do that again!' she spat at him. 'I won't be manhandled like a sack of coals! I won't! Do you hear me?' She swung on her heel and started to run down the slope towards the gate, but when he tried to follow her she turned on him like a virago. 'Go away! Leave me alone! I'll go home by bus!' she shouted.

But it was the sight of the tears pouring down her face, not her words, which stopped him. He hated to see her in such distress. He watched her as she vanished along the path and told himself savagely that there were plenty more fish in the sea. Theresa would be glad to have him back. He was a fool for caring.

Joanna knew, as soon as she entered the bedroom, that Theresa had been crying. Her sister's averted face was swollen and blotched with tears, and Theresa's voice, when she spoke, was unsteady, in spite of a gallant effort to make it sound natural.

'Thought you were watching "An Age of Kings" with Freddie,' she said accusingly.

'It's over.' Joanna sat down on the edge of her bed. 'Each episode's only about an hour long. They've cut the plays in half. Freddie's fuming, and Gramps says it's vandalism. Personally, I think it's a good idea. I don't have time to get bored. Or is that sacrilege?' Theresa gave a short laugh and, encouraged, Joanna went on: 'You ought to have come down to see it. You'd have enjoyed it. *Richard II*'s one of the more interesting plays.'

'I didn't feel like it.' Theresa searched beneath her pillow for a handkerchief and vigorously blew her nose.

Unbearably moved by this prosaic gesture, Joanna moved from her own bed to sit beside her sister, who was lying, fully clothed, on top of the counterpane. Beyond the sash windows, the light was slowly draining from the sky as the late-April day sank towards darkness. Joanna slipped an arm about Theresa's shoulders and squeezed them.

'Don't cry, Twin.' It was so many years since either of them had used the old phrase with which, as children, they had comforted one another that Theresa was forced to smile; but it was a smile which almost immediately vanished.

'How could she?' she asked thickly. 'How could Davey take him away from me like that?'

Joanna wondered why women invariably blamed the

other woman for breaking up a romance, and never themselves or the man.

'I don't think that's quite fair,' she reasoned gently. 'There was nothing serious between you and Anthony, was there? He wouldn't have stopped you going out with someone else.'

'She *lured* him!' Theresa howled, and Joanna was torn between the desire to laugh and a strong impulse to tell her twin to grow up and stop behaving like a baby. She was angry with Davina herself, but it was no use blinking the facts.

'Terry love, let's face it! Anthony Douglas was just a casual boyfriend. He's every right to take Davey out if he wants to.'

'He thinks she's prettier than me.' Her twin's voice was a savage whisper.

Joanna frowned. She hated unnecessary histrionics.

'She is. Admit it. Davey's prettier than all of us, but it's a fact which won't influence anyone who's really fond of you or me or Freddie. And, anyway, who wants to get serious at our age? There are years and years ahead of us for that.'

Theresa shook her head obstinately. Shadows were beginning to edge out from behind the heavy Victorian furniture, a legacy from the previous owner who had included it in the purchase price when Jean and Bernard had brought the house after their wartime marriage in the August of 1940.

'You'll understand one day,' Theresa said bitterly, 'when you're in love.'

'Oh, come on, Terry!' Joanna was losing her patience. She got off her sister's bed and went to find the library book she had come upstairs to fetch. 'I'm not staying to listen to that sort of nonsense. You're no more in love with Anthony Douglas than I am.'

'You know nothing about it,' Theresa answered sullenly, and there was a look of such pain in her eyes that her twin was prevented from making an acid rejoinder.

'All right,' Joanna agreed, with the hint of a grin.

39

'Anthony Douglas is a louse and Davey's a traitor. But look at it this way. She'll be back at Forest Moor in two weeks' time, and he doesn't strike me as the sort to be content with letters, however passionate. So the field will be wide open again. You'll be less than the girl I take you for if you can't manage to win him back.'

Theresa sniffed and tossed her head. 'I don't know that I want him back,' she said with an attempt at bravado.

But Joanna was well content with the glint of steely determination in her sister's eyes and the abrupt cessation of tears.

'What is it? What's upset you?'

Anthea Marshall held open the front door of her flat as Davina stepped inside. One glance at her niece's white face and distraught appearance was enough to warn her that something untoward had happened. It was unlike Davina to be anything but immaculately turned out and in complete control of her emotions. She ushered her into the big high-ceilinged living-room, whose long windows overlooked the cobbled road and grassy slope on the opposite side of the Crescent.

Anthea's flat was on the first floor of one of the Bathstone houses begun in 1767 by John Wood the younger: a magnificent sweeping curve of thirty dwellings joined by a symmetrical design of simple Ionic columns. It was beautifully furnished, with two glass-fronted Regency bookcases, one on either side of the white marble fireplace housing the original eighteenth-century steel grate. A small Regency library-table, with animal head and leg supports, stood in one window, with a Regency sabrelegged mahogany chair nearby. A hanging cabinet, with lyre-patterned doors, was the room's sole wall-decoration.

The rest of the furnishings were modern, but discreetly so: nothing was allowed to detract from Anthea's cherished period pieces. A beige Wilton carpet covered the floor, and a wide, deeply cushioned sofa, upholstered in dark brown velvet, faced the empty fireplace, with two matching armchairs drawn up at right angles to it. The long curtains, too, were velvet, a rich shade of garnet, giving the room its only touch of colour. A couple of convector heaters, discreetly placed, infused the room with some much needed warmth, but because the flat stood empty for months of each year it had, inevitably, the slight aroma of mustiness which comes from rooms too little opened to light and air.

'Sit down,' Anthea ordered, and Davina sank gratefully into the sofa's softly cushioned depths. 'I'll make some coffee. You can tell me about it when I come back.'

She crossed the hall to the kitchen and made coffee in an old earthenware jug kept especially for the purpose. Anyone guilty of using a metal percolator, like her sister-in-law, felt the rough edge of Anthea's tongue. She put two Crown Derby cups and saucers on a tray already spread with an embroidered tray-cloth, added cream-jug and sugar-bowl, and carried everything back into the living-room. Davina was still sitting where she had left her, staring into space.

Anthea placed the tray on a low table in front of the fireplace and poured the coffee before she spoke.

'Now, then,' she said bracingly, handing one of the cups to Davina, 'what's wrong?'

Davina sipped the hot liquid, and her colour revived a little. Then she returned cup and saucer to the table and clasped her hands together in her lap.

'Aunt Thea, I'm in love.'

Anthea amended coolly: 'You *think* you're in love. As I told you before, these schoolgirl crushes are bound to happen from time to time, but accept them for what they are and be on your guard against them. Who is the young man?'

'Anthony Douglas. One of Mother's pupils.'

'Ah, yes. I think I met him when I came to tea with you all on Easter Sunday. I had the impression, however, that he was Theresa's boyfriend.'

'He was. But there was nothing in it,' Davina assured her, a shade too quickly.

Anthea raised her eyebrows and laughed. 'I thought I

hadn't underestimated Mr Douglas's character. A handsome young man, and how he knows it! "A spoiled brat", I think, wouldn't be an uncharitable description. Isn't his father that vulgar man who made a fortune in pickles? Or sauces? Something like that. He pops up frequently in the worst kind of newspapers, or on the radio, telling everyone how he became a self-made millionaire.'

'Anthony's going to be a doctor.' Davina sounded defensive, and her aunt felt the first faint stirring of alarm; the first warning that this might be more serious than she had imagined. She put down her cup and saucer, leaning forward in her armchair to place one hand over Davina's.

'My dear, before you allow this ... this boy-and-girl affair to go any further, please stop and think. You are seventeen, with your whole life in front of you. No one falls in love for ever at that age. In fact I very much doubt if anyone falls in love permanently at all. People are attracted to one another, rush off and get married, and a few years later can't stand the sight of one another. Or, at best, are indifferent. Why do you suppose that all the great love-stories of history are tragedies? Because the couple involved haven't had time to get bored or to find that they like someone else better. Oh, I'm sure you think at the moment that I'm talking like a frustrated spinster – a phrase I've heard too often in my life. But I had a chance, once, to get married. I, too, thought myself in love.' Davina had a mental picture of the young airman in the photograph in her aunt's study at Forest Moor. Anthea went on: 'But I made a deliberate choice against it. I saw the pitfalls, and I wanted more for myself than a lifetime of slow disillusionment and possible regret.' Her hand tightened over Davina's. 'If you want an example, look at your mother, a qualified biology teacher, who married my brother when she was not much over twenty; forced into a life of domesticity which has never suited her.' Anthea added fiercely: 'I don't want to see you fall into that trap.'

5

'YOU'LL BE GOING BACK to school tomorrow,' he said. 'It'll be a whole term before I see you again.' The light from a street-lamp slanted down through the branches of a plane tree, illuminating Anthony's face as it turned towards her. There was a painful intensity in his blue eyes, and his hands gripped the steering-wheel of the Aston Martin. 'I love you, Davina,' he added slowly, as though the statement puzzled him.

He had told her that he was taking her out to supper for their final evening together, and then had taken her home to meet his parents – the last thing she had either expected or wanted.

Davina had continued seeing Anthony Douglas, in spite of Anthea's advice. She could not help herself. One part of her, perhaps the biggest part, wanted to please her aunt, but whenever she saw Anthony she seemed to lose the power to say 'no'. There was no avoiding him, because of his twice-weekly lessons at the house, and he had made no further attempt to kiss her or make love to her in any way. He had behaved perfectly over the past two weeks, taking her on trips around the countryside in the car, giving her lunch at expensive restaurants, doing no more than hold her hand in the cinema. He had surprised even himself. He was used to girls throwing themselves at his head and accepting their homage as no more than his due.

He was aware of the approach of the new school term, and Davina's imminent departure, like a lead weight, settling in his chest. He had made no progress, and he was conscious of something or someone coming between them as soon as he made even the slightest headway; some barrier that prevented them getting close. He had always intended that their last evening should be special, but didn't quite know what to suggest. So when his mother had said that morning, 'Why don't you bring your young lady home to dinner, dear?' he had jumped at the chance. To introduce Davina to his parents seemed a way of forcing her into a commitment she might not otherwise be willing to make.

The evening had not been a success. Lyncombe Manor, a few miles to the east of Bath, was an Elizabethan manor-house which had come on to the market five years earlier, about the time that Norman Douglas, having made his fortune with Douglas's Sweet Mixed Pickles and a range of bottled sauces, was looking for a retirement home in the West Country. He was then only forty years of age, but saw no reason to continue in harness any longer than was necessary.

'I've made my pile and now I'm going to take it easy,' he had announced, after a lucrative sellout to a big American food-manufacturing firm.

Davina had at first been overawed by the size of Lyncombe Manor, a fact which had added to her natural reticence. Norman and Cicely Douglas, both raised in the friendly atmosphere of a Yorkshire mining village, found her difficult to get on with. Her Forest Moor poise, her cool remote gaze irritated them, and they mentally dubbed her 'stand-offish'. Moreover, Cicely Douglas did not think Davina good enough for Anthony and constantly referred to his friendship with Claire Neville, the only child of their nearest neighbours, Sir Harold and Lady Neville at Green Top Farm.

As a result, conversation grew increasingly stilted as the evening wore on, and Davina resented Anthony's attempt to make her a part of his family before she was really sure how she herself felt. They had left as soon as the meal was finished, and Anthony had driven her back to Nightingale

Close in silence. They sat now, in his car, outside the house, trying desperately to make sense of their feelings for one another.

'I love you,' Anthony repeated, not sure if she had heard him the first time.

'Yes.' Her hands moved convulsively in her lap. 'I think I love you. No! Wait!' There was a note of panic in her voice as he tried to put his arms around her. She pressed her hands to her cheeks for a moment, then said: 'I can't think properly out here. Let's go in. They're all out this evening. Mum and Dad have gone to Bristol, to the theatre, and taken Gramps with them. The twins have gone to a local hop at Twerton, and Freddie's at her drama class. So we'll have the place to ourselves.'

Anthony followed her inside, into the big untidy kitchen, where she filled the kettle and set it to boil on one of the gas-stove rings.

'I'll make a cup of tea,' she offered, pulling off the pale-yellow cotton jacket she was wearing.

She seemed tired, and there were shadows under her eyes. The white-and-yellow striped cotton dress she had on made her appear more childlike than the skirts and sweaters or blouses she normally wore. She looked suddenly very vulnerable and young.

When the tea was made, they carried their cups and saucers into the deserted dining-room. It was getting dark, and Davina drew the heavy faded and patched brocade curtains. She was conscious tonight of the general shabbiness of the house, after seeing how Anthony and his parents lived at Lyncombe Manor.

As she turned, she found him standing close behind her. He put his arms round her and began to kiss her passionately, her hair, her eyes, her lips, her throat. She gave a half-strangled cry and, for a moment or two, tried to fend him off, before she was overcome by a whole host of strange new sensations. She had never known it was possible to feel like this, as if her bones were turning to water. She started to kiss him back, tearing at his clothes

45

with fingers that shook and refused to do her bidding. Then she was lying with him on the floor, her senses swimming, a great tidal wave of love and joy spreading throughout her body; a feeling that now was the only moment in the whole of her life that mattered; that the past was lost to her, and the future no more than a dream.

Lawrence Walden had accepted Jean's invitation to stay to supper yet again. He knew that he should not impose so much, but he had come to Nightingale Close to discuss Labour Party business with Bernard, and had stayed on afterwards to watch the day's play at Wimbledon on television. He did not have a set of his own since the break-up of his marriage, and had always found the flickering black-and-white images a distraction from his work. He used to sit with Emmy in the kitchen, after tea, watching the 'Tonight' programme, instead of hurrying away to mark books or prepare tomorrow's lesson. Between him and his wife, television had taken the place of conversation as their relationship had slowly died, but once on his own again he had sworn to do without it. But old habits died hard, and when he and Bernard had come downstairs from the study to find Jean and her father watching tennis in the living-room Lawrence had automatically taken a chair, his eyes riveted to the screen. It was less than four-teen years since the BBC had resumed their postwar tele-vision service, and an even shorter time since it had been transmitted to the provinces. For many people, it was still a novelty.

'You'll stay to supper, Larry?' Jean had asked as the programme ended, and he had said, 'Yes,' without a moment's hesitation. The prospect of leaving without seeing Joanna, who was upstairs with her sisters, doing her homework, was unthinkable.

When she and Theresa did at last appear, they were both gloomy, confronting the possibility of failed O levels.

'I'm never going to survive them all,' Theresa announced despondently, taking the seat next to Lawrence, which he

46

had been trying, unobtrusively, to save for Joanna. 'It's no use, Dad! Maths is a closed book as far as I'm concerned.'

'Me, too.' Joanna slipped into the chair beside her grand-father and squeezed his arm. She quoted: ' " O is a point inside a triangle ABC; parallelograms AOBP, AOCQ are completed. Prove that PQ is equal and parallel to BC." I mean, the mind boggles!'

'I've told you both a hundred times', Bernard reproved his daughters sternly, 'that geometry is mostly a question of logic.'

Freda grimaced cheerfully as she bounced into the room just in time to overhear this last remark.

'You and Mum shouldn't have given all your brains to Davey,' she said. 'How can you expect the rest of us to have our fair share? Thank goodness you don't need academic qualifications for acting. I shan't have to worry so much when my time comes.'

'You'll take your O levels whether you want to or not, young lady,' her mother retorted sharply. 'Acting is a very overcrowded profession. You'll need some decent qualifications behind you. Terry, if you need extra tuition in biology, you have only to say. If you're going to be a nurse, it's important you get it. You can share Anthony's evening lessons if you want to.'

Theresa flushed a dull red and was about to refuse when she caught Joanna's eye, across the table. She remembered her twin's advice. Davina had been back at Forest Moor for six weeks now; time enough for Anthony to have started to forget her. Now was Theresa's chance to try to win him back.

'OK,' she answered carelessly. 'Why not? But I'm not up to A-level standard.'

'There's not that much difference in the syllabus, and it'll give you a foretaste of what's to come.'

Jean handed round plates of ham with a limp salad and lumpy mashed potato. Bernard sighed inwardly, but resignedly. He had long ago given up all hope of improving his wife's cooking.

47

There was silence for a moment, while they ate or chased the food warily around their plates. Then Lawrence said: 'I'm thinking of leaving teaching. Well, eventually. I'd like to go into politics. I'd like to stand as a Labour candidate at the next election.'

Bernard lifted his head. 'My dear fellow, there won't be another general election for at least four years, and I doubt very much if you'd get in. The Tories have been in power now since 1951, and Macmillan and co. seem pretty well entrenched to me. An overall majority of ninety-eight will take some eroding. Work for a party victory, by all means, but don't go sticking your neck out.'

'A lot of things can happen in four years,' Lawrence said confidently. 'And I'd like to try. I've thought for a long time that it's something I'd really like to do. Naturally, I shouldn't resign my post at school until I knew I'd won. I'd apply for special leave of absence to fight the election itself.'

'Well, I think it's splendid!' Joanna exclaimed, her eyes shining with excitement. 'I hope, when the time comes, you can stand for a local seat, then I can come and campaign for you. I should like that!'

'Would you?' Lawrence's heart was beating ridiculously fast. He was sure everyone must be able to hear it.

'I trust that by then you'll be up at Oxford,' her father observed drily. 'Or have you changed your mind about trying for a place?'

Joanna's face fell. 'No, of course not.' She brightened again. 'But it depends when, in 1964, the election's called, doesn't it? If it's in the summer, I shall be down for the long vacation. I love politics. I think it's very stimulating.'

Freda yawned. 'Darling Jo, I don't know how you can. It's all such a crashing bore.' She smiled at Lawrence. 'But she means it, you know. She was absolutely glued to the television when they were giving out the results last October. She'd make a marvellous wife for any MP.'

Lawrence glanced suspiciously at her. He never knew quite what to make of Freda. She made him uneasy. Those china-blue eyes in the doll-like face missed very little. Had she, Lawrence wondered, guessed his secret? He must be careful. He devoted his attention for the rest of the meal to Theresa.

A rice pudding followed the ham and salad, baked so solid that it had to be cut in wedges, like cake, followed by coffee the colour of dishwater and tasting like nothing on earth. Her mother really was bad news for anyone who enjoyed food, thought Joanna.

The telephone rang in the hall. Bernard got up and went to answer it. He was not gone long, but when he returned he was frowning.

'That was Thea,' he informed Jean, puzzled. 'She said Davey's on her way home. To expect her later this evening.'

'Home?' Jean was equally puzzled. 'She can't be! You must have misheard . . . Unless she's ill. No! They'd have put her in the sick-bay at school, not sent her home. Are you sure Anthea said that? Didn't she give you any clue as to what's the matter?'

Bernard shook his head. 'Not a word. She just said that Davey would tell us about it when she got here, whatever "it" is. And she didn't want to see her back at Forest Moor until, and unless, she came to the right decision.'

Freda slipped into her sister's bedroom, her white cotton pyjamas clinging skimpily to her slender body. It was yet another source of grievance to her that she was not allowed to spend her pocket money on diaphanous nylon nightdresses from Marks & Spencer.

The twins were in bed, but still awake. Since their elder sister's arrival an hour earlier, there had been an atmosphere of tension throughout the house which precluded sleep. From the floor below, Joanna could hear the subdued murmur of her grandfather's radio, indicating that he, too, was awake. No one knew what was taking place in Bernard's study, but Davina had been shut up there with him and Jean for the past twenty-five minutes.

49

The June evening was drawing to a close, but neither Joanna nor Theresa had switched on the bedroom light. The darkness seemed somehow more fitting as they speculated in whispers as to the probable cause of Davina's unexpected return. She had looked very pale when she came in, but it was obvious that she was not really ill.

Freda had no such inhibitions and flicked down the switch inside the door, flooding the room with harsh fluorescent strip-lighting.

'Guess what?' she demanded.

'Pull the curtains, you stupid child!' Theresa made a dive beneath the bedclothes. 'Everyone will be able to see in.'

Joanna didn't bother with words, but got out of bed and drew the curtains herself. Then she plugged in the lamp which stood on the chest of drawers between the beds and turned off the overhead lighting. Freda was patently bursting with news, and asking her to do anything was a sheer waste of time.

'All right, what have you discovered?' Joanna enquired, climbing back into bed again. 'You might as well tell us at once because you know you'll never be able to keep it to yourself, and neither of us is in the mood for guessing games.'

'Spoilsports!' Freda sat on the edge of Joanna's bed, her eyes brimming with excitement. She hissed dramatically: 'Davey's going to have a baby!'

There was a stunned silence, before Joanna protested: 'What nonsense! She can't be! Who told you?'

'No one told me. I listened.' Freda was indignant at having the veracity of her statement doubted. 'I wanted to go to the bathroom,' she added virtuously, 'and as one of you two was in the one up here I had to use Mum and Dad's on the lower landing. And if', she went on, casting all pretence aside, 'you stand close up against the wall – well, actually I used a glass, you know, the way you can – and listen really hard you're able to hear quite a lot of what's going on in the study, especially if people are talking loudly. And most of the time Dad was shouting. I should

50

think they could have heard him in the Pump Room.'

'And you're sure that Davey's going to have a baby?' Even now, Joanna couldn't really take it in. 'But how? I mean, who's the father?'

'Anthony Douglas, of course!' Freda sighed. Sometimes her elder sisters were so slow. 'It must be him, unless there's some other boy we know nothing about.'

'But she wouldn't! Not that!' Joanna suddenly remembered her twin and turned her head sharply.

Theresa was propped against her pillows, her mouth set in a thin hard line, her eyes blazing with hatred.

'She's a little slag!' she rasped. 'Davey's nothing but a cheap little whore! Well, that'll finish her precious school career. What's Aunt Anthea done? Expelled her? I suppose that's why she's been sent home.'

'Not exactly.' Freda wrinkled her nose, making it look more retroussé than ever. 'I couldn't make out everything that was said, but I did gather that Aunt Thea's in favour of getting rid of the baby.' She lowered her voice and pronounced in her best stage-whisper: 'Abortion!'

Joanna was scandalized. 'Mum and Dad won't allow it. I mean, I know they don't go to church much nowadays, but Mum had a strict Methodist upbringing and Dad's family were Baptists.' She pushed her hair out of her eyes and stared blankly at the other two. 'They wouldn't! They'd simply never allow it.'

6

'IF LAD'S WILLING t' marry the lass, why not?' Norman Douglas stared defiantly at his wife. 'He's done wrong by 'er and he must pay.'

'That's fine talk from the boy's father, that is.' Cicely Douglas shifted angrily in her chair. Unlike her husband, the accent of her native Yorkshire dales did not thicken in moments of stress. 'And what about his career? He wants to be a doctor and he's worked hard for it. Is all that education to be thrown away?' She glared across the room to where Jean and Bernard Marshall were sitting awkwardly on the edge of the enormous cretonne-covered settee which dominated the drawing-room of Lyncombe Manor. 'It's my experience that the girl's just as much to blame in these affairs as the lad. More so, very often.'

Jean bridled. 'If you're implying that my daughters haven't been properly brought up—' she was beginning, but Norman Douglas silenced her with an apologetic wave of the hand.

'No, of course she isn't, Mrs Marshall. Cis knows as well as I do you can't keep young people in leading-strings once they're over a certain age. And I see no reason', he added, turning towards his wife, 'why it should affect Anthony's career. Good Lord! We've got more than enough room here t' accommodate lass, and the bairn when it comes. If Tony gets place at Bristol University, the way he wants, and deferment from National Service, he can go on living at home and travel into Bristol each day. After all, he's got the Aston Martin.' He beamed complacently.

'And what about my daughter's career?' Bernard asked aggressively. 'That's in ruins.'

For the first time since the arrival of their unwelcome guests, Norman Douglas looked annoyed.

'Well, I'm afraid there's nowt we can do about that. A mother's place is at home with the children. Always has been, always will be. Fair's fair, Mr Marshall. Or p'raps I should call you Bernard, now that we're to be related, like.' His good humour was returning, and he offered Bernard a fat Havana cigar, which was curtly refused. Hurt, Norman Douglas continued with more asperity: 'We're offering lass a home, which, without offence, is more than you and Mrs Marshall are able to do. We'll increase Tony's quarterly allowance – and it'll be a generous increase, I can promise you. Your lass and t' baby won't be wanting. And when he's qualified lad'll have a decent career to support 'em and any other chick that comes along meantime. And they do say National Service is coming to an end this autumn. It's likely that those deferred now will never have to do it, although I think it's a pity. Bit of army life never did a lad any harm. However, under those conditions, I don't think you and your good lady can complain about lass losin' her career. Any road, women and education don't mix, in my opinion.'

'That', said Jean hotly, 'is an extremely short-sighted, old-fashioned, reactionary attitude, and it's men like you who have retarded the cause of women's emancipation. You're still in the Middle Ages!'

'Calm down, Jean!' Bernard's tone was peremptory. 'It's no good carrying on like that. Davina's pregnant, and you don't like the prospect of all the gossip and disgrace that goes with it any more than I do. Marriage is easily the best and most respectable way out of the dilemma. Especially to the baby's rightful father. Adoption's all right in the final analysis, but there are nine months to be got through before then. So I agree with Mr Douglas . . . er . . . Norman. Anthony has to continue with his studies if he's to support a family.'

Cicely Douglas smiled thinly. She was forty, the same age as Jean, but with her beautifully groomed blonde hair, carefully made-up face and expensive clothes looked much younger. She thought Jean Marshall dowdy and untidy, and did not hesitate to let her feelings show. She said: 'I won't pretend this marriage is what we wanted for Anthony. We'd always hoped, Norman and I, that he'd eventually marry Claire Neville, the daughter of our neighbours, Sir Harold and Lady Neville, at Green Top Farm. The young people have been friends for a year or two now, and I fancy Anthony has a soft spot for Claire. However, he seems set on doing the right thing by your daughter, and we've nothing against Davina. She's a nice enough girl. So we'll stick by them both and do as Norman suggests. If, that is, it's what they both really want.'

'We can soon settle that. Let's ask 'em!' Norman Douglas walked across to the french doors which gave on to a terrace running along one side of the house, and opened them. 'Come in here a minute, you two,' he said.

Davina had accompanied her parents to Lyncombe Manor, where she was surprised to find Anthony waiting for her. He explained that his mother had telephoned his school to say that he was suffering from a heavy summer cold and would not be in for the rest of the week.

It was two days since Davina's return home, and since then the lines between Nightingale Close and Lyncombe Manor had been almost constantly engaged. Anger, distress, recriminations and a certain amount of bluster on both sides had gradually given way to planning the best way out of their mutual dilemma. In the face of Anthony's determination to marry Davina, there was not much else they could do.

As they waited together on the terrace in the hot June sunshine, he said pleadingly: 'It'll work out OK, Davina, you'll see. My parents'll love having you here. And the baby.' Then, as she made no immediate reply, he put an arm around her waist. 'Don't you want to marry me?' he asked.

Davina stared down the long grassy slope in front of her, still a brilliant green in spite of the last few weeks' lack of rain, thanks to an army of sprinklers. Part of her wanted desperately to marry Anthony Douglas: the part that told her she was in love with him and probably always would be. But she also felt trapped and degraded; denied a free choice. She had to marry him, whether she wanted to or not, for the sake of respectability; for the sake of all those shibboleths and prejudices of a society which still regarded the unmarried mother with horror, particularly an unmarried mother of only seventeen. And Davina knew that she was not strong enough to outrage convention. For one moment's physical self-indulgence, she had been robbed of her independence, shamed her family and, worst of all, betrayed Anthea to whom she owed so much. She would never forget the look on her aunt's face when she had told her she was pregnant.

But the look, compounded of disgust, revulsion, anger, had quickly faded.

'You must get rid of it,' Anthea had said firmly. 'An abortion. There are places where you can get these things done. I'll make enquiries, and you can tell Jean and Bernard that, whatever it costs, I shall pay. Meanwhile, say nothing to anyone else. I shall send you home on sick leave. I'll tell Matron and the rest of the staff that you're unwell, and that I've judged it best that you return to your family for a few weeks. Don't worry, I'll make it convincing. Pressure of work, too much study, something like that. As soon as I get the necessary particulars of where you're to go, and when, I'll let you know. You can come back to school as soon as you're fit, but you'll have to work extra hard to make up what you will have missed. It's essential that you get good A levels next year.'

It had not, however, worked out like that. Bernard had been horrified at his sister's proposal.

'Apart from the moral angle, abortion's against the law!'

It was a stand endorsed by Jean, who, for all her liberal views on the rights of women, was not prepared to countenance anything illegal. Moreover, in spite of a professed agnosticism, she still retained enough of her childhood Methodist teaching to be superstitious about the taking of life. She liked to hedge her bets, her father had once slyly accused her, in case, after all, there was a God somewhere out there.

Davina hadn't known whether to be glad or sorry at her parents' attitude. Aunt Anthea's way would have simplified matters, but if she had the baby, then she would have to accept Anthony's offer of marriage.

She looked at him and gave him a fleeting smile, but did not answer his question. 'What a mess,' she said.

'It'll work out,' he assured her again. 'My parents are loaded. They'll see we're all right.' He added confidently: 'You'll like living here, and I'll be home every evening. You'll be able to help me with some of my studies.'

'Doesn't it worry you', she asked, 'that your parents will have to subsidize not only you, but me and the baby as well, for the next five or six years?'

'Why should it? I've told you, they've pots of money and I'm their only child. My happiness is all they care about. And I shall be happy, because I'll have you. I'm glad it's worked out like this. It means we can be married straightaway without having to wait until we've both graduated.'

'But what about me?' she asked in a small depressed voice. 'I shan't be graduating at all.'

'Does that bother you?' He looked surprised and faintly hurt. 'Doesn't marrying me and having our baby more than compensate?'

Once more, she refrained from answering his question, but he didn't seem to notice; and when his father opened the french doors and invited them to go inside he said, 'Right! Let's get it over!' with the utmost cheerfulness. 'Let's make it absolutely plain that we love each other and that we're going to get hitched.'

As Bernard turned the Ford Prefect into the driveway of 4 Nightingale Close, the front door opened and Joanna came down the steps.

'Aunt Anthea's here,' she mouthed through the car window.

'Hell and damnation!' Bernard got out and slammed the door with unnecessary violence. 'What does she want? I hope she isn't going to make trouble.'

His sister was waiting for them in the living-room, drinking a cup of tea provided for her by Joanna, whose return from school had coincided with her aunt's arrival.

Without preamble, she remarked grimly: 'I understand you've all been at . . . what's it called? Lyneham Manor?'

'Lyncombe Manor,' Bernard corrected her and would have said more, but she interrupted him.

'Very well. Lyncombe Manor. The house, anyway, of the young man responsible for Davina's condition.' She directed her attention towards her niece. 'What does this mean, Davina?'

'It means that she and Anthony are going to get married,' Bernard said tartly, before his daughter could reply. 'Davey, go upstairs and lie down for a while. You look all in.'

Davina hesitated for a moment, avoiding Anthea's eyes, then slipped obediently from the room.

Jean said, taking off her lightweight summer jacket: 'I must go and get the girls something to eat. They're always hungry when they get in from school. Are you staying for tea, Thea?'

'No, thank you. When I've said what I have to say, I shall spend the night at Royal Crescent and catch the early train tomorrow morning. I can't afford to be absent from Forest Moor too long.'

'Suit yourself.' Jean headed in the direction of the kitchen.

Bernard closed the door behind her and turned resolutely to face his sister.

'It's no good you kicking up a fuss, Thea. What's done is done, and we have to find the best way out of the mess. The boy wants to marry Davey, and his parents, who, fortunately, are very wealthy, are willing to support them and give the pair a home until Anthony has qualified as a doctor. It might have been a damn sight worse.'

'In what way?'

'In every way!' Bernard exploded. 'If the father was some

57

penniless student, for example, instead of the son of a very rich man!'

'In my opinion, it's a great pity he isn't. You might then have been persuaded to do things my way.'

'Your way is illegal,' Bernard snapped. 'And I'm damned if I'm having my daughter fooled around with by some backstreet butcher.'

His sister glanced at him contemptuously. 'Do you think those are the only abortionists in the country? Good heavens, Bernard, be your age! It goes on all the time. For the right kind of fee, there are doctors willing and able to terminate a pregnancy all over the country. Her future in-laws would do much better to spend their money that way than in helping two young people, barely more than children themselves, to get married.'

'It's what Davina wants.'

'Is it?' Anthea's expression was dour. 'Or have you simply scared her to death, all of you, with your talk of the sanctity of life? Frightened her with your talk of breaking the law. For God's sake!' She slapped her palm down hard on the arm of her chair. 'Davina's a brilliant scholar! One of the finest I've ever known. Can't you get it through your head, Bernard, that she's exceptional? Destined for a great academic career! And you want her to throw it all away for a foetus that hasn't, as yet, any life as we understand it. Do you want to tie her down, at seventeen, to being a wife and mother?' Anthea rose to her feet. 'Where is she? I want to speak to her. I must make her see sense.'

Bernard got up, too. 'Leave her alone,' he warned. 'You're not interfering this time, Thea.' He added on a softer note, because he was fond of his sister: 'I promise you that if Davey herself was opposed to the marriage we'd have the baby adopted.'

'Adoption's not on!' Anthea retorted. 'It would mean nine months, probably a year off school. Even with her ability, Davina can't afford it. My way, she'd be back at Forest Moor within weeks.'

'What you mean', Bernard observed shrewdly, 'is that

she'd be out of your jurisdiction, beyond the range of your influence, for nine months or a year. But, in any case, this discussion is pointless. I told you, Davey's made up her own mind. She wants to marry Anthony Douglas and keep the baby. All in all, Jean and I think that's best. This way there won't be any gossip or whispering behind her back. And adoption's never satisfactory. She might regret it later on and wonder what had become of the child.'

'I want to see her,' Anthea insisted stubbornly.

'Oh, all right!' Bernard's resolution suddenly weakened. Jean told him, frequently and loudly, that he had no backbone where his sister was concerned. 'Top floor, front bedroom. But you won't get any joy.'

Davina was sitting on the broad window-ledge, staring out into the deserted close, when Anthea tapped on the door and came in. She looked wary and then defensive as she sprang to her feet. Her aunt went across to her and took both her hands.

'Davina my dear, you don't have to go through with this ridiculous charade, you know. Nor is there any need to endure nine months of pregnancy, only to suffer all the trauma of adoption at the end of it, when your child is a live human being. I've found someone, a doctor, who runs a clinic in Hertfordshire. You'd enter as one of his private patients, ostensibly for observation, for a couple of nights. There would be no record of what had actually been done. Now, please be sensible. For my sake, if not for your own.'

The appeal was too much for Davina, who started to cry silently. 'I don't know,' she said. 'I just don't know.'

'You've always trusted me before,' Anthea reminded her, a little more sternly. 'Has my advice ever been for anything but your own good?' Mutely, Davina shook her head. Her aunt persisted: 'My sole concern is for your welfare. If you'd listened to me, this would never have happened in the first place. You're special. You don't need a husband or a family or anything that distracts you for a moment from your chosen path. You have a marvellous career ahead of you.

Believe me, it will be more than enough. It will compensate for any other lack. It will fill your life in a much more satisfying fashion than the ephemeral nonsense we dignify with the name of *love*! It's your choice. Don't, I beg of you, make the wrong one.'

Davina looked down into the street again. A deep resentment welled up in her. All these people pushing her this way and that; forcing her into decisions she didn't want to make; didn't know how to make! She blamed her mother for not explaining to her more fully the facts of life; her father for always letting her do what she wanted; Norman and Cicely Douglas for making marriage to their son too easy; Anthony for getting her pregnant; and Anthea for complicating what otherwise might have been a simple choice. The only person Davina failed to blame was herself.

'Well?' Her aunt, still holding her hands, squeezed them hard. 'What have you decided?'

'I . . . I don't know. I suppose . . . I suppose I ought to have the baby.'

The last words were almost a whisper and Anthea had to lean forward to catch them. Abruptly, she released her niece's hands and straightened up.

'I see. You think you're in love with this boy, is that it?'

'I . . . I'm very fond of him.'

'It won't last.' Anthea moved towards the door. 'So I want to say one thing to you, Davina, before I go.' She paused with her hand on the door-knob. 'If you change your mind at any time, now or after the baby's born, I'm always there. I can't reinstate you as a pupil at Forest Moor once your condition becomes generally known. But I can see that you get sufficient coaching to get you through your A levels next year, and you can stay in my private flat as my guest. But you must come fully committed and alone. No encumbrances. No regrets. That's my offer, and it will stand for the next twelve months. After that, I wash my hands of you. What you do with the rest of your life will be up to you. Goodbye, my dear, and good luck. Think over carefully what I've just said.'

7

'IT'S LOVELY here,' Joanna said, looking out of the window at the soft green spread of English turf. In the distance, a copse of elegant beech trees caught the final rays of the bright March sun. The day had been brilliant, without a stain of cloud, the sort of day so rarely encountered in early spring, and Joanna had enjoyed the ride which had brought her from Bath bus station almost to the gates of Lyncombe Manor. She liked visiting Anthony and Davina, and was delighted by any chance to see her little niece. 'It's so peaceful here,' she added, 'after the Saturday crowds in town.'

The Douglases had put three first-floor rooms at their son and daughter-in-law's disposal, on the western side of the house. The big corner room, which also had south-facing windows, was used as a dining- and sitting-room; next door to it was the bedroom; and a small room across the corridor served as a nursery. The last was the only one which had been redecorated, in pastel shades of green and pink, with a frieze of lambs halfway up each wall. As well as the cot, from one of Bath's most expensive shops, a play-pen and high chair stood ready for future use, and every spare inch was crammed with toys. Norman and Cicely Douglas adored their grand-daughter.

Anthony and Davina had been married quietly at Bath register office at the end of June, and Samantha Cicely Jean had been born, two weeks overdue, on 2 February 1961. She was now almost six weeks old.

'How's everyone at home?' Davina asked, passing

Joanna her second cup of tea. The table was set in one of the window alcoves and caught the evening sun. Davina's face was in shadow; but it was not simply that, her sister thought, which made her look ill. Her movements were apathetic, her questions polite noises which, as a good hostess, she forced herself to make. Anthony, too, seemed morose.

'Oh, pretty much as you might expect,' Joanna answered cheerfully, in an effort to lighten the atmosphere. 'Freda's full of the Laurence Olivier – Vivien Leigh divorce, and his remarriage to Joan Plowright. Dad's worried about the situation in Cuba. Says there's going to be serious trouble there before long. Mum's furious about the new parking-meters that are springing up everywhere. Dad lent her the car to go shopping in Bath this morning, and she couldn't get the hang of them at all. Gramps has decided to write his memoirs, starting with his birth on Mafeking night, so that's keeping him busy and helping him to occupy his time. He says he's going to call it *The Diary of Another Nobody*, and that it's for us kids, so we'll know what life was really like at the beginning of the century.'

Davina smiled faintly. 'Things sound pretty normal, as you say.' She hesitated, then asked: 'How's Terry?'

'Oh . . . Twin's OK. Thanking heaven that "O"s are behind us and "A"s won't be until next year.'

There was a moment's awkward silence. Theresa had refused to attend either Anthony and Davina's wedding or the party held by Norman and Cicely Douglas to celebrate their son's successful application for a place in the medical school of Bristol University. She had steadfastly refused to visit her sister and had never seen the baby. The rift between them had widened into a chasm since Davina's marriage.

After tea, Anthony excused himself on the score of having studying to do.

'Dad lets me use the library, downstairs,' he explained, 'so you and Davey can chat to your heart's content, Jo. You won't disturb me.'

'What about the washing-up?' Joanna asked, after he had gone. 'The same arrangement?'

'Oh, yes!' Davina sounded bitter. 'We're allowed our own bathroom, but I still have to share the kitchen. The food's cold more often than not, by the time I get it up here to the table. What Cicely really wants, of course, is for us to take our meals with them. She's hoping I'll find it so awkward that, in the end, I'll give in.'

'It's a beautiful kitchen,' Joanna said wistfully. 'Not like ours at home.'

Davina grimaced. 'It's the constant supervision from Cicely I can't stand. Am I feeding her precious boy OK? Are Samantha's feeds at the right temperature? Oh, leave the dishes! I'll do them when you've gone. Tony'll be working all evening, and it'll give me something to do. Let's talk while the baby's asleep and we have the chance.'

'What's the matter, Davey?' Joanna asked, sinking into an armchair and peeling off the cardigan of her knitted twin-set. The central heating at Lyncombe Manor always proved too much for her, used as she was to the draughty and chilly rooms of Nightingale Close. She was overdressed and uncomfortable. 'Aren't you happy?'

Davina laughed scornfully. 'Why on earth should I be happy? This isn't the life I'd planned for myself, as you well know.'

'Don't you love Anthony?'

Davina leaned her head against the flowered back of the chintz-upholstered chair.

'How the hell do I know? I'm only just eighteen!'

'But . . . you must have wanted to marry him.' Joanna was confused. 'You must have loved him to . . . well, to do what you did.'

'Oh, Jo, don't be so naïve! Attraction and love aren't necessarily the same thing.'

'Maybe not. But nobody made you get married. You could have had the baby adopted.'

Davina sat forward, clasping her hands round her knees. The sun had dipped behind the trees, and the room was in shadow.

'I couldn't have stood the waiting, with everyone

63

knowing what I'd done. I should have had to stay in Nightingale Close – there was nowhere else I could go – and the neighbours would have gossiped. This way, everything is respectable. Samantha has her own father. Her proper father. What else could I have done? Except follow Aunt Thea's advice.'

'You could never have done that!' Joanna was upset. 'Think of Sammy, how beautiful she is. You couldn't have destroyed her!'

'That's talking with hindsight. We'd never have known Samantha as she is now, and what the eye doesn't see . . . For God's sake, let's change the subject! I'm sick to death of going over and over it in my mind, trying to convince myself that I did the right thing. Is Terry still determined to be a nurse?'

'Of course. And Freddie'll never be happy unless she goes on the stage. It's just me who doesn't know what to do with her life.'

'I thought you were going to try for a place at Oxford.' The note of envy had crept back into Davina's voice.

'I have to get suitable grades in A levels first. I know my O levels were OK, but I'm a bit weak in English Lit., which is one of the subjects I've opted to take. Mum says I ought to get some extra coaching.'

'Well, that's easy. Ask Lawrence Walden. He'll fall over himself to oblige.' It was dark now, and Davina got up to switch on the light and draw the curtains.

'What do you mean by that?' Joanna asked.

'Oh, come on, Jo!' Davina smiled teasingly over her shoulder. 'You know he's keen on you.'

Joanna sat very still. At last she said: 'No, I didn't know.'

'Didn't you? Honestly? I bet the others have noticed it. Not Mum and Dad. They don't see anything beyond the end of their noses. But Freddie. There's not much escapes her beady little eyes. And Gramps. He's pretty shrewd. And Terry's your twin. What's the matter? Don't you like the idea of a secret admirer?'

'It's not that. I like Lawrence a lot, but not in that way. I mean, he's years older than I am. And he had a rough time during the divorce from his wife. I'd hate him to get hurt again.'

'Don't give him anything that could be construed as encouragement, then. Don't be too friendly. Play it cool.' Davina crossed to the record-player, which stood against one wall. Moments later, the strains of Roy Orbison's 'Only the Lonely' flooded the room. She began to sway slowly to the music, her arms wrapped tightly around herself, a protection against the world.

Joanna watched her, a worried frown between her brows. It occurred to her that her sister was far more unhappy than she let on, and that there was nothing she could do to help.

The row blew up out of nothing, as so often happened, Joanna reflected, between her parents.

Jean and Bernard Marshall rarely quarrelled, but when they did no punches were pulled, no holds barred. It was a bit, Joanna supposed, mixing her metaphors, like lancing a boil, when all the poisons which had accumulated over months, even years, flooded out. But she wished this particular fight hadn't happened when Davina was staying in the house. She had wanted her sister's visit to be one of calm and quiet.

Davina had telephoned home a few days after Joanna's visit to Lyncombe Manor.

'She wants to come for the weekend,' said Jean, who had taken the call. 'She sounds a bit fraught. She says she needs to be on her own for a couple of days. She's going to leave Samantha with Cicely Douglas. Good job she decided not to breast-feed.'

Theresa had looked up from her homework. 'If she comes, I'm going out. I don't want her here.'

Jean had told her sharply not to be foolish, and had refused permission for Theresa to go and stay with a friend.

'A mistake,' Reginald Harding had said to Joanna, and

so it had proved. Theresa's determination to ignore Davina's presence had a lot to do with the atmosphere of ill-will that pervaded the house.

On top of everything else, Freda was having one of her frequent running battles with her father about the necessity of remaining at school beyond the age of sixteen.

'If I'm going to be an actress, what I need is experience!' she shouted at him on Friday evening, just as Davina arrived, and was promptly banished to her room as a punishment for her rudeness.

'Hardly an auspicious beginning,' Joanna whispered, kissing her sister, and noting that Davina looked even thinner than she had done the previous Saturday.

The following morning, Jean, as usual, took the Ford into Bath to do the weekend shopping. When she returned, complaining loudly about the iniquitous charge of a shilling for two hours' parking, there was a large dent in the offside rear door.

'You've pranged the bloody car!' Bernard exclaimed wrathfully, erupting into the kitchen, where she was unpacking her basket and an assortment of carrier-bags.

Jean glared at him. 'What a fuss to make about a little scratch!' she retorted scornfully.

'A little scratch!' Bernard was almost incoherent with rage. 'It's a bloody great dent! It'll have to go into the garage to be hammered out and resprayed. It means I'll have to go into Bristol by bus all next week, and you know what a pantomime that is! How the hell did you do it?'

'I was trying to pass a car in Milsom Street, and it wouldn't get out of my way.'

Bernard exploded, and the quarrel escalated to include Jean's untidiness, her abysmal cooking, her general sloppiness and total incompetence as a mother – charges which were met with equally virulent accusations concerning Bernard's notable lack of success in gaining a head-mastership, his unwillingness to help with household chores and the number of times a week he brought Lawrence Walden home to supper.

'I am sick and tired', Jean yelled, 'of feeding your damn friend!'

Davina was in the hall, speaking to Anthony on the telephone.

'When are you coming home?' he asked peevishly. 'Sam and I are missing you. You ought not to leave her, you know, Davey, while she's so young.'

'Is that your mother's idea or yours? And, anyway, I've only just got here. We agreed I could stay until tomorrow.' The continuing row in the kitchen, which she could hear plainly through the open door, was making her head ache. Her legs felt weak, and she thought for a moment that she was going to faint. 'Look, I must go now,' she said. 'Love to Sammy. I'll call you this evening.' Hurriedly she replaced the receiver.

Jean's voice had sunk to a sibilant whisper, but was still audible to Davina.

'And what about your affair with my sister, eh? Answer me that! My own sister, under my own roof! I don't think you've any right to complain about anything, Bernard Marshall!'

'Good God, that was years ago!' Bernard's voice, too, had sunk, and he sounded guilty and defensive. He counter-attacked with his own private grievance. 'And I'm fed up with having your father here. He didn't have to come to live with us. He's only sixty-one, and perfectly capable of looking after himself.'

There was another flurry of words from Jean just as the telephone rang. Davina answered it, only to find that it was Anthony again.

'I think you ought to come back, Davey,' he said. 'Sam's not been well all night. It's not fair to expect Mother to cope alone.'

Davina slammed down the receiver without answering and ran upstairs to her old bedroom at the top of the house, where she shut and locked the door. She sat down on the window-seat, trying to stop herself shaking.

She felt trapped. Everything had happened too fast in

the past eleven months. She had been given no time to think. She could see herself ending up like her mother: frustrated; imprisoned in a way of life which she had grown to hate; overwhelmed by a domesticity she could not handle. Would Anthony be unfaithful to her, as her father had been to her mother? With her own sister? Well, that, too, was on the cards. Theresa had been his first choice, and it was obvious that she was still very fond of him.

Davina stared down into the close. Because it was a Saturday morning, it was unusually busy. The girl from across the road – slender, pretty, Davina's age – was getting on to the pillion seat of her boyfriend's motor-bike. They were both carefree, laughing. The two boys from the centre house were charging up and down the garden path, playing a game, lost in some fantasy world of their own making. The man next door was just backing his Morris Minor out of the garage . . . Abruptly, Davina got to her feet. Her suitcase was lying open on the bed, still half-packed with the few clothes she had brought with her for the weekend. Hastily, she crammed the rest of her things in on top, changed her slippers for shoes, grabbed her handbag and coat and snapped the case shut. She raced downstairs, bumping into her youngest sister on the first-floor landing.

'Hey!' Freda looked annoyed. 'Where do you think you're going in such a hurry?'

Davina said: 'Tell Mum and Dad I've gone to see Aunt Anthea. I'll telephone tonight and explain but, if Tony calls, you don't know where I am. I'll get in touch with him myself.'

Before Freda could react to this astonishing piece of news, Davina had descended the last flight of stairs and wrenched open the front door.

'Mr Ingham!' she yelled, as the Morris Minor began to pull away from the kerb. The car stopped, and Gilbert Ingham wound down his window. 'Oh, Mr Ingham, thank goodness I caught you. Are you going into town? Can you give me a lift as far as the station?'

'I'm not going back,' she said. 'Never.'

The day was very warm for March, and one of the windows of Anthea's study was slightly open. The chattering of the birds, as they gathered in the trees outside, ready to fly to their evening roost, was deafening.

'What about your husband and child?' Anthea asked quietly.

Davina shook her head. 'I don't know. I can't think about them yet. All I know is that I've made a terrible mistake and I have to put it right before it's too late.'

All the way, in the train, she had been only half-aware of what was going on around her, of the other people in the carriage. She had telephoned Anthea from Southampton station. Her aunt had at once abandoned the hockey match she had been watching, between teams from the school's top two houses, and driven the four miles, at speed, to pick her up.

'I've been waiting for your call,' Anthea said, as she embraced her.

Such physical displays of affection on Anthea's part were rare, but today she was filled with satisfaction. Davina was hers now, as she should have been from the beginning. She had beaten Bernard and Jean, with their old-fashioned notions of morality, and that boy, who had thought he could take Davina away from her by making her pregnant. But Anthea had always felt that she would win in the end.

But she had to be sure.

'Are you absolutely certain', she asked now, 'about what you're doing?'

Davina smiled sadly. 'I don't think I can ever be absolutely certain. There will be times in the future when I'm bound to have doubts. But in the main, yes. I need to be here, to sit my A levels, to go on to Oxford, as you did. Samantha will be all right. Anthony's parents dote on her. She'll never miss me. She's too young. Tony can divorce me. Perhaps he'll marry Theresa, after all. I'm not cut out to be a wife and mother. I've come to realize that more and more during these past few months.'

Anthea drew a deep breath.

'Very well. If that's how you really feel, I won't pretend I'm not delighted. You can live here with me, although you can't, of course, come back to Forest Moor as a pupil. I shall make arrangements, however, with members of the staff to coach you as a private pupil. If you work really hard, there's no reason at all why you shouldn't sit your "A"s, as originally planned, this summer.'

Davina nodded. She felt happy and relaxed for the first time in almost a year. She felt as though a great burden had been lifted from her shoulders.

PART TWO

1964–5

8

IT WAS one of the hottest, longest summers anyone could remember, beginning in late spring and continuing well into the autumn. Mods and Rockers clashed on the beaches, women's dresses grew shorter, Vidal Sassoon and Mary Quant became household names, the Beatles conquered the United States and, in spite of the glorious weather, *Goldfinger* packed the cinemas.

Joanna and Davina travelled from Oxford to Bath, at the start of the long vacation, sharing an otherwise empty railway compartment. Davina was down from Somerville, her sister from Corpus Christi. It was so typical of Davey, Joanna reflected, to have chosen an all-women's college. It had been pure chance which had thrown them together, Joanna scrambling aboard the train at the very last moment, after a lingering farewell with her latest boyfriend.

Although Alex Ferrer was more than just a boyfriend as far as she was concerned; and, she felt convinced, as far as he was concerned, too. She could still feel the pressure of his mouth on hers as he had kissed her goodbye; the hard rough grip of his fingers as he had held her against him. He had seemed unmindful of the curious stares and ill-concealed smiles of other people on the platform, and Joanna wished she could be one half as indifferent to public opinion as he was. But she hadn't been brought up like that and had eventually pulled herself free, hurrying towards the waiting train with downcast eyes and hot flushed cheeks, aware of his amusement and hoping to

God she had not forfeited his good opinion. It was only after she had slung her case on to the rack and sunk, panting, into a seat that she saw her sister in the opposite corner.

'Davey!' she exclaimed, smiling broadly. 'How lovely to see you!' She was always genuinely delighted to see any of her sisters.

During term-time, their paths rarely crossed. They shared no lectures, Joanna reading English and Economics, Davina Saxon and Medieval History; they had no mutual friends, and their outside interests varied.

'Hello, Jo.' Davina gave a faint embarrassed smile. 'I saw you on the platform.'

Joanna blushed. She was already acutely and unhappily conscious of her untidy appearance. Her thin cotton dress was clinging damply to her body, and her hair was ruffled. Her sister, on the other hand, looked cool in a blue-and-white striped coat and skirt, her brown hair, cut into one of the new short styles, a shining cap framing the perfect oval features.

'That was Alex Ferrer,' Joanna said self-consciously. 'He's at Corpus, too. He's reading Economics. How ... how's Aunt Anthea?'

'Fine. We're going to Greece this summer. We're off as soon as the Forest Moor term ends.'

'Oh.' Joanna hesitated, wondering whether or not to say any more, then decided to take the plunge. 'That means you won't be seeing anything of Anthony and Sam.'

'No.' The coldness of Davina's tone was not encouraging. It seemed as though she had no intention of enlarging on the subject, but after a moment she went on irritably: 'You know very well I haven't seen either of them since I left.'

'No,' Joanna agreed quietly. 'I was just hoping that you might have changed your mind, that's all.'

Davina turned her head to look out of the carriage window, at the flying fields and trees.

'Leave me alone, Jo. I know what you all think of me and

I don't care. You won't make me alter my decision.'

Since her return to Forest Moor, three years earlier, Davina had refused to have any contact either with the Douglases or with her own family. Holidays she spent with Anthea, in Royal Crescent or, more usually, abroad. When they were in Bath, Anthea guarded her niece like a dragon. Anthony's early attempts to visit his wife had met with a polite but adamant rebuttal. His letters were returned unopened, and efforts to waylay her as she entered or left the flat had proved a waste of time. Anthea was always in attendance. By the time Davina went up to Oxford and became less well protected, Anthony had given up trying.

Davina added fretfully: 'Can't you make Tony understand that it's over between us? I've asked him to give me a divorce, but for some reason he seems determined not to co-operate. I'm sure he's doing it just to be difficult. To punish me. I should think he'd jump at the chance of his freedom.' She looked again at her sister, this time pleadingly. 'Won't you talk to him and try to convince him? I know you still see him.'

'Of course I still see him!' Joanna was growing angry. 'He's my brother-in-law. More important, Sam's my niece. If Mr and Mrs Douglas had their way, he'd have divorced you long ago and married that Claire Neville they're so fond of. But he's still in love with you. He wants you back on any terms, for Sam's sake as well as for his own.'

'How . . . how is Samantha?' Davina once more averted her head.

'She's beautiful,' Joanna said forcefully. 'She's three years old and chattering away non-stop. But she needs a mother, Davey. Mrs Douglas is wonderful with her, but she's too old. A little girl of three needs a younger woman.'

Davina's fingers tightened over the clasp of the handbag on her lap, but all she said was: 'In that case Anthony should give me my divorce, then he could provide Samantha with the mother you say she needs. I hear he's been seeing Terry again, or have I been misinformed?'

'Who told you that?' Joanna's tone was belligerent.

'Aunt Thea saw them together in Bristol, last Easter. She said Anthony had his arm around Terry's waist. She thought they looked . . . well, more than friendly.'

'Yes, he's seeing her again.' Joanna frowned at her reflection in the window as the train entered a cutting and threw the carriage into shadow. 'With him at the University and Terry at the BRI it would be surprising if their paths hadn't crossed. I know he's done duty on the wards at the Infirmary as part of his training.'

'You sound as though you don't approve.' Davina was curious. 'Why not? You always blamed me for taking him away from her. I thought you'd be pleased that she'd got him back.'

The train was pulling into Reading station, and they began gathering their things together.

'All change for Swindon, Chippenham, Bath Spa and Bristol, Temple Meads,' the guard was yelling.

Joanna was spared the necessity of a reply. She didn't feel like spending the rest of the journey in her sister's company and went off to the station buffet for a cup of tea. When the Paddington-to-Bristol train pulled in, she waited until Davina had boarded and deliberately chose a different compartment.

She managed to find another corner seat and, propping her elbow on the arm-rest, stared thoughtfully out of the window.

The friendship between Anthony and her twin disturbed her. Theresa was still in love with him and resolutely turned a deaf ear to all Joanna's warnings that, as far as Anthony was concerned, she was just another girlfriend.

'For God's sake,' Joanna had begged when she was home in the spring, 'open your eyes to the facts! First of all, Anthony's still hoping like crazy to get Davina back. Second, I've seen him on more than one occasion with Claire Neville. I saw them together at the Odeon in Bath, only last week.'

'Oh, I know all about *her*!' Theresa had exclaimed

dismissively. 'Tony only takes her out to keep his parents happy. His mother's a terrible social climber. As for Davey, I'm sure he doesn't really care for her any more. How could he, after the way she's behaved?' Theresa had smiled, a small, secret, self-congratulatory smile which made Joanna want to protect her and shake some sense into her at one and the same time.

She had said no more, either then or later, but had returned to Oxford for the Trinity term in a mood of profound disquiet. Within a few weeks, however, all thoughts of her twin's problems had been driven from her mind by the entirely new and breathtaking experience of falling in love herself.

She had first met Alexander Ferrer as she left the Bodleian Library one lunch-time, after a morning spent researching one of the minor Victorian poets. He was standing near the entrance with a group of friends, and Joanna's initial impression was that he was one of the ugliest young men she had ever seen.

Beneath a head of straight black hair was a square weatherbeaten face with a pugnacious jaw-line, brown eyes opaque in the density of their colouring, and, above them, thick black eyebrows which almost met in a straight line across the bridge of his nose. They gave him a heavy scowling appearance, and it was not until the fascinated Joanna took a second look that she saw the promise of humour in the strongly marked features. There was a lift to the corners of the long thin mouth and a twinkle in the eyes which suggested a light-hearted approach to life, a determination not to take its challenges too seriously, that conflicted with her own staid and solemn nature. From the beginning, it was an attraction of opposites.

Someone had called her name, and Joanna had realized, guiltily, that it was a boy she had been very friendly with during her first term at Oxford, and with whom she had remained on good terms ever since. Yet she had not even noticed him and, for a second, had difficulty in recalling his name. He introduced her to the others in the group, but no one registered except Alex Ferrer, who freed himself from the clutches of two girls, hanging one on either arm, and extended his hand, grinning.

'You've not been working on such a beautiful morning, have you?' he chided her gently. 'That's what I call dedication over and above the call of duty. Come on, I'll buy you lunch!'

At any other time, from any other person, such a peremptory order, such an assumption of her willingness to comply, would have elicited a prim refusal. Instead, 'Thank you. I'd like that,' Joanna heard herself answer like a breathless schoolgirl.

The affair had progressed from there, with visits to the cinema – he liked *Dr Strangelove* and *Goldfinger*, she preferred *Chimes at Midnight* and *For King and Country*; to the Oxford Playhouse – his choice was Shaw and Ionesco, hers Shakespeare or John Whiting; and to concerts – Alex was a Bob Dylan fan, Joanna's interest in music was strictly classical. Alex was a member of the Conservative Party; Joanna tried to get him to read Marx and Engels. They had absolutely nothing in common, and all their friends and acquaintances prophesied that it could not possibly last.

But when they went down for the long vacation in this summer of 1964 Joanna was more in love than ever and snapped her fingers at such gloomy prognostications.

'Where were you on Thursday evening?' Theresa was sulky and self-righteously angry when Anthony met her at the top of Christmas Steps on Saturday morning. 'I waited outside the cinema for over an hour.'

'I know. I'm sorry.' He took her hand in an effort to placate her and kissed her cheek. 'I did try to get in touch with you, but when I phoned, the Ward Sister said you'd just gone off duty. I could only have missed you by about five minutes.'

Theresa jerked her hand away. 'You could have phoned

the home. So where were you? What's your excuse this time? And why didn't you ring yesterday to explain?'

'I couldn't. I was too busy. I had lectures in the afternoon, and in the morning one of the local flea-pits was giving a special showing of films for us and members of the Red Cross and St John Ambulance Brigade.' He made no attempt to repossess himself of her hand, but as they started down the steep flight of steps leading into the ancient heart of Bristol city he said: 'You'd have laughed if you'd been there. They'd resurrected an old wartime film called *Behind Russian Lines*. Someone had set up a camera in a first-aid post just outside Stalingrad and let it run. Some of the injuries brought in were pretty horrific, and after less than fifteen minutes the cinema foyer was knee-deep in people who'd passed out cold.'

'What's funny about that?' Theresa demanded sullenly, but she put a hand through his arm in a gesture of forgiveness.

'The fact that ninety per cent were medical students. The toughies from the Red Cross and St John's, mostly women, didn't turn a hair. I wasn't one of the casualties, thank God, but at one point it was touch and go. Heaven knows what we'd be like if ever there was another war.'

'Road accidents can be just as bad. You've done work in Casualty. You ought to know. Anyway, why did you want to see me this morning?' Theresa glanced at her watch. 'I've only got an hour. I must be back on duty at one.'

'We'll grab a coffee and a sandwich at the Bay Horse in Bridewell Street.' Anthony added with some constraint: 'There's something I want to say to you.'

She caught the note of suppressed hesitation in his voice, and immediately all her suspicions were reawakened. Where had he really been on Thursday night? With Claire Neville? She realized that he had neatly side-stepped her question. She stopped and faced him.

'You haven't said where you were Thursday evening.'

'Ken Evans wanted me to help him with his notes on disorders of the nervous system. I couldn't refuse.

79

Honestly! He was in one hell of a mess with it. It would have been churlish not to do what I could.'

'I don't believe you,' she said flatly, as they resumed walking. 'You were out with Claire. You might as well admit it.'

'No, I wasn't,' he answered, curbing his impatience. He was getting tired of the jealousy and the accusations and the rows, but he felt guilty about Theresa. How could he explain that he had only renewed their friendship so that he could hear about Davina, and because, every now and then, she reminded him of her sister?

Perhaps, strictly speaking, that wasn't all the truth. He could, after all, have learned as much as there was to tell from Joanna, and it would have been less biased. The fact was that he had always liked Theresa, found her good company, a pleasant companion for an evening. She knew what he was talking about when he discussed his work, and had helped him swot for his exams. But that was as far as it went, where he was concerned. Lately, however, he had begun to suspect that Theresa's ideas about the nature of their relationship and his did not coincide. She expected a great deal more from him than he was prepared to give. And last week she had mentioned the word 'marriage'.

'I am married,' he had told her bluntly.

'I mean after you're divorced.' She had been confident of his intentions. He had begun to worry. Theresa, he realized, took too much for granted.

He had arranged to meet her outside the Whiteladies cinema on Thursday evening, but at the last moment he had ducked it. A stray remark from Ken Evans that he could do with a bit of help on disorders of the nervous system had been seized on as an excuse. The astonished Mr Evans had found himself hauled back to his Clifton lodgings – an unsavoury bed-sitter at the top of an old Victorian house – and virtually held prisoner for the evening. By the time Anthony left, to cover the sixteen miles to Lyncombe Manor, he had come to a decision.

The Bay Horse in Bridewell Street sold good filling sandwiches and followed the new custom of more trendy pubs by providing coffee for non-drinkers. It was a favourite haunt of perennially hard-up nurses from the Bristol Royal Infirmary.

Anthony steered Theresa to a table flanked by high-backed settles, and bought cheese-and-pickle sandwiches and coffee at the bar. He returned with his laden tray to sit opposite her and watched her bite hungrily into the wedges of soft white bread.

'Terry,' he said, stirring and restirring the liquid in his cup until the chink of metal against china began to jar on both their nerves, 'I don't want you to take this the wrong way.' What a silly thing to say! How could he possibly expect her to take it a right way? He paused, looking at her uncertainly, unsure of her reaction. 'Terry,' he went on, 'I've made up my mind. I'm going to see Davey during the long vac. I'll manage it somehow, in spite of that aunt of yours. One way or another I've got to make her see sense. I need her. Sam needs her. I want her back.'

9

HE ENLISTED Joanna's help, knowing that he was powerless to manage on his own.

'Get Davina to go shopping with you one afternoon. Surely that shouldn't be too difficult. Then you can make some excuse about being tired and steer her towards Henrietta Park for a rest. I'll be waiting there with Sam.'

Joanna was reluctant to deceive her sister, but at the same time she wanted to see Davina reconciled with her family for her niece's sake. After mulling the proposition over for a few minutes, she decided that without her co-operation there was no chance of Anthony and her sister meeting without Anthea being present. So when her brother-in-law called at Nightingale Close to make his request she felt there was nothing she could do but agree.

'It'll have to be soon,' she warned him, 'before Anthea gets home. And she and Davey are off to Greece at the end of next week. I shall be away myself at the beginning of August.'

'The sooner the better. How about tomorrow? You could go and ring her now.'

Joanna hesitated. She and Anthony were sitting in the garden at the back of the house, on the little patch of grass reserved by the Marshall ladies for sunbathing, walled in as it was by laurel bushes and one or two stunted trees. The rest of the lawn was mercilessly exposed to the upper storeys of the neighbouring houses, and a frieze of chimney-pots made a jagged line against the burning turquoise sky. The normal lush greenness of an English summer was yellowing in the heat, and the parched earth was cracked and fissured from too little rain. In the distance, a radio blared through an open window, 'Can't Buy Me Love', the Beatles' latest hit.

'Yes, all right.' Joanna frowned. 'But we won't meet in Henrietta Park. It's too far off the beaten track, and she might get suspicious. The Parade Gardens. We can get refreshments there, and there will probably be a band – there usually is – and deck-chairs. Besides, it's near the shops. It would seem more natural to go down there.'

'Anything you say, only go and speak to her now,' Anthony urged, 'while I'm still here, and then you can tell me whether she agrees.'

Joanna turned her head against the gaudily striped canvas of the garden lounger and asked sharply: 'Have you told Theresa of your intentions?'

A faint flush crept up her brother-in-law's neck and blotched the pale honey-coloured skin. Unlike most fair-haired people, Anthony tanned easily and evenly, radiating a healthy golden glow. It wasn't fair, Joanna thought enviously, knowing that she was turning an unbecoming mottled shade of red.

'Yes. I met her in Bristol last Saturday.' He added defiantly: 'I decided it was time she knew how I felt.'

'What was her reaction?'

Anthony grimaced. 'Not good. Bad, in fact. But you know your twin. Everything has to be larger than life, every gesture twice as extravagant.'

'In other words, she made a scene.'

'And how! Bloody embarrassing it was, too. She burst into tears in front of a pub full of people. Great noisy sobs like I'd just told her she'd two months to live. One man was ready to lynch me, I can tell you! Then Terry got up, bumped into the table and spilled all the coffee. I've never been so glad to get out of a place in all my life! Honestly, Jo, I haven't given her any encouragement to warrant that sort of reaction. She reads things into situations that just aren't there.' Joanna raised her eyebrows, but made no comment. Sensing her disbelief, he added belligerently: 'Anyway, Terry always over-reacts. It's her way. I'm sure she doesn't feel half of what she projects.'

'Who's talking about projecting?' Freda came through the french doors from the dining-room, still wearing her cotton school-dress. 'Hi, Tony! Long time no see. What brings you here?' And without waiting for him to answer she sank into the deck-chair Joanna had that moment vacated, and stretched luxuriously. 'Only three more days of school,' she exulted, 'and then it's behind me for ever. Look out, RADA, here I come!'

'You haven't been accepted yet,' her sister reminded her, 'and if you haven't passed your A levels Dad's quite capable of making you sit them again at Christmas. So don't count your chickens before they're hatched.'

'Cassandra!' Freda mocked her. 'If there's any justice in this world, I shall pass my "A"s with flying colours. Goodness knows, I've worked hard enough even to please Mum and Dad. And once I've done my audition the three-year course at RADA will be in the bag.'

'Such hubris,' Joanna murmured and went indoors.

When she emerged again, ten minutes later, she met Anthony's anxious eyes across her sister's head. She nodded and mouthed: 'Tomorrow afternoon.' For some reason, she didn't want Freda to know of her complicity in their brother-in-law's little scheme.

It was just like old times, Anthony reflected, except that Theresa was not there.

When Jean had asked him to stay for the evening meal, his first impulse had been to refuse, foreseeing too much embarrassment on both sides. He knew that Bernard had never really liked him; and, while not condoning Davina's behaviour, both his parents-in-law tended to blame him as the original cause of a disastrous situation. Their attitude towards their grand-daughter was ambivalent. When Cicely Douglas invited them to Lyncombe Manor or brought Samantha to visit them in Nightingale Close, they always appeared delighted to see her. But in between times they never made any attempt to interfere or to initiate any move which would bring them into closer contact with the child. Only Joanna and, to a lesser degree, Freda treated Samantha to any overt display of affection. As for Anthony himself, he tried to keep out of the Marshalls' way as much as possible, and only his need to enlist Joanna's help had brought him to Nightingale Close that afternoon.

It had therefore come as something of a surprise when Jean, coming into the garden about four o'clock, looking hot and harassed after an afternoon spent touring the summer sales, had pressed him to stay for supper.

'It's a long time since we've seen you,' she said.

'Er . . . yes, thank you, I'd like that,' he muttered, in response to an encouraging nod from Joanna.

'If you really want Davey back,' she had pointed out to him later, 'you might as well try to get everyone on your side.'

Reginald Harding, emerging from his room in time for the evening meal, seemed pleased to see Anthony again, although it was never easy to be sure what he was thinking. A naturally quiet self-effacing man, except where his job had been concerned, he had made up his mind when he first came to live with his daughter and son-in-law that he must never, on any account, interfere, whatever problems they had with the girls. In return for their hospitality, which exempted him from the inconveniences and traumas of living alone, he must never take sides. Sometimes he wondered if he had made the right choice; if, in insuring against the loneliness of old age, he had given up too much independence. There were occasions when the fear of becoming merely a cipher gnawed at the back of his mind.

When Bernard arrived home from school, it seemed somehow inevitable to Anthony that he should have Lawrence Walden with him; but the truth was that Lawrence had been a far less frequent visitor in the two years since Joanna went up to Oxford than previously.

There had seemed little point in running the gauntlet of Jean's increasing hostility without anything to recompense him. But this evening, suddenly recollecting that the long vacation must have started, he had practically invited himself.

'Larry, how nice,' Jean said, as though she meant it, and very nearly did. Now that she saw so much less of him, she could afford to be generous.

With Lawrence present, the talk at the supper-table naturally veered towards politics. A worsening crisis in Britain's balance of payments made it a racing certainty that the Prime Minister, Sir Alec Douglas-Home, would be calling an election very soon.

'I reckon October,' Bernard said. 'I'm going by that interview Reggie Maudling gave to the *Financial Times* back in February, when he admitted there were going to be difficulties later in the year. "A Serious Crisis in October" was the newspaper prediction. The Tories won't want to face that sort of situation without a new mandate from the country. In any case, an election's due. They can't put it off any longer.'

Freda remarked buoyantly to her sister: 'Larry's putting himself forward as a Labour candidate. Isn't that exciting?'

'What?' Joanna jumped when spoken to, as though her attention had been miles away. 'Oh, yes. I remember you saying you were going to try to get into Parliament at the next election.' She smiled vaguely at Lawrence. 'That was some years ago, now.'

'Yes. Four to be precise, a few months after the Conservatives took office again in 1959. You said then that you thought it a wonderful idea and would like to help me.'

'Goodness, did I?' Joanna, who had been day-dreaming about Alex, made a determined effort to focus her thoughts. 'Yes . . . yes, I do recollect something of the sort.' She looked back at this pre-Oxford, pre-Alex self with wondering detachment. She could no longer drum up any enthusiasm for Lawrence Walden's political ambitions. 'Well, if the election's not until the autumn, I don't suppose

I'll be able to keep that promise. I'll be up again by then. But I wish you lots of luck with the selection committees.'

'Thank you,' he said quietly, deflated by her obvious lack of warmth.

He was more in love with her than ever. Joanna was twenty now, and the gap between that and his own thirty-four years was, in marriage terms, lessening. But during the two years since she went up to Oxford the other gap, the spiritual gap, had widened. He had noticed her interest in him dwindling from the very first time she came home, and had told himself sternly that this was only to be expected as her horizons broadened and her acquaintances became more numerous. Her attitude towards him tonight, however, indicated that her indifference to him had deepened to the point where she was unaware of his presence unless it was drawn to her attention. It was apparent to Lawrence, if to no one else, that Joanna was head over heels in love. He supposed he should have foreseen the possibility and then he would have been better-prepared for the tide of desolation that washed over him. He wondered bitterly who the lucky man was.

Later in the meal, Reginald Harding made some remark about August Bank Holiday Monday.

'I shan't be here that week, Gramps,' Joanna said, squeezing his hand to lessen his disappointment. 'A friend of mine, Alex Ferrer, has asked me to stay with his parents for the first week of next month.'

Further questioning, mainly from Freda, elicited the information that Alex was the son of Sir Herbert Ferrer and Lady Pamela Ferrer, formerly Lady Pamela Goudge, younger daughter of the late Earl of Denby.

'You don't mean Ferrer's the road haulage people, do you?' Bernard demanded and, when Joanna nodded, added disapprovingly: 'Herbert Ferrer must be one of the richest men in the country. Why is it all my daughters have this penchant for bloated capitalists? No one would think you'd all been brought up to be good socialists.'

'Oh, Dad!' Freda laughed. 'Any minute now you're going

to start talking about grinding the faces of the poor! And, anyway, you can't help who you fall in love with, can you?'

'Who said anything about love?' Joanna asked too quickly and too brightly. 'Alex and I are just good friends.'

Freda crowed with delight. 'Not that hoary old chestnut!' she pleaded.

'Leave the girl alone,' Jean admonished her youngest daughter, coming unexpectedly to Joanna's defence, and turned the conversation with a reference to the recent collapse of the John Bloom Rolls Razor washing-machine company, with debts of over £2½ million. This had the desired effect of diverting her husband's attention from more personal matters; and, once the meal was over, Bernard dragged a reluctant Lawrence off to his study for a discussion about Labour Party strategy in the months ahead.

Anthony thanked his mother-in-law politely for supper and said that he must go. Joanna escorted him to the front door.

'Tomorrow,' he said, gripping her hand with painful intensity. 'The Parade Gardens at about . . . what time? Two o'clock?'

'Three-thirty,' Joanna amended firmly. 'I'm not meeting Davey until two.'

'All right. But you do promise to be there?'

'I can't promise anything, but I'll do my very best. Now, go home for goodness' sake and stop worrying.'

'I'm tired and my feet are hurting.' Joanna sat down on one of the seats near the Abbey and eased her feet out of a pair of new white shoes. 'What's more, I'm dying of thirst.'

Davina made sympathetic noises and nodded towards the Pump Room.

'Let's go in and have some tea.'

'OK.' Joanna appeared to consider the proposition. 'On second thoughts, wouldn't it be nicer to sit out of doors on a day like this? What about the Parade Gardens? There's usually a tea- and coffee-stall there. We can listen to the band at the same time. What do you say?'

She thought briefly that her sister was going to resist the suggestion, but Davina merely shrugged and said: 'All right.'

They skirted the Abbey and crossed the Orangery to Grand Parade. Joanna peered over the wide stone balustrade into the sunken gardens below.

The scent of river water and sun-warmed grasses made her breathe deeply, appreciatively, and the bright municipal flower-beds glowed like jewels against the newly mown lawns. To her left, Pulteney Bridge, with its twin rows of shops, spanned the sluggish weir and the slow-flowing Avon.

As she had predicted, a band was playing, selections from *The Student Prince, Lilac Time, Bitter-Sweet*, Souza marches and popular classics. People were taking their ease in council deck-chairs, on park benches, or just sitting on the grass. Small children – the bigger ones had not yet been let loose for the summer holidays – were chasing each other in and out of bushes, or growing fretful and restless in the heat.

Joanna's eyes darted from side to side, trying to locate Anthony and Samantha. If, after all, he had changed his mind, she didn't know whether to be glad or sorry. Then she spotted them, sitting in the layered shade of some trees.

'Come on,' Davina said impatiently. 'What are we waiting for? I'm broiled, standing around up here.'

They paid their entrance fee at the kiosk and descended the long slope into the gardens. Anthony, who had been on the alert since his arrival, half an hour previously, got to his feet. Lifting Samantha out of her collapsible push-chair, he began threading his way through the sunbathers towards them. Joanna thought that her niece looked enchanting, fair curls tumbled, blue eyes wide with interest, and wearing a blue-and-white floral Marks & Spencer dress which Joanna had bought for her at the beginning of the summer.

'I'll get the tea,' she said quickly to her sister. 'You see if you can find a couple of empty chairs.'

Before Davina could protest, she walked in the direction

of the counter, set back in the shadow of the Parade pavement overhead, not daring to glance over her shoulder for fear of giving the game away.

Davina looked helplessly around her. Every deck-chair seemed to have an occupant, not one of whom showed the slightest disposition to move. Someone tapped her on her arm.

'Hello, Davey,' said her husband.

Forest Moor closed its doors for the eight-week summer break on the last Thursday in July. Anthea Marshall caught the first available train from Southampton to Bath, anxious to see her niece, to hear all about Oxford and to make final plans for their imminent trip to Greece. Two hours after arriving in Royal Crescent, she realized she had a crisis on her hands.

'Tony wants me back,' Davina said unhappily, perched on the window-sill in her aunt's bedroom, watching Anthea unpack. 'He . . . he says he's still in love with me.' She recounted briefly the details of their meeting. 'He had Samantha with him.'

'And you had Joanna with you,' Anthea murmured thoughtfully, but she kept her suspicions to herself, accepting that this was not just one of Davina's periodic attacks of conscience, eventually to be soothed or reasoned away. She had apparently been left alone in her husband's company for over two hours – the tactful Joanna having, it seemed, withdrawn – and a great deal of emotional damage had been done. Of the two, Anthony and Samantha, it was obviously Anthony and his declaration of undying love which had made the most lasting impression on Davina. Anthea decided that her niece had very little maternal instinct, and Samantha's charms had barely dented her consciousness. Davina, however, did have a truly soft spot for Anthony Douglas; and had Anthea been more honest with herself she might have acknowledged that having a 'soft spot' was merely her euphemism for being in love.

The one thing she did acknowledge was that Davina was seriously considering returning to her husband.

'Tony says of course I must finish my time at Oxford. Get my degree.' Davina twisted her fingers together, the knuckles showing in a white line against the sunburned flesh. 'I can't bear to think of him being so unhappy all this time. I honestly thought he'd forget me. Divorce me and marry somebody else. I'm sorry, Aunt Thea, but I'm afraid I shan't be able to go to Greece.'

Anthea made no reply, continuing to put away her clothes. She saw all her dreams in danger of being wrecked. It was a desperate situation. And a desperate situation had need of a desperate remedy.

10

THERESA WAS OFF DUTY at five o'clock all that week and, on Friday, she emerged into the sunshine and traffic chaos of Upper Maudlin Street just in time for the rush-hour congestion. She had been on the women's ward all afternoon and felt tired. She found her own sex more difficult to cope with than men. Women seemed to lack a sense of humour when faced with illness, becoming fractious and far more inclined to find fault. Theresa guessed that this was because they were unused to a passive role during sickness. At home, whatever their own state of health, they were the nurses.

'*My* trouble', Theresa remembered her mother once saying, after Bernard had been in bed two weeks with a bout of flu, 'is that I don't have a wife to look after me when *I'm* unwell.'

Smiling at the recollection, dazzled by the bright sunlight, Theresa collided with a woman coming towards her, and had half-stammered an apology before she recognized her aunt. She broke off, staring in astonishment.

'Hello, Aunt Anthea! What a surprise! What are you doing in Bristol?'

'I might be doing a number of things,' Anthea replied reasonably. 'It's not off-limits to people who live in Bath. But, as a matter of fact, I came to meet you. The Ward Sister, or whoever I spoke to when I telephoned, told me you'd be free about now. I've been waiting for you. I thought we might go and have some tea.'

'Oh! Well . . .' Theresa hesitated, trying not to be rude. She could recall no precedent for Anthea's behaviour. Her aunt had never before singled her out. They did not particularly like one another, and their paths rarely crossed. When Anthea had visited Nightingale Close in the past, she had said less to Theresa than to almost anyone else, with the possible exception of Jean. Now, confronted with this unexpected invitation, Theresa did not know how to refuse. 'I ought to get back to the nurses' home,' she said desperately. 'I need to do some studying. My SRN exams are next year.'

Anthea raised her eyebrows and looked down her long aquiline nose in a way which never failed to intimidate the most presumptuous of her pupils.

'Surely', she said, 'an hour of your time isn't going to make that much difference to you.'

Theresa was hot and uncomfortable. All she wanted was a bath and a cup of tea in the peace and quiet of her own room. Her uniform was crumpled and clinging to her body in the heat. Anthea, on the other hand, was her usual elegant self, in a pale-blue linen dress with navy handbag and shoes. White gloves, a single strand of pearls and a smart navy-blue straw hat completed an outfit which admirably suited her tall trim figure, and made her appear even more efficient and formidable than usual. Theresa experienced the same feelings she had known at school when summoned to the headmistress's study.

'No . . . no, I suppose not,' she managed to stutter.

'Good.' Anthea took her niece's arm, steering her across the road and down Lower Maudlin Street in the direction of the Haymarket and Broadmead. 'I thought we'd go to Jones's.'

They went up in the lift to the restaurant on the top floor and found a table by one of the windows, looking out over the city skyline. When they had ordered – tea, sandwiches and a selection of cakes – Anthea remarked briskly, drawing off her gloves: 'You're probably wondering what this is about.'

93

'Yes,' Theresa agreed awkwardly.'I suppose I am.'

Anthea removed her hat, giving her head a shake. The beautifully cut, greying brown hair fell immediately into place. Theresa was even more conscious of her own untidy locks. She had made an attempt at the new beehive fashion, back-brushing and lacquering her hair into a messy-looking mound which had incurred the wrath of both Staff Nurse Wetherby and Sister Dukes. She had been sent to the cloakroom to comb it out and told never to come on the ward looking like that again. The result had been to make her hair look dull and unkempt. Tonight, she would have to wash it and let it dry straight. She wondered enviously if she would ever have the money to achieve a style like her aunt's.

Anthea leaned forward, linking her hands together on the tablecloth, and asked: 'How fond are you of Anthony Douglas?'

Theresa's face turned scarlet; a raw, ugly, blotchy colour, making her look young and vulnerable. She was the least mature of all the sisters, Anthea reflected; the eternal schoolgirl. She supposed it was that which had attracted Theresa to nursing. She liked the discipline, the sense of duty, the idea of being part of a team; the institutional way of life.

'What's that got to do with you?' Theresa asked bluntly, betrayed into rudeness by her sense of outrage. 'It's none of your business.'

'On the contrary, it's very much my business.' Anthea leaned to one side as the waitress arrived with their order and waited calmly while the girl laid the table, ignoring the seething impatience of her niece. When the waitress had departed, Anthea poured two cups of tea, her own without either milk or sugar, and pushed the plates of sandwiches and cakes towards Theresa. 'Please help yourself. This is my treat, so eat as much as you like. I know you young women always seem to be hungry. Meanwhile, let me explain.' She sipped her tea and then dabbed her lips fastidiously with the paper napkin provided by the restaurant. 'Did you know that Anthony has seen Davina and asked her to go and live with him again?'

Theresa's hand shook and she dropped the sandwich she was eating. Since the start of the long vacation she had seen nothing at all of Anthony, neither had he telephoned her. He had warned her that he intended, if he could, to salvage his marriage, but she had not wanted to believe him. She had tried to persuade herself that, once he had thought it over, he would change his mind. His protracted silence had begun to worry her, but she told herself that he was punishing her for the scene she had created in the pub. He could not possibly have meant what he said.

But now it appeared that he had.

Theresa's courage and optimism revived a little, however, as she considered the situation. Davina would surely not agree. She looked hopefully at her aunt.

'What . . . what did Davey say?'

'Ah! You did know, then. At least he had the grace to tell you in advance.' Anthea took another sip of tea and stared over her niece's head to the roof-tops beyond the window. The sky was gaining in transparency as it slowly drained of colour. A faint haze of light hung over the city, causing the buildings to lose definition; a painting which had been smudged by a thumb. She switched her gaze to meet Theresa's and drew in her breath sharply. 'Davina, it seems, is seriously considering the matter.'

'What?' Theresa's tone was taut with anxiety. 'She can't be! She's always said she'd never go back to him.'

'Then, she must have changed her mind.'

'But . . . I mean . . . how did it happen? When did he speak to her? I thought she wouldn't let him anywhere near her.'

Anthea replied bitterly: 'I fancy your twin could answer that question better than I can. Eat your tea and I'll tell you all that I know. Then I'll tell you what I think you should do.'

'You're very quiet,' Alex Ferrer said, putting his arm

around Joanna's waist. 'In fact, come to think of it, you've been preoccupied ever since you arrived. Is something worrying you, dear heart, that I wot not of?'

They had just finished lunch at the Ship Inn in St Martin's Lane, and were now strolling across the green towards the west front of Exeter Cathedral.

Joanna glanced up at him with a rueful grimace. 'I'm sorry. Has it been that obvious?'

' 'Fraid so. Even m' father, not the most perceptive of men, as you may have gathered, remarked last night, after you'd gone to bed, how quiet you are.'

'Oh dear. And I did so want to make a good impression.'

'Oh, you have, dear girl, you have!' Alex assured her, lying gallantly.

'A nice enough gel,' his mother had pronounced, the day of Joanna's arrival at King's Acre Court. 'But a bit of a pleb. What does her father do, Alex, did you say?'

'A schoolmaster. And you married a bit of pleb yourself, Mother dear, if it comes to that,' Alex had drawled. 'Doesn't seem to have done you much harm.'

'Your father had already made his pile,' Lady Pamela pointed out drily. 'And money, dear boy, makes up for any amount of deficiency in breeding and the social graces. This place could never have been kept going without Herbert's money behind it.' And she had given an all-embracing sweep of one thin arm to include the room in which they were sitting and everything that lay beyond it: the huge and rambling mid-Victorian pile which was King's Acre Court, with its fifty acres of woodland, parks and gardens. 'A mathematics teacher, isn't he? At one of those secondary modern schools, or whatever one calls them.'

'You're a snob, Mother,' Alex had chided, kissing her cheek affectionately. 'A hypocrite, too.'

Lady Pamela had remained unruffled. 'The only two possible things to be, my dear, if you're English, titled and married to new money.'

Alex had laughed and warned her to be nice to Joanna.

His mother had protested, with reason, that she was never anything else to the girls he brought home.

'Ah,' he had answered, his eyes twinkling in the way they had, so that she never knew whether to take him seriously or not, 'but Jo is different. Jo is the girl I hope to marry.'

They entered the cool echoing vault of the cathedral nave, suddenly blinded by the shadow, after the white glare outside, as the long hot summer proceeded on its relentless course.

'You haven't answered my question,' Alex whispered. 'Is something worrying you?'

'Only family matters.' Joanna shrugged dismissively. 'Nothing I should be burdening you with. Let's forget it.'

He murmured: ' "That care, though wise in show, that with superfluous burden loads the day . . ." '

She resented the ease with which he quoted Milton. She had never had a facility for producing apt quotations, and envied those who could. Poetry had been of low priority in a house dominated by the sciences, and even Freda found it difficult to repeat chunks of the playwrights and poets at will.

The week, now half-over, to which Joanna had looked forward with so much eagerness, had begun to seem like a mistake. She was ill at ease with Alex's parents, both of whom accorded her a polite old-world courtesy which was more unnerving than downright hostility would have been. It was the way those sort of people, as she stigmatized them in her own mind, treated inferiors.

'Never be rude to the servants or tradespeople, darling. It simply isn't done.' She could imagine Lady Pamela Ferrer saying precisely those words.

Alex laughed at her when she tried to explain how she felt.

'You really must stop being so damned sensitive,' he had said. 'It's just Mother's way. She's polite to everyone.'

Joanna had been left with a feeling of having made

herself ridiculous, and from then on kept her own counsel. She was anxious about what was happening at home between Anthony and her sister. She had left Bath for Devon at the beginning of August without having seen Davina again. She had thought it wise to let well alone; not to exert pressure in any way. Anthony had been hopeful after their meeting in the Parade Gardens.

'Davey's weakening, Jo,' he had told her over the phone. 'She's still fond of me.'

It confirmed Joanna's own impression during her brief conversation with her sister while they were walking home. Davina had been very quiet for most of the way, but when they had parted at the bottom of Gay Street, to go their separate paths, she had asked earnestly: 'Did I do the wrong thing when I left? Could I make the marriage work?'

'Plenty of women do find fulfilment in marriage,' Joanna answered, adding almost flippantly, afraid of sounding too intense: 'Even Mum's happy after her own fashion.'

'Is she?' Davina had considered the statement. 'Perhaps,' she conceded at last. Then she had turned and walked up Gay Street to the Circus without glancing back . . .

'I said', Alex hissed in Joanna's ear, 'that this is the tomb of Bishop Hugh Oldham, founder of Manchester Grammar School and co-founder of Corpus Christi.'

'What?' Joanna pulled herself together. 'Oh . . . yes.' She focused on the mitred effigy, hands piously folded together in prayer, lying on top of the stone sarcophagus, beneath its elaborately carved stone canopy. 'I heard you.'

'Liar.' Alex grinned. 'You haven't heard a thing I've been telling you for the past five minutes.'

Vaguely she recalled him pointing out the minstrels' gallery and informing her that the roof was the longest unbroken stretch of Gothic stone vaulting in the world. But, apart from that, she had to admit he was right. She could remember very little.

'I'm sorry,' she said. 'I'm not in a very receptive mood this afternoon. And I was so looking forward to you showing me round.'

'No problem. We'll come again another day, when you've less on your mind.'

Joanna turned her head quickly, suspecting sarcasm, but Alex rarely deliberately made people feel uncomfortable. His ugly features, which so many women found so attractive, were devoid of spite. He drew her arm through his and pressed her hand.

'What would you like to do instead?' he asked.

'I ought to go round the shops,' she suggested, 'and buy your mother a thank-you present.'

'No, don't,' he said, a shade too quickly. 'I mean, there's no need. She'd be embarrassed.'

He could see the quizzical lift of his mother's eyebrows; hear the trace of disdain in her voice.

'My dear Alex, what a terribly bourgeois thing for her to do.'

No one could be more devastatingly cruel, more gratuitously rude, when they put their minds to it, than members of the British aristocracy.

He said: 'Why don't we go for a drive? Dartmoor. Drewsteignton.'

They had been for so many trips in his battered little Chamois, which was as much a part of his image as an Aston Martin was of Anthony's, that Joanna had lost count of the places they had visited. She would have liked to explore King's Acre Court – the walled garden, the glade, the willow garden, Hollerton's wood, Sir Julian's wood, the pool garden, the terraces, the winter garden, the conservatories – but Alex seemed anxious to get her out of the house as much as possible; away, she suspected, from his mother. Sir Herbert was seen only in the evenings, at dinner, being in Exeter for most of the day, at the offices near Rougemont Gardens, still the hub of his huge industrial empire, in spite of the lure and greater convenience of London.

They had driven over the northern and eastern edges of Dartmoor so many times that Joanna was growing tired of them. Besides which, she found the moor eerie, with its empty boulder-strewn spaces, the uneasy quality of its silence, its hard metallic skies and strange silver-rimmed light.

Perhaps she wouldn't have minded so much if Alex had actually made love to her, but he hadn't. There were times when she had been absolutely certain that it must happen; when his embraces had been so passionate, so frenzied almost – although she shied away from that particular thought – that the final act of consummation had seemed inevitable. But at the last moment, just when she had been joyously ready to yield, he had broken away with a muttered apology or one of his slightly off-beat remarks, accompanied by a nervous little laugh.

Joanna was frustrated. She wanted him to make love to her, she admitted it freely to herself; and was also aware, in this year of 1964, that women were beginning to take the initiative in sexual relationships. But she still had what Freda called a very old-fashioned attitude towards romance.

'You're still living in the fifties, Jo,' her younger sister would reprove her. 'Nowadays, you've got to get out there and show them what's what!'

But Joanna found the new freedom difficult to cope with. For her, the decisive moves in the game of courtship and love had to be made by the man. And Alex was signally failing to take the final step. Did he regret inviting her to his home, now that he saw that she didn't fit in? At Oxford, the gulf between his political beliefs and hers had not seemed to matter; if anything, it had been a source of rivalry and amusement, scoring points off one another in endless late-night coffee-shop debates. But here, on his home ground, amongst his own kind of people, Joanna was aware for the first time that they were from widely different social backgrounds, and that he was as much a natural right-wing Conservative as she was a committed socialist. She felt confused and miserable. She loved him, but she had no idea if he really loved her.

She sighed and turned away from Bishop Oldham's tomb.

'Yes, let's go for a drive,' she agreed, smiling brightly. 'Why not? It would be a pity to waste such a lovely day indoors.'

11

'YOU'VE BEEN BAD-TEMPERED ever since you got home,' Jean complained, tipping cornflakes into a bowl. 'Didn't the holiday go as planned?'

Bernard glanced up from his perusal of the *Manchester Guardian*.

'I could have told you it wouldn't work,' he said, peering at Joanna over the rims of his spectacles. 'You've nothing in common with Sir Herbert Ferrer's son. Bosses and workers. Same old story.' And he went back to reading his newspaper.

It was one of the few wet mornings of this extraordinary summer, with a light wind sweeping across the garden, lifting the leaves and ruffling the grasses. But it was still warm, and the dining-room window was open, so that Joanna could hear the incessant chattering of the sparrows. After King's Acre Court, the house looked even shabbier than usual. The cracks and stains of the ceiling were like a world map, and one leg of the sideboard was propped up with books. The wallpaper, its yellowing background patterned with pale pink roses and dark blue birds, had been up for years, covering every wall and making no concessions to the fifties fad, still fashionable, for different colours and textures in different parts of the room.

Only Joanna and her parents were seated at the breakfast-table. Reginald Harding, suffering from a heavy summer cold, was having a day in bed. Freda had not yet put in an appearance.

Joanna ignored her father's remark.

'I thought I might walk up to Royal Crescent this morning,' she said, 'and see Davey.'

'What do you mean?' Jean paused in the act of swallowing and said thickly, through a mouthful of milk and cornflakes: 'She and Thea have gone to Greece.' She cleared her mouth and asked impatiently: 'Why are you so surprised? You knew they were going.'

'I just thought . . . well, that they might have changed their minds.'

'Why on earth would they want to do that?'

'No reason.' But as soon as the meal was over she must telephone Anthony.

The post clattered through the letter-box, and they heard Freda thump down the last flight of stairs into the hall. A few moments later, she appeared holding two official-looking letters, one of which she had already opened.

'Passed my A levels,' she announced, without much interest. 'Quite decent grades. Two Bs and a C.'

Bernard exclaimed wrathfully: 'You had no business to open that letter. It's addressed to me!'

Freda, however, was not listening to him. She had slit open the second envelope and was reading its contents. She gave an ecstatic whoop of joy.

'I'm accepted! RADA have accepted me for a three-year course!' She began dancing a jig around the table.

'I don't know,' Jean said doubtfully. 'I don't know about you living alone in London.'

'Oh, Mum!' Freda stopped in her tracks, staring at her mother in exasperation. 'I'm eighteen, for goodness' sake! I'll go to a YWCA hostel to begin with, if that'll make you feel any better. Later on, I expect I'll find a flat with some of the other first-year students.' She leaned over the back of her sister's chair and flung her arms around Joanna's neck. 'Congratulate me, Joey!'

'Congratulations on both achievements,' Joanna said, turning her head and smiling up into the eager face only a few inches from her own.

Even Bernard was looking pleased.

103

'Very good, Freddie. Very good indeed.' But there was no doubt he was really referring to the A-level results which he held in his hand.

Freda was far too excited to eat any breakfast and, as soon as everyone had finished, Joanna helped her mother wash up, then headed for the telephone.

Anthony was at home.

'I simply don't know what went wrong,' he said in answer to Joanna's questions. He sounded angry and unhappy. 'I could have sworn that Davey was ready for a reconciliation. I spoke to her the day before you went away, last Friday week. She came out to the Manor. It was quite voluntary. I mean, I hadn't pressed her to come. She was a bit quiet but, then, things were a bit strained all round. Maybe my parents weren't too welcoming, but Davey said she understood. We went for a walk, her and Sam and me. And then, when I phoned her the following morning, your aunt answered and said Davey didn't want to speak to me and please would I not ring her again. They were going to Greece, after all, she said. But Davey had told me, only the previous afternoon, that she had definitely decided to cancel the holiday.'

'Haven't you any idea what could have happened in the meantime? It must have been on the Friday evening, after Davey got home.'

'I've no idea at all.' Anthony sounded depressed. 'And frankly, Jo, I'm beginning not to care. That's it, as far as I'm concerned. I've done my best, and I'm not prepared to waste my life waiting for Davey to change her mind again. I've talked it over with my parents, and I'm going ahead with the divorce.'

'Oh, Anthony, no!'

'Sorry, Jo, but there it is.' His tone had taken on an implacable note, and Joanna realized that nothing she could say, no arguments she could advance, would make him change his mind. 'It's what your sister's wanted for a long time, and now it's what I want, too. And I have to think of Sam. I can't expect my mother to look after her for ever. Thanks for all your help, but there it is. Come and visit us whenever you like. You know you're always welcome.'

When she had hung up, Joanna stood for a while, staring at the receiver. She had been so certain that Davina wanted to mend her broken marriage that she found what had happened hard to credit. However much she thought about it, she was unable to see what had gone wrong. Except that Anthea had come home . . .

After a while, she went upstairs to help her mother with the usual Monday-morning chore of changing the beds. She had problems of her own, without spending any more time worrying about Davina.

Alex had seen her off from Exeter's St David's Station the previous afternoon with an affectionate kiss, a pat on the back and a promise to be in touch as soon as he returned from the family holiday in the south of France. The Ferrers had a villa just outside Juan les Pins. Joanna had wondered if they might ask her to join them there, later in the month, but she and Alex had said goodbye without anything being mentioned. She suspected that his mother continued to be the problem. The long vacation suddenly seemed just that, stretching ahead of her in a procession of empty dreary weeks.

She decided she must get a job, but the ones offered her by the clerk at the Bath employment exchange had no appeal.

'You've left it a bit late,' the girl said. 'The best temporary vacancies were all snapped up as soon as the universities came down.'

'Why don't you help Larry Walden?' her father suggested. 'He's been selected as prospective Labour candidate for Avonvale. He doesn't stand a snowball's chance in hell of winning it, of course. Solidly Tory. Always has been. But it'll be good experience for him and, if he acquits himself well, he'll get a stab at a marginal seat next time.'

'The Prime Minister hasn't even called an election yet,' Joanna objected.

105

'Home's got to go to the country soon, and October is everyone's bet. The papers are full of speculation, but they're all agreed on that.'

'What on earth could I do for him?' she demanded, interested in spite of herself. She remembered Davina's warning, all those years ago: Don't give him anything that could be construed as encouragement. Don't be too friendly; play it cool. But politics had always interested her; and just at present, feeling angry with Alex and his parents, the idea of doing something constructive for the Labour Party had a special appeal.

'Telephone him and ask,' Bernard said. 'I'll give you his number. If he's not at the Clifton flat, he's probably staying in the constituency with his agent. Fellow called David Nugent. Larry gave me his address. You never know, there might be something you can do.'

Lawrence Walden was at home when she rang, and his delight, once he realized who was speaking, made Joanna wary. But in her present vulnerable state she was not proof against the warmth of his tone. It was nice, she discovered, to be needed.

It was Theresa's day off. Having finished her spell of duty on the women's ward she came home to Nightingale Close.

'Men's ward on Thursday,' she announced with satisfaction. Joanna was sitting in the garden with her grandfather, and Theresa had wandered out to join them. She dropped into a spare garden chair and stretched out her legs. 'Fancy coming to the pictures tonight?' she asked her sister. 'Mum says *Goldfinger*'s on at the Beau Nash.'

'I'd love to,' Joanna said regretfully, 'but unfortunately I can't. Larry Walden's picking me up after tea and we're driving over to Avonvale. There's a residents' meeting at the town hall about the proposed new bypass, and as prospective Labour candidate they want to hear his views. I'm going along to lend moral support.'

'You're going along', her grandfather commented drily, 'as window-dressing. Constituents prefer a candidate with

106

a woman in tow. They're not keen on single men, whether they're bachelors, widowers or, like Larry, divorced. This is the third or fourth time you've been to meetings with him. If you're not careful, people will begin to get the wrong idea.'

'Nonsense!' But Joanna blushed uncomfortably, particularly when faced with her twin's look of curiosity.

'How long has this been going on?' Theresa wanted to know.

'Nothing's going on,' Joanna snapped. 'I was at a loose end, and Dad suggested Larry Walden might find me a temporary job helping in the Avonvale constituency. He's been adopted as prospective Labour Party candidate, in case you've not heard. As it turned out, with the election not yet called, there isn't much in the way of stamp-licking of leaflet-folding to be done. But his political agent asked if I could accompany Larry to one or two meetings. Last Saturday', she added with a laugh, 'we were at a vicarage fête.'

'I believe you're quite enjoying yourself,' Theresa remarked thoughtfully. 'You always liked politics.'

'Now, don't get me wrong!' Joanna begged sharply. 'I'm doing what little I am doing as a favour to Larry, because he's a friend of Dad's and because I'm sorry for him. Nothing more.' She added: 'As far as the future's concerned, there's not a chance he'll be elected. It's just good experience for him. Even David Nugent says that. It's solidly Tory country.'

Freda opened the dining-room window. In four weeks time she would be leaving home for London, and she could hardly wait for the day to arrive. Her impatience to be gone was making her almost unbearable to live with.

'Phone, Jo!' she shouted briefly, and withdrew her head before her sister could ask who it was on the line.

'She's really impossible nowadays,' Joanna grumbled, getting up. 'She's just discovered Webster, and we've been treated to speeches from *The White Devil* and *The Duchess of Malfi* all week.' She went indoors.

It was Alex. She couldn't believe her ears.

'I cut short my holiday in France,' he said. 'I missed you. I wanted to see you.'

'Where are you?' she asked, dazed, her heart slamming against her ribs.

'In Bath. Well, just outside. I'm staying with cousins of my mother. I was hoping I might see you this evening. Just tell me where exactly you live and I'll be there as soon as possible.'

Her stomach lurched sickeningly. 'Oh, Alex, I can't. Not this evening. I've made other arrangements.'

He was too polite to ask her what they were or suggest that she cancel them. 'Tomorrow, then,' he said. 'I'm here for several days.'

Damn Lawrence Walden! Damn this silly meeting she had let herself in for! She would ring him and say she couldn't go. Then she envisaged the hurt look on his face, the whipped hangdog look in his eyes. She could not do it to him. But she must make it absolutely clear that tonight was the last occasion she would be available as escort.

The meeting was over. The arguments for and against using valuable farmland to relieve traffic congestion on Avonvale's overcrowded roads had raged furiously back and forth. The sitting Conservative MP who had been present to back Tory councillors, and Lawrence Walden had both put opposing points of view, Labour for once coming out strongly in support of the farmers. Lawrence had done his homework, and been ready with a better and far less controversial route for the proposed bypass. Now the hall was almost empty.

David Nugent, who had been sitting in the front row, climbed on to the platform. A tall man with red hair and freckles, dark-rimmed spectacles perched precariously on the shallow bridge of his nose, he had a rare quality of being able to put people immediately at ease. It was his powers of persuasion which had coaxed Joanna into accompanying Lawrence on his recent forays into the

Avonvale constituency. She had sat beside him throughout the meeting, strongly aware of his very masculine presence. He was twenty-eight years old, married to a very pretty girl some years younger than himself and had two small children, a boy and a girl.

'That was great, Larry!' he said, flinging an affectionate arm around Lawrence's shoulders. 'You put up some very strong arguments, and that suggestion for an alternative route was brilliant. Caught the Council boys on the hop. I reckon this evening's been worth a few thousand votes for us in the election.'

Lawrence's thin face broke into a grin, and he glanced proudly at Joanna like a little boy seeking approval. She hardened her heart.

'I'm glad it went well,' she said briskly, 'because this is the last time I'll be able to come with you.'

His face crumpled ludicrously. 'But the Michaelmas term doesn't start until October,' he protested.

'A friend of mine has just arrived in Bath.' She avoided David Nugent's eyes. 'A friend I want to see a lot of. A man,' she added baldly. She saw the shuttered look descend on Lawrence's face and went on ruthlessly: 'When I asked you if there was anything I could do to help, I hadn't bargained on being offered the job of surrogate wife. If that sounds rude, I'm sorry, but I do have a life of my own to live, and I wouldn't want to give anyone the wrong impression.'

'No, of course not,' Lawrence agreed calmly, after a moment during which he fought to control his voice. But his disappointment was acute.

When Joanna had telephoned him three weeks earlier, he had been too excited and too happy to consider the motives behind her offer of help. She had never approached him or sought him out of her own free will before, and it never occurred to him to question her reasons. He remembered, earlier in the summer, thinking that she was in love; but, as far as he could tell, she seemed to have got over it. At university, these affairs were often so fleeting. And Bernard had never mentioned Alex Ferrer in their conversations.

David Nugent was looking embarrassed and kicking himself for having completely misread the situation. When Joanna had been introduced to him, he had received the definite impression that there was a close relationship between her and Lawrence Walden. Now it appeared he had been wrong, and he was disappointed. He had recognized Joanna at once as a political animal, who would be an invaluable partner for any aspiring MP. She was bright, intelligent and a potential Honours graduate, unless he was very much mistaken. The disparity between her and Lawrence's ages hadn't seemed to matter. She was a serious girl, older than her twenty years.

He said smoothly, long training at papering over awkward cracks coming to his rescue: 'I'm sorry that we won't be seeing you again, Jo, but I think Larry's proved tonight that we're both redundant. He can stand on his own two feet without support from either of us.' She was looking relieved, and he knew that he had said the right thing. A naturally demonstrative man, he bent down and kissed her cheek. 'We shall miss you. Thanks for all your help. Enjoy the rest of your vacation. Now, there's an all-night café next door. Let's go and get ourselves a cup of well-deserved coffee.'

12

JOANNA HAD NOT REALIZED, until he asked her to a party at Green Top Farm, that Alex was related to the Nevilles. Lady Neville and Lady Pamela, it seemed, were some sort of cousins and, although not close, they were nevertheless on sufficiently friendly terms for Alex to be welcome at the farm whenever he wished to stay there.

'It's Claire's twenty-first birthday,' he told her. 'You've been invited.'

'You mean you've wangled me an invitation,' Joanna said, laughing.

The past week, since his arrival, had been one of mixed happiness. She had found the same contentment in his company that she always did, and had shown him her patch of ground with as much pleasure as he had felt in showing her north Devon. They climbed Glastonbury Tor and explored the abbey ruins. They went to Weston and played the penny-in-the-slot machines on the pier. They fed the ducks and swans on the moat of the Bishop's palace at Wells and did a tour of the Roman baths at Bath. They had tea in the Pump Room and experienced the same difficulty in crossing Cheap Street, opposite Union Passage, that Jane Austen had complained of in *Northanger Abbey*.

Even Alex's visit to Nightingale Close passed off without a hitch. Bernard and Jean were uninhibitedly themselves, but managed to avoid the vexed subject of politics. Perhaps both of them sensed how important Alex was to her, Joanna thought gratefully. And he was soon on easy terms with her grandfather and Freda, the latter going out of her way to charm him.

'Your sister's a scamp,' he said later, with an affectionate grin. 'She'll go through life doing the most outrageous things, and people will simply indulge her.'

'You mean she'll get away with murder,' Joanna retorted caustically. 'Mmm. That sounds like Freddie.'

But, in spite of everything going so well, her own relationship with Alex seemed to progress no further. He kissed her passionately, snuggled up to her in the cinema, put his arm around her when they walked, but never said that he loved her or suggested going to bed together. And, more than anything else in the world, Joanna wanted him to make love to her. So why didn't he? Was it because he had old-fashioned values? Was his occasional coldness because he couldn't trust himself not to? Did he really think that she would mind?

Her head spun with unanswered questions. She would wake at night from dreams of him that made her blush when she recalled them in the cold light of day. She still, however, found it difficult to take Freda's advice and make the first move.

Yet nowadays women were making the running all the time. There was a different atmosphere abroad. The raising of their hemlines to a height not seen since the twenties had given women a sense of freedom never before enjoyed by their sex. To add to the confusion, men were growing their hair and starting to wear bright colours for the first time in nearly a century. But with women also wearing trousers – or tunic-like dresses and tights, which made them look like medieval page-boys – there was an androgynous look about the young which was beginning to blur the dividing-line between the sexes. Women were beginning to usurp men's roles, both physically and mentally, and vice versa. Joanna, unlike Freda, was finding it hard to adapt.

She also continued to fret about her elder sister. She wanted to know what had changed Davina's mind, but

Davina and Anthea were still in Greece. It seemed likely, therefore, that Joanna would have to wait for an explanation until the start of the Michaelmas term, when they had both returned to Oxford. Meanwhile, Theresa was also full of plans for the commencement of the new university term, when Anthony would once more be in Bristol every day. She had already invited herself, on several occasions, to Lyncombe Manor, and from time to time Anthony took her to the cinema or the theatre, or for an evening meal at a pub or a restaurant. It was obvious to Joanna that her twin's hopes were again riding high, but after Claire Neville's twenty-first birthday party at Green Top Farm she could not help wondering how justified those hopes were.

'You're not enjoying yourself,' Alex accused her, as they swayed together to the number one Cilla Black hit, 'Anyone Who Had a Heart'. 'Come on, kid! Give us a smile.' He did his Bogart imitation.

The communicating doors between the dining- and drawing-rooms of the farm had been thrown wide open, with the record-player and a stack of records sited, more or less centrally, against one wall. Joanna reckoned there were about thirty couples crammed into the space thus provided, and noted grimly that Anthony had been invited as Claire's partner. They displayed all the ease of an acquaintance with stretched back over a number of years; but there was, Joanna considered, more to the relationship than that. Anthony seemed genuinely fond of Claire, while it was fairly obvious that she was very much in love with him.

Claire Neville was a pretty girl with dark hair and dark melancholy eyes, rather too heavily made up, and fringed by thick lashes which gave her a permanent look of suppressed surprise. She was wearing a dress of flaring scarlet which made her thin body seem even thinner and accentuated her general waif-like appearance. Whether this was natural or contrived, Joanna was unable to decide, but it was clear that a number of men, including Anthony, found it very appealing. All Claire's movements were controlled and delicate. She was the antithesis of Theresa.

'I said you're not enjoying yourself,' Alex hissed again in her ear, as they paused for breath. They leaned against a corner cupboard containing sets of beautifully carved ivory chessmen and one or two exceptionally fine pieces of dark-blue Bristol glass.

'I am!' Joanna protested indignantly. 'Very much indeed!' She nodded towards Anthony, as he danced by with Claire. 'That's my sister Davina's husband, did you know?'

'Someone mentioned it,' he answered lightly. 'She left him for the groves of academe, or so I was given to understand.'

It got under her skin sometimes when he spoke in that slightly stagey fashion, and she said irritably: 'If you mean for a university career, why don't you just say so?'

'Sorry.' His lips brushed her hair, and she could feel that he was laughing at her. It annoyed her even more.

'I'm going outside for some air,' she announced brusquely and headed for the dining-room door without waiting to see if he was following her.

A long stone-flagged passage led to a garden at the back of the farmhouse, with an unrivalled view of distant Bath, nestling in its marshy valley. An evening breeze, blowing across the high ground, soothed her flushed cheeks. To her left, a tangle of shrubbery made a wind-break for a worn and weatherbeaten seat; and, behind that again, the grey creeper-hung walls of the house provided yet further shelter. It was still very warm, and menacing banks of cloud were building up on the horizon. The hot early-September day was threatening to end in thunder. A group of barns and the distant spire of a church, together with an occasional tiled roof, showed beyond the slope of the parched fields, stubbled now after the harvest.

Joanna sat down on the bench and waited. After a moment or two, Alex joined her, slipping his arm around her waist and kissing her cheek.

'What's the matter?' he asked gently. 'You've been in a funny mood all evening.'

She turned her head to look at him. It was dusk, and the lights of the distant city were coming to life one by one, spangling the darkness. Lights had also been switched on in the farmhouse, sending the shadows, which had been lurking like predatory jungle beasts, springing across the flower-filled borders. Alex's saturnine face was close to hers. Tentatively, she put up a hand and stroked it. He took it in one of his own and pressed his lips against the palm.

Joanna said: 'That's a very pretty gesture, Alex, but does it mean anything?'

He regarded her quizzically. It was a look she knew well, and it always had the power to make her feel weak at the knees.

'Does it have to mean anything?' he asked.

She summoned up her courage and decided it was time to speak plainly.

'I should like it to mean that you love me.'

'You know I do. I thought I'd made that obvious.'

'Not to me. You've never said so in so many words.'

'Haven't I? Ah!' There was silence for a moment while he stared, almost absent-mindedly, ahead of him. Then he said: 'That first night after you arrived at King's Acre, after you'd gone to bed, I told my mother that you were the girl I was going to marry.'

Joanna felt breathless. It was difficult to speak. 'I . . . wish you'd told me,' she eventually managed to stammer.

He grinned. It was strange, she reflected, how most women, after they had known him for even the briefest period, ceased to think of him as ugly.

'I thought I had,' he said. 'In deeds, if not in words.' He quoted Goerge Herbert. ' "Words are women, deeds are men." '

Once again Joanna experienced a prickle of irritation at his refusal to be straightforward.

'Are you saying you love me?' she demanded. And without waiting for his answer she continued: 'Are you saying you want to marry me?'

There was an even more protracted silence than before. The sky had turned the colour of smoked glass, and there was an ominous rumble of thunder overhead. A few drops of rain, the size of large hailstones, fell on the back of Joanna's hand. Alex drew her closer so that her head was resting in the hollow of his shoulder.

'I suppose I must be,' he agreed at last.

On 16 October the Labour Party, after thirteen years in opposition, and after a night of nail-biting tension, won the general election with an overall majority of four. Joanna, watching the results as they came in on a friend's television, noted with a surge of pride that Lawrence Walden had increased the Labour vote in Avonvale by more than five thousand – no mean achievement in a traditionally Conservative stronghold.

She returned to her own room, bleary-eyed and yawning, in time for a belated breakfast. She decided to cut the morning lecture and concentrate instead on finishing her essay for the afternoon's tutorial. But her enthusiasm for the Victorian poets was at a low ebb, and it was with an overwhelming sense of relief that she called, 'Come in!' in answer to a knock at her door just before lunch-time.

Relief turned to delight at the sight of Alex, standing beaming at her, framed in the doorway. He made her an elaborate bow, less mocking than usual.

' "To the victor belong the spoils," ' he quoted, adding with a grin: 'Personally, I prefer the Scott Fitzgerald version: "The victor belongs to the spoils." '

Joanna scrambled to her feet and went over to kiss him. 'If I were one for gloating . . .' she began.

'You should see your face!' he retorted. 'It has "gloat" written all over it. However' – he laid a finger gently against her lips – 'I have not come here for a political

116

discussion. So, woman, hold your tongue.' His eyes were very bright and, for a moment, she wondered basely if he had been drinking. But there was no smell of alcohol on his breath, and she came to the conclusion that he was simply enjoying himself.

'What are you doing here?' she asked. 'Did you cut Claydon's lecture, too?'

'Alas, yes. But unlike you, who, I imagine, have frittered the night away watching the sad decline of the ruling classes, I have the best of excuses. I had some very important shopping to do.'

'Shopping?' She frowned.

'Shopping. For this.' And he produced from his jacket pocket a small red leather box, embossed with gold lettering, which he handed to her with a flourish. 'Voilà! Sweets to the sweet.'

The thought touched the edges of Joanna's mind that the whole quotation was *Sweets to the sweet: Farewell*. But the sight of a very beautiful opal in an antique gold setting drove all other considerations from her mind. Under the gem's milky surface, the colours gleamed and shifted.

'Oh, Alex, it's *wonderful*,' she breathed as he ceremoniously lifted it from its bed of white satin and slipped it on to the third finger of her left hand. But yet again she could not help remembering the old wives' tale that opals were unlucky. Whatever was the matter with her this morning? This was the moment she had been waiting for ever since that evening at Green Top Farm.

She had secretly resented the fact that there had been no immediate formal recognition of their engagement. She had suspected a reluctance on Alex's part to commit himself further than he had done already. But now it seemed that she had been wrong. On a morning when she might have expected him to be sulking over the Conservatives' defeat, here he was, apparently unconcerned, surprising her with an engagement ring and in the mood for celebration.

'I shall take you out to lunch,' he said, stooping to kiss her. 'Champagne. All the trimmings.'

There was a knock at the door and, without waiting for an answer, Davina came in.

'I hear you've been looking for me,' she announced. 'So as I had to come to Corpus this morning I thought I might as well find out what it's about.' She became aware of Alex. 'Sorry. Am I in the way?'

'Oh, no. It's only our official betrothal.' Alex smiled distantly and drifted towards the door. He was not fond of Joanna's elder sister. He had met her once or twice at parties in the rooms of mutual friends, and thought her self-centred and cold. 'Jo will show you the ring.' He blew a kiss at Joanna. 'I'll be back to pick you up in half an hour. I'm afraid I can't spare you longer than that.' Then he was gone.

'You can certainly pick your moments!' Joanna exclaimed in some dudgeon. 'I've left messages for you all over the place, but you have to choose this particular morning to come barging in. As Aunt Dora would say, your sense of timing is way off beam.'

Davina shrugged and sat down in a basketwork chair. She looked neat and businesslike, as always.

'So why do you want to see me?'

Joanna asked bluntly: 'What went wrong, Davey, between you and Anthony? When I went away at the beginning of August, I was sure everything was set for a reconciliation between you two.'

She thought Davina wasn't going to answer, but after a moment's hesitation her sister said: 'Well, if you must know – although I don't see it's any of your business – I had a visit from Theresa. She called at the flat one Friday evening. It was the day after Aunt Thea came home for the summer holiday. I remember because Aunt Thea had gone into Bristol for the day and then went on to visit a friend in Clifton for the evening. I'd been over to Lyncombe Manor that afternoon.'

'So what did Twin want?' Joanna asked as Davina fell silent.

Her sister stared sightlessly at an old brass jug, brought

118

by Joanna from Nightingale Close, filled with big pink chrysanthemums, their shaggy heads like mops. After a while she said slowly: 'Did you know that Terry and Anthony had been sleeping together? That he'd mentioned marriage to her? Not just once, but on several occasions.'

'I don't believe it!' Joanna exclaimed forcefully. 'Twin's making it up.'

'Why should she? What has she to gain?'

'For heaven's sake!' Joanna leaped off the bed and began pacing about the room. 'Terry thinks she's in love in him. Maybe she is. I don't know! But I do know that she always resented the fact that he preferred you to her. She'd do anything, say anything, to prevent a reconciliation between you. Why would he ask her to marry him, when he was planning all the time to get you back?'

'She refused him.' Davina put up a hand and smoothed a strand of sun-bleached hair into place. 'As a matter of fact, Terry was the one who told him he ought to try for a reconciliation, for Samantha's sake. But even after he'd decided to do his paternal duty' – Davina spat the last word scornfully – 'he was still pestering her to sleep with him.'

'Rubbish! She's lying!' Joanna was sceptical. None of this sounded like her twin. Theresa could get angry and say hurtful things she didn't mean, but she was never devious or calculating. Either she had indeed been telling the truth, or someone had primed her with the story . . .

Anthea! It had to be. She had been in Bristol, it seemed, that day.

Davina got up to leave.

'Davey,' Jo urged, 'have you thought . . .?'

'I've done with thinking.' Her sister cut her short. 'I made a decision about my life three years ago and I should never for a moment have considered changing it again.' She turned on Joanna almost savagely. 'I'll tell you what I don't want, Jo! I don't want an unfaithful husband, and I certainly don't want one who's unfaithful with my own sister! I have no intention of being like Mother. Did you know that Dad and Aunt Dora had once been lovers? No, I can see by your face that you didn't. I overheard Mum and Dad quarrelling that day I ran away. I couldn't stand being humiliated in that fashion!' Davina opened the door and stood, framed in the doorway. She was looking very beautiful, her skin glowing with health and tanned to a warm honey colour by the Aegean sun. She wore a black-and-white check skirt and a white Angora sweater, black stockings and low-heeled shoes. Tiny diamond studs, a present from Anthea, gleamed in her ears. Her grey eyes were cold as she glanced at her sister. 'I've made up my mind, Jo. From now on, there's no going back. I've told Terry that if she wants Anthony she can have him!'

13

'IT'S TIME that man got married and had a proper home of his own.'

Jean removed the turkey from the oven and began to baste it. The kitchen, as always on Christmas Day, looked as though it had been struck by a whirlwind. Joanna, standing at the sink, looked up from the bowl of potatoes she was peeling.

'Dad hasn't asked Lawrence Walden for dinner today, surely!' she protested.

Her mother nodded glumly. 'What could I say? The poor man hasn't anyone else to turn to. That's what I mean about him getting married. It must be six years now since he and Emmy were divorced. High time he was thinking about another wife and relieving me of the burden. Besides,' Jean went on, ladling hot fat over a scrawny-looking bird, 'he'll need a wife if he ever gets into Parliament, and he seems determined to try again at the next election. Your father says Wilson's bound to go to the country soon. He can't hang on very long with only a majority of four.' She paused, frowning. 'Jo, this bird is terribly thin. There's no breast on it. It's never going to feed six of us. I'm sure it wasn't like this when I brought it home from the butcher's.'

Joanna abandoned her potatoes and came to stand by her mother. After a moment, she started to laugh.

'What's funny?' Jean demanded suspiciously.

'Nothing, except that you're cooking it upside down.' Joanna kissed her mother's flushed cheek and went back

121

to the sink. 'A pity Terry couldn't get time off for Christmas.'

Jean shrugged. 'We don't see much of her at all these days.' She seized the bird between two pieces of grease-proof paper and hoisted it over. 'Oh, yes, that's more like it! What a silly thing for me to have done. All Terry's spare time', she went on, 'is taken up with studying for her finals and chasing Anthony Douglas.'

'She still sees him, then?' Joanna's tone was neutral. 'When does the divorce go through?'

'It becomes absolute at the beginning of February. A divorce in our family! Whoever would have thought it!'

'It's common enough nowadays.' Joanna dropped the last potato into the saucepan and lit a gas-ring. She put the saucepan on to boil. 'You don't see Sam very often.'

'Oh, she's all right.' Her mother replaced the turkey, right side up, in the oven. 'The Douglases spoil her and give her everything she wants. There's not much we can do for her. She comes here occasionally for the day.' As though suddenly conscious of how offhand her remarks sounded, Jean embarked on a flustered self-justification. 'I don't know! It's just that ... well, Sam doesn't seem like our grand-daughter. We've never had a lot to do with her, after all. And we can't keep on going to Lyncombe Manor and poking our noses in. It wouldn't be good for the child. And then there's ... how shall I put it? Loyalty to Davina.'

'I shouldn't think you owe Davey anything!' Joanna retorted with asperity. 'She rarely comes to see you, even when she's in Bath and only a quarter of a mile away.'

'She and Thea go abroad a lot. They're in Innsbruck this Christmas.'

And you really don't care whether you see her or not, Joanna thought, emptying the potato peelings into the pedal bin next to the sink. There had always been something lacking between Jean Marshall and her eldest daughter.

Jean asked: 'When are you going down to Exeter? You did tell me, I know, but I've forgotten.'

'Sunday. The day after tomorrow.'

Freda wandered into the kitchen. She had not arrived home until late Christmas Eve, having spent the first few days of the holiday with friends. Joanna considered that the freedom of London and the heady intoxication of RADA had not improved her. It seemed to her that Freda had even more theatrical airs and graces than before she went away.

'It's a phase,' Reginald Harding had protested, when Joanna had aired her opinion earlier that morning. 'Freddie's free of the restrictions of home for the first time in her life. Naturally it's gone to her head.'

'When are we giving the presents?' Freda wanted to know. 'And don't expect anything spectacular from me, folks. Pockets are absolutely to let. Everything in London's so bloody expensive.' She perched on a corner of the kitchen table and waited to be reprimanded. Both Jean and Joanna wisely ignored her. Freda looked disappointed and swung her legs.

She was wearing a very short red skirt and a black top with a matching red roll-neck collar. Her black tights were patterned with flowers and disappeared into white boots, decorated on the front with bows. Her hair had been cut, by a talented fellow-student who had missed his vocation, in one of the new geometric styles, originated by Vidal Sassoon, and her face was adorned by furry false eye-lashes, very pale, almost colourless, lipstick and a liberal coating of Max Factor panstick.

'We're giving them after lunch, as we always do,' Jean snapped, growing more harassed and bad-tempered by the minute, overwhelmed by the sheer logistics of preparing Christmas dinner. In domestic terms, the festive season remained the biggest trap of the year.

Bernard popped his head around the door. 'Your father's asking for his coffee,' he said, 'and I could do with mine. I shall be in the study until Larry arrives.'

When Joanna had made the coffee, she volunteered to carry the cups upstairs to the two men, but her mother shook her head and grabbed the tray. Any excuse to escape from the heat and panic of the kitchen for five minutes was too good to miss.

Freda unhitched her leg from the table-corner and sat down opposite Joanna, who had made a start on the Brussels sprouts.

'Gramps says you're going to stay with Alex and his parents the day after Boxing Day. Incidentally, congratulations. I haven't really looked at the ring.' Joanna held out her left hand, and Freda grimaced. 'Pretty. But I thought opals were supposed to be unlucky.'

'An old wives' tale.' Joanna pushed a knife across the table. 'Here. Make yourself useful and help me with these sprouts. Take off the outer leaves and split the stump across, like this.' She demonstrated, but she might as well have saved her time and breath.

'Sorry, darling.' Freda pushed the knife back again. 'I must look after my hands.' She sighed. 'Lucky old Davey, eh? Innsbruck and all those bronzed ski instructors. Posh hotels and drinks in the bar. It's got to be better than this.' She glanced disparagingly around her, at the chaos and the mess. 'I think today I'd even rather be Terry, struggling with bed-pans on the wards. And that shows you how much I wish I wasn't here. At least you've got King's Acre and the delectable Alex to look forward to.'

'He's ugly,' Joanna said, laughing. 'And he'd be the first to tell you so.'

Freda stretched her arms above her head, the thin black material of her bodice straining across her breasts. At eighteen, she was developing into a very attractive woman, Joanna noted.

'There's ugly and then there's ugly,' Freda answered cryptically. She lowered her arms and looked thoughtfully at her sister. 'He's very attractive and he knows it. I'd watch him, if I were you. There's an elusive quality about your Alex. Remember that song Judy Garland sang in *A Star Is Born*? "The One That Got Away".'

Anthony Douglas was doing part of his practical training

124

on the wards of the Bristol Royal Infirmary, known simply to all Bristolians as the BRI.

He had not been looking forward to the separation from his daughter and parents over the Christmas period, nor, if the truth were told, from Claire Neville. They seemed to be seeing a great deal of each other during his free time these days; and, although study devoured most of his spare waking moments, he nevertheless found himself frequently in her company.

He liked Claire, and had recently begun to suspect that liking was ripening into something deeper. He was not in love with her in the way that he had been in love with Davina, but that had been a once-in-a-lifetime emotion, and not one that he wished to repeat. It had brought him nothing but unhappiness and, as far as he was concerned, it was over; something to be put behind him and forgotten.

Claire was a quiet gentle girl; not brilliant academically, but that was all to the good. Her outside interests would never conflict with her husband and home. She had left school with a couple of indifferent CSEs in English and Geography, and now decorated the reception desk of a Bath dentist, doing what was expected of her extremely well. Nervous patients found her reassuring, charming and easy on the eye.

Anthony was on good terms with Sir Harold and Lady Neville. He had known them for many years and always found them completely devoid of 'side'. As the inheritor of an ancient baronetcy, Sir Harold could have been expected to look down his aristocratic nose at the self-made Douglases and, had he ostracized them, the rest of the county would probably have followed suit. Instead, he had positively encouraged the friendship between Anthony and Claire, and had never been heard to make a derogatory remark about either Norman or Cicely to anyone. Some of his friends sneered that he had his eye to the main chance and the Douglas fortune, and had been inclined to laugh when Anthony got married in a hurry to the daughter of a Bath schoolmaster. What could you

125

expect? they had asked one another. Blood would tell. But now it was a different story. The Douglas boy would soon be divorced, and it looked very much as if his friendship with Claire might lead to something more permanent. Except that several of them had seen him about in the company of his soon to be ex-sister-in-law: the one who was the nurse. It sometimes seemed as if he could not make up his mind.

The wards and corridors of the BRI had been decorated with a mass of coloured balloons and paper streamers. All the lights were switched on after a lunch of turkey and Christmas pudding, for those patients who could eat it, to add a little sparkle to a cold grey day and to bring some added warmth to the austere interiors, which the Edwardians had considered suitable for the care of the sick. Nurses and doctors alike started to relax as afternoon visitors began streaming in with parcels and magazines and bunches of hothouse flowers.

Anthony and a fellow-student, Brian Bickerstaff, were in the sluice near the main women's ward, chatting up a couple of nurses, when Theresa appeared. She was looking flushed, her cap slightly awry, and she was carrying a sprig of mistletoe.

'Right!' she said. 'Who's next?'

She ignored Anthony and made straight for Brian Bickerstaff, putting her arms around his neck and giving him a long hard kiss, to cheers of encouragement from the other nurses.

'Go it, Marshall! That's the ticket!'

'Watch your hands, love, you're making him blush!'

Grinning, Theresa released her embarrassed victim and made once more for the door.

'Hey!' Anthony protested. 'What have I done? Don't I get a kiss?'

'Sorry.' She smiled at him provocatively. 'I didn't think you cared.' She shot a pleading glance at the other two girls.

The smaller of them nudged the other in the ribs. 'Come

126

on,' she murmured, 'it's time old Mrs Duffey had her medicine.' And when her friend seemed inclined to linger she seized her arm in a vice-like grip. 'Come on! And *you'd* better come with us,' she added to Brian Bickerstaff. 'Mrs Duffey's a very interesting case.'

When they were eventually alone, Theresa made no attempt to approach Anthony. Instead, she leaned against the sterilizer and said accusingly: 'You've been avoiding me lately.'

'Nonsense! I've been busy, that's all. And you've been studying for your exams.'

He was uneasy. He hadn't expected Brian and the other two nurses to disappear like that, and wasn't quite sure why they had. His remark to Theresa had been an idle one, in keeping with the general hilarity and laxness of the season. He would have said it to any nurse walking around with a sprig of mistletoe in her hand. It hadn't been intended in any specific context. He heaved himself away from the wall and asked, with an attempt at jocularity: 'Well, am I going to get that kiss or not? It may be Christmas, but there's still work to be done. I can't stand here all day.'

Theresa looked at him for a long moment. Then, slowly and deliberately, she moved towards him, put her arms around his neck and her lips on his. It was a sensuous embrace, her tongue probing his mouth, her body pressed close against his. He had never known she could be like this. In the hospital, among the male students and nurses, she was referred to as 'flash-bang-wallop Terry', and he had come to think of her that way himself. Flighty Terry Marshall, uniform always slightly askew; jolly, bouncing, good for a laugh. Very few people realized how bright she really was. They thought her good examination results simply a matter of luck. She hid her intelligence under the mask of a clown.

She was kissing him harder now, her lips demanding a response. He was aroused and his arms closed round her. He kissed her in return, the lobe of her ear, the base of her

127

throat. He felt excited, as though he were making love to her for the very first time.

The door of the sluice opened, and Brian Bickerstaff's voice whispered urgently: 'Knock it off, you two. Matron's doing her rounds, wishing all the patients a merry Christmas. For Pete's sake, come on!'

Davina stood at the window of her hotel bedroom and looked out at Innsbruck's snow-covered peaks. Down in the courtyard, people were returning for drinks and early dinner, after a day spent on the ski slopes. A thin sun was showing through the clouds as it sank behind the mountains, and a flurry of snow, grainy and dry like salt, spattered momentarily against the glass, blown loose from the overhanging eaves. Somewhere a dog was barking; probably the smelly aggressive little terrier belonging to one of the elderly residents.

Davina turned back into the lighted room and looked at herself in the wardrobe mirror. She was wearing a short black lace Courrèges dress, which had been Anthea's Christmas present to her. She had never owned a Paris frock before, and although it was an off-the-peg model from the boutique, and not an *haute couture* original, it had cost a lot of money and she was still nervous of putting it on. Anthea told her not to be so silly. French clothes were made to last.

'It's time you had something decent, my dear,' she had observed, when her niece had protested against such extravagance. 'You're going places, Davina. You must look the part.'

Going places. Now that she was in her last year at Oxford, it was her aunt's perpetual theme. Davina occasionally woke in the middle of the night in a cold sweat, in case she somehow failed Anthea's expectations. She owed her too much to face with equanimity the prospect of letting her down. And she had almost done so last summer, when she had seriously considered going back to Anthony. If she hadn't found out in time about Theresa, she would probably have thrown everything away.

But would it really have been throwing everything away? Was she that certain she wanted the brilliant academic career her aunt had mapped out for her all those years ago? Didn't she want Anthony even more? And what about her child? Why was she so lacking in maternal feeling? If it came to that, why was she so lacking in filial emotions? She had never felt anything very much for Jean. Perhaps, Davina thought resignedly, she was just incapable of love.

But that wasn't true, either. She had loved Anthony. She still did, if she were honest with herself, which wasn't very often nowadays. It was simply that it had all come too soon, love and motherhood, before she was ready for them. And now she would shortly be divorced, a free agent once again. Except that a woman who had had a child could never really regard herself as free . . .

There was a knock on the door which separated her room from Anthea's. Her aunt came in.

'You're wearing it,' Anthea said with approval, looking at the dress. 'I must say it's shorter than I remember it in the shop.'

Davina smiled. 'All the fashion magazines are predicting even shorter skirts this coming year. You're looking very smart yourself. Very *grande dame*.'

Her aunt laughed. 'I'm not sure that that was the intention, but thank you all the same.' She did indeed look extremely handsome in a plain black Balmain dress, with pearls. The dinner-gong sounded. 'Shall we go down?'

Davina hesitated. It was as if, just for a moment, a curtain had been lifted and she could see herself clearly, living a life chosen for her by somebody else, manipulated like a puppet, with her aunt pulling the strings . . .

But, of course, it wasn't like that at all. It was what she, Davina Douglas, wanted. It had to be. It was what she had chosen.

She decided to revert to her maiden name.

14

REGINALD HARDING was watching the television transmission of Sir Winston Churchill's funeral, the pageantry of a nation's homage to one of her greatest heroes, and yet a man whom Reginald himself had never really liked. He could never forget the fiasco of the Dardanelles during the First World War, or the tragedy of Greece in the Second.

Reginald Harding had almost been too young to fight in the 1914–18 conflict, but he had scraped in by the skin of his teeth to join the RNVR in the very last months of the war. After three hectic days at Crystal Palace, where he was issued with his naval uniform, he had found himself on a train bound for Lerwick, in the Shetland Islands, where a wireless station had been set up. Even now, after all these years, any mention of Lerwick brought to mind the stone-flagged streets and the smell of the herring drifters moored in the harbour. Later, he had been transferred to Longhope in the Orkneys, for final briefing as an Ordinary Telegraphist, but the Armistice was signed before he could complete his course.

He had been released early because he intended to train as a teacher, and in 1918 teachers were in short supply. Before the end of the following spring, he was engaged on an Honours course in Modern History at Bristol University. He had already met his future wife, and shortly after that, poor as the proverbial church mice, they had married. Jean had been born nine months later. The next year Dora had arrived.

With a First Class Honours degree, he had fondly

imagined that he would easily secure a post in a grammar school, but by that time the situation had changed and there were too many teachers. Desperate for money, he had written to the Board of Education asking to be relieved from his commitment to teach, on the grounds that no vacancies were available; but to his astonishment he had been told that the commitment must stand unless he repaid the cost of his training. In desperation, he had applied to the Admiralty Schoolmaster branch and joined the Royal Marines as an instructor, teaching almost illiterate recruits to read and write and pass simple exams. He and his family had moved to Deal, where, apart from six weeks' training in HMS *Defiance* – two hulks moored in the Hamoaze, an inlet of Plymouth Sound – and a brief spell at Chatham, he had remained for the next seven years.

During his stay in Deal, Reginald had found time to finish the thesis which earned him his MA degree, and when he eventually returned to Bristol he managed to find a job as junior history master at one of the grammar schools. After the Second World War, he had moved to Bath, and in the mid-fifties had successfully applied for a vacancy in the Inspectorate, advertised by the Ministry of Education.

And it was as one of Her Majesty's Inspectors for Schools that he had ended his career, sufficiently comfortably off to buy the pleasant airy house overlooking Henrietta Park, and to have savings put by. But he had never forgotten the early poverty and struggles, and all his life tended to resent people who, through an accident of birth, were born to wealth and privilege. It was this attitude of mind which had led him to join the burgeoning Labour Party in the early 1920s, and to raise both his daughters as socialists.

Reginald had been proud when Jean followed him into teaching, but secretly he was even prouder of Dora and her acting career. He and his wife had always been ardent theatregoers, and when their younger daughter announced her decision to go on the stage neither of them

131

had tried to dissuade her. She had made some sort of success at it, too, in an overcrowded profession where so many sank without trace. And now Freda was following in Dora's footsteps, and likely to make an even bigger name for herself if her grandfather was any judge of the matter. It would not be an overnight success – there were far fewer of those than the public imagined – but he had no doubt that she would make it in the end. Freddie had a star quality about her, combined with natural talent, which augured well for the future.

No, Freda was all right. It was the others he worried about. He stared at the television screen, watching President Eisenhower standing on the deck of a ship with a knot of other VIPs, but not really taking in the scene. He was too busy thinking about his grand-daughters. A bad business, that of Davina and Anthony Douglas. She should never have left him and the child like that. They should have worked something out. Times were changing. It would soon be the norm for a woman to have a family and a career. It wasn't healthy, either, for two women to be as close as Davina and Anthea Marshall. He blamed Jean for that. She should have nipped that relationship in the bud, before it had time to blossom. But she had never had much feeling for her eldest daughter. She had resented Davina's arrival in 1943, because she had been forced to give up her own career. Bernard had been away in the Army, and she had had to struggle on alone.

Joanna didn't seem really happy, either. Reginald Harding shifted restlessly in his chair, and it was not just because, today, his hip was painful. He got on well with Alex Ferrer, whenever Joanna brought him home, but there was something not quite right about that engagement. It was difficult to define exactly what was wrong, but, if pressed, Reginald would have said that there was too much giving on one side and too much taking on the other. There was a lack of purpose about Alex: he struck Reginald as a man who found himself in a situation almost against his will, but was too much a gentleman to object.

But there again it was such a nebulous feeling that he often upbraided himself for being too fanciful.

It was Theresa, however, who really exercised his mind, causing him sleepless nights, when he tossed restlessly on his pillows. She was still seeing Anthony Douglas – inevitable, Reginald supposed, when their work brought them so often into contact – and lately, to her grandfather at least, she had mentioned the word 'marriage'. Primed by Joanna and following his own instincts, Reginald had tried to persuade her not to be too sanguine. He saw nothing in Anthony's manner to suggest that he had any really serious intentions towards Theresa. Reginald had hinted to him once that he should stop seeing her on anything but a strictly family basis, but Anthony had only laughed.

'I like Terry,' he said. 'She's fun and a good sport. One of the boys.'

Hardly a lover-like encomium, Reginald had thought sadly.

In a few weeks' time, Anthony and Davina would be divorced, and Reginald wondered what would happen then; how things would work out . . .

He realized that for more than ten minutes he had been completely unaware of what was happening on the screen. He levered himself out of his chair and switched off the set.

'I thought we were going to the pictures,' Theresa said. 'You agreed to see *What's New, Pussycat*. You know how I like Peter O'Toole.'

She sounded petulant, even to her own ears, but she had just finished a spell of night duty and this had been her first day-shift back on the wards. She still hadn't adjusted properly to the new routine and was tired. What was more, her final SRN examinations loomed on the horizon, only weeks away, and she knew she should have stayed in her room this evening to revise. Instead, as soon as she was free, she had rushed back to the nurses' home, changed her uniform for a pale-green linen dress and matching jacket, and hurried out to meet Anthony. He was waiting for her in their usual place, by Neptune's statue, overlooking the old harbour in the city centre.

'Sorry I'm late,' she panted, the warmth of the June evening and her last-minute panic-stricken rush making her hot and flustered. 'Are we going to miss the beginning of the film?'

It was then that Anthony had suggested going for a walk instead.

'There's something I want to say to you.' Ignoring her protest, he took her firmly by the elbow and guided her in the direction of College Green.

'What ... what do you want to talk about?' Theresa asked, her breath catching in her throat. Her excitement mounted. This was it. He was going to propose.

'Wait,' he said. 'We'll go up on Brandon Hill.'

In the eighteenth century, Brandon Hill had been a fashionable residential district. Now it was a pleasure garden; lawns and flower-beds, rockeries and waterfalls, winding paths, rustic seats and shady trees. Dominating everything, on the crest of the hill, was Bristol's tribute to John and Sebastian Cabot, the tower which bore their name.

'Let's sit down,' Anthony said, indicating a seat near the children's swings. It was only seven o'clock, and there was still a number of youngsters enjoying themselves in the little playground.

'Well?' Theresa asked. Her voice sounded thick and unlike itself. 'What is it you want to say?'

Anthony made no response for a moment, apparently absorbed in watching two small boys attacking another with all the robust brutality of the young. The city sprawled below and around them, islanding them on their mound. There were a lot of people about, enjoying the first real hint of approaching summer. The sun, flaming in the west, filtered through the overhanging trees, making golden fans of the horse-chestnut leaves.

Theresa stirred restlessly. Why couldn't he just come

134

straight to the point and ask her? He must know what her answer would be.

He turned his head at last to look at her, and took one of her hands in his. She waited tensely, returning the pressure of his fingers.

'We've been good friends, Terry, you and I, over the years.' She nodded mutely, and he went on: 'Your friendship's meant a great deal to me since Davey and I split up. We've had some good times together. So' – he drew a deep breath and smiled – 'I wanted you to be the first to know that I'm getting married again. I can't bring Sam up on my own. She needs a mother.'

Theresa sat in frozen silence. Somewhere close at hand a bird was singing. The heavy scent of elderberry flowers, just coming into blossom, hung pungently on the air. The three boys had stopped fighting and were screaming with laughter over something one of them had said.

'What do you mean, you're getting married again?' she asked at last. Her lips felt bloated, and she was feeling sick.

'I've asked Claire Neville to marry me, and she's agreed.' There was a short pause. 'Aren't you going to congratulate me?' he said.

Theresa withdrew her hand. She was suddenly shivering, desperately cold. Shock, she thought automatically; hot sweet tea, blankets, keep warm. She began to laugh, quietly at first, then wildly, letting herself go in complete abandon. Anthony was looking astonished, and she dabbed her eyes with her handkerchief.

'Sorry!' she gasped, trying to pull herself together. 'I'm not laughing at you.'

He avoided asking her for an explanation in the same way that he avoided looking her straight in the eye. He said stiffly: 'I thought you'd be pleased for me.' And at the back of his mind a voice nagged: 'Liar! Liar! Liar!'

That made her laugh harder than ever. 'Oh, I am!' She struggled for breath. 'Delighted!'

Anthony began to feel embarrassed. Passers-by were staring at them and grinning or looking concerned. He

135

exclaimed angrily: 'For God's sake, shut up! It's not that funny!'

'It's not funny at all.' Suddenly, Theresa was perfectly sober. She was twisting her handkerchief round and round between her fingers. 'What is it I'm supposed to say? Oh, yes. I hope you'll both be very happy. But don't bother asking me to the wedding.' She forced herself to stand on legs that were still unsteady. 'I'll be seeing you around, I expect. Now I must get back and do some studying.'

'We could still go to the pictures,' he offered.

He spoke almost without thinking. Theresa's reaction to his news had been worse than he had feared, having spent days convincing himself that she felt about him as he felt about her; simply as a very good friend. Just good friends. The trite phrase made him wince as he reflected how many times, in how many cases, it had proved to be untrue. He should have taken Joanna's advice, her grand-father's hints, and made a clean break with Theresa. He had been selfish. She had been useful as a casual girlfriend when others were unavailable. He deserved to feel every bit as miserable and as guilty as he did.

'No, thank you,' Theresa said quietly, in answer to his invitation. She had herself in hand now and was behaving with a maturity and dignity totally at variance with her usual rather childish, tomboyish style. 'I'll say goodbye. As I said, I expect I'll be seeing you around.'

'Almost bound to,' he agreed sheepishly. 'Are you sure you're all right? I think perhaps I ought to come with you.'

'No!' Once more there was the hint of hysteria in her tone, which she heard and quickly suppressed. 'I'll be fine on my own.'

She moved stiffly away from him, like someone recovering from an illness and not yet sure of the strength of her limbs. Then she began to hurry, stumbling at first, before breaking into a run. He got up and followed her to the top of Great George Street, but she was already too far ahead for him to catch up. The last he saw of her was the pale green of her dress, her hair flying loose about her shoulders, the ridiculous strappy high-heeled sandals making her appear taller than she really was, vanishing round the corner into Park Street.

'Your mother really doesn't like me, does she?' Joanna asked, linking her arm through Alex's. 'She wants you to marry that Olwen creature.'

She was spending the first week of August, as always, at King's Acre Court. Ahead of her lay her last year at Oxford and a future which, for the moment, remained distressingly blank. She had no idea what she wanted to do except marry Alex, but he was as elusive as ever about setting a date. They were engaged, he said. Wasn't that enough?

As far as Joanna was concerned, nothing would ever be enough until he was hers alone, and removed from Lady Pamela's sphere of influence. She acknowledged herself completely baffled by Alex's relationship with his mother. Never once had she seen him behave like the downtrodden son; nor did Lady Pamela, as far as she could tell, ever seek actively to coerce him. They sparred verbally, argued fiercely, but good-humouredly, laughed at the same jokes, but never at any time did they encroach on one another's independence. And yet, Joanna felt, his mother did, in some subtle way, influence Alex's actions.

This evening, for instance, at dinner, without doing or saying anything overt, she had made it perfectly plain to everyone that Olwen Bruce was the girl she would really like him to marry. Dick Bruce was Sir Herbert Ferrer's senior accountant, a large florid man with an acute business sense and aristocratic connections, which made him acceptable to both the self-made man and the Earl's daughter. Selma Bruce was a silly fluffy woman, but their only child, Olwen, while inheriting her mother's doll-like prettiness, with cornflower-blue eyes and soft blonde hair, had her father's drive and acumen. Joanna could see for

137

herself that Olwen Bruce would make the ideal wife for the heir of Ferrer's International Haulage.

After dinner, the other four had settled down for a rubber of bridge; and Alex, knowing how card games of any kind bored Joanna, had suggested taking a stroll in the gardens. She had agreed with some misgivings, knowing how he, too, enjoyed his bridge.

'You don't want to take too much notice of Mother,' Alex replied lightly. 'I never do.'

They were strolling along the terrace outside the house, where a magnificent *Magnolia Grandiflora* climbed the wall of warm red Hensley stone. It had been raining hard all day, but now the sun was out, bathing the lawns and flower-beds in a brittle transitory glory.

Joanna glanced sideways at Alex. 'Don't you want to go to bed with me?' she asked abruptly.

He did not answer immediately, but paused, bracing himself against the stone balustrade which edged the terrace and staring out across the gardens. After a moment or two, he said harshly, in a voice totally unlike his own: 'Don't you think that sort of thing is best left until after marriage?'

Joanna was disconcerted. 'Perhaps ten years ago . . .,' she began uncertainly, then went on: 'Alex, these are the "swinging sixties". Everyone's doing it, or so we're told. The old taboos have been lifted.' She pressed herself against his back, slipping her arms around his waist and hugging him. 'But, in any case, I love you, you love me. We're engaged to be married. Surely that's a sufficient reason.' Once again there was silence, broken only by the twittering of some birds in a nearby tree, gathering to fly back to their roost. 'Alex?' she queried softly, giving him another gentle squeeze.

He turned suddenly, breaking free of her arms and pulling her roughly into his, covering her face, her eyes, her throat with kisses. For a moment she was delighted, before panic at the violence of the onslaught began, once more, to substitute fear for pleasure. She could feel his fingers biting

138

into her shoulder-blades, bruising the flesh. Her lower lip was torn and bleeding. Her dress was ripped at the neck. This was far worse than his previous attempts at making love, and it occurred to her that perhaps the reason why Alex normally held himself on so short a rein was because he was a man of overmastering sexual drive and passion. Perhaps his mother knew what he was really like. Perhaps that was why she was so protective towards him.

He was crushing her so tightly she could scarcely breathe. She tried to push him away, protesting on a gasp which was half laughter, half hysteria: 'Alex! Let me go! Please! Not like this. Gently! What on earth is the matter with you?'

Her words seemed at last to penetrate his consciousness, and he dropped his hands, backing away from her and leaning, panting, against the balustrade.

'But isn't that what you wanted?' he demanded.

'Yes . . . No! Not like that! You must know it isn't.'

He wiped his mouth with the back of his hand, then made a little half-gesture in her direction.

'Jo, I'm sorry.' The proffered hand sank back to his side and, to her horror, she saw his eyes slowly fill with tears. He repeated wearily: 'Jo, I am so sorry.'

She was beside him at once, her arms about his neck, her head resting on his shoulder.

'Don't be, my darling. Don't be! I understand.'

'Do you?' he asked quietly. She raised her head to look at him, and the old rueful smile crept back into his eyes. He was once more the Alex whom she knew and loved. He would have added something further, but just at that moment the french door leading from the drawing-room opened. Sir Herbert appeared, bluff and genial.

'Telephone, Joanna my dear,' he announced. 'Your mother, so Higgs informs me. Take it on the library extension.'

Joanna was confused. She could think of no good reason why Jean should be ringing her – it was only two days since they had said goodbye – and she was acutely conscious of Sir Herbert's curious stare, followed by his hurriedly averted glance. With her torn dress and bleeding lip, she was only too well aware of the appearance she presented. She slipped past him into the house.

The library was on the other side of the building, overlooking the drive; a high-ceilinged room with walls covered in walnut bookshelves of an elaborate Gothic design. On the floor was a fine Indian carpet from Amritsar, and George II mahogany chairs surrounded a late eighteenth-century drum table. Between the windows was a French bracket clock in Louis XVI style but, so she had been told, with an English fusee movement.

The telephone, incongruously modern in bright blue plastic, stood in the middle of the table. Joanna picked up the receiver, and there was a click as Higgs, the butler, replaced the one in the hall. Alex, sensing her anxiety, had followed her and now hovered close at hand.

'Mother? Is something wrong?'

'Oh, Jo . . . Oh, Jo! It's so awful, I still can't believe it!' She heard her mother start to cry.

'Mum!' Her voice was sharp, laced with terror. 'Mum! What's happened? What is it? It it Gramps? Is he ill? Is he . . .?' She could not bring herself to finish the sentence.

'No. No, it's much worse than that. It's . . . it's . . .' Jean was becoming incoherent.

'Mother!' Joanna shouted down the phone. *Tell me what has happened!*

'It's Terry,' Jean managed to get out at last. 'Matron's just rung me. She . . . Terry . . . she's taken an overdose of sleeping tablets. Oh, Jo! Oh, God! Theresa's dead!'

PART THREE

1966–71

15

THE TRAIN was only half as full as it normally was on a Saturday afternoon at the height of the summer season. On this 30 July, people had postponed all but the most necessary journeys unless, like Joanna, they lacked any interest whatsoever in football. For today England had reached the finals of the World Cup and were playing West Germany at Wembley.

Taunton station and suburbs were left behind as the train moved once more into open country; the lush fields and farmlands lying along the borders of Somerset and Devon. Joanna, in the corner seat of her otherwise empty compartment, stared out of the dirty window. The very last of the houses, with their neat lawns, bright and close-cut, gave place to a long overgrown bridle-path and a stream, whose water was dark and brackish. Willows over-hung the bank, and in the distance was a building which might have been stables. Rooks cawed and swooped high in the trees, and woods bounded the horizon. Deep green fields and brick-red earth indicated they were crossing into Devon.

Joanna, locked inside her thoughts, saw none of it. She was going, as usual, to spend the first week of August with Alex and his parents, but this time there was a difference. This time they were finalizing arrangements for the wedding. A year, eighteen months ago, she would have been thrilled at the prospect. Now she was apathetic. She had been in that state, that half-twilight world, since Theresa died. She was burning up with hatred of Anthony Douglas.

143

The coroner had brought in a verdict of suicide while the balance of the mind was disturbed. Several nurses had testified to the fact that Theresa was swotting hard for her SRN examinations, and had been taking sleeping pills to help her relax after long hours of study. One or two close friends said she was depressed following what they presumed was a row with a boyfriend. She had also, earlier on the evening of her death, been drinking in a pub with a couple of medical students from the University. One of these, Brian Bickerstaff, gave evidence that although Theresa left not later than seven o'clock she had already had three large whiskies.

On entering the nurses' home, she had met two other nurses on their way out. One of these said she thought Theresa was crying, but could not be certain, as Nurse Marshall had brushed past them and run quickly upstairs. The girl who occupied the neighbouring room had heard Theresa slam the door of her own room and then move about for five minutes or so, after which it had all gone quiet. She thought nothing of this until, at about eight o'clock, she went to ask if Theresa would like to join her for a mug of coffee. She had found the door locked, and there had been no answer to her knocking. For some reason, she had become uneasy and fetched the Warden, who had spare keys for every room. When the door was opened, they had discovered Theresa in bed and had thought, at first, she was asleep, until her unnatural stillness and the empty bottle lying on the coverlet had alerted them to the truth. All attempts, both immediate and at the hospital, had failed to revive her. The parents had been informed at once.

Throughout the proceedings, there had been no mention of Anthony Douglas by name, and although the coroner had touched on 'the row with the boyfriend' he had been decided in his opinion that pressure of work for her forthcoming exams had been the cause of Theresa's final breakdown. He had made a few well-chosen remarks about the stresses of modern life and the inadvisability of putting young people under too much pressure, and the case had been closed. Joanna, who attended the hearing, thought that Anthony got off far too lightly.

From the beginning, she had been positive in her own mind that his marriage to Claire Neville was the cause – and the sole cause – of Theresa's suicide. She did not believe for one moment that pressure of work would have given her twin even a fleeting qualm. She remembered the ease with which her sister had passed exams at school, and knew that almost everybody underestimated Theresa's scholastic ability because she played the fool. If Theresa had been taking tablets to make her sleep at nights, it had been because she was unhappy about Anthony Douglas and for no other reason.

Joanna, who had always liked Anthony, who had always warned her twin not to take him too seriously, began to hate him. Grief-stricken by the thought of the loneliness and despair which must have driven Theresa to so final an act, and blaming herself for being so wrapped up in her own affairs that she had been too blind to see or to help, her guilt and desperate need to find a scapegoat had made her ex-brother-in-law a natural target. It was useless to tell herself that she was being unreasonable and unfair. Her intelligence knew it only too well, but even now, after a year, she was still unable to think of Theresa's death with any kind of rational detachment. Anthony must have been aware of Theresa's feelings for him, and should have made a clean break with her once he realized that he had no intention of marrying her. And added to all this was Davina's story that Anthony had slept with, and actually proposed to, Theresa, who, in what her twin could only presume was a fit of conscience, had sent him to make peace with his wife. It was all such a muddle, the only clear fact to emerge being that, from the first, Anthony had acted badly by Theresa.

Joanna's own antidote to unhappiness had been hard work, which had resulted in a Double First. She had come down from Oxford loaded with honours and without the slightest idea what she wanted to do with the rest of her life except marry Alex, with whom she was as much in love as ever. There had been no repetition of the scene on the terrace the night Theresa died. All Joanna's emotions were temporarily blunted, and Alex seemed willing ro respect her grief.

Alex, who had obtained a Second Class degree in Economics, had gone into his father's firm to learn the haulage business 'from the bottom up', as he put it, but no one had any illusion that he was just an ordinary employee. Bernard grumbled that there were better men on the dole, but at a time when it was taken for granted that a person who found a job boring or uncongenial would simply move on to another nobody paid much attention to his strictures.

And, indeed, even Bernard had very little to grumble about since the March general election had returned a Labour government for the second time in slightly less than eighteen months, and on this occasion with a respectable overall majority of ninety-six. Lawrence Walden had fought and been elected for West Yorkshire Moors constituency, and taken his seat in Parliament on the government backbenches. Joanna had been pleased for him and written him a very nice letter, to which he had not replied: a fact which she had not even noticed, being by then deep in plans for her wedding.

Alex's announcement that they might as well get married now as wait until later had taken her by surprise. She had always assumed that she would be the one to chivvy him into setting a definite date, and she was still not sure why he had come to this sudden decision. She resolutely held at bay a growing suspicion that his mother was putting pressure on him to break off the engagement, and that this was the only way he could think of to resist her; because, if that were so, what did it imply about the true state of Alex's feelings?

Joanna sighed and began gathering up her things – handbag, jacket, magazines, her unread book – as the train drew slowly into St David's Station. She lifted her case off the rack and made her way into the semi-deserted corridor. The train doors opened, and the inky ribbon of platform stretched before her. Alex was standing in front of a poster advertising Torquay and displaying a couple of garishly painted palm trees. She waved, and he moved forward to greet her.

'Hello, love,' he murmured, and his lips lightly brushed her cheek.

Freda was delighted when Dora invited her to stay for the first two weeks of the summer vacation.

'I'm resting, darling, and it'll be marvellous to have some young company,' her aunt had assured her over the phone.

Freda, standing in the cluttered hallway of the house in Notting Hill Gate, where she shared the three attic rooms with two other drama students, thought it would be marvellous, too. She liked London, but her grant didn't run to remaining there for pleasure. Normally, as soon as term ended, she headed for home and the employment exchange, in the hope of finding a temporary job to eke out her allowance. The thought of the big garden flat in Holland Park filled her with delight.

Besides, going home these days wasn't what it had been. Since Theresa's suicide, there had been a sombre feel to the house, and although nobody talked about it very much Freda knew that it was in all their minds. Her grandfather had taken it particularly badly, and seemed to blame himself for some reason. But, then, all of them, in one way or another, did that.

'We should have seen it coming,' Bernard had said once, out of the blue and in the middle of a completely unrelated conversation. It had been at Christmas, Freda remembered, and she and Joanna had both been at home.

They had all known immediately what he was referring to, and Jean had cried: 'I don't see how we could have! I really don't!' And then they had all carried on talking as though there had been no interruption, except that the

147

subject under discussion, whatever it had been, no longer seemed important any more.

Another time, Freda had discovered her mother crying quietly to herself as she peeled the potatoes for dinner; and, although Jean's cooking was as bad as ever, Bernard had stopped complaining. The heart had gone out of the house; and, even though it must one day return, Freda preferred to stay away as much as possible until that happened.

Dora had a ground-floor flat in a street near Ladbroke Grove, a legacy from her second husband. Freda loved the houses in Holland Park, with their porticoes, stuccoed frontages and wrought-iron railings. She liked the chestnut trees in Holland Park itself, and the intellectual undercurrents of its famous past. Henry and Charles James Fox had lived there; so had Lord Leighton, the artist, and Ford Madox Ford. She remembered someone telling her that there had been pig-sties and potteries there once, and even a racecourse. Hippodrome Place now marked the site of the stables.

'Darling!' Dora said, opening the door and smothering her niece in a warm embrace. 'Lovely to see you!'

It made Freda feel instantly at home. Most actors, she presumed, were extroverts, and what she missed most in Nightingale Close was the constant touching, the kissing, the extravagant expressions of delight or despair, which, however insincere, were as necessary to her as breathing.

She liked, too, the well-ordered luxury of her aunt's flat, compared with the disorganized clutter of home and the near-squalor of the Notting Hill attics. She settled down to enjoy her week with Dora.

One evening Dora said to her: 'You're not into all this drugs thing, are you? LSD or whatever it's called.'

It had been a wet day, with skies of tumbling clouds which had not yet cleared, and they had decided not to go out after all.

'I'll cook us something,' Dora had volunteered, and had produced two wonderfully fluffy omelettes, packed with

148

tiny button mushrooms in a rich cream sauce. She had always been, ironically, more domesticated than her elder sister.

'Poor Jean,' she used to remark, 'she never could work out which way up to hold a frying-pan.'

She and Freda ate their meal on their knees, sitting in front of the big gas-fire in the drawing-room, which Dora had insisted on lighting because it was chilly.

'I feel the cold,' she said.

It was a room full of pale floral chintzes, flower pictures adorning the walls. The huge sofa was like a deep feather bed, and the armchairs almost as bad. Freda always felt she might get lost and never be found again every time she sat in one. There was a fire-screen, canvas, embroidered in brightly coloured wools, which was used to mask the fire when it was not in use, and a pale-pink wall-to-wall carpet. Freda, who adored soft and pretty things, loved it.

'This room is so typical of you, Aunt Do,' she said, glancing around her.

'Yes, I suppose it is,' Dora answered, 'but you're avoiding my question. You're *not* into this drugs thing, are you?'

'Not into it, exactly. I've made a couple of trips, we all have, but you needn't look so worried. I didn't enjoy it.' Freda stared down at her plate. 'If you want the truth, I was frightened. It didn't work for me the way it does for a lot of people. I didn't get all the wonderful experiences they talk about. It was like being in a nightmare. I can't really describe it. I wouldn't want to do it again.'

'I'm glad to hear it,' Dora said quietly. 'Drugs are a mug's game. Like you, I tried it once or twice when I was young. It was mainly cocaine in those days. But I had the sense to stop before it became a habit. Don't let other people shame you into doing it. That's always a danger. You get called a coward, a spoilsport, names like that. Promise me you'll ignore that kind of taunt.'

'OK,' Freda agreed lightly. She could not resist adding: 'This is a very serious conversation, Aunt Do.'

149

Dora grimaced. 'I am capable of being serious, you know. Being on the stage doesn't preclude you from having a brain or even common sense. I was thinking of Jean. She's had all the trauma of one daughter's suicide. She doesn't want another addicted to drugs.'

Freda stopped eating and stared at the flickering gas flames of the fire.

'Jo blames Anthony Douglas,' she said. 'For Terry's death, I mean. She's quite paranoid on the subject.'

'Is that Davina's ex-husband? That handsome boy I met one Easter when I came to Bath? I remember now. At that time he was going out with Terry. What does he have to do with it?'

Freda resumed eating. 'If you don't mind, it would take too long to explain. But I think Jo's wrong. Taking your own life is a personal decision. It's a matter of choice. I don't see you can blame anyone else, do you?'

'Perhaps not.' Dora put aside her empty plate. 'But Terry was Jo's twin. Jo's bound to take it harder than the rest of you. What about Davina? What does she feel?'

Freda shrugged. 'I don't know. In the past few years, I've only seen her once, briefly, at Terry's funeral. If she was upset, you wouldn't have known. Aunt Thea was with her. They both had their emotions well under control.'

Dora rested her chin on her hand, waiting for her niece to finish her omelette.

'Your father tells me she's got a job at Forest Moor.'

Freda laughed shortly and laid her knife and fork together. It was raining heavily again. The houses on the opposite side of the street looked mysterious and romantic in the damp evening mist.

'Junior history mistress,' she said. 'As soon as the post fell vacant, Aunt Thea had Davey apply. And she got it. Surprise, surprise! Aunt Thea must have that Board of Governors in her pocket. Goodness knows what the rest of the staff must think. Nepotism isn't in it!'

'Have you ever thought', Dora suggested gently, 'that

Davina might simply have been the best-qualified candidate for the job?'

Freda regarded her aunt affectionately. 'You're a very nice person, do you know that?' She leaned across and kissed Dora's cheek. 'I much prefer my mother's sister to my father's.'

'Thank you, darling.' Dora gathered up the dirty plates. 'It's a tribute I don't deserve, however. And now, in true British fashion, let's not get too emotional, even if we are rogues and vagabonds. Did I tell you that I've been asked to play the Countess in a Radio Three production of *The Cenci*?'

'I don't know it,' Freda admitted cautiously. 'Who's it by?'

'It's the poet Shelley's only play, based on the real-life case of a noble Italian family. Briefly, the father, Count Cenci, rapes his daughter, Beatrice. Together, Beatrice, her step-mother – that's me – and her brother murder the Count. Then they're all arrested and executed. *Charlie's Aunt* it ain't, and it's pretty tough going on the ear. But lovely from an actor's point of view.'

'Sounds grim. Well, this time next year, I shall be in the market for a job.' Freda gave a nervous laugh. 'Probably waitressing or washing up in an all-night café.'

Dora put her arm around her niece's shoulders.

'You'll be all right,' she said. 'I won't pretend it isn't a tough life, but from what I've seen you've got what it takes. A certain spark. But don't expect it to be a bed of roses to begin with.'

16

'NO. I'M SORRY, but I will not, under any circumstances, have Anthony and Claire Douglas invited to the wedding.' Joanna stared defiantly at Alex and his mother.

The three of them were in the library at King's Acre Court, drawing up a list of guests, already too long for comfort. Joanna knew her parents could ill afford a wedding of such a size, but knew also that Bernard would reject Sir Herbert's well-meant offers of financial assistance. She had kept her own friends and family to a minimum, but the number of people whom Lady Pamela found it necessary to invite had run into several pages. Joanna had been going through the pencilled names, in her future mother-in-law's spidery writing, trying to put a brave face on things. Alex must surely realize that a wedding of this magnitude would embarrass her father. She was wondering when he would intervene, when she read: 'Sir Harold and Lady Neville. Dr and Mrs Anthony Douglas.'

Lady Pamela frowned. 'What do you mean? Of course Anthony and Claire must be invited. Winifred Neville is my second cousin. And as Claire and her husband live near Bath it would be the height of discourtesy not to ask them.'

'No,' Joanna repeated mulishly. 'I will not have Anthony at my wedding.'

'It's Alex's wedding as well!' Lady Pamela was beginning angrily, jerked out of her normal detachment by what she regarded as a studied insult to members of her family, but her son interrupted her.

'Mother! Please. I've already explained to you why I

thought Jo would object to their presence.'

Lady Pamela's lips set obstinately in a bloodless line.

'You told me some nonsense or other about Joanna holding Anthony Douglas responsible for her sister's death, but I can't say I took much notice.' She addressed herself again to Joanna. 'You really must try to pull yourself together. Be realistic. Your sister was plainly neurotic or she would never have taken her own life.' Her voice resumed its customary smooth tone. 'I want Claire and her husband invited. I assumed you would have wished to have the little girl, your own niece, to be a bridesmaid.'

Joanna's anger threatened to choke her, but when she spoke it was slowly and distinctly, with no trace of the emotion she was feeling.

'If Anthony Douglas is at the wedding, then I shall not be.'

The two women sized each other up. Lady Pamela was shaken to find that here, in this particular instance at least, was a will every bit as implacable as her own. The discovery, however, made her even more determined to get her own way. She raised her eyebrows.

'Is that a threat? Alex my dear, try to explain to Joanna the rudiments of good behaviour.' She got up and went out, closing the library door firmly behind her.

'Your mother is *insufferable*!' Joanna choked, on the verge of tears.

Alex was silent for a moment or two, nor did he, as she expected, come round the table to comfort her. Instead, when he did speak, it was to say rather coolly: 'Mother has a point, you know. This dislike of Anthony Douglas is growing into an obsession.'

She stared at him, half-blinded by unshed tears but too proud to make a bid for his sympathy by openly crying.

She took a deep breath to steady her voice. 'Terry was my sister. My twin sister. I care about her death. And, whatever you and your mother think about it, I shall continue to hold Anthony responsible. He went on stringing

153

her along, glad of her company when no one else was available. He even asked her to marry him while he was still married to my other sister. He's a shit.' She spoke with quiet venom.

'Have you talked to him about it?' Alex asked reasonably. 'Have you bothered to listen to his side of the story?'

'There's nothing he could say that I should want to hear.'

Alex sighed. 'I didn't know you could be such a bigot, Jo. That's the sort of attitude that starts wars, burns books, creates extremism . . .'

She jumped up from her chair, furious because she knew that he was right.

'How dare you preach at me! I suppose I might have guessed that you'd side with your mother. You never try to see anything from my point of view, only hers. And you have the nerve to call *me* a bigot!' She flounced over to the window, shaking with rage, and turned her back on him.

He moved at last, getting up and walking across to her, holding her by her hunched shoulders and nuzzling her hair.

'Come on, Jo, that's being unfair. I'm only siding with Mother because she's being reasonable and you're not.'

'Reasonable!' She twisted round to face him. 'You call any of this wedding she's planned reasonable? She must know that my parents can't possibly afford this sort of thing. She's only insisting on it to embarrass them.'

'That's not true. My father is only too willing and ready to help.'

'To dispense charity to the poor, you mean!'

For a moment, she could see an anger to match her own blazing in his eyes. Then the light died and he put his arms around her, kissing her and murmuring endearments. There was a kind of desperation about him which she could not understand.

But for some reason she was unable to respond to his embraces as she usually did. She felt old and cold and disillusioned.

'Let me go, Alex!' She pushed him away. 'Let me go!'

Joanna could hear her voice, shrill and vindictive, and shut her ears to the import of what she was saying. Everything was coming to a head, like a boil bursting open to spill out its poison: her grief over Theresa's death, her festering dislike of Alex's mother, her disappointment and confusion that, after five years, she and Alex had never made love. She must, she had long ago decided, be the only twenty-two-year-old virgin of her acquaintance, and yet there was something about Alex that frightened her a little; disturbed her enough at any rate to prevent her making an issue of the matter. Nothing seemed to have point to it any more. Somewhere in the deepest recesses of her mind, she knew she was still suffering from the shock of her sister's suicide, but she was suddenly too tired to drag the fact to the surface and consider rationally what it might entail. She badly wanted to hurt someone as she had been hurt, and the person nearest to hand was Alex.

She dragged off the opal ring and flung it on the floor.

'There!' she panted. 'Opals are supposed to be unlucky, and this one certainly is! You're free now. You can marry Olwen Bruce and make your mother very happy. I'm going upstairs to pack and I'd be grateful if you would order me a taxi. I'd like it here in half an hour.'

'Go and stay with Aunt Do,' Freda advised, sitting on the edge of Joanna's bed and swinging long, bare, brown legs. 'She's rehearsing a play for Radio Three just at present, so she'll be living at home for a while. I'd have stayed longer if I'd been able to pay my way. But until next term's grant arrives I'm skint, and I didn't think it fair to expect Aunt Do to support me.'

Joanna gave a short laugh. 'What makes you think I'm not? I haven't even found myself a job yet. I don't know what I want to do. I suppose I'll have to arrange to see someone at the Appointments Board.'

'You might stand a better chance of finding a job in London,' Freda suggested.

The house was quiet. Jean was at one of her

Townswomen's Guild meetings, Bernard was in his study, preparing work for the forthcoming autumn term, and Reginald had gone to a matinée at Bath's Theatre Royal.

'Old-age pensioners half-price this afternoon,' he had said at lunch. 'And now and then I do like a good Agatha Christie.'

It had been a typically English summer day, starting with an insipid morning, a whisper of dampness in the air, slipping quietly into an afternoon of dreamlike unreality, and had now turned wet, rain lashing against the windows. After lunch, Joanna had retired to her room to sort through her clothes, to see what dresses and skirts could be easily shortened now that everything was being worn a good four or five inches above the knee. But she had soon tired of the exercise – she seemed unable to sustain interest in anything these days – and had lain down on her bed, hands linked behind her head, staring into space, doing nothing.

Alex had not telephoned or made any move to contact her since she left King's Acre. It had been Higgs who had tapped at her bedroom door to say the taxi had arrived and to help her downstairs with her cases. Even now, Joanna found it hard to believe that Alex had made no attempt to persuade her to change her mind; that he had let her go so easily. And yet it was typical of him, somehow. He had never made allowances for the art of dissimulation: he always took people at their word. But would she have wanted to be coaxed, had he tried? Hadn't she reached the point where she clearly, if reluctantly, recognized that her relationship with Alex wasn't going to work? That it had been a one-sided relationship from the start? That he and his mother were too close for comfort? That there would always be animosity between their two families?

Jean and Bernard, while sympathetic, had found it hard to disguise their relief that the engagement was over, the wedding off; a relief that was only partly financial.

'You marry one of your own sort,' Bernard had said,

giving Joanna an unaccustomed hug. 'A good socialist.'

'You wouldn't have been happy, you know,' Jean had assured her. 'Those sort of people resent outsiders. And it can be very uncomfortable when husband and wife disagree politically. You'd have been the one, eventually, to compromise for the sake of peace and quiet. Women can't afford too many independent principles, believe me!'

'Oh, Mum!' Joanna had exclaimed impatiently. 'Don't tell me that for all these years you've really been a closet Conservative!

'I used to vote Liberal before I married your father,' Jean replied, adding: 'I still do, only I don't tell Bernard for the sake of my sanity. I couldn't stand all the arguments it would entail.'

And Joanna, lying on her bed, watching the rain teeming down the windows, thought that her mother probably had a point. Things were certainly changing for women, but not nearly fast and far enough.

Freda's arrival had forced her into more practical considerations, such as what she was going to do in the immediate future. Freda had no time for theorizing. She liked to be up and doing, making plans, getting on with things. OK: Joanna wasn't going to marry Alex after all! So what *was* she going to do? It was pointless to sit around and mope.

So she sat herself down on the end of her sister's bed – the other single bed, Theresa's bed, had been removed, Joanna noted, some time during the summer – and offered suggestions.

'Do you think Aunt Do really wouldn't mind if I went to stay for a couple of weeks?' Joanna asked at last, finding the idea more attractive than wrestling with officials at the Appointments Board and being forced into some kind of decision. Although she would have to make one soon. Her parents couldn't be expected to support her for very much longer. She had a hundred pounds in her Post Office savings account, money saved from odd jobs done during various vacations: waitressing, delivering Christmas mail, even bottle-washing. She could at least offer Aunt Dora something towards her keep.

'I'm sure she wouldn't!' Freda bounced to her feet. 'She told me she enjoyed having young people around her. Ring her this evening. There! That's settled. All it needs is a little positive thinking.'

'Come in, Davina,' Anthea said, greeting her niece at the door of her study. 'I want to talk to you. I hope I haven't dragged you away from anything important.'

'I was due to take the second form for prep, but Miss Mablethorpe has kindly agreed to do it for me.'

'Good.' Anthea held the door wide, and Davina realized that this was a purely social occasion, otherwise she would have been kept waiting outside before being summoned with a formal 'Enter!'

The summer evening was cold, and a fire had been lit, bathing the marble swags of ivy and bunches of grapes surrounding the grate in a fitful glow.

The yellow ribbons adorning the frilled and flounced dress of the lady leaning over the rail of HMS *Calcutta* made a streak of colour against one wall; and a cut-glass sherry-decanter of Waterford crystal, with matching glasses, stood on a low table drawn up in front of the fire.

'Sit down, my dear,' Anthea invited, indicating the tapestry-covered couch.

Davina did so awkwardly, wondering what was coming. She disliked it when her aunt singled her out for special treatment. She knew that the other members of staff whispered behind her back. It was difficult, too, to make friends amongst them. They distrusted her, suspecting her, unjustly, of running to Anthea with their indiscretions. Nevertheless, she enjoyed her job at Forest Moor. She liked the atmosphere. She was conversant with its ways.

Anthea seated herself at the other end of the couch. Davina regarded her enquiringly and with a little apprehension. She accepted a glass of sherry.

After a moment's silence, Anthea asked: 'Are you happy doing what you're doing? You don't ever feel you've made a mistake?'

'No, of course not. I'm very happy. I love it.' Davina was aware that her tone lacked conviction, but it was only because she couldn't see where the conversation was leading. She was feeling her way.

'You're certain?' Anthea glanced sideways at her niece, the blue eyes glinting beneath the half-closed lids. She exuded an air of suppressed excitement which Davina found strangely puzzling. 'You don't regret the past? Your husband?' The word was uttered with barely concealed distaste. 'Your . . . your daughter?'

'No.' Davina was more puzzled than ever. It was a long time since her aunt had alluded, even obliquely, to Anthony and Samantha. Sometimes, the whole episode of her marriage seemed like a dream; something half-remembered from a previous existence. When she saw other women with their children, she felt only a guilty sense of relief, and even the guilt had lessened with the passing years. 'Why should I? I'm doing what I want to do.'

There was another silence while Anthea twisted the stem of her empty glass between her fingers.

'I expect', she said at last, 'you're wondering what this is all about. The fact is I have something on my . . . conscience.' This time, the intonation was derisive, and Davina wondered if her aunt knew the true meaning of the word. Or cared, if she did. The idea did not shock her; rather, she felt a stirring of response. She, too, could be ruthless in order to gain her own ends. Her aunt continued, raising her head and looking Davina full in the eyes: 'I'm afraid *I* was responsible for putting Theresa up to that story she told you.'

'What story?' Davina was totally at a loss.

'The story that she and Anthony had been sleeping together. That he had asked her to marry him and that she had refused. We concocted it together.'

'You and . . . Terry? But how could you? You never saw one another.'

'I went into Bristol especially to see her that afternoon, when she came off duty. She went over to Bath to see you the same evening. You were on the very brink, or so it seemed to me, of returning to your husband. I was desperate to prevent what I believed – still believe – would have been a tragedy. I felt that what I did was justified to save a brilliant academic career.'

Anthea waited, outwardly calm, but inwardly tense, as her niece struggled to assimilate this shattering news. Had she believed in anything beyond her own powers of survival, she would have prayed: 'Don't let her fail me now.' As it was, she could only sit quietly, waiting for Davina's answer. She had made her confession coldly, calculatedly and after a great deal of thought. She had hesitated more than once, but she had to know for certain that Davina was hers again; that no trace of Anthony's influence remained; that no vestige of regret lingered for the child who had been given up. It had seemed to Anthea that the only way to be absolutely sure was to present her niece with the truth. If she could accept that, then Anthea had nothing more to fear.

Davina was confused. Her uppermost emotion was anger, not because Anthea had done what she did, but because she would have preferred not to be told. Anthony was in the past, and belief in his duplicity had enabled her to forge ahead with a clear conscience. Now it appeared she had not been second-best. He really had wanted her back and, but for Theresa's story, she would have gone. Anthea had once more manipulated her life, robbing her of the freedom to choose . . .

Davina closed her mind to the thought. Anthea was the one person who truly cared what happened to her, who wanted the best for her, who admired and loved her. Her mother had never really liked her. It was time to face up to that fact. For some reason, Jean resented her eldest daughter. And what had Anthony wanted? To turn her into a *hausfrau* and mother . . .

She smiled reassuringly at Anthea. 'I don't suppose it matters now. Anthony's remarried, and he and Claire have a child of their own. It's impossible to go back, even if I wanted to. What happened is probably all for the best.'

Anthea was triumphant.

17

AFTER LUNCH, a quick ham sandwich and a cup of coffee at a pub in Victoria Street, Joanna made her way back to Victoria Tower Gardens. It was one of her favourite places in London, and she spent as much of her lunch-hour there as the autumn weather permitted. For some reason, she found the Buxton drinking-fountain and the two statues – one of Emmeline Pankhurst and the other a copy of Rodin's 'The Burghers of Calais' – supremely satisfying. The fountain commemorated the freeing of the Empire's slaves in 1834, and there seemed so much of British history crammed into that thin triangle of ground. She liked to think of Queen Philippa throwing herself at the feet of Edward III and pleading for the lives of those wretched starving men. And when her husband had finally said, 'Very well, do what you will,' she had reminded him of St Augustine's words: '*Love* and do what you will.'

Joanna liked, too, to remember the suffragettes and the stories her grandmother Harding had told her about the women who chained themselves to railings and were force-fed in prison in order to get women the vote. Sometimes she felt very close to those early pioneers. She believed that, had she been alive then, she would have been one of them; in the same way that she hoped she would have been an Abolitionist a hundred years before.

The garden today had the slightly dishevelled appearance that came with autumn. The first breath of frost had crisped and tufted the grass, and there was a drift of leaves around the base of the fountain. Joanna glanced at her

162

watch. Twenty minutes before she need be back in the office.

Her fortnight with Aunt Dora in Holland Park had stretched into almost three months after she had landed herself a job in Whitehall, at the Home Office. She wasn't established yet, and sometimes she wondered if she really wanted to become a permanent civil servant. She quite enjoyed her work and she had grown attached to the little room which she shared with another Oxford graduate, overlooking the Cenotaph and New Scotland Yard. All the same, it wasn't what she had seen herself doing in those heady undergraduate years; but, then, what had she envisaged, except marriage to Alex?

Joanna hunched her shoulders against a sudden north-easterly wind blowing across Westminster Bridge and ruffling the grey spume-flecked waters of the Thames. She wouldn't think of Alex. He had dropped out of her life as though he had never been a part of it. Except for the empty ache in her heart and the sharp sense of loneliness that assailed her every morning on first waking, she prided herself that she had successfully got over him. There were times when she found herself, involuntarily, looking for him among the pavement crowds, because she knew that Ferrer's International Haulage had offices in Mincing Lane; but if either he or Sir Herbert did visit London – and, in the nature of things, they must do – then they did not come sufficiently far west to make a meeting possible.

She was still, at her aunt's pressing invitation, living in Holland Park.

'There's no point in you even thinking about getting your own place', Dora had pointed out, 'until you know whether or not you're going to stay on. When I'm here, we're company for one another, and if I'm away on tour you can have the place to yourself. You won't find a better arrangement.'

Joanna had agreed, and paid her aunt three pounds a week towards the housekeeping. Her colleague at the office, a bright bubbly blonde called Selina Driver, told her she was 'a lucky sod'. She was the same age as Joanna, who vaguely recalled seeing her on one of the rare occasions she had visited a friend at St Hilda's.

'You ought to see where I'm living,' Selina said feelingly, 'for twice that money.'

Joanna had no difficulty in imagining it, after having seen Freda's flat in Notting Hill Gate. One of the reasons why she had decided to remain in Holland Park was to keep a discreet eye on her younger sister.

'Have you been inside that place?' she had demanded of Dora in horrified accents.

'A couple of times,' her aunt admitted cautiously. 'Many London landlords are real racketeers, but there's not much you can do about it, I'm afraid. It's one of the hazards of living in a capital city. Besides, Freddie'll be gone next year, and the rent is extremely low.'

'I'm not talking about the general state of the house,' Joanna had answered. 'It's no more than I expected, considering what the three of them are paying. It's the rooms themselves I'm on about. The untidiness and squalor and downright filth. Just because they're actors and fancy themselves as Bohemians doesn't mean they have to live like pigs. And that young man, Derek Conway, it wouldn't surprise me if he were on drugs.'

'I think they probably all are,' Dora answered calmly. 'I know for a fact that Freddie's tried LSD once or twice, but she swore to me she didn't like it and wouldn't touch it again. I told her it was a mug's game.'

'Aunt Do!' Joanna had been appalled. 'Why on earth didn't you tell me?'

'What was the point? What could you have done?' Dora asked sensibly. 'And you know, my dear, whether you believe me or not, actors are a little bit different from other people. For so many hundreds of years we really were rogues and vagabonds. It was only in the last century that the profession started to be even slightly respectable. The bulk of us still lead semi-nomadic lives on tour. Sleazy digs.

Grubby dressing-rooms. Eating when everyone else has gone to bed. It's the part of Freda that makes her want to be an actress that lets her put up with, or ignore, those sorts of conditions.' Dora added shrewdly: 'You can go round and kick up hell's delight if you like, but it won't make a bit of difference. Freda's twenty now. She can do as she likes.'

And Joanna, thinking things over, decided that her aunt was right. Any interference on her part would simply drive a wedge between herself and her younger sister, the only one who really remained to her. Theresa was dead, and she rarely saw Davina. She couldn't risk losing Freddie as well. So she said nothing, but worried all the same; and worried even more because she hadn't the courage to risk a breach and speak out.

She was still worrying, almost subconsciously because it had become a way of life to her, as she stood looking up at the statue of the six emaciated burghers, halters round their necks, the original of which was in the Musée Municipal des Beaux-Arts in the rue Richelieu in Calais. But for the humanity of a woman, those poor wretches would have died, to appease the wrath and pride of a king who had been defied for eleven long months. And yet Joanna could never quite bring herself to believe that women were a softer touch than men. Nor did she subscribe to the theory that, if women ruled the world, war and pestilence and famine would vanish overnight. Nevertheless, she did most fervently believe that it was time they had more of a say in the affairs of government . . .

Someone tapped her on the shoulder.

'Jo,' said a familiar voice, 'how lovely to see you. What are you doing in London?'

It was Lawrence Walden.

He was looking thinner, his naturally small-boned body seeming to have shrunk under the responsibility of being an MP. He would be a conscientious one, Joanna thought, taking seriously all the problems and complaints of his west Yorkshire constituency. The soft curling brown hair had receded even further back from his forehead, giving greater prominence to his deep brown eyes. He must be thirty-six now, she reckoned. He was still unmarried.

He was on his way to the House of Commons for the afternoon debate and Prime Minister's Question Time. He walked her back to the Home Office before retracing his steps.

'Why haven't you looked me up?' he asked, hurt. 'I had no idea you were staying in London.'

'I didn't know where you lived,' she excused herself, not wanting to wound him even more by telling him the truth, that the idea just hadn't crossed her mind.

'You could have left a note for me at the House,' he said. 'I should have got it.'

Joanna was apologetic. 'That never occurred to me,' she admitted. 'I've never set foot inside the Palace of Westminster, I suppose that's why. It's like a foreign country as far as I'm concerned.' There was a pause before she enquired diffidently: 'Do you know that Alex and I are no longer engaged?'

They crossed Abingdon Street and made their way past St Margaret's Chapel towards Parliament Square.

'Your father wrote and told me. I'm sorry,' Lawrence added, trying to sound sincere.

'There's no need to be,' Joanna said quickly. The last thing she wanted was his sympathy or to be told that she was 'well out of it'. She had had enough of that sort of talk from her parents. She changed the subject, saying the first thing that entered her head. 'I'd love to hear a parliamentary debate.'

'As a matter of fact,' he answered, delighted, 'I'm speaking on an amendment to the Town and Country Planning Bill on Thursday afternoon. If you can get the time off, I'll make sure you get a front-row seat in the Strangers' Gallery. Then, later, we can have dinner in the Strangers' Dining-Room.'

Joanna hesitated. Then: 'Right,' she agreed. 'I think I

might just have qualified for a half-day's leave by now. I'll see what I can do.'

Why not? she thought, as she entered the portals of the Home Office and made her way up to the second floor in the lift. What did it matter if she gave Lawrence some encouragement now? He was a nice man, and she realized that she was fond of him.

Selina Driver was already working at her desk, but she glanced up as Joanna came in.

'You're late,' she said. 'Sweeting's been on the warpath, but I said you'd gone to the ladies' cloaks. I think he believed me, but you know how he resents university types. What kept you?'

Joanna hung up her short red leather coat. 'I met an old friend and we got chatting. And, yes, it was a man; and, no, he's not married – divorced – but you needn't look like that. He's a friend of my father, fourteen years older than I am.'

'I like older men,' Selina ruminated. 'They know how to treat a girl. I'll have him if you're not interested. Pass him on to me.'

'He's an MP,' Joanna told her. 'Very respectable. Not your sort at all.'

'Oh, I don't know.' Selina sucked suggestively at the end of her pen. 'Not all MPs are respectable, you know. Rumour has it that the House of Commons is a veritable hotbed of naughty goings-on.'

Joanna burst out laughing. 'Well, if it is, Lawrence Walden won't be part of it, that's all I can say.'

Selina grimaced. 'If he's a friend of your father, I don't suppose you'd know. Look, it's desperately hard to meet decent men in London. How about arranging me an intro?'

Joanna considered the proposition, but suddenly found she didn't want to introduce Lawrence Walden to anyone. Selina was right. It wasn't that easy to meet eligible men; men you could trust. 'Swinging' London was beginning to boom, and there was a growing assumption among the male population, probably justified, that every woman was just waiting to fall into bed with any man who took her out for the evening. An active and diverse sex life was becoming obligatory for anyone who wanted to think of herself as 'in'. Joanna, used to the stricter moral climate of the fifties and early sixties, her sexual self-confidence eroded by Alex, felt she could not cope with the general promiscuity. No doubt Freda was having a ball.

Lawrence Walden – quiet, gentle, dependable Lawrence – who had been in love with her, so devotedly and for so long, seemed very safe. Alex had never shown the slightest need of her. Lawrence did. Joanna suddenly found that she wanted to be wanted.

'Sorry,' she said, sitting down at her desk and taking a file from the 'in' tray, which she had cleared this morning, but which had mysteriously filled up again during her lunch-break, 'but I've decided, after all, to keep Lawrence to myself.'

The following day, Joanna telephoned Lawrence at the House of Commons and invited him to go to a concert with her that evening at the Festival Hall, and during the second half they rediscovered a shared enthusiasm for the music of Haydn. When they parted at the door of the Holland Park flat, he leaned forward and kissed her tentatively, obviously half-expecting to be repulsed. Joanna responded by putting her hands on his shoulders and returning his kiss.

During the next three weeks, their meetings were as frequent as the demands of his job allowed. For the first time in years, Joanna felt she was really important to someone. She saw the way Lawrence's eyes lit up at her approach, was touched by the fact that he always put her comfort before his own and was grateful for the normality of their conversations, with none of Alex's slightly camp and mocking overtones. It was, nevertheless, still something of a shock when Lawrence proposed. Part of her had been expecting it. The other part had shied away from the possibility, hoping it would not happen.

Lawrence was paired for the ten o'clock division and had booked a table at Locket's, in Marsham Court, a restaurant close to the House and popular with MPs. Joanna sensed his awkwardness whenever they dined out, and something which she would have found embarrassing a few years earlier she now thought of as endearing.

They had finished their Lamb Shrewsbury and refused a sweet, asking simply for coffee, when Lawrence said abruptly: 'Jo! I love you . . . But, then, you know that. I always have. Will you . . . will you marry me?'

She sat very still; the stillness, he thought fancifully, of a wounded animal, turning in upon itself to conceal the hurt. Then she glanced up and gave him a brilliant smile, reaching out her hand across the table.

'Of course I will,' she said.

She gave a little gasp as she finished speaking, almost as though she had taken herself by surprise. He clasped her hand in his, not guessing at the panic she was feeling.

What in God's name had prompted her to say it? she wondered. Why had she suddenly decided to say 'yes'? But Lawrence's radiant expression gave her the answer. If ever a man deserved to be made happy, to be rewarded for years of patient devotion in the teeth of slights and neglect, he did. He was everything that Alex was not, and for that she should be grateful.

And she was! Oh, she *was*! People like Alex and his parents were not for her, nor she for them. She and Lawrence came from the same sort of background, spoke the same language, shared the same attitudes. Surely that was important! Surely that should be enough!

She did not love Lawrence; at least, not in the way that he loved her. But over the past weeks she had grown very fond of him. He had eased a little of the pain which bruised her spirit each time she thought of Alex, something she would not have thought possible a month or two ago. She promised herself that she would make him happy; that she *could* make him happy. He was a good man, and she was lucky to have realized it before it was too late . . .

They were married on 3 December at Caxton Hall by special licence. Joanna told herself resolutely that it was the most wonderful day of her life.

'I don't know how you can live in this dump,' Joanna said, looking around the living-room of the flat in Notting Hill Gate.

The furniture, all made of cheap plywood and thinly veneered, was sparse; nothing had been added to the bare essentials supplied by the landlord. A table, four chairs, one with a broken seat, a rather grubby three-piece suite upholstered in a bilious shade of green moquette, and a small occasional table which had seen better days were crammed into three-quarters of the available space, while the remaining area served as a kitchen. A few cupboards and a gas-stove stood on a square of black-and-white check linoleum, together with a sink and an Aga boiler which was supposed to supply hot water, but which, in Joanna's experience, usually ran from tepid to cold. A line of underwear dripped steadily on to the floor, and a pile of unwashed dishes was stacked on the draining-board. The other two rooms were bedrooms. The bathroom, shared with the house's other occupants, was situated on the floor below.

'You really could make an effort to keep this place tidier,' she said.

'Stop nagging, Jo.' Freda, curled up on one end of the sofa, looked sullen. 'You're getting very pious since you married Lawrence. I don't think he's doing you any good.'

'Leave Larry out of this,' Joanna retorted, seating herself, uninvited, in one of the bilious armchairs.

Her arrival had been the signal for the other two students to slope off to another room, with muttered excuses of having lines to learn. Joanna wondered uneasily if she was becoming too censorious; if her perspective was getting too narrow. She would wake in the night with a sense of being trapped and the fear that she had rushed into marriage on an impulse.

She told herself firmly that she did not know why. Lawrence was a loving and considerate husband, and everything was fine. Her parents, who had come up to London for the wedding, three months earlier, had been delighted by the marriage, and even Aunt Dora had been mildly approving. Only Freda had sounded a sour note, making a moue of distaste and sighing: 'Oh, *not* boring old Lawrence!' Joanna had ignored her sister, but the words kept on coming back to trouble her dreams.

'Why have you come?' Freda's voice broke in impatiently on her thoughts.

'What? Oh, sorry. I was miles away.'

'I said, why have you come? Apart, that is, from your constant desire to criticize the conditions I'm living in.'

Joanna grimaced guiltily. 'Sorry,' she apologized again. 'I didn't mean to carp. I know I've said it all before. The thing is, Larry and I are giving a little party on Thursday evening and we wondered if you might like to come.'

Freda swung her legs to the ground. She was wearing a very short brown skirt, which barely covered her thighs, and a large floppy man's sweater which was vaguely and disturbingly familiar to Joanna, but which Freda, when quizzed on the point earlier, swore belonged to Derek Conway.

' 'Fraid I can't,' Freda answered abruptly, adding on a softer note: 'Sweet of you to ask, but we're rehearsing madly at the moment for the third year's final production. Oddly enough, we're doing that Shelley thing Aunt Do was in last year on the radio. *The Cenci*. I've landed the role of Beatrice, and it's difficult stuff to learn. Anyway, your party will be all boring political people. Not really my scene.'

As she spoke, she stood up, obviously expecting her sister to leave now that the matter was settled. It wasn't like Freda, Joanna reflected, to be so inhospitable. She

171

usually offered at least a mug of coffee. Perhaps she was waiting for someone.

Then two things happened simultaneously. With a shock, Joanna remembered buying the yellow sweater three years ago as a present for Alex, just as, using his own key, he turned the lock of the door and walked in.

18

'HELLO, Jo,' he said, showing no sign of embarrassment other than a slight lowering of his lids over the opaque brown eyes. He continued easily: 'I read the announcement of your marriage in *The Times*. Congratulations.'

'Thank you,' she answered stiffly, and switched her gaze accusingly to Freda.

Freda shrugged. 'Honestly, Jo, it's not the way it seems. What I mean is, there was nothing going on between us in the past. We met quite by chance, just before Christmas, outside Selfridge's. Alex took me for a cup of coffee and . . . well, it just went on from there. He comes to see me whenever he's in town.'

'And has his own key to let himself into the flat?' Joanna enquired icily. 'I understand.'

'No, you don't.' Freda, in contrast to Alex, was getting hot and flustered. 'I gave him a key so that he could let himself in to leave a note or make himself a drink if I wasn't here. It seemed a shame for him to come half across London without being able to get inside the door.'

Joanna raised her eyebrows. 'I suppose he could always telephone to find out if you were in.'

'Most of the time the phone's out of order or the landlord's forgotten to pay the bill. Anyway,' Freda added heatedly, 'it's none of your damn business!'

The argument was irrefutable, and Joanna lapsed into silence. The question to which she desperately wanted an answer – 'Are you sleeping together?' – would have to remain unresolved. She had broken off their engagement.

She was the one who had married someone else. She had made Alex a free agent and now had no right to demand any sort of explanation.

She glanced from her sister to Alex and back again, hoping to get some clue, but Freda was wearing a mulish expression, which Joanna remembered only too well from their childhood, while Alex's ugly features, as usual, gave nothing away. Joanna thought bitterly that she had never known what was going on in his head, not from the very beginning.

She picked up her handbag and gloves, a nice conservative pale grey to match the darker grey suit she was wearing. The only splash of colour she had allowed herself was a maroon silk blouse, tied in a bow at the neck, and her skirt-length was a mere two inches above her knees. Alex, on the other hand, was looking far trendier than she remembered him. For a start, his hair was much longer than it had been, covering his ears, and, at the back, straggling over the collar of a jacket which owed far more to the influence of Carnaby Street than to Savile Row. His black trousers were corduroy velvet, and there was the hint of a ruffle at the neck of his collarless shirt. In contrast to him and to Freda, Joanna felt dowdy and, what was worse, middle-aged. She had to remind herself sharply that she was still only twenty-two. Marriage to a man fourteen years her senior was, she thought, making her old before her time.

'I must go,' she said, trying to speak coolly. 'Sorry you can't come on Thursday, Freddie, but I quite understand. Don't work too hard.' She gave her sister's cheek a quick dutiful peck and held out her hand to Alex. 'Goodbye. It's nice to have seen you again.'

'Goodbye, Jo,' he answered, with one of those half-smiles which had always irritated her and which were so reminiscent of his mother. He raised her hand to his lips and kissed it lightly. 'Take care of yourself, my dear.'

She let herself out of the flat, letting the front door slam. She found herself out in the street without quite knowing how she got there, the echo of her feet on three flights of uncarpeted stairs dying away behind her. The February night was cold and the streets deserted. From the basement flat came the strains of the Monkees' hit 'I'm a Believer', and in the house next door a long blue-and-red stained-glass window glowed like a jewel, high up on one wall. In the garden, Joanna could make out the spiky branches of a monkey-puzzle tree and laurel bushes, blurred, masses in the darkness.

Since her marriage, Joanna had learned to drive and, to her astonishment, had proved to have an aptitude for it. Her instructor had told her she was a 'natural', and she had passed her test at the first attempt. Lawrence had bought her a secondhand blue Volkswagen, which she had parked tonight in Campden Hill Road. She unlocked it and got into the driving-seat, fumbling with the ignition. It was then that she realized she was crying.

'You've been very quiet these past few weeks,' Lawrence said, squeezing Joanna's hand. 'Is anything the matter?'

They were spending the weekend in Lawrence's Yorkshire constituency, something he liked to do as often as possible.

'Yorkshiremen, particularly the country folk, are very suspicious of southerners,' he would explain, 'and I feel they've done me a bit of an honour to elect me. If I want to increase my majority next time, I have to win their confidence and I can only do that by going there as often as possible.'

He and Joanna rented a tiny terraced house in Haverthwaite, a village as central as possible to such a scattered community. Lawrence knew that it would have been a mark of his good faith and commitment had he been able to buy it, but he had only his MP's salary and what he had managed to save from his years as a schoolmaster, which was not very much. The furnished flat in London was also rented and took a large chunk out of his £3,400 stipend. Joanna had been forced to continue with her job at the Home Office in order to make ends meet, and was now seriously considering applying for permanent status.

'It'll be different in a few years' time,' Lawrence assured her, 'when I'm offered a post in the Government.'

That made her laugh. 'You're very certain.'

'I know my potential,' he replied.

It was a confidence which did not altogether surprise her. She used to think of Lawrence as a diffident man, but having heard him speak in several debates in the House she knew that he could be both trenchant and pithy. The questions he put during Prime Minister's Question Time were clear and logical, and often gave Harold Wilson the chance to dilate upon some point of policy which otherwise might have remained obscure. Lawrence, she had discovered, was very ambitious.

Joanna had begun to enjoy herself. Her old interest in politics had been reawakened, and she found it exciting to be at the hub of things instead of on the periphery. It still thrilled her to see in the flesh men who, until a few months ago, had simply been names in the newspapers: Harold Wilson himself, James Callaghan, Roy Jenkins, George Brown, Sir Frank Soskice, Patrick Gordon Walker, Richard Crossman and Denis Healey. One or two of them, although not as yet the Prime Minister, had been to the flat for a meal, and Joanna was relieved to find that, in general, Labour MPs tended to prefer supper or high tea to dinner or cocktails. Whether this was a genuine preference or a nod in the direction of their image as the working man's party, she did not know, but accepted it thankfully. She was a better cook than her mother – as Bernard so often asked, 'Who wasn't?' – but she was still no culinary expert. The sensible practical meals she had been brought up on presented no problems.

Until her meeting with Alex, three weeks ago, Joanna had been congratulating herself on how well she had settled into marriage with Lawrence. The sexual side of it had been disappointing, but she had no previous experience

176

with which to compare it. She had frequently heard her mother complain that she would rather read a good book, so she presumed that Lawrence's rather prosaic approach was that of most men. Common sense told her that sex could, and must, be better, but she decided that it was probably her fault. If she had been more highly motivated, she might have broken through Alex's defences. That they could be breached was demonstrated by his appearance in Freda's flat. It had not taken her younger sister long to seduce him.

The thought rankled, and Joanna was consumed by jealousy. She tried to put both Freda and Alex out of her mind, but was haunted by images of them in bed together. The last few weeks had been a nightmare. Her lack of concentration at the office had called down her supervisor's wrath upon her head and made her almost impossible to live with. Lawrence, instead of telling her not to be a bitch, had solicitously enquired about her health. When she had snapped she was 'Fine! OK!' he had recommended a course of iron tablets.

'I've always thought you're a bit anaemic. I tell you what,' he went on, 'let's bring forward our visit to Haverthwaite to this coming weekend, instead of the one after. The break will do you good. All that moorland air. I'll wire Ken Crosby that we'll be arriving Friday evening. Janet will see there's food in the house.'

Ken Crosby was Lawrence's constituency agent, and Janet, his wife, a fat, jolly, obliging woman, kept her eye on the little two-up-two-down house in Balaclava Terrace and saw that the rent was paid on time. This, because the whole street belonged to the local Labour Party committee chairman, was no more than nominal. Joanna had reservations about this arrangement and had once asked the landlord, Tom Birkenshaw, why he was a socialist.

'I should have thought that with all your investments you'd have voted Tory.'

Lawrence had been horrified at such plain speaking, but Tom Birkenshaw had only laughed.

'Don't worry, Larry. I like a lass who says what she thinks. Look here, my girl, no one on this earth is ever going to make us all equal. Not Marx. Not Lenin. Not even "our 'Arold", God bless 'im! I don't see anything wrong in a man bettering himself and acquiring a bit o' brass. What I want to see is a world where the best jobs and opportunities aren't given to a man just because he's wearing the right school tie.'

It was a point of view with which Joanna found herself in complete agreement, but she could not like Tom Birkenshaw. There was something too familiar in his attitude towards her, as though he owned both her and Lawrence, that annoyed her. It was he who had suggested, on this cold March Saturday evening, that they drive across the moors to the Malt Shovel at Baildon, but at the last moment, to her relief, he had telephoned to say he was unable to come. Joanna did not mind in the least driving herself and Lawrence in Ken Crosby's borrowed second-hand Sunbeam, instead of travelling in comfort in Tom Birkenshaw's Buick.

She had been looking forward to her evening out, but now Lawrence was once again beginning to fret and fuss.

'There's nothing the matter with me,' she said in answer to his question. 'Stop worrying, Larry.'

'You're not . . . pregnant, are you?'

Joanna shook her head. She wanted children badly. It was a great disappointment to her that she showed no signs, so far, of having any.

Lawrence professed equal disappointment, but seemed relieved.

'Perhaps it's just as well,' he would say. 'We should miss your salary.'

He said it again now, and she smiled wryly. 'Yes, I know. You'll have to hurry up and get that promotion to the front benches.'

Lawrence grimaced. 'Early days yet. I'm still a new boy. Wet behind the ears.'

She said suddenly: 'I saw Alex a few weeks ago. He was

visiting Freda. I'd called in to ask her to that party we were giving, and he arrived while I was there. He let himself in. He has his own key.'

'Ah!' Lawrence looked relieved. 'So that's it. I was afraid you were ill.'

'Yes, that's it,' she agreed.

One of the things she had learned not to do with her husband was to play those verbal I-don't-know-what-you-mean games which wasted so much time and energy. He was one of the most direct and open people she had ever met, and after Alex's slightly camp, sideways approach to things she found it a refreshing change.

Lawrence sipped his beer, watching the people in the busy lounge-bar as they good-naturedly eased their way through the crush surrounding the counter. The soft Yorkshire burr, so different from the flat hard-edged tones of the West Country, sounded pleasantly in his ears. He had the two things in life he had always wanted: a seat in Parliament and Joanna for his wife. He wasn't going to let himself feel threatened, not even by Alex Ferrer. Besides which, he knew something which, it appeared, Joanna did not.

A man on the neighbouring table was reading that morning's *Times*. When he had finished, Lawrence leaned across and tapped him on the shoulder.

'Excuse me, could I borrow your paper for a moment? There's something in it I want to show my wife.'

The man beamed. 'Ay, lad, tak' it. I've finished wi' it. Keep it if thee likes.' He and his companion, a large black and white collie dog, who had been asleep under the table, rose to their feet and ambled out of the pub.

Lawrence turned to the long columns of personal announcements and, having carefully folded the paper to a more manageable size, handed it to Joanna, stabbing with his finger at an item under the heading 'Engagements'. She read it with growing disbelief.

'Richard and Selma Bruce of The Old Barn, Drewsteignton, Devon, are pleased to announce the engagement of

179

their daughter Olwen to Alexander James Ferrer, only son of Sir Herbert and Lady Pamela Ferrer of King's Acre Court near Exeter.'

Joanna glanced up, dazed. 'But ... but what was he doing in Freda's flat? He must have known that he was going to ask Olwen Bruce to marry him.'

Lawrence said gently: 'My love, this is the new age of sexual freedom. I don't suppose Freddie cares what his future plans are.' He put an arm around her shoulders and gave her a hug. 'Don't look so shocked. Life's moving at a faster pace than it's ever done before. Like Alice and the Red Queen, you have to run fast these days just to stand still.'

She was very quiet during the drive back to Haverthwaite. This time Lawrence took the wheel.

'You're tired,' he said. 'You can doze.'

But she didn't sleep, staring instead out of the car window into the darkness, at the dimly seen shapes of rocks and trees. She liked Baildon Moor, what little she had seen of it during their flying visits north. It reminded her of holidays on Dartmoor when she was a child. There was the same clarity of air and the same sharp green colour of the land. The high and distant hills always seemed so delusively near. Here and there, a jigsaw pattern of houses and cottages broke the monotony of the landscape; and there was the sense of silent soft-footed menace which primeval stretches of moorland, such as this, always gave her.

It was raining by the time they reached Haverthwaite. Balaclava Terrace was a turning off the main street. Lawrence parked the Sunbeam outside the Crosbys' house, where the stone-built cottages gave way to open fields.

Then he and Joanna walked the hundred or so yards to their own front door, which gave straight on to the living-room from the pavement. Before she went inside, Joanna stood for a moment, drinking in the sweet-smelling air. The only sound was the trickle of water from the little stream at the back of the house, as it seeped down from the fells.

'Lovely, isn't it?' she said. 'I can't believe that this time tomorrow we'll be back in noisy smelly old London.'

Lawrence chuckled. 'Give me "noisy smelly old London" any day. I'm not a country boy. I find the quiet too oppressive. I like to be where there's something going on.'

Joanna closed the front door and grinned. 'You're too honest, Larry, that's your trouble. Are you sure you're cut out to be a politician?'

They had not yet switched on the light, and the room was dark except for the glow of the fire, still burning brightly in the grate. Joanna slipped off her coat, and suddenly Lawrence was beside her, taking her in his arms, covering her face with kisses. This was what she had longed for; this was passion. But now that at last it had happened she discovered that she didn't want it, not from Lawrence. She preferred their marriage the way it was, prosaic and undemanding. This sort of loving, this desperate hunger, was what she had wanted from Alex and never received.

But even as she made a move to push her husband away she knew that she couldn't do it. She had chosen to marry him. She could not, now, impose her own limitations on their relationship. They went upstairs to the tiny front bedroom and she let him undress her without any protest. When they were both naked, they lay on the bed together and she felt him enter her as he had done so often in the past few months. Tonight, it was different. She thought of Davina and Anthony Douglas and, for the first time, realized that no marriage was ever simple or straightforward. It was a mess of complicated emotions: desires and frustrations, cross-purposes and low cunning, deviousness and oppressive designs.

19

FREDA SCRABBLED among the sticks of greasepaint, cotton-wool, false eyelashes and a pair of someone's tights which littered the dressing-table of the pocket-sized dressing-room she was sharing.

'There's got to be more to acting than touring the north of England with a third-rate production like this,' she complained bitterly. 'Which of you bastards has pinched my tissues? I bought a new box only yesterday.'

She looked accusingly at the fair girl who was seated next to her, wearing the costume of a nun. The girl had removed the coif and wimple to reveal her own short hair. A cigarette dangled from lips still, like the rest of her face, caked with stage make-up, and she had kicked off her black buckled shoes, replacing them with pink furry slippers. The whole effect was faintly bizarre.

'I haven't taken your rotten tissues,' the girl answered calmly, 'so stop bitching. What's this?' And she pulled a blue cardboard box from beneath a denim jacket which had been tossed down carelessly on top of the general clutter. 'All the same,' she went on, 'you're right, this is a third-rate production. And apart from Roxanne and her boring duenna there are no decent parts in it for women. My agent said it would be good experience, but experience for what?' The girl, whose name was Julia Archer, eyed Freda's basket of fake oranges which lay on the floor between them. 'At least you get separate billing on the programme. "Orange girl – Freda Marshall." I'm just one of the "Ladies in Box" and then a follower of de Guiche and finally a nun.'

Freda, having smeared grease over her face, was now wiping it off with a handful of tissues.

'The orange-seller's hardly a memorable part. Not much more than a walk-on. After that, I'm just an anonymous member of the *commedia dell'arte*. I feel sometimes that I'm never going to get my name up in lights.'

A third girl, also wearing a nun's habit, and who had at that moment entered the dressing-room, looked surprised.

'You're a bit of an optimist, aren't you, Freddie? In this business, think yourself lucky to be working at all.'

Freda grimaced at her reflection in the mirror. 'Oh, I'm going to be famous,' she said. 'I've made up my mind.'

Julia Archer burst out laughing. 'And pigs might fly. Do you know how many trained actors are out of work in this year of Our Lord 1969?'

Freda finished wiping off her make-up and dropped the stained tissues into the wastepaper-basket. She stood up and reached for her denim skirt and sweater, hanging on the back of the door.

'No, and I'm not interested. I intend to make it big. That's all that matters.'

'Get *her*!' the third girl said, taking Freda's place at the dressing-table and starting to unpin her wimple. 'Who do you think is coming to see a second-rate production of *Cyrano*?'

'Third-rate,' Freda corrected her, running a comb through her hair and bending down to catch a glimpse of herself in the mirror. 'Julia and I have agreed on that. Where are we eating this evening?'

'I'm not going back to the digs, that's for certain.' Julia Archer glanced at her watch. 'Ten-thirty. There must be an all-night snack-bar somewhere, surely. Our landlady is definitely the boiled-cabbage-and-bacon-sandwich type, isn't she, Fred?'

Freda groaned. 'Worse, I shouldn't wonder. God, I hate touring! Strange cities, lousy digs. Here it is, midsummer, but do they know that in Bradford? I haven't seen a glimpse of sun since we arrived. Folkestone was bad enough, but this is a thousand times worse.'

There was a tap on the dressing-room door, and the three girls glanced enquiringly at one another. Other members of the cast were in the habit of simply wandering in.

It was the doorman, a small morose man who gave the impression of constantly smouldering ill-temper. He was panting from his climb up the stairs.

'Which of you is Miss Freda Marshall?' he demanded dourly in a strong Scots accent.

'I am,' said Freda. 'Why?'

'There's a bloke downstairs askin' t' see ye. Says his name's Tom Birkenshaw. Says he's a friend o' your sister, Mrs Walden.'

'A friend of Jo's?' For a moment, Freda was nonplussed, then light dawned. 'Oh, I know. My brother-in-law's MP for West Yorkshire Moors. I think this Birkenshaw is one of his constituents. OK. I'll come down and see what he wants.'

As she clattered down the bare stone steps, lit by unshaded light bulbs, Freda recalled enough of various conversations with Joanna to recollect that Tom Birkenshaw was their landlord and one of the big wheels in the local branch of the Labour Party. Lawrence always spoke of him as someone who had great influence over his continuing career as a Yorkshire MP.

'So, whatever he wants, just be nice to him,' Freda told herself sternly. He was probably as old as Methuselah and just wanted to impress his friends with the fact that he knew a real live actress. It never ceased to amaze her how glamorous and prestigious other people found it to mix socially with members of her profession. If they only knew, she thought with a tiny smile, how generally seedy and tawdry the life was: the miserable Sunday journeys, the unappetizing meals, the going to work just as everyone else was coming home, the dreadful uncertainty of ever getting another job when the present one finished. Most people wouldn't put up with the conditions actors endured.

As she reached the ground floor, Freda paused by the notice-board to see if her name was down for rehearsal call the following morning, but the only people mentioned were those in Act II, scene II, the Siege of Arras. That let her out, and she heaved a sigh of relief. At least she could have an extra hour in bed.

The man waiting for her at the stage door was, she judged, about fifty: a big broad-faced man with dark wavy hair and an easy charm of manner. He was, Freda noted at once, expensively dressed in fawn cavalry-twill trousers, silk shirt and a discreetly checked sports-jacket which could have been made in Savile Row. Not so much old, she thought, as mature, and definitely attractive in an obvious kind of way. Square, of course; old-fashioned as befitted his age group, but perfectly presentable. She decided that if he asked her out to a meal she would go. Anything was preferable to a cold supper at her digs or an all-night snack-bar.

'So you're young Freda,' Tom Birkenshaw said, eyeing her closely and taking in at a glance the brief skirt and figure-hugging red sweater. 'Jo's talked a lot about you.'

'Nothing good, I hope,' Freda responded flippantly, a remark which Tom Birkenshaw appeared to ignore.

'She wrote and told me you'd be in Bradford this week, so I found out what time the show finished and here I am.'

'You mean you haven't been to see it?' Freda tried to look pained.

' 'Fraid not. History isn't my subject, and I bore easily. But I'll come one night if you can get me a complimentary ticket.'

Freda laughed. 'Jo said you're rich. I can see why.'

'All Yorkshiremen are skinflints, is that it? Well, just to show you you're wrong, let me take you out to supper. My club. Hot meals served until midnight.'

Freda had half-expected a working-man's club: plastic-topped tables and blue cabaret acts, performed on a small dais at one end of the room. She had seen the type of place often enough on television. But the Carlton Club, off Manningham Lane, was a discreet Victorian house, with a dining-room boasting crimson plush-upholstered furniture, subdued wall-lighting, Irish linen tablecloths and gleaming cutlery. Freda began to feel awkward from the moment Tom Birkenshaw signed her in as his guest, uncomfortably aware of her clothes and her cheap plastic handbag.

'You might have warned me,' she said reproachfully, as they took their seats at a corner table. 'I'd have gone back to my digs to change.'

Tom smiled as she took the wine-list from a hovering waiter. 'You look very nice as you are.'

His brown eyes flickered across the expanse of tight red sweater, and Freda, for some reason, found herself blushing. She felt a sudden antipathy towards the big, smooth, well-fed man sitting opposite her, but told herself firmly not to be so silly.

'Are you married?' she asked coolly.

'There is a Mrs Birkenshaw somewhere,' he admitted, 'but we haven't seen one another for some years. She lives with her sister in Keighley. We go our separate ways.'

'No children?'

'Never wanted any. Life's easier without 'em, don't you think?'

The waiter arrived to take their orders, and the next ten minutes were spent in deciding what to eat. It was no surprise to Freda that Tom Birkenshaw chose steak: he looked to her like a man whose diet consisted mainly of meat. She asked for the Dover sole.

'Fish!' he exclaimed scornfully, when the waiter had gone. 'That won't put lead in your pencil.'

'It's gone eleven o 'clock at night,' Freda pointed out tartly, rattled by his last remark. 'If I eat too much, I'll never sleep, and I have an afternoon as well as an evening show tomorrow.'

She was beginning to wish she had refused his invitation and gone to the snack-bar with the others. When she had returned to the dressing-room to tell where she was going, they had all been envious, and she had preened herself on her good fortune. Now she was not so sure of her luck.

Tom Birkenshaw ordered the wine, then said: 'Tell me about this play you're in. This *Cyrano de Bergerac*. Wasn't he the bloke with the big nose?'

Feeling herself on safer ground, but wishing that her companion would stop staring at her breasts, Freda launched into a description of Rostand's masterpiece, trying to keep the conversation light by recalling as many amusing incidents as possible connected with the tour so far. By the time they rose from the table at midnight, she felt a little more reassured, in spite of the fact that Tom Birkenshaw's knees had touched hers several times during the course of the meal. But he had made no more vulgar remarks to embarrass her and had proved an intelligent listener, interested in the technical side of the theatre. Perhaps, she thought, she had misjudged him. After all, he was a friend of Jo and Larry. He would hardly try anything on.

When they emerged into the street, it was raining. The lamps showed drowned reflections in the wet surface of the road. It had turned chilly, and Freda, with only her sweater for warmth, shivered in the cold night air. Tom Birkenshaw put an arm around her.

'The car's parked just round the corner. Come on. Let's make a run for it.'

He moved forward, impelling her to go with him. His grip tightened, almost as if he were afraid she might try to get away. The thought of actually making a run for it had crossed Freda's mind, but once again she told herself she was being stupid. It was damp and cold, it was gone twelve o'clock at night and she was in a strange city. The sensible thing to do was to let Tom Birkenshaw drive her back to her lodgings.

She slipped into the Buick's front passenger-seat and began dabbing at her rain-smeared face with a paper tissue which she had found in her skirt pocket. She told Tom

Birkenshaw the address of her digs and settled back against the leather upholstery, feeling slightly sick. She should never have had that second piece of Black Forest gâteau. She prayed that her landlady didn't lock the front door at midnight.

Tom Birkenshaw switched on the car radio, and 'The Ballad of John and Yoko' filtered through on Radio 1.

'Do you like pop music?' he asked, as he eased the Buick away from the kerb.

'Some of it. Not indiscriminately.' Freda closed her eyes, feeling extremely tired. It had been a long day, with a rehearsal call this morning and then the meal with Tom Birkenshaw this evening, after the show. She thought longingly of bed. Her eyes closed, and she began to doze.

She jerked awake with a sudden sense of panic, peering through the window at the rows of houses.

'Where are you taking me?' she demanded shrilly. 'We're going away from the centre of the town. That sign said Shipley.'

'I thought you might like to see Baildon Moor by moon-light,' her companion answered smoothly. 'Or Shipley Glen.'

'There isn't a moon. It's bloody raining!' Freda sup-pressed a growing sense of fear.

Tom Birkenshaw lowered his left hand from the steering-wheel to her thigh.

'I was speaking figuratively. Who's interested in the scenery anyway?' He added: 'I wish you girls would give over wearing these tights. Stockings and suspenders were much more exciting.'

Freda pushed his hand off and yelled: 'Take me back to Bradford immediately!'

'Oh, come on! Don't start playing hard-to-get,' he pleaded.

Anger was rapidly replacing Freda's initial panic.

'Just because I'm an actress doesn't automatically mean I'm a tart,' she hissed at him.

She leaned across and seized the steering-wheel, wrenching it in her direction. The car lurched and the front near-side tyre bounced off the kerb. Fortunately, there was nothing behind them.

'You crazy bitch!' he shouted, prodding her in the chest with his elbow. Freda was thrown back into her seat, temporarily winded, but she recovered quickly and lunged at the wheel again.

'You let me out!' she panted.

With a curse, Tom Birkenshaw pulled in at the side of the road. It was very quiet, and there were no lights in any of the houses. Freda scrabbled at the door-handle with shaking fingers and managed to depress it. The damp night air rushed in to greet her.

A hand gripped her arm.

'Now, be a good girl,' Tom Birkenshaw wheedled, but she sensed a note of menace beneath the pleading. 'You had a nice supper, didn't you?'

'And now I'm supposed to pay for it, is that it?' Freda got her left foot out of the car and firmly planted on the road. 'Get stuffed!' she added viciously.

He clicked his tongue in mock disapproval. 'Not a very lady-like remark. But, then, in that get-up, I never did take you for a lady.'

Freda swung her handbag, catching him on the side of the face, and he flinched, loosening his hold. She eased herself completely out of the car and slammed the door shut. She had no idea exactly how far out of Bradford they had driven, but she knew that Shipley was almost a suburb of the main city and that the distance between the two wasn't much more than three miles. She hitched the strap of her handbag over her shoulder and set out determinedly back along the road towards Bradford.

Tom Birkenshaw watched her retreating form for a moment or two, then slewed round in his seat and stared through the windscreen. Bloody stuck-up little bitch! he thought savagely. Didn't she realize who he was? How important he was to her brother-in-law's career? Members of Parliament didn't necessarily have to lose an election to be ditched. Lawrence Walden might well find himself replaced with another Labour candidate at the next election.

Tom rubbed his cheek where the strap-buckle of Freda's handbag had struck him. He switched on the car's interior light and saw that there was a trace of blood on his fingers. He was conceited about his looks and hated any cut or scratch to mar them. He returned to his original theme. Who the hell did Freda Marshall think she was? She was just some tuppenny-ha'penny little actress no one had ever heard of!

He put out the light again and let in the clutch. The car moved forward. Within minutes, he was through Shipley and heading up Baildon Road towards the moors. In Baildon itself he had to stop again to dab at the trickle of blood which was oozing down his face on to his collar. Come to think of it, he had never much liked the way Joanna Walden looked at him, and had more than once detected a gleam of something like contempt in her eyes. And she was always having a dig at him about his money, implying that he couldn't be a true socialist because of it. She must, he decided, be a bigger fool than she looked if she thought that he supported the Labour Party out of principle. He supported it because, in these parts, it was the only thing to do.

As he dropped his blood-stained handkerchief on the floor of the car and once again let in the clutch, the idea came to him of going into politics himself. Why shouldn't he put himself forward as the prospective party candidate for West Yorkshire Moors at the next election? Why not, indeed?

He passed the Malt Shovel and increased his speed as he came out into open country. The notion of becoming an MP was growing on him the more he thought about it. He wondered why he had never considered doing it before.

20

FOREST MOOR was always at its most beautiful in the spring. Davina, standing at the window of her room, with its white-painted walls, well-stocked bookshelves and comfortable solid oak furniture, wondered if she would really have the courage to leave it. What was even more important, would she have the courage to tell Anthea that she had decided it was time to move on?

The shining April morning had an uneasy glitter, presaging rain. The pollarded trees along the path leading to the science laboratory were bursting into bud, fuzzed with a tender green. Davina had lowered the old-fashioned sash window at the top, and the early birdsong dropped into the quiet. She felt a sudden surge of optimism, heady and intoxicating. It was time to do something different with her life; time to make her own decisions.

Four girls, in dark green shorts and white Aertex shirts, were returning along the main drive after their pre-breakfast run, a form of exercise greatly approved of by the school hierarchy. They were young girls, first-formers, moving with a sort of graceless pre-adolescent strength, giggling and laughing. There was no doubt that it would be a wrench, leaving Forest Moor, which had been so much a part of her life, both as pupil and as teacher.

Fifteen minutes ago, Marlene, the little live-in housemaid assigned to look after the staff, had knocked on Davina's door.

'Morning post, miss,' she had announced in her broad Hamphire accent.

There were two letters, but it was the top one, with its Exeter postmark, which had immediately claimed Davina's attention. She had been expecting it, and had thought that, almost certainly, it must come today with its message of either acceptance or rejection. She had woken early, in the grey spaces of the dawn, and lain sleepless in her bed, watching the daylight slowly penetrate the thin blue curtains. When Marlene had handed her the official-looking envelope, Davina had nearly dropped it in her nervousness.

She had been unable to bring herself to open it for at least five minutes, staring at it, where she had placed it, on her desk by the window. But finally, upbraiding herself for being a coward, she had picked up the thin silver letter-opener from her pencil-tray and slit the envelope across.

It was dated 3 April 1970. Her heart began to pound.

'Dear Miss Marshall,' she read, 'We are pleased to be able to offer you . . .'

She had done it! At the age of only twenty-seven, she had obtained, against stiff competition, the post of headmistress at Haddington Grange.

But Haddington Grange, in spite of a name which conjured up memories of Angela Brazil and Joyce Lankester Brisley, was a modern glass-and-red-brick comprehensive school on the outskirts of Exeter, with between five and six hundred pupils of both sexes; a far cry from the exclusive, and exclusively female, haunts of Forest Moor. It was the reason why Davina knew her aunt would not approve and would actively oppose her taking up the offer.

This time, however, Anthea would lose. Davina contemplated the fuss there was bound to be as soon as she handed in her resignation. If she had been offered the headship of a school like Forest Moor, it would have been a different matter; Anthea would have been proud and delighted. But in that case it would probably have been Anthea who had encouraged her to apply in the first place. This, on the other hand, was something Davina had achieved on her own.

The day she had travelled to Exeter for her interview, her aunt thought she had been in London, shopping. Davina remembered, guiltily, wandering about the shuttered streets of Southampton for an hour after her return from Devon, in order that her arrival back at school should be twenty minutes after the arrival of the London evening train. Feeling like a traitor, she had confined her shopping in Exeter to Marks & Spencer, and had destroyed the tell-tale receipts.

It was the first occasion she had deceived her aunt in this way, but she had felt for a long while now the need to make her own decisions, to have control over her own destiny. It was only lately, during the past year, that the need had grown so strongly, but Davina suspected that it had its origins in Anthea's confession of the way in which she had persuaded Theresa to lie about herself and Anthony. At the time, it had not seemed very important, but it had, Davina supposed, prompted her into an awareness of how manipulative her aunt could be, and how little compunction she had in using people to further her ends. The memory of it had certainly strengthened Davina's determination in recent months to break free of Anthea's leading-strings.

But she still felt badly about it. She still felt she owed her aunt enough not to treat her in this underhand fashion, and had to remind herself constantly that in doing so she was only paying Anthea back in her own coin. And mixed with the self-reproach was resentement that her aunt forced her to act in this way.

She must not, however, waver in her resolution. She picked up the telephone on her desk and pressed the interhouse button, which connected her at once with the school secretary.

'This is Davina Marshall. I'd like an appointment to see Miss Marshall some time today. I have free periods starting at eleven-thirty this morning and again at three this afternoon.'

She was given an appointment for a quarter to twelve

and replaced her receiver with a sense of having burned her boats behind her. She glanced at her watch. There were still ten minutes before the bell summoned pupils and staff to breakfast in the oak-panelled dining-room, which had once been the main living-room of the old Forest Moor House. Davina picked up the second envelope which, so far, she had not even glanced at. The postmark on this one was London, and in the bottom left-hand corner, in red lettering, was the printed legend 'Smith & Greatorex, Publishers'.

Her mouth went dry. This was a letter on its own; not, like the previous ones, packed in with a regretfully returned typescript, which was why she had paid it no attention. Clumsily, she tore the envelope open, not even pausing to use the letter-opener. She couldn't, surely, be the recipient of two such strokes of good fortune in one day . . .

It seemed, however, that she could. Smith & Greatorex professed themselves deeply impressed with *Jack Straw and His Menie*, her 'very lucid and extremely interesting account of the Peasants' Revolt', and offered her an advance of eight hundred pounds on signature of contract. They also wanted her to visit their offices in Covent Garden in order to discuss suitable illustrations.

Davina sat down abruptly at her desk. Her knees felt weak, and she was trembling. This news should deflect at least some of her aunt's displeasure over her acceptance of the Exeter appointment.

The Tube had been packed, and Joanna had been forced to stand all the way from Westminster to Kensington. She had had a long and very tiring day, with Gerald Sweeting on her and Selina's back from nine until five-thirty. Joanna had likened him to a slave-master in a Roman galley, a remark which he had unfortunately overheard and which had done nothing to lighten the general atmosphere. To make matters worse, it was extremely warm for late April, but in government offices the heating was never switched off until the first day of May, just as it was never switched on again until the beginning of October – a law as immutable as those of the Medes and the Persians.

The three-roomed flat above a greengrocer's shop in Kensington High Street was hot and stuffy, the windows, having been shut all day, and the bed had been left unmade, Joanna having overslept that morning. She covered it quickly and was still unpacking her lunch-time shopping when Lawrence came in. She had not expected him home until late, knowing that there was an important debate that evening. But as his comings and goings were always erratic she expressed no surprise.

'Look at this lot!' she exclaimed in exasperation, indicating the tins and packets laid out on the red melamine work-surface of the tiny kitchenette, little more than a good-sized cupboard leading off the main room. 'Everything's going up by leaps and bounds. Five pounds three and sixpence halfpenny that cost me! A year, eighteen months ago, it wouldn't have been much over two pounds. And everyone says it's bound to get worse after next February when decimalization comes in.' She glanced up and saw how ill and strained Lawrence was looking. 'What's wrong?' she asked, all other concerns immediately brushed aside. 'Here, come and sit down and I'll make some tea. You've been overworking.'

She led him into the sitting-room and pushed him gently into an easy chair, part of the three-piece suite which had been her parents' wedding present to them. Then she hurried back into the kitchen and put the kettle on to boil.

'Now,' she said, returning to fuss over Lawrence, 'stay there quietly and put your feet up. Take it gently for once in your life.'

'I'm not ill,' he said abrasively, in what she thought of as his schoolmaster's voice. 'I've had a bit of a shock, that's all.'

'A shock? What about?'

'Ken Crosby phoned me this afternoon. He'd just come from the annual general meeting of the WYM Labour

195

Party. Tom Birkenshaw proposed a vote of "no confidence" in me, and the motion – with the help of his cronies, I don't doubt – was carried by a substantial majority.'

Joanna sank down on to the edge of the sofa, staring at him in bewilderment.

'A vote of no confidence? In God's name, why? You've been a marvellous MP. You've knocked yourself out for those people.'

'Ostensibly, they objected to my support, last year, of Barbara Castle's White Paper *In Place of Strife*.'

'That's ridiculous!' Joanna's blue eyes snapped furiously. 'I know the big unions were against it on the grounds that it would introduce the element of criminal proceedings into industrial relations, but West Yorkshire Moors is primarily a farming community. And there have been so many strikes these past few years I should have thought they'd be glad of any legislation to curb them.'

'That's why I said "ostensibly". Ken thinks there's something else behind the move. He's heard rumours that Tom Birkenshaw wants to stand himself as Labour candidate at the next general election.'

The kettle was whistling, and Joanna dashed into the kitchen to make the tea, continuing the conversation long-distance.

'Can they do that? Get rid of you, I mean?'

Lawrence gave a dry little laugh. 'Oh, yes. MPs aren't permanent fixtures. They can be given the order of the boot just like any other unsatisfactory employee.'

'But you're not unsatisfactory!' Joanna carried in the tray of tea things and poured out two cups, handing the one with sugar to Lawrence. 'Surely Tom Birkenshaw can't get away with it. There must be loads of people in both the constituency and the party who'll speak up for you.'

Lawrence shrugged resignedly. 'Outsiders can't do any more than try to persuade people that they're making a mistake, but Tom Birkenshaw is the chairman of the local

196

selection committee, and he's more clout than anyone else in the local party. He's already managed to get his vote of "no confidence" passed, and that's a very serious matter for any MP. Particularly as close to a general election as we are at the moment. It's common knowledge that the PM's going to announce one within the next few weeks.'

'Isn't there ... well, any hope of finding another constituency? If they do give you the push, I mean.'

Lawrence shook his head. 'Not this time, I'm afraid. I might be lucky the next time around.'

Joanna drank her tea without tasting it. 'It's wicked. Can't Ken Crosby do anything?'

'Of course he has some influence, but not enough to over-ride the decision of the committee.' Her husband smiled wryly. 'Sorry, my dear. It looks as though it's back to the blackboard for a while, at least.'

'It hasn't happened yet,' Joanna answered fiercely. 'Maybe it never will. Where are you going?'

Lawrence had risen to his feet. 'To the House. I'm still an MP, remember?' He looked down at her sadly. 'I'll be sorry if I have to give it all up. I know most people go on about inflation, and I admit it's a problem, but we've done some good things in this Parliament.'

And on this pessimistic note he left. Joanna heard his footsteps on the uncarpeted stairs and his exchange of greetings with the greengrocer, whose inner door was open because of the fine spring weather. Then the front door banged. Joanna got up and watched Lawrence from the window, as he disappeared in the direction of the Underground, before returning to her seat and pouring herself another cup of tea.

She had never liked Tom Birkenshaw, and she had the feeling that he didn't care much for her, but he had never been openly hostile and had seemed quite fond of Lawrence. What could have happened to turn him against them in so dramatic and positive a fashion?

The more she thought about it, however, the less an answer presented itself. She felt angry and resentful on

Lawrence's behalf. He had done so much for his constituents. But, for her own part, she wouldn't be sorry to leave London and go home to her beloved West Country. They would buy a house in either Bristol or Bath, depending on where Lawrence found a job, and she could settle down to being something that so far she had never been: a proper wife. Perhaps if life were less frenetic, and Lawrence's hours more regular, they might be able at last to start a family. The doctors they had consulted, separately and together, had all assured them there was nothing wrong with either of them. What they needed was a more relaxed existence.

Joanna replaced her empty cup and saucer on the tray and tried to direct her attention to immediate concerns, like putting away her groceries and getting herself something to eat. She realized suddenly that she was hungry. It was almost seven o'clock, and her last meal, a bar snack, had been at twelve-thirty. As she got up and headed for the kitchen, she saw the little pile of mail which she had had no time to open that morning and had left on the sitting-room table. When she had washed up the tea things, and before she cooked herself bacon and eggs, she returned to glance through it.

There were a couple of bills, the inevitable circulars, a long buff envelope from the Inland Revenue and a pale blue one, addressed to her in Davina's handwriting. Joanna pushed the rest aside and curled up on the sofa with her sister's letter. Written on Forest Moor notepaper, it contained two pieces of startling news: Davina's first book, a detailed account of the Peasant's Revolt of 1381, had been accepted for publication by Smith & Greatorex, and she had been appointed to the headship of a large comprehensive school in Exeter.

'You can imagine', Davina wrote, 'that Aunt Thea is disgusted and has more or less washed her hands of me. She finds it particularly hard to take in the wake of my breaking into print. She is, of course, over the moon about that, but it only makes it more difficult for her to accept my other decision.

'To tell you the truth, Jo, I don't really know how I found the courage to stand up to her. I've only done it once before, when I married Anthony, and that was rather different. I didn't even have the nerve to tell her when I went for the interview. I swapped my day off with Peggy Martin and said I was shopping in London.

'Incidentally, the Treasurer of the Board of Governors of Haddington Grange – I think the name of the school as well as its Devon location has done a very little to appease Aunt Thea's wrath – is a Mrs Olwen Ferrers, whose mother-in-law, I was informed in a hushed whisper by one of the other candidates, is the daughter of an earl. But I'd guessed she was Alex's wife long before that. Apparently there aren't any children and they don't spend much time together. The formidable Olwen seems to serve on a great many committees and does a lot of charity work in the city. Alex, I also learned from my informant – a local woman, as you have probably gathered – immerses himself in the family business. My general impression was of a not very happy marriage.

'Perhaps I shouldn't be telling you all this, but after all this time I don't suppose you've more than an impersonal interest in the Ferrers and their doings, and I thought you might like to know.

'Remember me to Lawrence. I expect you're both looking forward, with your usual campaigning fervour, to the next election. It seems it will be another Labour win with a substantial majority. That's something else which won't please Aunt Thea. Take care, Yours as ever, Davey.'

Slowly, Joanna raised her head from the letter and stared out at the London sky beyond the window.

21

ON 18 MAY the Prime Minister called an election for one month's time, and everyone was convinced that it would be Labour's third consecutive win over the Tories. Everything pointed to it, and the opinon polls gave the Government a substantial lead over all its rivals.

The Sunday before the election, Joanna and Lawrence were staying in Nightingale Close, preparatory to their move from London. Tom Birkenshaw was the elected Labour candidate for West Yorkshire Moors, and the newspapers had had a field-day with their stories about the 'sacked' MP. Lawrence had borne it all with the quiet dignity Joanna had come to expect from him, but she knew how much he was hurting inside. She grieved for him, and spent long hours devising new and ever more horrendous forms of torture to inflict on Tom Birkenshaw and members of the British press. She let Lawrence make love to her almost every night, even when she was so tired she could hardly think straight, because it seemed to be the only way he could forget his unhappiness. Afterwards, she would hold him quietly in her arms until he relaxed, and the steady rhythm of his breathing told her that he had at last fallen asleep.

Bernard and Jean had invited them down for the forthcoming week so that they could begin the long wearisome rounds of the estate agents. Joanna had not, as yet, mentioned to her mother that they would be looking for accomodation in Bristol rather than in Bath. How could she say that she did not want to live too near to her parents without sounding churlish? Her father, she knew, would understand and even be secretly relieved to have her and Lawrence at a comfortable distance. But perhaps, after all, her mother wouldn't mind: Jean could often be surprising.

They had all spent the early part of Sunday evening watching the World Cup from Mexico: England's quarter-final against their old adversaries, West Germany, a game which ended in defeat for the former World Champions. The house in Nightingale Close, like millions more all over the country, was plunged in gloom. Bernard groaned as he switched off the set.

'There goes the election,' he said, throwing himself back in his chair.

'Oh, come on, Dad!' Joanna protested. 'That's a bit far-fetched! Don't tell me you're getting superstitious.'

'Your father could well be right, Jo,' Lawrence put in gently. 'It's a fact that all sorts of things influence the way people vote. Do *you* like football? Do you normally care who wins or loses? But look at you now! You're just as miserable as the rest of us; and that despair, that sense of national defeat, is being multiplied all over the land.'

'It won't influence me on Thursday!'

'Of course not, because you're committed. But what about the floating voter? He needs to take his frustration out on someone. And because we've this tradition of never blaming our losing teams – it wouldn't be sporting! – who better than the Government?'

Joanna was irritated. 'I've never heard such nonsense!'

'Wait and see,' was her husband's reply.

'You ought to write a book on the subject, Larry,' Reginald Harding remarked quietly from his armchair in the corner. ' "Outside Influences on the Floating Voter" – something like that.' He chuckled. 'It wouldn't do your reputation any harm in the party, and I'm sure you'll want to stand again the next time round.'

Joanna smiled at her grandfather and squeezed his hand. She thought he was looking frail, and his arthritis was getting worse. Ten years ago, at sixty, he had been a vigorous, well set up man for his age, but the last twelve months had seen a rapid deterioration in his physical health. Mentally, he was as alert as ever.

'Don't encourage him, Gramps.' She stood up, stretching. 'To start writing a book, I mean. One author in the family is quite enough, and we have our hands full at present moving house and finding Larry a job. Besides, I don't believe in all these external influences. I'm naïve enough to believe that people listen to what politicians say and vote on policies. Come on, Mum, let's go and make supper. England may be out of the World Cup, but Labour will be back on Thursday with an increased majority. You'll see.'

But Thursday, against all predictions to the contrary, brought a Conservative government to power with an overall majority of thirty. A quiet election, with one of the lowest turnouts since the war, had ousted Harold Wilson and put bachelor Edward Heath into 10 Downing Street.

Tom Birkenshaw held the West Yorkshire Moors seat for Labour.

'It's nice having you so close again,' Jean said, pouring her daughter a cup of very thick, very dark brown coffee.

Joanna sat down at the kitchen table and glanced around her: the room was in its usual state of chaotic muddle. Nothing much ever changed in Nightingale Close, she thought. That, for her, was its chief attraction and charm.

'I'd hardly call Clifton Wood close,' she objected. 'We're right on the far side of Bristol.'

'It's closer than London,' Jean said, sitting down on the opposite side of the table. She cleared aside the various items of shopping which she had been in the process of unpacking before Joanna arrived, to make room for her cup and saucer. 'And it doesn't take long in a car. It was the best thing you ever did, learning to drive. Larry still liking his new job?'

'Mum, we've been back for almost a year, and Larry's

been in his present post nearly as long. And teaching English to fourth-formers can hardly be classified as new, when it's what he's been doing for the best part of his adult life. Yes, he's contented enough, but he won't be really happy until he gets back into Parliament again.'

'What happened up in Yorkshire?' Jean asked curiously. 'Why did that Birkenshaw man suddenly take against him? Did you ever find out?'

'No, and I don't suppose we ever shall. Just one of those things we have to accept and hope that it won't affect Larry's chances in the future. Finish your coffee and I'll take you to Bath for lunch. We'll go to the Old Red House.'

'It's closed,' Jean told her mournfully. 'It closed last year. You must remember. No one seems at all sure about the fate of New Bond Street. They're tearing down the whole of Southgate Street at this very moment. The Odeon cinema and those little Victorian shops! We're going to have a big new shopping mall, instead, all glass and breeze blocks. God knows where it'll end. Bath will soon be unrecognizable! And this decimalization! I can't get to grips with it. It's all right for your father. He's a mathematician. But I have to convert everything back into pounds, shillings and pence before I know what I'm spending.' Jean paused in her catalogue of woes and then sighed. 'That's how old people talk, isn't it? Always resisting and moaning about changes. Still, I suppose I am old.'

'You're fifty-one,' Joanna replied bracingly. 'That's no age at all nowadays. And, if it's any consolation, I agree with you. It's high time someone brought the Bath City Planning Department to its senses. Well, if the Old Red House is closed, we'll go to the Francis Hotel. Don't tell me they've started mucking about with Queen Square.'

'Of course not! They wouldn't dare!' Jean beamed at her daughter. 'Oh, it *is* nice to have you popping in occasionally, and to be able to go over and see you and Larry now and then. I never seem to see anything of Freddie. When she's resting, or whatever they call it, she goes to stay with Dora. Says it's better for her to be at the hub of things, in

London.' The beam slipped and became a wry smile. Jean looked down at her hands, curling the long, slightly arthritic fingers more tightly about her empty cup. 'I haven't made much of a go of things, have I, Jo? Davey always preferred Anthea's company, and Freddie'd rather be with Dora. As for Terry . . .' Her voice became suspended for a moment, and she made a brave effort to blink back the tears. 'I didn't even know enough about her to stop her killing herself. She didn't feel she could confide in me, I suppose.'

Joanna came round the table and put her arms around her mother as Jean began to sob; a hard, dry, grating sound, more shocking than tears.

'Mum! Mum, don't! It wasn't your fault. You mustn't blame yourself. Terry and I were twins, and I always thought we shared everything. But she didn't confide in me, either. It was Anthony's fault, all of it. He'd asked Terry to marry him. I know, because Davey told me. He was stringing them both along. He didn't know what he wanted. And in the end he married Claire Neville, Alex's cousin.'

And because of that I quarrelled with Alex, she thought. Well, she was glad that she had. He must have been carrying on behind her back with Freda. He must have! Alex and Claire! As a family they were all the same, and she was glad she was shot of them. There were times when she wished she could be rid of her own family just as easily.

Sisters! They were nothing but trouble, when she came to think of it. Her mother's sister. Her father's sister. Her own sisters. Love and jealousy, concern and resentment all mixed up together! What a mess it all was. Relationships were the very devil! Here she was, married to one man, a good man, a fine man, and still in love with another. Lawrence deserved better of her than that, but she couldn't control her feelings. Not that she regretted what had happened, she told herself fiercely. She had made the right decision. It would never have worked with Alex; not with a man who was so influenced by his mother's opinions.

Hadn't Davey told her that his marriage to Olwen Bruce wasn't happy? And there weren't any children.

But in that she and Alex were alike. She and Lawrence seemed unable to have a child, dearly as they would have loved one. Or was the longing one-sided? Joanna had an idea that perhaps she was enough for Lawrence. He was forty-one now and often said jokingly that he was too old to be a parent. But was he joking? Wasn't she all that he had ever really wanted? Whereas she was still young, only twenty-seven, and needed children, not just to cement her marriage more firmly, but because she loved them for their own sake. Unlike Davina, she had a strong maternal instinct. She thought suddenly of Samantha.

Her niece was ten years old now, growing up fast, but no one had seen her since she was a toddler. After Theresa's death, all connections between the two families had been severed. Jean had mentioned once that Anthony and Claire had a second child, a daughter Jacqueline, and that he was a partner in a large lucrative group practice in Bath. Widcombe, was it? Joanna could not remember. She automatically shut off whenever her former brother-in-law's name was mentioned. But now and then her conscience pricked her. Surely someone ought to show some interest in Samantha. Whenever she brought up the subject with Lawrence, however, he always made the same answer.

'Mind your own business, Jo. If she's anyone's responsibility, she's Davey's. Besides, I don't suppose Anthony and his wife would thank you for interfering. As far as Samantha is concerned, Claire is her mother. Your appearance at this stage in her life would only complicate matters.'

It seemed, on the face of it, sound advice, but somewhere at the back of her mind Joanna entertained a lingering doubt. There must come a time when her niece would have to be told the truth, and then she might well resent her mother's family's lack of interest. But in the end the prospect of having to contact Anthony and Claire

205

Douglas always stood between Joanna and her instincts. Lawrence was right, she decided. It really was Davina's business.

Jean had, by this time, regained control of her emotions. Gently, she pushed Joanna away, smiling apologetically.

'I'm sorry about that. I didn't mean to break down. Terry died so many years ago now, I thought I'd got over it.'

'I don't think you ever completely get over a thing like that,' Joanna said quietly. 'I know I haven't. Now, what about lunch? Are you on?'

'Yes, it would be nice. I haven't been out for ages. I'm sure your grandfather won't mind getting himself something just for once.'

As if on cue, the kitchen door opened and Reginald Harding came in, brandishing the newspaper and grinning all over his face.

'Jean! Have you read the *Guardian* this morning?'

'I haven't had time. Bernard always hogs our copy at breakfast.'

'Hello, Gramps.' Joanna went over and kissed him.

'Hello, my dear.' He returned her kiss, but perfunctorily. For once, a visit from his favourite grand-daughter was of secondary importance. 'I didn't see you. Keeping well?' Without attending to her reply, he thrust the newspaper at her. 'Here! Read this! There's a piece about Davey's book.'

Joanna grabbed the paper, almost tearing it in her eagerness.

The review was glowing, with only one slight reservation as to the choice of title.

'*Jack Straw and His Menie* – the unwieldy title is a quotation from Chaucer and, ironically, the poet's only known reference to what must have been the most traumatic event of his lifetime – is one of the best books ever written on the subject of the Peasants' Revolt. Davina Marshall brings to it a clear, analytical and, above all, unsentimental eye, and makes the telling point that, had John Ball and his "communistic law" succeeded in overthrowing the government of the day, England might well have anticipated the Russian Revolution by almost six centuries. Her lucid prose, her carefully reasoned arguments for the causes of the rebellion and her own obvious enthusiasm as she takes you, step by step, through the events which culminated in the confrontation of the young king and Wat Tyler on Saturday, 15 June 1381, at Smithfield, make this one of the most compelling books of 1971.'

Joanna handed the paper to her mother, expecting Jean's reaction to be the same as her own and Reginald's: one of pride and excitement. Instead, Jean merely nodded briskly.

'Very nice,' she said. 'Anthea will be delighted with it.'

'Oh, Mum!' Joanna's anger was apparent in the sharp tone of her voice. 'Can't you be generous about Davey just for once? It isn't her fault that Aunt Thea's always shown more interest in her than you have.'

'I said it's a nice review.' Her mother's response was clipped. 'Your father will be pleased, and cross with himself that he missed it this morning.' She turned to Reginald. 'Dad, you won't mind fending for yourself today, will you? Jo's offered to buy me lunch in Bath.'

'Of course I can manage on my own.' Her father was indignant. 'It'll do you good, so go and change. Jo and I can put the shopping away. We know where things are kept.'

Jean smiled gratefully and, a few seconds later, was hurrying upstairs. While Joanna washed the coffee-cups, her grandfather began stacking the various tins and packets into the already overflowing and untidy cupboards. He sighed.

'Your mother was always the same as a girl. No sense of order.'

Jo asked quietly: 'Gramps, why doesn't she like Davey?'

She thought for a moment that he was going to protest, to cling to the convention that parents loved all their children equally, but he didn't. He shrugged and sat down at the table, looking old and careworn.

'I don't know, my dear. I wish I did.' He rubbed the side of his nose, as though it might produce inspiration, like a genie from a lamp. 'She wasn't very happy at that time. Your father was away in the Army, and she was very restless. In the autumn – this is 1942 I'm talking about – she went up to London to stay with Dora for a few months. The Blitz was over by then, and it was well before the V1s and V2s. Dora wasn't married. It was before she met Ralph Whitlock. She was living in a small flat in Earls Court and she'd landed her first West End part the previous May. I remember how excited she was about it. She came home just before the production opened – we were still living in Bristol in those days – and took us out for a meal. Your father was on leave, and he and Jean came along as well. Even though it was wartime, the restaurants never seemed short of food.' He drifted off into a reverie, as he was apt to do lately, Joanna had noticed.

'You were saying about Mother going to London,' she prompted gently.

'Ah, yes.' Reginald shifted uncomfortably, as if his joints were hurting him. 'Dora wrote to say that she was nervous living on her own and would be glad of some company. A load of poppycock, if you ask me! Dora was never nervous of anything. It was something they concocted between them, I reckon, because Jean wanted an excuse to get away. Your grandmother was very unwell at the time, and of course I was teaching all day. I think Jean was afraid she was going to be asked to come over to Bristol and look after her mother, so she just upped and went. She didn't even tell us she was pregnant until it was nearly time for the baby to be born. We were extremely hurt by that. Neither of us could go to London to be with her because by that time your grandmother was seriously ill and in hospital. It was months before she recovered. Jean came home with Davina a few weeks later, at the beginning of March 1943. Dora was going on tour and didn't need her any more.' Reginald got to his feet again and started to shift the remaining groceries. 'And that, my dear, is all that I can tell you, I'm afraid. It doesn't really have any bearing, as far as I can see, on why your mother doesn't like Davey.'

Joanna finished drying the coffee-cups thoughtfully, and was just hanging them up on the old-fashioned kitchen dresser when the telephone began to ring in the hall. She could hear her mother still moving about in the bedroom overhead, so she went to answer it.

It was Freda. Even before Joanna could repeat the number and say who was speaking, her sister had plunged straight in.

'Mum!' Her bubbling excitement exploded in Joanna's right ear. 'Guess what! I've been offered the juvenile lead in a new play opening next month at the Adelphi! Mum, this is it! My big break! I've *arrived*!'

PART FOUR

1974

22

'IT'S LOVELY!' Joanna exclaimed, looking round appreciatively. 'I don't know how you discover these places. I
suppose you just bat your eyelids and the estate agents fall
over themselves to find you something special.'

Davina's self-contained flat, over a fancy goods and
knitting-wool shop, fully justified her sister's approval. On
the corner of a narrow alleyway, off the Close, she had an
unrivalled view of Exeter Cathedral's west front, flanked
by its twin Norman towers, and the surrounding green. On
this late-April evening, it was bathed in sunshine, the pale
Beer stone turned almost golden in the dying rays of light.

'I was just lucky,' Davina disclaimed modestly; although
there was no doubt in Joanna's eyes that her sister was
more beautiful than ever. At thirty-one, Davina had
matured into an extremely handsome woman. She set
down the dark-blue leather case, which she had insisted on
carrying upstairs from the taxi, and beamed at Joanna. 'It
really is good to see you,' she said.

Joanna sent her a quizzical glance. 'You could have
asked me before. Now that Larry's an MP again, I've plenty
of time on my hands, unless I find myself another job.'

'I know, but I haven't long moved in here. To begin with,
I was living near the school. I had a rented house in a
neighbouring road. Very convenient, but in the end I
couldn't take it any longer. It was all too bright and clean
and modern. I wanted something with more atmosphere.
I've started another book on the Black Death of 1348, and I
needed to be closer to the past. This place is perfect. Come

and look around, then you can unpack before we have supper.'

As she obediently trailed her sister from room to room, Joanna reflected that Davina's invitation to stay with her for a couple of weeks had arrived at just the right time. She had been low and depressed after a winter of fuel crises and power cuts, which had almost blacked out the whole of Britain. Then Edward Heath's decision to let the country resolve the issue of his long-running battle with the striking miners had meant all the hard work and grind of a general election. Lawrence, who had put himself forward, and been accepted, as the no-hope Labour candidate for the Avonvale constituency – the seat he had fought and lost once before – astonished everyone, including himself, by scraping in, after three recounts, with a majority of twenty-two.

For this miracle, as he was the first to admit, he was deeply indebted to the constituency agent, David Nugent, and to Joanna, both of whom had worked night and day on his behalf, pounding pavements, knocking on doors, distributing leaflets, attending meetings and button-holing people in the streets. Neither of them had dreamed of doing more than increase the party's share of the vote, particularly as the Conservative section of the local press had been quick to remind its readers that Lawrence had left his last constituency under something of a cloud, after suffering a vote of 'no confidence'. The leader and editorial writers had discounted the fact that, in the meantime, Lawrence had become a minor 'name'; the author of a book entitled – with due acknowledgments to Reginald Harding – *Outside Influences and the Floating Voter*. It had been well received in government circles and earned him attention from the media. And, if very few people in Avonvale had actually read the book, they had at least heard of the title, and his mild fame offset any adverse publicity which came Lawrence's way. He just managed to scrape in ahead of his Tory rival.

This narrow margin of victory had been reflected in the

national result. Labour had five more seats than the Conservatives, but no overall majority. There were days of uncertainty while Edward Heath refused to resign, but in the end he was persuaded to step down, and it was Harold Wilson who was sent for by the Queen to form a government. It had been touch and go, and everyone knew that there was bound to be another election before the year was out. For Joanna, the prospect of going through the whole process again was daunting, especially with possible disappointment lurking at the finish. Such a fragile majority could so easily be wiped out, and she had refused, point-blank, to give up the Bristol house and move to London, at least for the time being. In consequence, she saw even less of her husband than she might have done, and was at present looking round for a job which, as well as filling the empty hours, would also help to support the additional expense of Lawrence's tiny bachelor flat near Westminster. And, to add to everything else, she had recently suffered a miscarriage.

She had discovered, to her great joy, that she was pregnant just after Christmas, and had been warned by her doctor to take things quietly.

'You're thirty, Mrs Walden,' he had pointed out gently, 'and, although nowadays it's considered no great age, a first child is never that easy. Go home, put your feet up and let your husband help with the household chores. Especially in those long school holidays.'

But in February had come the election and Lawrence's acceptance as candidate by the Avonvale Labour selection committee. Knowing how much re-election to Parliament meant to him, and how dissatisfied and unhappy he had been for the past four years, Joanna had thrown herself heart and soul into the campaign. It had proved worth all her efforts, but at a price. Three weeks after Lawrence had again been sworn in as an MP, she had woken up one morning with stomach pains. Two hours later, Joanna found herself in Southmead Hospital minus the baby. Summoned by her mother, Lawrence had rushed down

215

from London, concern vying with relief on his face. He had never really wanted to be a father, and Joanna knew instinctively that her last chance to have a child had gone. Lawrence would make sure that she never had another.

Then, out of the blue, had come Davina's invitation. Her elder sister, with whom she had had so little contact for so many years, wrote that she had moved into a new flat near the cathedral.

'I know you like Exeter, and this place is so pretty I can't resist showing it off. It's time, anyway, that we renewed our acquaintance, and I can't think of a pleasanter location for doing it than this. I'm sure Lawrence can spare you for a couple of weeks. And Gramps tells me that you need a holiday. He says you're looking "peeky". Do come if you can. I truly would look forward to your visit.'

There was nothing, as far as Joanna could see, to prevent her going. Except at weekends, Lawrence rarely left London, having to be always within sound of the division bell. Without an overall majority, the Prime Minister needed every one of his MPs continually to hand. And Lawrence, when consulted, had said it sounded to him like a good idea: there were no engagements in the constituency over the next fortnight where her presence might be needed.

'It will do you good,' he had assured her over the phone.

It was the general consensus of opinion.

'Put the roses back in your cheeks,' her grandfather had said, kissing her fondly.

Bernard, who was fifty-eight and within two years of retirement, had remarked bluntly: 'Wish your sister would ask *us* down occasionally. I'd enjoy it more than all these foreign holidays. But there, Davina and your mother don't get on.'

Surprisingly, even Jean had urged her to go. 'You and Davey used to be friends, and you'd better make the most of her company before she becomes really famous with these books of hers. Look at Freddie! How often do we ever see her nowadays?' She added, in a tone in which

216

pride and bitterness were inextricably mixed: 'The well-known actress, Freda Marshall! Now about to break into films! I suppose we shall see even less of her once she becomes a star.'

So, thought Joanna, peering out of her window at the varying architectural styles of the buildings clustered around the sprawling green, here she was, with two carefree weeks stretching ahead of her.

Supper – a home-made lasagne and a Waldorf salad, washed down with a bottle of Beaujolais – was over and cleared away. As so often happened in April, a warm sunny day had turned to rain, laced with an evening chill. Davina switched on the electric fire, and she and Joanna curled up companionably in front of its comforting warmth. Through the still uncurtained window, Joanna could glimpse a gabled roof and, beneath it, a narrow Gothic wall-slit. The food and wine had induced in her a tranquil haze of well-being. She felt happier than at any time since she lost the baby.

The room they were sitting in, like the rest of the flat and Davina's clothes, bore the imprint of London rather than of the slower-moving and more conventional provinces. The long sofa was strewn with cushions in Liberty print patchwork and upholstered in a Provençal patterned material from Brother Sun. There was a Tiffany art nouveau lamp on the Habitat table, and Davina was wearing a loose dress in Indian cotton from Monsoon. Ethnic kitsch had long ago replaced the space-age look of the mini-skirt and its subsequent and short-lived sister, the maxi. In Joanna's bedroom there was a brass bedstead, rattan furniture and a couple of trailing plants on stripped-pine shelves. It was all very 'with it' and 'in', to use the current jargon, and consequently very expensive.

'You must be doing very well for yourself, Davey,' Joanna remarked without rancour, stretching her stockinged feet towards the electric fire. She had kicked off her shoes, and the feeling of warmth between her toes was almost sensuous. 'We all watched you on television again the other evening.'

'What do you mean, "again"?' Davina demanded, embarrassed. 'It was only my second-ever appearance. You make it sound as though I'm never off the box.'

'It may be only your second appearance, but I doubt if it will be your last.' Joanna smiled lazily at her sister. 'You made quite an impression. Last Sunday's *Observer* described you as one of the few intelligent voices at present to be heard on television. It said you were the best thing on that programme.'

'Rubbish!' Davina tried hard not to look too pleased. 'Anyway, I doubt if many people were watching a minority programme about education on BBC2. The vast majority were glued to "It Ain't Half Hot Mum" on BBC1.'

'You undersell yourself and the programme. There are a lot of people with teenage children who must have been interested enough to tune in. And who can talk with more authority about the differences between the comprehensive and private school systems than you, who have had firsthand experience of both? It was nice to hear you speak up for the state schools. Dad was delighted, especially as he was expecting you to take the opposite view. He's very proud of his famous daughter.'

'One book and a couple of television appearances don't constitute fame!' Davina protested, distressed by the notion. 'Now, Freddie, yes! She really *is* someone you could call famous without fear of contradiction. Two brilliant West End successes, one after the other, and now a part in a major British film! There was a piece in the *Guardian* about her, only this morning. Apparently, there's some talk of bringing Jeff Warwick over from Hollywood to play the male lead.'

Joanna raised her eyebrows and whistled. 'If that's true, then she'll certainly be made. The film will be a sellout in the States. Jeff Warwick is currently America's blue-eyed darling. You can't open any woman's magazine these days without coming across yet another article about him and his ecstatically happy marriage to Gabriella Richardson. They're the world's latest sweethearts. The most popular married couple since Debbie Reynolds and Eddie Fisher.'

'And look what happened to *them*,' Davina commented drily. 'One glance from Liz Taylor's big violet eyes and the whole thing was blown wide open.'

'Ah, but Jeff Warwick's marriage is made in heaven,' Joanna laughed. 'I have it on the indisputable authority of both *Woman* and *Woman's Own*. The Ideal Marriage is how most Americans see it, and woe betide anybody who tries to break it up. Not, according to the same impeccable sources, that anyone could.'

They both laughed this time, before Joanna introduced a more serious note into the conversation. 'Has Aunt Thea forgiven you yet? Are you still good friends?'

Davina got up from the sofa and went to pull the curtains, shutting out the lights of Cathedral Close.

'Oh, yes, she's forgiven me. Everything's all right between us now.' She returned to her place on the sofa, curling up once more in the corner. She looked, her sister thought, like a sinuous cat. 'The success of *Jack Straw and His Menie* went a long way towards reconciling her, and the two television panels have done me no harm. She's convinced herself that I only take the stand I do on comprehensive education in order to safeguard my job; and that I only want to safeguard my job in order to justify my decision to accept the headship of Haddington Grange. And who knows? She might well be right.'

Joanna was jolted out of her lethargy. She sat bolt upright. 'Davey! You can't mean that, surely!'

Her sister shrugged, the light from the Tiffany lamp softly gilding her hair. With her grey eyes and pale transparent skin, she had an ethereal quality which Joanna had only half-remembered.

'Why not? Privilege is the hardest thing of all to give up. Much harder than money. Privilege cocoons you against the world. It gives you self-esteem. It lifts you above the common ruck. Without it, you're just one of the faceless majority: people who can be, and are, conned and cozened and generally pushed around; who haven't the ability to speak up for themselves. Part of the process of private education is to convince you, from an early age, that you are one of the élite. The *crème de la crème*, as Miss Brodie put it. Deep down, it's what everyone wants, and after three years at Haddington Grange I'm not sure that it's such a bad thing.'

Joanna was horrified. 'You sound just like Aunt Thea. And we all thought you'd been converted.'

Davina sighed. 'I'm muddled, Jo. At one time I used to know exactly who I was, where my loyalties lay, what I thought. Not any more.'

'What changed you?'

Somewhere a dog was barking. Someone, just below their windows, called a loud 'Good-night!' and from further along the narrow alleyway came a muffled response. On the other side of the green, the cathedral crouched, as it had done for nearly eight hundred years, ever since Bishop William Warelast, the Conqueror's nephew, initiated the building of its twin Norman towers. And, long before that, the Romans had built their baths, houses and halls at Isca Dumnoniorum, until they had been recalled to Rome and the place was left to the marauding Saxons. For the first time, Joanna could see clearly why Davina liked history. It was gone, it was past, it was safe. No decision of hers or anyone else's could change what had happened. And that was the essential difference between them. Joanna wanted to make history; to have a hand in shaping the future. Which was why she enjoyed politics so much. She suddenly felt restless, wondering what she was doing here, cosseting herself like an invalid, when she should be in London or in the constituency, helping Lawrence.

Davina was speaking in answer to her question.

'I suppose what really unsettled me – although I didn't think it had at the time – was when Aunt Thea admitted to me that she had been responsible for that story Terry told me, about her and Anthony. Oh, Terry went along with the idea, but Aunt Thea had put her up to it.'

'What story?' Joanna asked, suddenly tense.

'The story that she and Anthony had been sleeping together. That he wanted to marry her, but she'd nobly sent him back to me. It was all a pack of lies. Aunt Thea knew me well enough to guess how I'd react, and she didn't want me going back to Anthony. She didn't want me coming down from Oxford with a decent degree to become just a doctor's wife and a mother. A waste, she called it, and maybe she was right. I shouldn't have done all I've done if I'd been married. Anyway, at the time I agreed with her, but I think the feeling that I'd been manipulated and robbed of free choice must have sunk into my subconscious and made me rebellious. I think it was probably the real reason why I was so set on getting the headship of Haddington Grange. By doing something I knew she wouldn't approve of, I was revenging myself on Aunt Thea.'

Joanna linked trembling fingers around one knee. 'Let me get this straight,' she said. 'Anthony and Terry were never lovers? He never asked her to marry him? He never, in short, gave her any reason to suppose that she meant more to him than she actually did?'

Davina nodded. 'Yes. Or no, according to how you view the question. The story was a fabrication, concocted by Terry and Aunt Thea.'

Joanna said nothing. For years, she had hated Anthony Douglas because she believed he had given Theresa cause to think that he loved her. She had broken off her engagement to Alex because she would not have Anthony and Claire invited to the wedding. (She was not, at the moment, rational enough to admit that the incident had merely been the culmination of a string of other reasons.) Alex had asked her if she had bothered to listen to Anthony's side of the story, and she had said . . . What was it she had said? 'There's nothing he could say that I should want to hear.'

How wrong she had been.

221

23

JOANNA had spent the morning, as she had spent the last three, shopping and sightseeing. She felt calm and unhurried, living in limbo; a big golden bubble of contentment which she had deliberately constructed around herself so that she wouldn't have to think – about Anthony Douglas, about Theresa, about Alex. Her newly acquired knowledge had deeply disturbed her, but for now she was protected against its pressures.

Davina was spoiling her. Each morning, before leaving for Haddington Grange, she brought Joanna her breakfast in bed; coffee, muesli, brown rolls and marmalade, and butter in a small blue-and-white porcelain dish. And in the evenings, on her way home from school, she stopped at the local delicatessen and bought delicious home-made pizzas, quiches, salads and steak-and-kidney pies. A woman came in twice a week to give the flat a thorough cleaning, so there was nothing for Joanna to do all day except amuse herself. She got up, dressed, covered the bed with the unfamiliar Continental quilt and went out. To begin with, she had loved it. Now, on this fourth morning, she was beginning to be bored. The bubble was starting, ever so slightly, to break, uneasy memories, thoughts and cares crowding in.

She had been round the cathedral twice already, and although it would repay a third, even a fourth, visit Joanna felt it was too soon to go again. She had visited the Maritime Museum and viewed the seventeenth-century Custom House, inspected Wynards Almshouses in Magdalen Street and window-shopped her way along High Street towards Fore Street. She was almost abreast of the magnificent thirteenth-century Guildhall, conscious of being hungry and wondering where to go for lunch, when she saw him turning out of a side-street opposite. Alex Ferrer!

It had always been a possibility she might run into him; a chance which had seemed unimportant when considering whether or not to accept her sister's invitation. Even if she did run into him, she had nothing to say to him. He was still Claire Douglas's cousin, and her feelings about Theresa and Anthony had not changed. Rather, they had hardened over the years. But now all that had altered. Davina's revelation had forced her to change her mind about both Anthony and Alex. She had wronged them both and, now that she saw him again, all her old feelings for Alex came surging back. She still loved him. But they were both married now. It would be better if they did not meet . . .

But he had already seen her. There was no possibility now of slipping unnoticed along the crowded pavement and hurrying down North Street. He was purposefully crossing the road towards her.

'Jo!' He was blocking her path. 'How good to see you again after all this time.' Only his eyes betrayed his uncertainty about his reception.

'Alex.' She grasped his outstretched hand, feeling the old familiar pressure of his fingers.

'I'm just going to have lunch,' he said. 'Will you join me?'

'Yes . . . yes, thank you,' she stammered. 'That would be lovely.'

If he felt surprise at her eager response, he concealed it. While they made their way back across the road and into St Martin's Lane, she explained her presence in Exeter, even though Alex had made no enquiry. Embarrassment and guilt were making her garrulous. She lapsed into a defiant silence. Glancing sideways at him, she found him smiling at her in complete understanding.

'Oh, damn you, Alex!' she laughed. 'You always knew too much about me.'

His hand came up to grip her elbow as he guided her across the threshold of Sir Francis Drake's old haunt, the Ship Inn.

'I've brought you here before,' he murmured. 'Remember?'

'Yes, of course. I haven't forgotten anywhere I went with you.'

He raised his eyebrows, but said nothing. The pub was packed with the usual crowd of business people, having lunch, and they had to fight their way through to the bar. When they finally had their food and drinks, all the tables were occupied. The only seats available were a couple of tall stools in front of a wide shelf running along one wall. Joanna perched precariously on one stool, while Alex seated himself on the other. They were in closer proximity than she would have wished, and throughout the meal their arms and legs were constantly touching.

'How is your wife?' Joanna asked politely, after she had assuaged the first pangs of hunger.

'Olwen's fine,' Alex answered noncommittally. 'I'm in London a fair bit these days. I have a permanent office in Mincing Lane. I have to deputize for my father a great deal. He had a stroke two years ago and, although he's made a truly miraculous recovery, he has to take life more easily than he did before. And, then, Olwen has her various charities and committees, so we don't see all that much of one another. She's a governor of Haddington Grange school. Did your sister tell you?'

'Yes.' Joanna speared a piece of ham on the end of her fork. 'I'm sorry to hear about your father. Do you still see a lot of him and your mother, now that you're married?'

After the briefest of hesitations, Alex replied smoothly: 'Olwen and I have never had a home of our own. We have rooms – self-contained, of course – at King's Acre.'

'Oh.' Joanna sipped her beer. 'I see.'

'Yes, I expect you do, but it was what we all wanted, Mother and myself and Olwen included. It wouldn't have

224

suited you, Jo my dear, which is why I let you go when you broke the engagement. I know you thought that perhaps I ought to have fought to keep you, and don't think that I didn't want to try. The temptation was overwhelming. But I knew that it really wasn't going to work for us. It was far kinder just to say goodbye. You were always much too independent for me.'

Joanna had a feeling that he wasn't telling her all the truth, but she had no right to quibble. She pushed the remains of her salad around her plate. 'And Freda?' she couldn't prevent herself asking.

'Ah, yes, Freda,' Alex said thickly, through a mouthful of cold roast beef and mustard. There was a momentary silence while he cleared his throat. 'My friendship with Freddie really wasn't what it seemed. She was telling the truth, you know, when she said it only dated from the previous Christmas.'

Joanna laid her knife and fork together on her plate, still half-full of quiche and salad. The size of pub meals invariably defeated her, and in any case she was not as hungry as she had thought.

'I don't see why I shouldn't believe you,' she conceded after a moment or two. 'And as, during the whole of our acquaintance, you never made love to me, perhaps it was foolish to have suspected that you were going to bed with Freddie.'

'Very foolish,' he answered gently. His right hand clasped her left one and squeezed it, but if Joanna had expected any further explanation or self-justification she was disappointed. He went on: 'As your time's your own, let me drive you somewhere. One of our excursions.'

'Can you take the afternoon off, just like that?'

Alex laughed. 'My dear, I'm the boss's son. Now, don't look so deeply disapproving! I don't make a habit of it, I promise you. In my way, I'm every bit as hard-working as the new MP for Avonvale. Please note that I do keep *au fait* with the important events in your life. I always have. I felt for you when your husband lost his Yorkshire constituency. I was going to write to you. Then I thought that perhaps it was as well to let the matter lie.'

'You wouldn't have known where to write.' Joanna finished the last of her drink. The crescendo of noise in the pub had reached unbearable proportions as the number of lunch-time clients approached its peak.

'I've always known where to reach you, wherever you are,' Alex answered simply, but once again volunteered no further information.

Joanna supposed, thinking over their meeting later that evening, that she could have asked how he knew; insisted on him revealing his sources. But, for some reason, she hadn't wanted to know. Instinct warned her not to pry too closely. Instead, she said merely: 'Yes, I should very much like you to take me somewhere. That would be nice, if you're sure you can spare the time. If you're not too busy. We could drive out over Dartmoor, just as we used to do in the old days.'

Alex nodded. 'Wait here', he instructed, 'while I telephone my secretary at the office. Then we'll stroll round and pick up the car.'

'Hey!' Jeff Warwick exclaimed. 'Is this it? It looks pretty old-fashioned to me. What's all the fuss about?'

He stared round him a little contemptuously at the narrow windowless basement room, its walls covered with pictures. There were long sofas and plush banquettes, and one or two display-cases featuring jewellery from local shops. The bar was illumined by a warm orange glow, and the atmosphere was thick with cigarette smoke. At the far end, he could hear music, a tune he identified as 'Vincent', a Don McLean hit from two years earlier.

The receptionist, who had greeted Freda and watched her sign in, returned Jeff's look of disparagement with interest.

Freda said shortly, 'It's Annabel's,' and seemed to think no further explanation was necessary. With a spurious air of meekness, Jeff Warwick followed her to a table further along the room.

Heads turned as he passed, and a number of people who greeted Freda affectionately by name regarded him curiously. There was probably no one present who failed to recognize the unmistakable blue-black hair, the high oriental cheekbones, the thickly lashed brown eyes – which, according to the worst of the publicity handouts, had 'set a million female hearts on fire' – and the flashing white smile, splitting the olive-tinted skin.

Born twenty-nine years earlier in Los Angeles, and christened Giovanni Antonio Alberoni, the son of an Italian immigrant father and Chinese mother, he had changed his name to Jeff Warwick at the age of seventeen, when he had first begun to haunt the film studios looking for work as an extra. A talent scout had spotted him and signed him for Twentieth Century-Fox in 1965, a day or two before his twentieth birthday. His first part, in a low-budget movie about a rock group, had made very little impact, but his second, in which he played the leader of a gang of rebellious teenagers, all riding motor-cycles and kitted out in black leather, had made him an overnight sensation with young America, and his fame had quickly spread across the Atlantic.

But it was his marriage three years previously to the singing star Gabriella Richardson which had made him a universal favourite with young and old alike. Gabriella – known to an adoring public simply by her Christian name – was a purveyor of sentimental ballads, sung in a soft sweet voice which matched her plump, fair, all-American prettiness, and sounded an echo from the forties and fifties, at variance with most of the current musical scene. She had once been unkindly described by the *Melody Maker* as a dinosaur, but every disc she cut turned, literally, to gold. In the late sixties, early seventies, she made two films for the Walt Disney studios, and met Jeff Warwick at a Hollywood party. What happened after that, as the PR men were never tired of printing, was history. The greatest romance of the decade. The Great Rebel tamed by the shrinking gentle rose. The hell-raiser giving up his wild roistering ways to settle down in domestic bliss with his young Born-Again Christian wife. The classic case of the Bad Man tamed by the love and devotion of a Good Woman.

When they had been served with their drinks, Jeff asked tersely: 'What are we doing here?'

'We're doing as we've been told. We're being seen.' Freda's tone was as edgy as his. She had decided from their first introduction that she did not like him. 'Publicity. Ever heard of it?'

'Here?' His attitude was still disparaging.

'Here,' she answered flatly, sipping her Bacardi and Coke. 'This place has been going for eleven years and it's the most famous nightclub in London.'

Jeff raised his eyebrows. 'Doesn't seem much of a joint to me. Where are the topless waitresses? The Bunny Girls?'

Freda was about to snap a sarcastic answer, when she caught his eye and detected a glint of suppressed laughter.

'You're having me on!' she accused him angrily. 'I bet even in LA they've heard of Annabel's. All the most famous people come here.'

He smiled lazily at her. 'Yeah, sure. But it isn't quite as I imagined it would be. A bit slow. Terribly British.' He mimicked a passable English accent, and moved closer to her on the plush banquette. 'I damn near told my agent I didn't want to be in this film. I'm glad now that I didn't.'

'Why?' asked Freda, her hostility evaporating slightly.

'Why to what? Why didn't I want to be in the film? Or why am I glad now that I came?'

Freda shrugged. 'Both, I suppose,' she answered.

She had taken a lot of trouble tonight with her appearance. It was one of her idiosyncrasies that the more she disliked an escort, the more she dressed up for him. Her hair, nowadays lightened to a soft reddish blonde, was loose and curling, restrained only by a plaited Indian band, worn straight across her forehead and tied at the back of her head. Her frock was garnet-red lawn cotton, hand-embroidered with sprays and circles of white and green flowers. Rows of black silk braid circled the hem and the wide floating sleeves. The bodice was heavily smocked. Her face was carefully made up, the metallic blue eye-shadow complementing the blue of her eyes and making them look enormous against the sun-tanned skin. The lashes were thickly mascaraed.

'OK, then,' Jeff said. 'I didn't want to be in the film because I didn't particularly like the script, and I didn't want to spend the summer in Britain. I've heard about your summers. They're wet and they're cold and they're miserable. I could've been in LA. I've a beach-house on Malibu. So that's your first question answered.'

'And the second?' Freda spoke idly, making conversation while her eyes roamed the room, noting which members of Annabel's famous clientele were in tonight, and flicking every now and then towards the door to appraise the new arrivals.

'Be nice to Jeff,' the studio bosses had warned, apprised of a certain coolness in her manner towards her famous co-star. 'We're fortunate to get him.'

She knew that, of course, for herself. When she had been told who was playing the male lead opposite her, she could hardly believe her luck. Her agent had been over the moon.

'Freddie darling,' he had crooned ecstatically into the phone, 'this is it. The big one. Don't blow it, please, whatever you do.'

Maurice's voice had held a pleading note. She wasn't the easiest of his clients, and among theatre managements had a definite reputation for being difficult. However, her two West End successes had been so enormous, and had given her so much clout in the profession, that people were prepared to make allowances and handle her with kid gloves. But Maurice Benson knew that the film moguls would be less tolerant. Freda had yet to prove herself as a film actress, and until she did she would be expected to toe the line. Jeff Warwick was the star of the picture, and his comfort and peace of mind would take precedence over Freda's

'You've got to make him happy,' Maurice had begged her.

Jeff's importance on the lot of Pinewood had been apparent from the very first day, and although it was only what Freda had anticipated she had not expected to be so openly relegated to second place as she had been. She was annoyed and made the fact obvious. Jeff Warwick – she stubbornly insisted on pronouncing the name the English way, not War-wick in the American fashion – could not act his way out of a paper bag, she announced loudly, within his hearing.

There had been rumblings from his entourage, and word had got back to the American studio bosses in Los Angeles, who were putting up most of the money. Freda was given a broad hint that she was not indispensable, and that there were plenty of other, more established British actresses who could be used in her stead. The PR men suggested a night out together on the town, not just for publicity purposes, although they were important, but also in the hope that the two stars of the film *Watershed* might get to like one another a little better. So far as Freda was concerned, the experiment was not yet working.

She became conscious of Jeff's right hand pressed against her left thigh, and could feel its warmth through the thin material of her dress. She turned her head sharply and enquiringly in his direction. He had moved even nearer, and his face was now so close to hers that her nose accidentally brushed his cheek.

'The answer to the second question', he murmured dulcetly in her ear, 'is because I've met you. That's why I'm glad I didn't turn down the offer.'

24

MAURICE BENSON left his Austin Rover in the Pinewood Studios carpark and asked the way to Miss Marshall's dressing-room. He discovered Freda resting between takes and learning her lines for the following day's scenes. Her dresser, a large, comfortable, motherly woman called Enid Boyce, opened the door in answer to his knock.

'Mr Benson's here to see you, love.'

Freda sighed audibly and muttered something which Maurice preferred not to hear.

'Let him in, Enid,' she said. She got up from her armchair and came towards him, hands outstretched, stooping a little to kiss him on both cheeks. She was wearing a pink georgette twenties dress and matching felt cloche hat, which did not look really authentic on her curvaceous figure. 'Maurice darling, great to see you. It must be something important to bring you all the way out here. Another film offer? The lead in a Broadway show?'

Maurice smiled perfunctorily and patted her shoulder. Setting out from his office in Gracechurch Street that morning, he had decided that the time for the oblique approach was past. From now on, plain speaking, even at the risk of alienating his most important client, would have to be the order of the day.

'Freddie,' he said, sinking down into the chair she indicated and refusing her offer of a drink, 'I'm afraid I have to be blunt. Stop making a bloody cake of yourself with Jeff Warwick.' Maurice slapped his briefcase on to the low wooden table, undid it and produced a sheaf of that

231

morning's newspapers. He stabbed at them with a nicotine-stained forefinger. 'Headlines about you and Jeff in every one of them. All about how you're breaking up his marriage with Gabriella.'

'Oh, for goodness' sake!' Freda's tone was dismissive, but Maurice noticed that she avoided looking directly at him. 'What do you expect from those rags? You know perfectly well that if they can't uncover a story they'll invent one.'

The agent leaned back in his chair, his eyes searching her face. He knew from experience Freda's every expression, every nuance of her voice. And she was quite definitely on the defensive.

'What are you telling me?' he asked at last. 'That there's nothing between you and Jeff Warwick?'

She shrugged and sat down again, calling over her shoulder to her dresser. 'Bring me a drink, Enid, there's a dear. A Bacardi and not too much Coke. Are you sure you won't join me, Maurice?'

He shook his head. 'Too early in the day for me. But I'd be grateful if Mrs Boyce could find me some coffee.' A quick glance round the room from his bright shrewd eyes told him that, apart from the drinks-trolley, in one corner, there were only tea-making facilities, and recollected that Freda disliked coffee when she was working. His request meant that, in all probability, Enid Boyce would have to go to the canteen.

Freda hesitated, then laughed. 'All right. Fetch Mr Benson a cup of coffee, would you please, Enid?' And when the door had closed behind the dresser she said: 'So now you've got me on my own, Maurice, what is it that you've come to say?'

He leaned across to seize one of her hands, clasping and unclasping it in his agitation. The gold-and-agate signet ring, which he always wore on the little finger of his left hand, bit into her flesh.

'Freddie! If it were anyone else, I wouldn't say a word, I promise you. But Jeff Warwick! You'll be reviled and hated all over America. You'll be worse than a scarlet woman. *Watershed* will be a no-no at the box office before it even hits the screen. Remember how Liz Taylor was pilloried when she broke up the Fisher – Reynolds romance? She only survived because she was a great big enormous star. You're nobody, Freddie – at least, not in the States, and that's where it counts. You'll be blamed for the break-up of Jeff's marriage far more than he will. You know how anti-woman most women are, particularly when a handsome man's involved. And in this case the Morality Brigade will be backed up by the Sob Sisters. Jeff Warwick is their living embodiment of redemption from a misspent youth by the Christian faith. The whole Bible Belt of America will be up in arms.'

Freda sipped her Bacardi, regarding her agent over the rim of her glass.

'My, my! That was a long speech, Maurice dear,' she observed at last. 'You must have been rehearsing it all the way from town.' He flushed uncomfortably, and she laughed. 'Yes, I thought so. But you've had a wasted journey. Jeff asked me to marry him last night, and I said I'd think about it. He said it didn't matter what answer I gave him. He's sick of Gabriella. He's instructing his lawyers this morning to ask her for a divorce.'

Freda couldn't recall the exact turning-point in her relationship with Jeff Warwick. She rather fancied it had been that evening at Annabel's. It was not long after that, at any rate, that they had first made love.

Freda had given a party for the entire cast, director and producer at her flat in Charles Street. She had a suite of rooms on the first floor of one of the eighteenth-century houses which lined both sides of the road, sumptuously, if impersonally, furnished throughout in shades of olive, cream and a soft pale blue by her ex-flatmate Derek Conway.

Derek had found the cut and thrust of the theatrical world too harsh for his liking and had opted out soon after leaving RADA, where, in his last year, he had been specializing in décor and design. Renting a couple of shabby rooms in Beak Street, he had advertised himself as a design consultant, offering, for an extortionate fee, to advise people on what to buy and where to buy it, for which he also took commission from the shops. He had started in a modest way, but his natural flair in such matters soon earned him a reputation which ensured that business grew at an astonishing rate. By the time Freda had need of his services, his fame was equal to hers and Conway Interiors were a regular feature of all the glossy magazines. His presence at any party was a social cachet, and Freda had had no hesitation in asking him to hers. He was renowned for leaving such functions at a relatively early hour, and Freda was therefore secretly very flattered to find that, on this occasion, he was one of the last to go.

But not quite the last. When she finally closed her front door on what she assumed to be all of her guests, she returned to the living-room to discover Jeff Warwick lying full length on one of the three huge cream-upholstered sofas.

'Hi!' he said, waving his empty whisky-glass. 'I helped myself. Hope you don't mind. I've been waiting for them all to leave. I've been hiding in the bathroom.'

'I see.' She crossed to the drinks-cabinet, where she poured herself a Bacardi and Coke. 'Won't your henchmen be looking for you, wondering where you can be?'

'My what?' He laughed, only very slightly drunk, in spite of the double whiskies he had been putting away all evening.

'Those three gorillas who normally dog your every footstep, and keep the fans and other undesirables at bay.' Freda spun round and walked towards him, drink in hand.

She was wearing a long shimmering Zandra Rhodes dress in ice-blue chiffon, heavily encrusted with bugle beads sewn in a chevron pattern, over an under-dress of darker blue silk. The carefully tinted reddish-blonde hair floated in a cloud about her face. At twenty-eight years of

234

age, she was a very beautiful woman.

'Oh, them!' Jeff waved dismissively. 'I told them they could have the rest of the night off. I know where I can reach them, if it proves necessary.'

Freda moved his legs and curled up in the vacant corner of the sofa. The long glass table in front of them reflected the olive green of the carpet.

'To what do I owe this honour?' she asked, kicking off her silver shoes.

'Hey!' He turned his head lazily towards her. 'Say that again. It's so God-darned British.'

'I *am* British,' she reminded him sharply. 'What do you expect?'

Throughout this brief exchange, she had been aware of a mounting sexual excitement, which she had never experienced in any of their on-set clinches. It was a well-known fact that stage kisses were highly unromantic, but Freda had played opposite several leading men who, at times, had aroused her physically. Until now, Jeff Warwick had not been one of them. Her present feelings, her suddenly heightened awareness of his presence, took her by surprise, and she found it unsettling.

He said: 'I loved your Aunt Dora. A real gutsy lady. Who was the queer in the tight velvet suit?'

'Derek Conway', she answered coldly, 'is a friend of mine. He's an interior designer. He advised me on this flat.'

'Yeah. I can imagine. As a matter of fact, he told me so. Conceited little guy. Told me he won't move from his original offices in some place called Beak Street, because it's where Canaletto lived during a stay in London.' Jeff again exercised his talent for mimicry, imitating with unnerving accuracy Derek Conway's high light voice. ' "What was good enough for Canaletto is good enough for me, I always say." He's a junkie, too, did you know that? He insisted on taking off his coat and rolling up his sleeve, to show me the tattoo of a ship on his left wrist. I could see the needle marks higher up his arm. What's he on? Snow?'

'Yes,' Freda said shortly. She added: 'At least, it used to

be. I don't pry into my friends' affairs. What they choose to do with their lives is their business.'

'OK! OK! I wasn't implying any criticism.' Jeff sat up straight. 'In fact it's one hell of a relief not to be surrounded by sweetness and light. A guy can get pretty sick of all this Jesus-loves-you stuff and praying for sinners.'

Freda giggled, the Bacardi and Coke she was drinking adding its fumes to its forerunners' and making her feel light-headed. 'Why did you marry her?'

'Gabriella? Shit, *I* didn't marry her. It was a shotgun wedding, with the media and the studios and my agent all holding the rifle. It was one helluva story. Gabby weeping all over the Hollywood gossip-writers and telling them what a really sweet guy I was underneath, and how Jesus had chosen her, singled her out, as the means of my redemption. They couldn't possibly risk losing a story like that. Everyone nagged and nagged at me until I proposed. As far as I was concerned, the wedding was just a publicity stunt. Unfortunately, for everyone else it was fairy-tale time. And-so-they-lived-happily-ever-after time. And did they? Fuck!'

He got up, putting down his glass and stretching until his bones cracked. He had discarded his jacket in the heat of the room, and the white silk of his evening shirt clung, here and there, to his body. As he lifted his arms above his head, it moulded itself to the shape of his ribs and the hard flat pectoral muscles. He watched the tell-tale expression on Freda's face through half-closed eyes, then sat down again, close to her, on the sofa. She was still curled up in her corner, nursing her three-quarters-finished drink. He removed the glass from her unresisting hand and placed it on the table before moving even closer and kissing her.

Freda raised a hand and passed it over the shining cap of blue-black hair. With one finger, she lightly traced the line of his high oriental cheekbones. Then she was in his arms, her lips on his, while he fumbled with the zip down the back of her dress. She had less difficulty with the one on his flies. They rolled off the sofa on to the olive-green carpet, the long tufted pile tickling Freda's bare back . . .

When it was over, and she was sitting, propped against the base of the sofa, wearing nothing but her stockings and a narrow gold bracelet, she asked: 'So? Where do we go from here?' She knew instinctively that what had happened between them wasn't just a one-night stand or the beginning of a casual duration-of-shooting affair.

Jeff went over to the drinks-cabinet and poured himself a stiff whisky and soda, the light from the wall-lamps bleaching his sun-tanned skin. He downed the alcohol in one gulp.

'I want you, Freda,' he answered unsteadily, without turning his head. 'I want you more than any other woman I've ever met. And I hope to God you feel the same way about me.'

The flat in Clifton Wood smelt musty and damp, as though it had been shut up for far longer than the ten days she had been away. There was a box of groceries, together with a note from Jean, on the kitchen table. Joanna put down her case and picked up the half-sheet of pale blue notepaper, bearing yesterday's date.

'Dear Jo, Hope you had a good holiday – again! You and Davey seem to be getting very pally all at once. Two visits in as many months! Came over to water plants as requested, so brought a few things with me. Guessed you'd be home late. All well in Nightingale Close. Love, Mum.'

Joanna smiled to herself, crumpled the note and threw it in the kitchen waste-bin, pocketed the spare key, which her mother had left beside the food, and carried her case into the bedroom.

This was pleasant, light and airy, as were most of the first-floor rooms of Victorian and Edwardian houses. It could, Joanna acknowledged, have been pleasanter still, as could the rest of the flat, if either she or Lawrence had had the slightest interest in interior decoration. But although she liked things neat and tidy – ship-shape, she supposed, and Bristol fashion – Joanna had no flair for

237

making a house a showplace. Everywhere was furnished in an agreeable but fairly characterless style. In that respect, she was more like their mother than either of her sisters. She thought Davina's flat quite beautiful, knowing that in a year or two, when tastes and fashion changed yet again, its décor would all be altered. Davina, surprisingly, considering Anthea's influence, liked to be 'with it' – a phrase which most certainly would not appeal to their aunt. As for Freda, she could now afford to pay someone else to plan her furnishings for her. Joanna had been in the Charles Street flat only once, and had come away with mixed feelings. She could not help but be impressed, yet it had seemed so alien and impersonal. Nothing about it had reminded her of her younger sister.

Joanna humped her case on to the big double bed she shared with Lawrence, when he was at home, unlocked it and threw back the lid. But she made no immediate attempt to unpack, instead wandering over to the window and looking out into the street. There was a Cupressus tree in the front garden and, beneath it, a delicate blue-and-white carpet of wood-anemones, past their best now but still pretty enough to catch the eye. They had seeded themselves from their wild habitat, somewhere on the Downs, and none of the tenants had had the heart to uproot them. A low-clipped yew hedge was contained by an even lower boundary wall, crumbling now along the edges, where weeds were beginning to triumph, pushing their way through the cracking mortar. Joanna sighed and turned back into the room.

She had wanted to leave Exeter this time even less than the time before, because at long last she and Alex had become lovers. Even now, she couldn't quite believe it; wasn't at all sure exactly how it had happened. They had driven out across the eastern flank of Dartmoor one afternoon, towards Castle Drogo, the mock-medieval castle designed by Lutyens for Julius Drew, founder of the Home & Colonial stores. They had parked within sight of the house, its crenellated 'battlements' visible through the pale green tracery of trees.

By mutual consent, they left the car and strolled towards the lip of the ridge, peering down into the Teign gorge below them. It had been very quiet and quite breathtakingly beautiful, with not another soul anywhere around. A whinchat, from its perch on a neighbouring gorse bush, felt safe enough to ignore them, ruffling its feathers and making its odd distinctive call like the tapping together of stones. Alex had brought a rug from the car and spread it on grass still damp from yesterday's rain.

For a few minutes, they sat side by side, not speaking, but both as suddenly and self-consciously aware of their physical proximity as if they were on a first date.

It won't happen, Joanna had thought, holding her breath. It hasn't before, so why should it now?

But it had. Alex had reached for her, forcing her down until she was lying full length on the rug, his hands fumbling with her clothes. Then he was astride and she felt him thrusting inside her . . .

Abruptly, it was all over and they were separate entities again; a strange and unrewarding experience, almost brutal. Alex was lying on his back, an arm thrown across his face as though shielding it from her gaze. Joanna had the momentary, and surely ridiculous, impression that he was crying, but a second later he sat up, turning to her with his customary grin.

'Well, now you know,' he had said. 'I'm not the world's greatest lover.'

She swallowed her own sense of bitter disappointment and answered gently: 'It'll be better next time.'

She could not suppress the thought, however, that he must have made love to other women. Olwen. Freda. What had it been like for them? Was there something about her that made him feel uneasy? Did she lack some response which he found necessary to arouse him? By the time they had returned to the car, she had been ready and willing to shoulder all the blame. Years of abstinence, followed by marriage to a man with whom, however hard she had tried, she was not in love, must have left their mark; must have inhibited her in some way which Alex sensed and found distressing.

But things would change. Now that they had once made love, there were, as she had said, bound to be other times and she would get to know what it was he needed. And in every other way they were so happy together. She could willingly have stayed with her sister another week, but Davina had been displaying signs of restlessness, of wanting the flat to herself. This second visit had been at Joanna's suggestion, not hers, and had not been so convenient for her. She needed peace and quiet in her spare time, to get on with her book.

Joanna walked through the flat's empty rooms, feeling cold and lonely. The silence was deafening, and she wished that Lawrence would ring, but it was unlikely. His time nowadays was completely swallowed up by parliamentary business. There was the threat of another general election in the offing. Joanna suddenly felt that she could not face it.

Before she and Alex had parted, they had promised each other to keep in touch. Joanna had decided to move back to London. That way, whenever Alex was in town, they could meet. They would have to be very careful, that went without saying. She was not prepared to hurt Lawrence or to jeopardize his career. She was too fond of him, but with the protective love a mother feels towards her child.

She went into the kitchen to make herself a much needed cup of tea. As she did so, the telephone in the entrance-hall of the flat began to ring.

25

IT WAS Lawrence.

'Jo! I was hoping you'd be home.' She could tell by his voice that he was excited, but he remembered, punctilious as always, to ask if she had enjoyed her holiday.

'Yes, but never mind that. Why are you ringing?'

'Does the name Bill Skinner mean anything to you?'

Joanna thought hard. 'The MP for North Wallingford,' she said slowly. 'One of the PM's blue-eyed boys . . . Oh, I know. He was appointed Secretary of State for Industrial Reorganization, one of those new posts that Harold created. Shirley Williams got the other one. Secretary of State for Prices and Consumer Protection. Am I right?'

'Yes.' Lawrence sounded almost breathless now. 'Jo, Skinner's asked me to be his PPS.'

Her brain wasn't functioning properly tonight; it took her all of fifteen seconds to recollect that PPS stood for Parliamentary Private Secretary.

'Larry,' she murmured, 'that's wonderful. Congratulations.'

She knew what the appointment must mean to her husband: that those four years out of Parliament had not counted against him; a tacit acknowledgement that Lawrence had been badly used by his former constituents; that the vote of 'no confidence' which had led to his being dropped had been the result of some kind of behind-the-scenes wheeling and dealing. Joanna's thoughts flicked to Tom Birkenshaw, and she wondered how he would view the appointment.

241

Lawrence was speaking again. 'Skinner was kind enough to mention the book. Said he'd found it excellent reading. I expect he was only being polite, but it may have been a contributory factor to my being asked.'

'I'm sure it was.' Joanna hesitated. 'Listen, Larry. I've been thinking that I really ought to come back to London to live. It's silly me being down here and you being there. We hardly see anything of one another. I know it'll be expensive, but no more than it is at present. And we needn't rent a place in Avonvale. David Nugent has said we can always stay there. He and Eileen and the children are always delighted to see us.'

'But you said, with another election this year a racing certainty . . .'

'I know what I said, but this appointment changes things.' She didn't stop to specify how, but hurried on: 'Why don't I come up tomorrow and have a look around? Do a tour of the estate agents and see what we can afford.'

He caught something of her enthusiasm. 'That'll be splendid. I'll be at the House all day, but I'll leave the key to this flat in the usual place, and if you want to have lunch here there's food in the fridge. I restocked it yesterday. If we don't have time to meet, give me a ring after you get back to Bristol in the evening. You'd better write to the landlord as soon as you can and give the statutory one month's notice. I must go now, love. Tomorrow's going to be a busy day.'

'All right. And Lawrence – congratulations!'

'Thanks.' He hung up, and she was left staring at the silent receiver.

She telephoned Bath to give her parents the news. Bernard was delighted, as was her mother, although Jean's pleasure was tempered by Joanna's decision to give up the Clifton Wood flat and return to London.

'You know it doesn't agree with you. Besides,' her mother added plaintively, 'I shall miss you.'

'You'll probably see me just as often,' Joanna consoled her. 'I'll be down on constituency business pretty frequently.

242

I'll have to take the strain off Larry's shoulders.'

'Avonvale's not as near as Bristol,' Jean objected. 'And you haven't a house there. Where will you stay?'

Joanna patiently told her of the Nugents' offer, and eventually even her mother had to concede that the good news outweighed the bad. When she finally cleared the line, Joanna rang Davina to say she had reached home safely and to tell her about Lawrence.

'Splendid,' her sister said, with more warmth than Joanna had expected. 'He'll make Prime Minister yet. What a famous family we're becoming. Freda, Larry . . .' Modesty forbade her going on.

'You,' Joanna supplied with a little edge to her voice. 'I know. I'm the only one who seems to have achieved absolutely nothing. I can't even manage to have a baby!'

There was a brief silence before her sister replied with a brittle laugh: 'Motherhood isn't all it's cracked up to be. There are plenty of other worthwhile things you can be doing.'

She hung up, and Joanna could picture her going back to her desk by the window, overlooking Cathedral Close, momentarily upset by Joanna's unthinking remark, but soon losing herself in the manuscript of her new book. The Black Death would provide a sufficient antidote to unwelcome thoughts.

Joanna returned to the kitchen and her abandoned efforts at making tea. She reheated the kettle and, realizing that she was hungry, rummaged in the pantry for something to eat. Her mother had provided bread, butter and half a pound of ham among the groceries she had left, so Joanna made herself a sandwich and carried it into the living-room, where she switched on the electric fire. The late-May evening had turned cold, with a mist rolling in from the Bristol Channel, and she was glad of the warmth. She thought again of Alex, and the desire to telephone him at King's Acre Court was overwhelming, but she knew it would be foolish. His mother might answer. Or Olwen. She would have to be patient and contact him only in the way they had arranged: telephone calls to his Exeter office. His secretary, he had assured her, was the soul of discretion. But she must tell him as soon as possible about her change of plans.

Joanna recognized that she was playing with fire, but had sufficient faith in her own common sense and good judgement to imagine that she could get away with an illicit affair without doing any harm to Lawrence. It did not occur to her at the time how arrogant she was being. All she knew was that her affection for Alex, suppressed for so long, had been reawakened and was even stronger than before. She felt certain that he needed her just as much as she needed him. It did not cross her mind that this might be another rash assumption.

She picked up that morning's *Guardian*, which she had bought at St David's Station and then not bothered to read. Northern Ireland and the activities of the IRA continued to occupy most of the headlines. Joanna turned the pages apathetically until she was suddenly arrested by a photograph of Freda, clutching Jeff Warwick's arm. The caption underneath read: 'The actress Freda Marshall and Jeff Warwick, her co-star in the film *Watershed*, seen leaving Annabel's nightclub in Berkeley Square. There are rumours of a rift in Warwick's three-year-old "dream" marriage to Gabriella, and Miss Marshall is thought to be the cause. She recently refused to confirm or deny the reports, saying "Wait and see".'

Joanna shrugged the gossip aside, regarding it as no more than the customary tittle-tattle which had surrounded her younger sister ever since Freda had achieved star status. But the picture did serve to remind her that she had informed everyone except Freda of Lawrence's news, and they had always been fond of one another. Without much expectation of finding her sister at home that time of the evening, Joanna went to the phone and dialled Freda's number. There was a long pause during which the bell continued to shrill, unanswered, at the other end of the line. Joanna was about to replace the receiver, when the noise ceased abruptly. A man's voice sounded in her ear.

'Hello. This is Freda Marshall's apartment. This is Jeff Warwick speaking.'

Within three weeks, it was almost impossible to pick up a newspaper, however staid and respectable, without finding at least one reference to Freda and Jeff Warwick and their now notorious affair. Even the death of the Queen's uncle, the Duke of Gloucester, on 10 June, and the IRA bomb which exploded alongside Westminster Hall seven days later, injuring eleven people, were only momentary distractions, and barely succeeded in driving the story off the front pages. Screaming headlines pilloried Freda as 'the Woman Who Destroyed a Dream' and Jeff as the deserter of wife and child. There were pictures from Hollywood of a distraught Gabriella, surrounded by a cohort of gimlet-eyed lawyers, nostrils flaring at the prospect of a 'kill'; Gabriella in tears – 'My life is wrecked'; Gabriella clutching her year-old son by the hand – 'I must rebuild my life for Jeff junior's sake'; Gabriella peering soulfully at a photograph of Jeff – 'I still love him. I always shall.'

Affection, however, did not deter the singing star from demanding a million dollars alimony – 'I have to think of my son's future' – along with her petition for divorce. Jeff, between frantic phone calls to his own lawyer in Los Angeles, informed Freda gloomily that he saw little hope of contesting the claim.

'Every judge in the States will be firmly on that vulture's side.'

The film was nearing completion. Only one or two scenes remained to be shot and put in the can. Whether *Watershed*, in view of its attendant publicity, would prove to be a smash box-office hit or a total failure was in the lap of the gods. Meantime, Jeff was faced with the looming possibility of near-bankruptcy.

On the day after the film was finished, he put his arms around Freda and have her a long open-mouthed kiss.

'It'll be worth it, though, honey, just to be free of that

bitch and to be with you. We'll be married in LA as soon as the final decree comes through.'

Freda slid gracefully out of his arms and smoothed her hair into place, where he had ruffled it. She was wearing a pale-grey linen dress, in sharp contrast to the shocking-pink accessories she had chosen to go with it. She presented a confusing image of demureness and brash vulgarity which was not entirely unintentional. She was not sure, herself, at the moment who she really was. She constantly failed to recognize the pen-portraits of her painted by the tabloid press.

'We'll discuss it when I come home,' she said, picking up her pink gloves and handbag. Jeff had been living permanently in her flat for the past month.

'You going out?' His tone was sulky. 'You might've told me. Am I invited?'

'I did tell you. I'm having lunch with my sister Jo. Family gossip. You wouldn't be interested.'

She met Joanna at Chez Solange, in Cranbourne Street, not far from Leicester Square and Shaftesbury Avenue, the heart of London's theatreland. It was an unpretentious but elegantly furnished restaurant, the cooking authentically French.

'I feel safe here,' Freda murmured, drawing off her gloves. 'René Rochon and his wife are old friends, and make sure, in that courteous Gallic way of theirs, that their customers aren't harassed by the press. Thank God eating is a sacred business to the French.'

Joanna laughed. 'I'd be careful they don't throw you out, then. I should think that hat of yours, not to mention the shoes, handbag and gloves, might be considered a hazard to your fellow-diners' digestion.'

Freda grimaced ruefully in reply. 'They *are* pretty ghastly, aren't they? I just felt like wearing them.' She shoved the offending handbag and gloves down by her feet and removed her hat. 'There! Is that better? Oh, Jo! It is good to see you. How's everyone at home? What are they all saying about me?'

'We-ell ...' Joanna shrugged expressively. 'I haven't really been in touch with Nightingale Close that much, since coming to London. I've been too busy flat-hunting. Those rooms that Larry has in Morpeth Terrace are far too tiny. I think we're finally settled on a flat across the river in Lambeth. Crozier Street, not far from St Thomas's Hospital.'

Freda looked down her nose at the address, but said gallantly: 'You must ask me round to see it before I go to LA.'

Joanna raised her eyebrows. 'You really are going, then? To America?'

'I haven't much choice, have I?' A waiter approached to take their order, and it was not until he had gone that Freda was able to enlarge on her theme and satisfy her sister's curiosity. 'Well, I mean! What the hell can I do, Jo? The publicity's been horrendous. If I backed out of marrying Jeff now, I'd make him look the most God Almighty fool in creation. And he doesn't deserve that of me. The affair is as much my fault as his, and it's no good me trying to kid myself otherwise.'

'You mean you don't love him any more?' Joanna broke open a hot bread roll and spread it lavishly with butter.

'No.' Freda broke open her own roll but avoided the butter. She had her figure to think of. 'To begin with, I didn't even like him. Then I found he could be funny, quite amusing really when he wanted to be, and that the publicity image of arrogant superiority wasn't truly him. We became friends and then lovers. Well, you must admit that physically he's bloody attractive. And when I discovered that he'd got himself pushed into this marriage with Gabriella, that it had all been arranged by the PR boys and taken up by the media, I was sorry for him. Pity's a dangerous emotion, Jo. It can so easily be mistaken for something that it isn't.'

'I know,' Joanna agreed quietly, thinking of Lawrence. She drank a spoonful of vichyssoise, wondering if she should say anything. But Freda was not interested in anyone's problems but her own just at present.

'So here I am, with all this hoo-ha going on, both sides of the Atlantic, and particularly in the States, trapped into marrying Jeff in the same way he was trapped into marrying Gabriella. Ironic, isn't it? Serve me right, I guess Mother would say, for fooling around with a married man.'

'How does Jeff feel about you?' Joana sipped her soup again, letting it trickle, cold and smooth, over her throat.

Freda sighed. 'That's just it. He's crazy about me. And I can't deny that the prospect of arriving in the States already known – however dubious the reason – with immediate entrée into the main Hollywood scene, is pretty alluring. I mean, I'd be a fool to pass it up.'

'Even if it entails marrying someone you don't really fancy?'

Freda's eyes were suddenly shrewd as she glanced at her sister across the table.

'You should know all about that, Jo. Don't try to pretend that you ever really fancied Lawrence Walden.'

'We've had our moments,' Joanna answered defensively.

'That's not an answer, and you know it. Never mind, I won't press you. After all, I invited you out today to talk about me.'

'Thanks,' Joanna murmured and made a moue of resignation.

'Sorry.' Freda was at once contrite. 'I honestly didn't mean it to sound quite like that. Of course I want to hear all about you and Larry. It's just that . . . well, I wanted you to know how matters really stand between me and Jeff. There's no one else I can talk to, apart from Aunt Do, and she's on tour at the moment. Mrs Malaprop in *The Rivals*.'

'She keeps working pretty steadily, doesn't she? Gramps said in his last letter that the production's going to Bath. He and Mum and Dad have booked to see it.'

Freda's wave of the hand dismissed this information along with her empty soup-plate, as the waiter deftly removed the latter. Deep-sea bass in a fennel sauce replaced it.

'Jo,' she said earnestly, 'whatever happens in the future, whatever you read about me in the papers, you must believe that I really am going to try to make this marriage work. If it fails, it won't be because I haven't made an effort. And now for goodness' sake shut me up before I become one of those bores who talk about nothing but themselves. Tell me your news. Spill the beans.'

But when they at last emerged from the restaurant into the hazy sunshine of a June afternoon, and began strolling in the direction of Charing Cross Road, Joanna realized that she had talked to her sister about Davina and the new book, about their grandfather's worsening arthritis, about Lawrence's appointment as PPS, about her own role as a political wife, but nothing at all, not a word, about Alex Ferrer.

26

JOANNA ASKED anxiously: 'Are you feeling all right? You look extremely pale.'

The kitchen of the flat in Crozier Street was flooded with sunlight. She and Lawrence sat at the breakfast-bar, drinking coffee. The air which stole throught the open window, ruffling the Liberty print curtains, was sharp and full of the scents and sounds of the early-morning city.

'Yes, of course I'm all right.' Lawrence replaced his yellow-banded cup in its plain white saucer, sounding tetchy. 'I've a lot on my plate at present. Tom Birkenshaw's been on the warpath lately, with some damned awkward questions about the Industrial Reorganization programme. Bill Skinner, understandably, gets a bit uptight about it and wants all the information at his fingertips. The PM, however vigorously he denies it, tends to lend an ear to fellow-Yorkshiremen, and of course the Opposition love to hear our own back benches having a go at us, especially with another election in the offing.'

'I wish I knew what Tom Birkenshaw has against you,' Joanna said musingly. 'I suppose he's never dropped you a hint?'

'Not a word. To give him his due, he's a good debater and, one way or another, is making quite an impression.'

Joanna selected a piece of toast, spreading it thickly with butter.

'I suppose it's certain there will be another election this year? Ted Heath and the Liberals don't seem to be pressing.'

Lawrence laughed shortly. 'Heath's afraid of what will happen if he loses for the second time in twelve months. There are plenty of other members of the Tory Party eager and willing to step into his shoes.'

He put up a hand to his thinning hair, pushing it back from his prominent forehead. At forty-four, a few curling tendrils remained on the top of Lawrence's head, but it would not be long, Joana reflected, before his crown was completely bald. His brown eyes, those dark liquid eyes which were his most outstanding feature, looked enormous in his small-boned face, and there were bruised circles underneath them. His skin had never had much colour, but in recent weeks it had begun to look almost waxen. She had tried to persuade him to see a doctor, but he had angrily refused. If he was right, and another election was imminent, he had to prove his stamina and his ability, not only to the Government, but also to his constituents. A fear that literally haunted his dreams, giving him restless nights and causing him to talk in his sleep, was of finding himself once more without a parliamentary seat after a tenure of only a few months. Bill Skinner had demonstrated his confidence by offering him the post of his Parliamentary Private Secretary, after his four-year absence from the House, and now Lawrence had to maintain and justify that confidence, which Tom Birkenshaw and others sought to undermine.

The trouble was, they were being handed plenty of ammunition. The daily papers were still full of Freda's affair with Jeff Warwick, and although Lawrence could hardly be held accountable for his sister-in-law's love life it did nothing, either, to redound to his credit. There had already been one or two oblique references to the story by Tom Birkenshaw, which had set the Chamber laughing slyly at Lawrence's expense; and that sort of remark, however humorously received, in the long run left a bad impression. No one wanted an MP who was the butt of crude jokes behind his back, even if they were about his wife's sister. For Lawrence's sake, Joanna wished Freda would hurry up and go to America; but there were, it appeared, some scenes of *Watershed* to be reshot which could not be done with stand-ins, so Jeff Warwick was still in England, still living in Freda's flat, and the story rumbled on, spinning out yet more mileage.

Lawrence himself said very little about the newspaper articles, but Joanna knew he read them. She had seen the angry way he tossed them aside when there had been a resurgence of interest in the affair. But he was fond of Freda. He always had been. Davina was the sister-in-law he did not care for.

Joanna glanced at the kitchen clock. 'You'd better get dressed. It's nearly eight-fifteen.' She wanted to beg him to take life more easily, but she knew it was an impossible request. She was seeing the pressures of political life at first hand these past few months, and realizing what it took to survive them.

Lawrence got up from the table, swallowing the dregs of his coffee. 'What are you doing today?' he asked her.

'Oh, this and that. Nothing much.' To herself, Joanna sounded deliberately evasive, but Lawrence was too pre-occupied to notice. He was already halfway to the kitchen door; heading for the bedroom.

Half an hour later, he was gone. Left alone in the flat, Joanna poured herself more coffee, sitting at the breakfast-bar to drink it, and contemplating the hours ahead of her.

Alex was in town for the day. In all probability he had already arrived, travelling up on the early-morning train from Devon. She found it irritating, and had said so, that neither he nor his father had ever bought a house or a flat in London, preferring to stay at a hotel when necessary.

'Why should we?' Alex had asked, when she put the question to him. 'Most of our business is conducted from Exeter. The offices in Mincing Lane are really for show. To inspire confidence in foreigners who equate England with London.'

Today, he had promised to be through with business by one o'clock at the latest.

'We'll meet for lunch,' he had said three days earlier, when she had telephoned him. 'How about the Tate Gallery? I hear the food there is very good, and we could look at the pictures afterwards.'

She had demurred. Millbank was too close to the Houses of Parliament for comfort, but Alex had gently pooh-poohed her objection.

'Our revered MPs don't go swanning down to the Tate, love. Half of them probably don't know what the place looks like. Your half especially. White City Stadium is more their line of entertainment.'

She had let the jibe pass and felt a traitor for doing so, but all she wanted was to be with Alex. She was more in love with him than ever, she told herself, yet she still had not managed to seduce him a second time. They had made a disastrous attempt one afternoon in a hotel bedroom, but the seediness of their surroundings had defeated Joanna. Alex had seemed less affected but, remembering the conditions of Freda's flat, she felt that this should not have surprised her. Once again, she had felt miserably to blame, but Alex had merely smiled his winning, crooked, sidelong smile and said: 'All in good time, love. All in good time.'

The fact that they were scarcely having an affair in the usual sense of the word in no way made Joanna feel less guilty. And the intent was there, at least on her part. She could not answer for Alex. She continually worried that someone she knew, somewhere, someday, would see them together and was ready with half a dozen plausible explanations. She very occasionally wondered if it was all worth it but, apart from being in love, she felt she owed Alex something. She had broken off their engagement because of her unreasoning hatred of Anthony Douglas, which had been founded on a lie; and, although Alex said very little on the subject, it was obvious that his marriage to Olwen was unhappy. They led totally separate lives and slept in separate bedrooms at King's Acre. That much, at least, Joanna had been able to discover. And it was all her fault. If she had not been so blindly prejudiced, if she hadn't blundered into marriage with Lawrence, she could have married Alex and made him happy. She pushed to the back of her mind all the other reasons she had had for ending their association. She could only see that, thanks to her foolish actions, he had been forced to turn first to Freda and then to Olwen Bruce. There were times when she felt burdened down by guilt; guilt for deceiving Lawrence, guilt for deserting Alex.

But today, she decided, glancing out of the window at the buildings opposite, benign beneath a bright blue sky, she was going to forget all her worries and just enjoy herself. She was going to meet Alex. That was all that mattered.

'I'm told the food is based on traditional English dishes,' Alex said, leaning back in his chair and studying the menu. 'Some of the recipes are those of Elizabeth Cromwell. Oliver's wife.'

'Yes, I do know who Elizabeth Cromwell is,' Joanna snapped.

For some reason, she had felt uneasy ever since they had walked into the Tate Gallery restaurant. She found her eyes continually searching the room. Perhaps it was the consciousness of the proximity of Westminster, and so many people who knew her as Lawrence's wife. Caesar's wife, who had to be above suspicion. She had arrived outside the Tate far too early and, to kill time, had walked along Millbank as far as Victoria Tower Gardens and looked once more at the copy of Rodin's 'Burghers of Calais'. She should not have done it. It had been too sharp a reminder of that meeting with Lawrence, eight years ago.

'What's the matter?' Alex asked quietly. 'You seem on edge. It's not like you.'

'Isn't it? That's all you know. I'm always nervous during our meetings.' She went on: 'I must be mad to put myself through all this. It's a form of masochism. I couldn't bear to hurt Larry. I'm too fond of him, and any scandal so close to home could damage his career. It's been bad enough for him with Freda making the headlines every morning.' She paused. She had not meant to mention her sister's name. It was a subject she tried to avoid when with Alex. But he exhibited such a total lack of embarrassment that it annoyed Joanna. 'So why, I ask myself, am I doing it?' she added angrily.

Alex answered in that evasive camp way of his: 'May I suggest, dear heart, because you cannot resist *mes beaux yeux*?'

A waitress arrived to take their orders, and Joanna used the pause to summon up her courage. When the girl had departed, she leaned across the table and said in a low voice: 'Alex, I want to go to bed with you. I realize the past two failures were my fault, but please let us try again. I love you. We won't go to a hotel next time. You must get a flat in town. Surely your father can't object when you're here so often.'

He looked amused, tilting his head to one side and grinning at her.

'Darling, please! This is neither the time nor the place. You do choose your moments.'

'You're prevaricating, Alex!' Joanna suddenly felt sufficiently angry to say a number of things which she had kept bottled up over the years. 'Why was it so much easier for you to sleep with Freda? Don't bother to deny it. You forget I know you had a key to her flat. I was there once when you let yourself in, and you surely don't think I'm stupid enough to have swallowed Freddie's explanation! Men don't have keys to girls' flats in order to make themselves cups of cocoa.'

'Did Freddie really say that?' Alex picked up one of his forks and began to trace patterns with it on the tablecloth. 'It does sound a bit far-fetched. I mean, I simply loathe cocoa.'

Joanna's fingers tightened over the clasp of her handbag, which she was holding in her lap. 'Alex!'

She got no further. A man, on his way out, had paused by her table, and a familiar Yorkshire voice said: 'Eh! If it isn't Mrs Walden! Hello, Jo lass.'

It was Tom Birkenshaw, in company with another man whom Joanna recognized as a fellow Labour MP.

The day was ruined for her. But, as Alex pointed out later, there was no reason why it should have been.

'You're a fool, love,' he said exasperatedly, as they stood in front of John Bettes's portrait of 'A Man in a Black Cap'. 'As far as that man Birkenshaw knew, I was just an old friend you'd bumped into, who'd invited you out to lunch. All you had to do was to introduce me and play it cool, and he wouldn't have thought another thing about it. Instead, you behaved like a schoolgirl caught at the back of the games pavilion, snogging with the under-gardener. Of course the blasted man was suspicious. I should have been, in his shoes.'

'Do you really think he was?' Joanna enquired anxiously. 'Suspicious, I mean. Do you really think he thought there was something between us?'

Alex sighed as he linked an arm through one of hers and urged her on towards the Van Dycks, the Lelys and the Knellers. 'Jo love, I've told you. The way you reacted was enough to raise doubts in the most unsullied of minds, and I doubt very much if your Mr Birkenshaw has one of those. Fancies himself as a man who knows what's what, does our Honourable Friend, or I'm no judge of face and character.'

'Do you think he'll say anything to Larry?'

'God, Jo, what does it matter? Just get your act together. Get in first. Tell Lawrence tonight that we bumped into one another and I took you to lunch for auld lang syne. It's all so simple.'

'I don't like deceiving Larry, and I don't relish telling him lies.'

'But you're deceiving him all the time. Dear God in heaven! I'll never understand how women's minds work.'

She stared up at William Dobson's painting of Endymion Porter, without registering a single detail. Then, slowly, she turned and faced him.

'What are you doing it for, Alex? Why do you want to

keep meeting me like this? I find our relationship incomprehensible. I always have. Do you think you could explain it to me, after all these years?'

He bent forward and kissed her lightly between the eyes.

'Don't start making demands, Jo. That's one of the things I've always loved about you. You never harass me, or badger me, or try to use emotional blackmail. You're the most restful person I've ever known. Don't change now. Just take life as it comes. You're my best friend. Don't try to alter me.'

It wasn't an answer to her question, but it was sufficient to silence her. If she persisted in trying to make sense of their relationship, she would only disappoint him, and that, as he had probably gambled on, she could not bear. So they resumed their inspection of the Tate Gallery's British Collection, and Joanna listened with half an ear while Alex enthused over Hogarth and Turner and Constable and sniped at the romantic portraits of Zoffany and Romney and Raeburn.

Later, back at the empty flat in Crozier Street, she was free to wonder, as always, what the day had been about, and to indulge her misgivings over the meeting with Tom Birkenshaw and his friend. She didn't trust Tom and wished, for the millionth time, that she had the glimmering of an idea what it was he had against herself and Lawrence. She didn't suppose it took very much to turn a man like him into an enemy. Alex was right: Tom Birkenshaw had always had a high opinion of himself. Either she or Larry had unwittingly slighted him at some time; not shown him the deference he considered to be his due.

The telephone rang. It wouldn't be Lawrence. He was speaking in a debate that evening and would be at the Commons until late. And it wouldn't be Alex. He never contacted her at home and, in any case, he would by now be on his way to Paddington. Her encounter with Tom Birkenshaw had unnerved her, and it was with a sense of trepidation that she lifted the receiver.

But it was only Freda, inviting her to a party.

'It's a farewell do, I'm afraid. Everything's finally settled and I'm off to the States with Jeff in a couple of days' time. There's so much to do, and it seems the best way to say goodbye to all my friends. I'd ask Lawrence, but it won't be his sort of thing.' Freda broke into a giggle, and for a moment Joanna was reminded of the impish schoolgirl, the perpetual thorn in the flesh of Theresa and herself; always borrowing their clothes without permission, declaiming lines at the top of her voice when they were trying to get to sleep. 'Not your scene, either, Joey, if it comes to that, but I'd love it if you could drop in for a while. Tomorrow, around nine o'clock. Come early, then you can leave before the party really gets going.' She added pleadingly: 'Do say you'll come.'

'Yes, all right,' Joanna agreed, laughing. In the relief at hearing her sister's voice – although what she had been expecting, she hardly dared guess at – she would have promised anything. 'You're really going, then? With Jeff.'

'Yes.' The voice at the other end of the line was suddenly studiedly neutral. 'We'll be married over there, as soon as his divorce comes through.'

27

As SOON AS JOANNA got out of the lift, she could hear the noise of the party from further along the door-lined corridor. 'She', sung by Charles Aznavour, was just coming to an end, to be succeeded by Gary Glitter and 'Always Yours'. She reflected that it was just as well that Freda's flat occupied the whole of the first-floor level.

Joanna was later than she had meant to be. A glance at her wrist-watch showed that it was nearly eleven. Her original intention had been to call in early and to leave before most of the guests arrived and the party really got under way. But Lawrence had been so unwell since arriving home at six o'clock, after a gruelling three-hour committee meeting, that only his insistence and her promise to Freda had at last persuaded her to go.

'I shan't stay long,' she had told him, emerging from the bedroom in the new pale-green chiffon dress she had purchased at Harvey Nichols that morning. 'I shall just look in and say my goodbyes to Freddie, then come straight home again. For goodness' sake, go to bed, Larry, please. You look dreadful and you're short of breath.' She stood irresolute in the middle of the living-room. 'I really ought not to leave you. Tomorrow, you must see the doctor.'

'I am perfectly all right,' Lawrence said through bloodless lips. 'Just tired, that's all. All I need is a good night's rest, and I promise I'll go to bed as soon as you've gone. I'm paired for tonight's ten o'clock vote, so I shan't have to return to the House. By the way, I have to go down to the constituency again this weekend. Will you come with me?'

'Yes, of course. Apart from anything else, you need me to see that you don't overdo things. I take it the Nugents know we're coming?' Lawrence nodded, and she went on: 'I've left hot milk and brandy in a Thermos in the kitchen. Mind you drink it before you turn in.'

'Stop fussing, Jo!' he exclaimed irritably. 'Stop treating me as though I were your father.'

She knew how sensitive he was about the fourteen-year gap in their ages, so she let the subject drop. The buzz of their doorbell told her that the taxi had arrived. She stooped and kissed him.

'Take care of yourself,' she urged gently. 'You don't want poor health ruining your career chances.'

He smiled up at her. 'I'll be careful, I promise.' But it was an empty promise, and both of them knew it. Ambitious politicians could not afford to take things easily or to complain too much of illness.

Twenty minutes later, the taxi dropped her in Charles Street, outside the house where Freda had her flat, and she went up in the lift to the first floor. As the automatic doors closed softly behind her, Joanna saw Dora coming towards her along the corridor.

'Aunt Do! How lovely to see you! You're not leaving already?'

Dora, in a navy-blue silk dress, which could have been a Jean Muir or just a very clever imitation, flung her arms around her niece and hugged her.

'Jo darling! Freddie's given you up. She decided an hour ago that, after all, you weren't coming.'

'I was delayed.' Joanna knew that Lawrence would not want his health discussed with anyone. An incautious word could so easily get back to Westminster, especially from Dora, who numbered among her acquaintance so many influential and semi-influential people. The border-land between the show business which was politics and the genuine article had always been blurred. 'But why are you running away like this? I thought you had more stamina.'

'I'm fifty-three, darling,' her aunt replied evasively, as though she had something on her mind. After a brief pause, Dora seemed to arrive at a decision. 'As a matter of fact, you're right. Late nights don't trouble me. I'm used to them, after all, and I don't usually wake up properly until evening. But . . .' She hesitated, before blurting out: 'There are always drugs at Freddie's parties.'

'Drugs?' Joanna was shocked. 'I thought Freddie told you years ago that she'd kicked that habit.'

Dora shrugged. 'Oh, Freddie, bless her, just sticks to booze. But I know from experience that she allows pot to be smoked at her parties. Point is, you can't do much nowadays to prevent it.'

'Marijuana's illegal,' Joanna said sternly.

'It's all illegal.' Dora shrugged again. 'But in a gathering of that size' – she jerked her head in the direction of the open door giving on to the main room, where Gary Glitter had given place to the Rubettes and 'Sugar Baby Love' – 'you can't keep an eye on everyone, even if you wanted to. You can't stand at the door and search people's pockets.'

'You can be careful who you ask.' Joanna was still censorious.

Her aunt gave a gurgle of laughter. 'Darling, not at this sort of do, where practically everyone brings along a couple of gatecrashers. Well, I must be off. Come and see me soon. I'm resting at the moment, now that my tour of *The Rivals* has finished, and I need cheering up.' She kissed Joanna's cheek and pressed the button for the lift. 'I stayed in Nightingale Close last week, while we were in Bath with the show. Jean and Bernard looked very well. Your father's looking forward to his retirement in two years' time. But I thought Dad looked poorly. But, still, he is seventy-four. What can one expect?' The lift bumped quietly to a halt and the doors slid open. Dora got in and, with a final wave of her hand, disappeared from view.

Joanna heard the lift descend and was tempted to summon it back and leave with her aunt, but that would

261

mean losing her chance to say goodbye to Freda. Reluctantly, she turned and walked towards the door at the end of the corridor.

The room, big as it was, seemed to be bursting at the seams. People, standing, sitting, sprawling on the floor, filled every inch of space, and the atmosphere was thick with cigarette smoke. The music, blaring from an outsize stereo system, was louder even than it had sounded outside. The noise of conversation was almost deafening, and only the lighting was subdued.

Judging from the number of entwined bodies and passionate embraces, the party had obviously been well under way for some considerable time. Hired waiters, their faces blandly impersonal, circulated with trays of drinks. Freda was nowhere to be seen.

Joanna touched the arm of the nearest person, a young woman in a bright orange dress.

'Is Miss Marshall anywhere about?' she asked formally, striving to make herself heard above the din.

The girl looked vaguely around her. 'Freddie? Anyone seen Freddie?' she demanded of the members of her immediate group. Most of them shook their heads, then someone recalled having noticed her at the other end of the room, near the window. Joanna thanked them and began pushing her way through the crush, waving aside a persistent waiter who was trying to give her a glass of champagne. This was going to be a very short stay. She wished she hadn't gone to the expense of buying a new frock. Stepping awkwardly over the recumbent figures littering the floor, she was just despairing of ever finding her sister when she heard her name called. Freda, elegant in a long dress of dark-red crushed velvet, diamonds sparkling in her ears and on her fingers, was standing a few feet away from her, nursing her usual Bacardi and Coke.

'Jo! Darling! I'd given you up.' Freda moved to give her sister the customary salute on both cheeks, but with more warmth than she exhibited towards friends. She held

Joanna at arm's length. 'And what a tarty dress! I love it. You ought to wear things like that more often.'

'I'm not staying,' Joanna said, her desire to get out of the flat and away from the party as soon as possible robbing her of her usual good manners. 'I only came to say goodbye.'

Freda pulled a comically rueful face, but made no effort to change her mind.

'You really should have come earlier, before things got hectic. I told you it wouldn't be your scene.'

'It wasn't Aunt Do's, either,' Joanna retorted before she could stop herself.

Freda's eyes narrowed. 'What's that supposed to mean?'

'Well, if you don't know, I'm not going to tell you.' Joanna realized that they were coming perilously close to a quarrel, and went on quickly: 'Anyway, all the best in the States, Freddie. Don't forget to keep in touch. And with Davey.'

'Oh, Davey!' Her sister shrugged. They were still having to speak at the top of their voice to make themselves heard. 'We were never great friends. OK, Jo. Just to please you I'll be the dutiful sibling and write when I can. Are you sure you won't stay longer? It seems a shame, now you're here, not to show off that dress.'

'No, I must go.'

Jeff Warwick strolled up at that moment and put a proprietorial arm round Freda's shoulders, then gave her a long, lingering, slightly maudlin kiss. He began feeling her breasts through the thin velvet cloth, but Freda pushed him impatiently away.

'Later, lover,' she said brusquely. 'I'm just going as far as the lift with my sister. I don't know when I shall be seeing her again. Do you think you could make yourself useful and phone for a taxi?'

She put down her glass and took Joanna's arm, guiding her skilfully through the mass of humanity and into the comparative quiet of the corridor. A door in the opposite wall opened on a flash of bathroom tiles and the sound of flushing water. The girl in the orange dress emerged, evidently having just been sick. She gave her hostess a watery smile and gushed, 'Great party,' just as a young man erupted from the living-room to take her place.

Freda cocked a quizzical and knowing eyebrow at Joanna, murmuring:'Definitely not your scene.'

Another door opened, clearly revealing the disordered bed beyond, and a couple strolled out, the man still hitching up his trousers, the girl draped sensuously about his neck. They did not even bother to acknowledge Freda's presence, but slid straight back into the crowd, calling for champagne.

Joanna returned her sister's look, but all she said was: 'It must be costing you a fortune.'

'Oh, Jeff's paying,' Freda responded airily. 'He likes to keep me happy.'

A third door, at the end of the corridor, was pushed wide, and although this time the bed was invisible from where Joanna was standing the soft pink décor and old-fashioned silk-draped dressing-table made the room's function immediately apparent. It took Joanna a second or two to assimilate the fact that the two people coming out were both men.

She recognized Derek Conway immediately, not only from his years as Freda's flatmate in Notting Hill Gate, but also because his face was so often to be seen nowadays in all the colour supplements and glossy magazines. Conway Interiors. Way beyond her and Lawrence's means.

It took her a few moments longer to focus on his companion, but when she did the shock was like several thousand volts of electricity, rocking her from head to foot. She stretched out a hand, blindly feeling for the wall to give her support. Through the haze of disbelief and horror, she heard Freda mutter, 'Oh dear God!' and felt herself being gently but firmly propelled back the way she had come.

She tried to say something, but couldn't. Her feet refused to obey her, and she stumbled. She was feeling sick. Freda's arm was clamped about her waist, half lifting, half dragging her into the kitchen. She was pushed into a blue-cushioned rocking-chair, where she stared stupidly at the stripped-pine units and rows of immaculate never-used gadgets which was supposed to be every housewife's dream. Freda had filled and was plugging in the electric kettle, searching for coffee, sugar and milk in one of the cupboards, taking down two blue mugs from brass hooks on the wall.

When Joanna spoke at last, her voice was barely more than a croak.

'That was Alex.' Alex, who was supposed to be safely back in Devon, but who, after leaving her yesterday, had presumably gone straight round to Derek Conway's flat, where he had spent the night.

'I blame myself,' Freda said. 'I should have warned you. But I thought you knew Alex was AC/DC. Whatever you said at the time, I assumed that was why you called off the wedding.' She placed one of the blue china mugs, full of steaming coffee, in front of her sister and ordered: 'Drink it!' Then she hitched one leg over a tall pine stool and went on: 'Of course, after that little scene at the Notting Hill flat, I realized you had no idea, but as you and Alex were through by then I didn't think it mattered. In fact it seemed better to let sleeping dogs lie. He didn't come to see me, as I don't need to tell you now. He came to see Derek Conway. Derek was with me when I ran into Alex the previous Christmas. It was a mutual attraction right from the start.'

Joanna sipped her coffee, and the strong hot liquid restored some of her equilibrium. The shock was beginning to wear off, and she had stopped shaking. Alex being a homosexual explained a great deal. But not everything.

'Why', she asked, 'did he get engaged to me? Why did he marry Olwen Bruce?'

Freda grimaced. 'My dear, there are a lot of men like Alex; men who don't really want to admit what they are. They desperately want to believe that they can have a normal relationship with a woman, and some of them even succeed. For a while.'

'Alex's parents . . . do they know?'

Freda drank a mouthful of her own coffee. 'I gather from Derek that his mother does, and accepts the situation. Unreservedly. Those old aristocrats are virtually unshockable. They've experienced it all in their own families over the generations. But his father has no idea, and would probably cut Alex off with the proverbial shilling if he ever found out. He was born in the backstreets of Exeter and pulled himself up by his boot-laces. Parents were Plymouth Brethren. Alex's mamma protects him like a hen with one chick, but I think even she might have her work cut out to protect him indefinitely. Oh, Jo! I wish to God you'd told me that you and Alex were seeing one another again. I wouldn't have told Derek he could bring him this evening. And there again, if you hadn't been late, if you'd arrived when I expected you, the party wouldn't have had time to get going.'

Joanna grinned ruefully. ' "If all the earth was paper and all the sea was ink . . ." It isn't your fault, Freddie. None of it. So stop blaming yourself. Shouldn't you be getting back to your guests?'

'Sod the guests!' Freda spooned more instant coffee into her mug and poured on hot water from the kettle. 'I don't know half of them anyway.' She looked around her. 'This kitchen is the only room in the flat that I really like. I shall miss it. I've sold the place, by the way.'

The door from the hall swung open and Alex stood framed in the doorway. After a moment's hesitation, during which he found himself under the scrutiny of two pairs of unwinking blue eyes, he advanced further into the room and let the door close behind him.

'Am I allowed in?' he asked warily.

Freda put down her mug and slid off the stool.

'It looks as though you are in. I take it you want to talk to Jo alone.'

'If she'll let me.'

'Jo?' Freda raised her eyebrows. 'I'll stay if you want me to.'

Joanna shook her head. 'No. I'm all right now. You get back to the party.'

When she had gone, leaving the faint scent of her perfume lingering on the air, Alex said abruptly: 'I'm sorry, Jo.'

'Why, Alex?' she asked. 'Why bother to take up with me again, after all these years? What did you expect to get out of it? More to the point, what did you expect *me* to get out of it?'

He looked at her sadly. 'I like you, Jo. I like you more than I've ever liked anyone in my whole life. You're my best friend. When I'm with you, I feel whole and sane. But I can't love you the way you want me to. I'm sorry. That's the real reason why, when you broke our engagement, I let you go. It was the only time I've been unselfish enough to put your interests in front of my own.'

'And Olwen?'

'I've never cared a straw about Olwen. I married her – or, rather, my mother pushed me into marrying her – to allay any suspicions my father might have had.'

'Does she know? About you, I mean.'

'She's always known, but she doesn't care. All she's ever wanted is King's Acre Court and my father's money. She's perfectly happy with her committees and her good works.'

'And where does that leave me?'

'Only you, my dear, can tell me that.' Alex came across and took both her hands in his. She made no attempt to withdraw them. 'I hope we can still be friends. I need you, Jo. I need you more than I've ever needed anyone. Now that I've found you again, I can't let you go.'

'Just good friends?' she enquired mockingly, raising her eyes to his.

He returned her gaze steadily. 'If you'll allow it.'

She sighed and briefly lifted one of his hands to rest against her cheek.

'I've no option,' she said bitterly, 'as long as you need me. I love you. I always have.'

28

IT WAS a few weeks later, on a Monday morning in late July, that the story broke, and Joanna was sharply reminded of Freda's words; words which had barely dented her consciousness at the time.

'Alex's mamma protects him like a hen with one chick, but I think even she might have her work cut out to protect him indefinitely.'

Joanna and Lawrence were again spending the weekend in the Avonvale constituency, staying with David Nugent and his wife, Eileen. The two Nugent children, Stuart and Laura, both now in their early teens, were away on a school camping holiday, so the talk had been almost uninterruptedly about politics, ever since Joanna and Lawrence's arrival on the Friday evening. It was fairly certain that the Prime Minister would call a second election in October. He had soldiered on since March with a minority government, and it was generally felt to be impossible to carry on much longer.

'Unfortunately,' David Nugent said over supper on Sunday night, 'it's not the very best of climates at present in which to hold the second general election of the year. People are bored with politics. They don't want to be subjected to yet more party propaganda. After the hassle of last spring, they just want to get on quietly with their lives, And at the best of times Labour Party supporters are notoriously more apathetic about voting than the Tories.'

'What do you reckon my chances are of being reelected?' Lawrence asked anxiously. 'A majority of twenty-two is really no majority at all. It can be wiped out just like that.'

'True,' David Nugent agreed. He helped himself to more cold roast beef and pickles. But behind the dark-rimmed glasses his hazel eyes were reassuring. 'However, you've been an excellent MP. You've proved your worth both in the constituency and in the House. So all we have to do between now and October is to keep our heads down and our noses clean.' He glanced apologetically at Joanna. 'Forgive me for saying this, Jo, but I can't help feeling relieved that your sister has finally gone to America. All the newspaper stories about her and Jeff Warwick don't seem nearly so bad when she's a few thousand miles away in Los Angeles. And I read this morning, in one of the Sunday scandal-sheets, that they'll be getting married soon, now that Gabriella is the ex-Mrs Warwick.'

Lawrence asked eagerly: 'You think I'm certain to be returned, then?'

David Nugent shrugged. 'Nothing's certain. Larry. Not where a seat as marginal as this one is concerned. But if you want my honest opinion ... well, then, yes. I feel pretty confident you'll be re-elected. Jo is very popular, and has been from the start, which is more than could be said for the wife of the previous MP.' He smiled. 'And those two big council estates, which have been built at Shipp's Causeway, have done a lot to swing the vote in our favour. So try not to worry. Be like me and smile more.'

But Joanna, lying beside Lawrence as he tossed and turned all night on the strange mattress in the Nugents' spare bedroom, knew how deeply worried her husband really was about once again losing his parliamentary seat. These last few months back at Westminster, treading once more the 'corridors of power', had merely confirmed Lawrence in his true vocation. And yet, even knowing how much politics meant to him, Joanna could almost wish that he would be defeated in the forthcoming election. His health was suffering, but he refused to consult a doctor because he must not be seen to be ill.

Joanna sighed and reached out to him in the darkness, trying, by the comfort of her presence, to infiltrate his uneasy dreams and stop his restless twitching. After they had made love, he had eventually fallen asleep, holding her, as he liked to do, in a tight embrace. He needed the reassurance of her body pressed against his, as though he were afraid that she would somehow escape him. After a while, she had freed herself, very gently, so as not to wake him, and was at once ashamed of the feeling of relief which flooded through her. Dear God, she prayed desperately, please make me love him more than I do! You know that he deserves it. She stroked Lawrence's back, now hunched towards her, tracing the outline of a protruding shoulder-bone beneath the striped cotton material of his pyjama jacket. He was growing far too thin. He muttered something in his sleep, but she was unable to make any sense of it. But the tone was anxious; worried.

Joanna rolled on to her back, her hair fanning out across the pillow. It was moonlight, and through the uncurtained window she could see it dappling the wood behind the Nugents' house: a little copse that ran down to the banks of a small muddy stream. She thought of Alex, as she had thought of him every night for the past few weeks, just before falling asleep. They had had no contact with one another since they had parted that night in Freda's kitchen.

'If you want me, if you ever get desperate, you know where to find me,' she had said.

He had nodded, understanding. She would always be present in the background of his life, for those moments when it became unbearable to him and he felt he could not go on. Then he had only to contact her and she would be there to comfort him; to give him strength and support .

But, otherwise, they would not meet. From now on, as they had done for so long in the past, they would go their separate ways.

Joanna found that she was crying and she put up an impatient hand to brush the tears away. She despised self-

270

pity, both in herself and in others. It was her husband she should be sorry for: Lawrence, who had given her more love than she had ever returned, who was making himself ill with worry that this second election of 1974 would once again scotch his parliamentary career. The excitement of having won Avonvale from the Conservatives in March had been constantly overshadowed by the size of his own and the Government's majority. Joanna told herself she should be glad events had turned out as they had. She owed Lawrence her wholehearted and undivided support.

They were catching the midday train back to London, and Eileen Nugent did not wake them until late. By the time Joanna and Lawrence sat down to breakfast in the Nugents' sun-filled dining-alcove, it was nine o'clock, and David had already left for the local Labour Party committee rooms. With an election in the offing, there was a great deal of organizational groundwork to be got through.

'I just have to cook the eggs,' Eileen said cheerfully, arranging tea-pot and milk-jug on the table. 'Amuse yourselves by looking at the morning papers.'

There was a pile of three beside Joanna's plate; the *Guardian* and two of the more scurrilous tabloids, which David Nugent, much to his wife's disgust, insisted on taking each morning.

'You need to know the worst of what your enemies are saying about you,' was his philosophy. 'The distortions, the lies, the slanders. These two rags can always be relied on to keep you up to date.'

Joanna handed the *Guardian* to Lawrence and prepared to enjoy some scandal. She spread open the first of the remaining papers, and found herself staring at a front-page photograph of Derek Conway, one hand outflung to ward off the eager reporters, being escorted from his Beak Street offices by two plain-clothes policemen.

'Interior Designer Arrested on Drugs Charge,' proclaimed the headline.

Quickly, she skimmed the following paragraphs. Words and phrases leaped off the page to meet her.

'Derek Conway, fashionable interior designer ...
consulted by royalty, film stars ... flat above his office
premises in Beak Street raided after tip-off ... quantity
of heroin found ... arrested in company of friend,
Alex Ferrer, only son of Sir Herbert Ferrer of Ferrer's
International Haulage ...'

Joanna's heart began to pound. She went back and read
the last dozen words again. There was no mistake. Alex
Ferrer ... Ferrer's International Haulage. With trembling
fingers, she turned to the second of the two tabloid dailies.
The heading here was in even bigger and thicker type:
'Designer and Friend Arrested on Drugs Charge.' And,
underneath, a much clearer picture of Derek Conway
getting into a police car, followed by Alex.

It was two days later, just as Joanna was getting ready to
go out after lunch, that the doorbell of the flat in Crozier
Street was rung. Cursing under her breath, because she
was in a hurry, she went to answer it. A young man, in grey
trousers and a tweed jacket, stood outside. He smiled
ingratiatingly.

'Mrs Walden?'

'Yes.'

'Mrs Lawrence Walden? Wife of the MP for Avonvale?'

'Yes.' Joanna's acknowledgement was more cautious
this time.

'I'm Ken Dudley of the *Clarion Express*. I'm one of the
researchers for the Bartlett Miller column.'

It took Joanna a moment or two to place the name, but
when she did it was to remember that Bartlett Miller was
the *Clarion Express's* gossip columnist, and one of the
most savage in the business.

'What do you want?' she asked shortly.

'We have reason to believe' – the smile grew even more
ingratiating – 'that you are a friend of Alex Ferrer.'

Joanna hesitated, but only for a second. 'Alex Ferrer
and I were engaged once, but that was many years ago.'

'Quite. But Mr Miller understands that you still see him.

In fact you've been seen in his company quite recently.'

Reason to believe ... Mr Miller understands ... Joanna's mind went back to that scene in the Tate Gallery restaurant: herself and Alex lunching together, Tom Birkenshaw stopping by their table. It was he, of course, who had put Bartlett Miller on to her. It could not possibly be anyone else.

The palms of her hands were sweating. She did not know what to do. If she denied everything, neither this young man nor his vitriolic boss would believe her, and would scent an intrigue. Bartlett Miller and his henchmen would never stop hounding her. And if 'honest' Tom Birkenshaw, the straightforward, no-nonsense, hard-hitting MP for West Yorkshire Moors, was not prepared to be quoted they would sniff around until they found other people who were: waiters, barmen, museum custodians who might recognize them.

On the other hand, if she admitted to it, the story still would not go away. She could see the newspaper headlines now. 'MP's Wife Friend of Alex Ferrer ...' 'Joanna Walden, Wife of the MP for Avonvale ...' What was it David Nugent had said? 'We must keep our heads down and our noses clean.' This could provide just that hint of scandal needed to overthrow a majority of twenty-two.

She had to get hold of someone. She had to talk to someone. This was not a decision she could make on her own. She thought again of David Nugent.

'I'm sorry,' she said. 'I'm in a hurry. I can't stop now.' And she slammed the door shut before one of Ken Dudley's heavy brown brogues could wedge itself against the jamb. Then she half-ran, half-stumbled over to the phone and dialled the Nugents' Avonvale number.

'Make a clean breast of everything to Lawrence,' was David Nugent's advice, given in a clipped unsympathetic voice, 'and I'll be with you this evening. I'll catch the five-ten train.'

So Joanna did something she had never done before.

She rang the House of Commons and left a message asking Lawrence to come home as soon as possible. He arrived in Crozier Street just after six, worried and afraid that she was ill.

'What's wrong? What's the matter with you?' he asked anxiously, as she met him at the front door.

'Nothing. Come in and sit down. I have to talk to you. I've made tea and cut some sandwiches. David will be here around half-past seven.'

'David?' Lawrence was puzzled, but he followed her through to the living-room and dropped, pale with exhaustion, into one of the grey velvet-covered armchairs. 'What's he coming for? Jo! What's happening?'

So she told him. There seemed no point in trying to lead up to it gently. She told him everything; about her meetings with Alex over the past few months; about Tom Birkenshaw seeing them lunching together at the Tate; about Freda's farewell party; about Bartlett Miller and the reporter who had cornered her that afternoon.

When she had finished, there was silence in the room for several minutes. Lawrence lay back in his chair, eyes closed, thin body hunched against adversity. Joanna could feel the scream rising inside her: 'Say something for God's sake! Say something!' But she kept silent, watching him tensely.

'Well, that's that, then,' he said at last, opening his eyes again and staring blankly in front of him.

But David Nugent, when he arrived, took a less pessimistic view.

'It all depends', he said, drinking his tea strong and black and sugarless, the way he liked it, 'if, on election day, the Great British Public is in one of its puritanical holier-than-thou moods, or if it's wearing its other, liberal-minded hat. Champion of the underdog. And you will be the underdog in this election, Larry; it's no use my pretending that you won't. Once this story hits the papers – and, as far as I can see, we haven't a snowball's chance in hell of preventing that happening – your Conservative opponent is bound to make capital out of it. And as you've said yourself, so often, a majority of twenty-two is easily overturned.' The agent put his cup and saucer back on the tray, carefully not looking at Joanna. 'Until today, I was hopeful of you increasing your majority; but, as the author of *Outside Influences and the Floating Voter* knows only too well, these sorts of things do have an effect. However,' he continued more cheerfully, 'there's no saying but it might work to your advantage. As I've already pointed out, the British are never predictable over moral issues.'

Joanna asked in a low voice: 'What do you suggest I do about this reporter, Ken Dudley?'

David Nugent looked her full in the eyes for the first time since entering the flat, half an hour before. 'Nothing at all. Refuse to comment. Remember the French dictum: "Qui s'excuse, s'accuse". Let Bartlett Miller and his minions dig their own dirt. That way, it will smack more of a smear campaign. Visit the constituency as often as possible. Be seen doing good works!'

Joanna laughed, but commented bitterly: 'You think I've been all sorts of a disloyal fool, don't you? Be honest!'

'I think you've been unwise,' he answered steadily.

The three of them spent the rest of the evening, through a belated dinner until bedtime, discussing revised strategy for the election campaign, whenever it came; the government White Paper on Northern Ireland, which aimed to find a constitutional solution to the Province's difficulties; and, inevitably, but unproductively, the reasons for Tom Birkenshaw's animosity towards Lawrence.

'I'm afraid it might have been my fault again,' Joanna said. 'I was too outspoken about his business interests.'

David Nugent finally retired, some time after midnight, to the flat's only spare bedroom, and Joanna found herself alone again with Lawrence. When she returned from the kitchen, where she had been doing the washing-up, he was still sitting beside the empty fireplace, holding a half-full tumbler of whisky. Joanna hesitated, then went over and sat on the arm of his chair.

'Larry, I'm sorry.'

He glanced up at her. There were black circles under both eyes.

'No, *I'm* sorry. I shouldn't have over-persuaded you into marrying me.' He sighed and leaned sideways, resting his head against her shoulder. 'I've loved you ever since you were a schoolgirl. There's never been anyone else for me. I was never very fond of my first wife. You've always been the one that mattered. No! You don't have to say anything. I've always known that you don't feel the same way about me. I knew you were still in love with Alex Ferrer. I can't tell you how grieved I am that it's turned out the way it has for you.'

Joanna bent and kissed him. 'I'm an ungrateful idiot!' she said huskily. 'I don't know a good thing when I've got it. But it's all going to be different from now on, I promise. It's just going to be you and me.' He smiled faintly and squeezed her hand. 'Come on!' Joanna got to her feet. 'Let's go to bed. You're worn out.' He nodded and stood up. She put her arms around him, feeling how thin he was. 'I meant what I said, Larry. Just you and me.'

She drove David Nugent to Paddington station the following morning and saw him off on the train.

'Thank you for all you've done. For all you've still to do,' she said, reaching up to shake his hand as he leaned out of the carriage window. 'Nothing like this will ever happen again.'

'It's my job,' he answered briskly, without giving any of his thoughts away. But Joanna sensed his underlying animosity towards her and was saddened by it. She liked David Nugent and had, in the past, valued him as a friend.

When she got back to the flat, the telephone was ringing. She lifted the receiver, expecting it to be her mother, or perhaps Davina.

It was Bill Skinner himself. He had insisted on speaking to Joanna in person. Lawrence had collapsed while speaking in a debate on the government proposals on Northern

276

Ireland. He had been taken to St Thomas's Hospital. It appeared to be a heart-attack of some sort. No doubt the hospital authorities would confirm . . .

Joanna summoned a taxi, not trusting herself either to drive or walk the short distance from Crozier Street. At St Thomas's, she was met by a deputation of three doctors, including the senior cardiologist, all looking extremely grave. Lawrence had suffered a massive coronary and was in intensive care. They regretted that they could not hold out much hope . . .

Joanna was at Lawrence's bedside, holding his hand, when he died, without regaining consciousness, at four o'clock the following morning.

PART FIVE

1978–80

29

'WE'RE GOING TO LOSE the next election,' Joanna said. 'Callaghan made a fatal mistake when he decided not to go to the country last September. People are getting fed up with all these strikes, particularly in the public sector. When you can't get buried, and the refuse is standing shoulder-high in the streets, it begins to hit home. When the Ford workers were out last month, it didn't really matter to anyone who wasn't waiting for a Ford car, but my constituents don't like it when they're personally affected.'

'Who does?' David Nugent asked with a crooked smile. 'But I don't think you need worry about losing your seat at the next election. You've done wonders since becoming Avonvale's MP.'

It was over four years ago, now, in the October of 1974, that Joanna had fought and won her husband's parliamentary seat, increasing his twenty-two majority to more than a hundred. Labour had been returned to power with an overall majority of three, a slight improvement on their showing earlier in the year, but not significant enough to make running the country any easier. And the surprise resignation of Harold Wilson as Prime Minister, eighteen months into the parliamentary session, had done nothing to bolster the Government's fragile confidence. But: 'You'll do better with Callaghan as PM,' David Nugent had told Joanna. 'He's not a Yorkshireman – Irish descent – and he won't pay so much heed to the Yorkshire Mafia.'

This was his name for the half-dozen or so MPs who were close friends and colleagues of Tom Birkenshaw, now promoted to the front benches as Under-Secretary of State for Housing. His attitude towards Joanna was one of contained animosity, a covert emotion which she sensed, in spite of his general air of affability whenever they came into contact.

It was still a source of wonderment to her to find herself at Westminster at all. When David Nugent had first proposed that she put herself forward as Labour candidate in Lawrence's place, she had laughed at him.

'How can I? Nothing has changed because of Larry's death. Even if the selection committee approve me and I contest the seat for Labour, the Tory press will simply go ahead with the story of my involvement with Alex. Particularly Bartlett Miller.'

David Nugent had worked hard to reassure her. 'There's a lot of sympathy for you at present, because of Larry, and I think, on that account alone, they might drop it. If they don't, and decide to go ahead with their smear campaign, there's no one to be hurt by it now, but yourself, and we'll fight it together. If they insinuate that you, too, take drugs, or have ever done so, we'll slap an action for libel on any newspaper that prints the story. Come on, Jo! You've nothing to lose. Larry had. You owe it to him to try to hold Avonvale for Labour.'

So, burdened by guilt, Joanna had allowed her name to be put forward to the selection committee, who had, by a narrow majority, chosen her from a shortlist of herself and three other candidates. And in October 1974 she had found herself taking her seat on the government back benches with a surprising sense of belonging. This, she suddenly realized, was what she was meant to do with her life. This, without knowing it, was what she had always wanted.

Just over a month later, she had risen to give her maiden speech on the subject of farming subsidies; a speech which, as was the custom, was non-controversial and which was listened to, for the first and last time in an MP's career, in complete silence from the Opposition benches. Her parents,

Davina, both her aunts and David Nugent were all in the front row of the Strangers' Gallery. Her grandfather had badly wanted to be present, but his arthritis was making him increasingly housebound, and Eileen Nugent had sent her apologies by her husband. She was extremely sorry to miss the occasion, but she had been committed for some months to spending a week with friends in Birmingham.

After Joanna had left the Chamber, she took the Members' lift up to the public gallery and invited her family to tea in the Harcourt Rooms. It turned out to be an unexpectedly pleasant occasion, Anthea striking the only sour note by pronouncing the food uneatable and informing Dora that her hat was far too frivolous for someone of fifty-three. But, other than that, her mood was congratulatory .

'You did very well, my dear,' she said, pecking Joanna's cheek. 'I was proud of you.'

It was the first time in her life that Joanna could remember receiving any word of praise from her father's sister, and she grimaced at Dora behind Anthea's back. She suspected that it had been intended as some kind of snub to Davina, but during tea she noticed that her elder aunt and sister seemed to be on excellent terms. And when Anthea had announced that she would be retiring the following year, at the age of sixty-five, Joanna's suspicions had been aroused – suspicions which had proved to be well founded when, in 1975, Davina had applied for and won the vacant headship of Forest Moor. For the past three years, she had been back where she belonged – in the place which in spirit she had never really left. All inducements by the Haddington Grange governors to persuade her to remain had failed. In the end, it had proved no contest.

All in all, Joanna could remember the occasion of her maiden speech with great clarity, because of the plot she sensed was hatching beween Anthea and Davina, because of the way fellow-MPs had congratulated her afterwards, because of the family party. But most of all she remembered it because of the events of the following day, 21 November 1974.

She had returned home to the flat in Crozier Street, after a gruelling twelve hours, and switched on the late-evening television news. The scenes of carnage which had met her eyes had engendered feelings of disbelief and outrage. The IRA were already claiming responsibility for the bombing of two Birmingham pubs, and she had sat on, appalled, letting her supper go cold, as she watched bodies being lifted clear of the rubble. Finally, unable to eat anything, she had gone to bed, but at five the next morning her telephone had rung. It was David Nugent.

Barely coherent, he had told her that Eileen and her friends had gone for a drink at one of the pubs hit by the bombing. All three were missing, but enough had been found of Eileen to confirm that she, at least, was dead. Joanna had gone straight to Avonvale on the earliest train, but there was little that she or anyone else could do. It was a situation which David Nugent had to come to terms with himself, and, at the time, he had needed only the company of his children.

Looking at him now, four years later, Joanna thought how marvellously he had coped. There were grey hairs among the red, and the hazel eyes behind the dark-rimmed glasses were, in unguarded moments, shadowed by pain, but other than that he gave no sign of the terrible tragedy which had torn his life in two. The measure of his success was reflected in his children. They had been shattered by their mother's death, and for some time afterwards both had needed psychiatric help. But it was their father's love and understanding which had really pulled them through. Nowadays, Joanna reflected, it would be difficult to find two happier, better-adjusted teenagers than Laura and Stuart Nugent.

Joanna still stayed with them whenever she was in Avonvale on constituency business, Laura's presence protecting her and David from any ill-natured gossip. Not that there was any foundation for any such kind of gossip. She and David had an almost entirely professional relationship, and, if pressed, Joanna would have said that the agent, who had done so much for her and her new career, did not really like her. He had never forgiven her for what she had done to Lawrence. She suspected, deep down, that he still considered her responsible for her husband's death.

She tried to visit the constituency most weekends, and twice a month held a Saturday-morning 'surgery' at the local Labour Party headquarters. Sometimes she found the experience rewarding, sometimes depressing, depending on how able she was to assist her callers. Today had fallen into the second category, and she had returned to the Nugents' house in Oxford Road feeling tired and miserable. Elsie Nugent, David's mother, had called in some time during the morning and prepared lunch, which she had left, to keep hot, in the oven. Neither of the children had come home yet, and David suggested starting without them.

It was toad-in-the-hole with boiled potatoes and carrots, not one of Joanna's favourite meals, but after years of her mother's cooking she was able to eat almost anything. David Nugent watched her admiringly, pushing his own food around his plate and swallowing hardly anything. The conversation, as always, was politely impersonal, mainly about the subject which interested them both most: politics.

In response to his last remark, Joanna said: 'I wish I could feel as confident as you do about my chances of retaining this seat. The PM has to go to the country next year, and it's my feeling that we're in for a drubbing. All I heard at the "surgery" this morning was complaints about things about which I can do nothing. There was a man from the Shipp's Causeway estate, whose father had died five weeks ago and who still hasn't been buried because of the gravediggers' strike. And there was a woman of eighty, who lives in an isolated cottage on the Banbury road, who's at her wits' end because she hasn't had her ashbin emptied in over a month. She says the smell is shocking. They want to know when the Government's going to get to grips with the unions. People like that, who've worked hard for a pittance all their lives, and have never dreamed of striking for higher wages, see themselves as victims. And with cause. Suddenly, the Conservative Party, especially with a woman at its head, seems an attractive proposition. Margaret Thatcher's projecting the image of an ordinary down-to-earth housewife who wants to run the country as she'd run her household economy, and the idea is very appealing. It's only people like us who know it's a sham; a publicity stunt thought up by her advisers.'

'You don't like her,' David Nugent said, laying down his knife and fork, his eyes twinkling.

'Do you?'

'No. But I wish to God she was on our side. Like you, and unlike some of our more blinkered colleagues in the party, I think we're going to lose the next election, and I'm very much afraid that if that happens we shall be out of office for a very long time. People are looking for something different. Suddenly, they want a more authoritarian form of government.'

'Why?'

'Because people like change.' David gathered up the dirty plates and carried them into the kitchen, returning with a bread-and-butter pudding. 'People get tired of too much liberty, as they get tired of everything else. They had that up to the hilt in the late sixties and early seventies. Now they want someone else to shoulder the responsibility for their lives. They want to be told what to do, what to think. It wasn't coincidence, you know, that the Victorian era followed hard on the heels of the French Revolution and the Age of Reason.'

The front door banged. There was the sound of voices in the hall. A moment later, Stuart Nugent poked his head round the dining-room door.

He was eighteen now; a good-looking boy with his

286

father's red hair, but in a lighter shade of auburn. The widely spaced eyes were hazel – again, like David's – and the freckled skin was pale. No amount of sun produced a tan. For the two years since he left school, he had worked in the Job Centre in Bath, travelling the fifteen miles there and back every day in an ancient Triumph Herald. Unlike his sister, who would be sitting her A levels in a year's time, and who was then hoping to go up to university to read Political Science, Stuart had never been academically inclined. He had always had a wide circle of friends and enjoyed the sort of social life which precluded much study. He was talking of moving to Bath as soon as he could find accommodation at a price he could afford on his Civil Service pay. He had already joined one of the city's amateur dramatic groups, and had been out this particular Saturday morning at a rehearsal. He was as indifferent an actor as he had been a student, but his universal popularity ensured him a small role in nearly every production. He was at present rehearsing the butler, Merriman, in *The Importance of Being Earnest*.

'Your dinner's in the oven,' his father said by way of greeting. 'Toad-in-the-hole. Probably burned to a cinder.'

'Not stopping,' Stuart said, coming further into the room. 'Hello, Mrs Walden. How was the "surgery"?' Without pausing for an answer, he went on: 'I shan't be home this evening, Dad. Been invited to a party.'

David Nugent groaned. 'When haven't you? I don't know why you bother to tell me when you'll be out. It would be more to the point to tell me when you'll be in. Where's the party this time? Anyone I know?'

'No. It's the girl who plays most of the leads with the Walcot Players. She's really good. She's doing Gwendoline Fairfax in the Wilde. She's with me now, as a matter of fact. I've been singing the praises of the Tradesman's Arms at Camberley Green. Especially their steak-and-kidney pie. She wants to try it.'

'Well, it'll beat your grandmother's toad-in-the-hole.' David Nugent had risen from the table. 'But for goodness'

287

sake bring her in and introduce us. Don't keep the poor girl hanging around in the hall.' He shrugged despairingly at Joanna. 'Honestly! Kids of today! No manners.'

It was her turn to laugh. 'I fancy parents have been saying that since the Stone Age.'

The girl who followed Stuart Nugent into the dining-room was, Joanna judged, about seventeen, tall, grey-eyed, with fair hair scraped back into a pony-tail, and with very clear, almost translucent skin. She was wearing a pair of tight faded blue jeans, white canvas trainers, a black leather jacket zipped up to the throat against the December cold, and a tan leather handbag was hoisted negligently over one shoulder. The jeans and trainers could have been bought by anyone of her age in any market or leading chain store in the country. The bag and jacket, on the other hand, spoke loudly of money. And the way she moved and spoke indicated the sort of confidence which came from an expensive education and a privileged background. Without waiting for a formal introduction, she held out her hand to David.

'So you're Stu's father. He's told me a lot about you. A political agent. I find that quite fascinating. My name's Samantha Douglas, by the way.'

Joanna found herself shaking hands with her niece as in a dream. Dazedly, she waited for some sign of recognition on Samantha's part, but none came, adding to her sense of unreality. Did the girl truly not know that Joanna Walden, MP, was her aunt? How much, if anything, had Anthony told her? She had been very young when her father remarried; young enough for the memory of those early years to be quickly expunged. Perhaps she had been brought up to believe that Claire was her real mother. On consideration, Joanna reflected that would have been the sensible thing to do. There would have been no reason to burden the child with a mother who had so positively rejected her, when she had another one, who presumably loved her, ready to hand.

Samantha's next words seemed to confirm this impression. She was frowning slightly as she released Joanna's hand.

'You know,' she said, with an uncertain laugh, 'you seem vaguely familiar, Mrs Walden. I feel as though we'd met before, a very long time ago. It must be all those pictures I see of you in the newspapers.' She went on: 'You and your two sisters are quite famous, aren't you? Davina, Joanna and Freda Marshall. I do so admire you all, although of course', she added ingenuously, 'Freda's the one I'd really like to meet. I thought her last picture, *Lovers' Meeting*, was absolutely terrific. The story was trite, but she was marvellous. Is it true that she and Jeff Warwick are getting divorced? Just wait until the girls at school hear that I've met her sister! They'll be green with envy. I'm working hard at trying to be like her. If one local girl can become a famous actress, why can't another? Because that's all I want to be. An actress.'

30

THE TAXI drove out of Southampton on the Romsey road,
leaving the sprawling suburbs of the town behind it. Here
and there, the winter-coloured woods were patched with
snow, and to the left of her Joanna could see the scar of an
old railway line. A pale sun gilded the wings of some
screeching gulls, foraging inland. An isolated cottage still
sported its Christmas decorations, long after the Twelfth
Night which decreed they should be taken down.

The taxi swerved suddenly to the right, between laurel
bushes dripping from a recent squall of rain, and sped
along an avenue of lime trees towards the square Georgian
house at the end. Joanna craned out of the window for a
better view. It was the first time she had seen Forest
Moor.

The head girl was standing by the open front door,
waiting to escort her famous headmistress's equally famous
sister up the broad flight of stairs to Miss Marshall's study
and private living-quarters. She greatly admired Mrs
Walden, who wrote a regular weekly column in both the
Guardian and *The Times*, and whose speeches in the
House of Commons were frequently reported.

A junior materialized, seemingly from nowhere, to take
Joanna's overnight bag. She followed her and the head girl
upstairs.

'Jo!' Davina greeted her sister with a firm handshake
and a quick peck on the cheek. 'It's good of you to give up
your time. I know how busy you must be in the run-up to a
general election.'

Joanna smiled her thanks at the two girls, and took her case out of the junior's hand.

'In the face of your pressing invitation,' she said to her sister, 'how could I possibly refuse? A chance to talk about one's self must always prove irresistible.'

Davina laughed. 'Come and sit down. We'll have tea first, then I'll get someone to show you your room and you can unpack your things.' She moved towards a low table set in front of the fire. Joanna noted the rich gleam of silver and the transparency of fine bone china. Davina added: 'This, by the way, is the study. I usually have afternoon tea here because of the splendid view over the park. My private sitting-room, by contrast, is rather cramped.'

The study, although Joanna had no means of knowing it, had changed very little since Anthea's day. The big leather-topped desk and book-lined walls were still the same. The marble swags of ivy and vines still gleamed in the light from the fire. The marquetry table remained in its accustomed place, but the photographs had disappeared, giving place to both the hardback and paperback editions of Davina's two books: *Jack Straw and His Menie* and the even more highly acclaimed *Black Death; Black Prince*. The two pictures, 'The Road to Sydenham' and 'The Gallery of HMS *Calcutta* (Portsmouth), 1876', had gone to grace the walls of Anthea's flat in Royal Crescent, and in their place Davina had hung copies of 'Les Laveuses' by Leon-Augustin Lhermitte and one of Archibald Thorburn's magnificent bird paintings, 'Tree Sparrow and Bullfinches'.

'This talk I've asked you to give', Davina said, motioning her sister to a seat on the large green leather settee, 'is part of our winter careers programme for the sixth form. You're our third speaker in the series.' She began to pour tea. 'I persuaded Aunt Dora to come down last month and talk about acting. She was very good. I was pleasantly surprised.'

'I don't know why you should be.' Joanna accepted the Crown Derby cup and saucer and selected a sandwich from the matching Crown Derby plate. She couldn't help sparing a thought for Haddington Grange. 'Aunt Do's an intelligent woman. The trouble is, you've always seen her through Aunt Thea's eyes.'

'Maybe.' Davina sipped her tea. 'We certainly got on better than I'd expected. I've never cared for her very much, I'm afraid.'

'Aunt Thea again.' Joanna hesitated, then said: 'Mum and Dad were disappointed that you didn't come home for Christmas.'

'You mean Dad was disappointed. Aunt Thea asked me months back to go with her to Salzburg. Now, don't start lecturing me, Jo. Tell me about yourself instead.'

Joanna nibbled at a *langue de chat* biscuit. 'What do you want to know?'

Davina shrugged. 'Well . . . when's the election, for a start?'

'May, perhaps, or June. I think Callaghan will hang on as long as he can. I don't think he realizes quite how unpopular the Government has become. He made a fatal mistake in not going to the country last autumn before all this trouble blew up. The newspapers are calling it the "winter of discontent".'

'They would!' Davina exclaimed contemptuously. 'It's a pity they can never come up with an original phrase. You think Labour will lose, then? What about Avonvale? Are you going to be out of a job?'

Joanna sighed. 'I'm keeping my fingers crossed. David Nugent, the agent, is optimistic.' She paused for a moment; then, before her sister could change the subject, hurried on: 'Talking of David, his son, Stuart, has a girlfriend. I met her first before Christmas, and I've . . . I've seen quite a bit of her over the past two months.'

'Really?' said Davina, her voice flat with uninterest.

'Yes. She . . . she belongs to the same Bath amateur dramatic group as Stuart Nugent. She's still at school at the moment, studying for her "A"s, but she wants to be an actress. She's extremely keen in fact, although her father, she tells me, is against it. Davey!' Joanna, who had been staring down at her hands, folded in her lap, glanced up. 'Davey, her name is Samantha Douglas.' There was a long silence, broken only by the hissing and crackling of the logs in the grate. As her sister made no effort to speak, Joanna went on, in a desperate bid to provoke some reaction: 'She doesn't know I'm her aunt. She believes Claire is her mother. Anthony doesn't seem to have told her the truth yet, though I suppose he'll have to one day. Sooner or later, she's going to need a copy of her birth certificate. I'm just surprised that in these days of foreign travel and passports she hasn't wanted it already.'

'What . . . what's she like?' Davina asked at last, a little unsteadily. She was looking very pale.

'She's tall and fair, like Anthony, but she has your eyes and skin. Very intelligent, but, then, you'd expect that, wouldn't you? I gather Anthony wants her to go to university and give up what he calls "this acting nonsense". But she's very determined.'

Davina smiled faintly. 'I was the same. We all were, I suppose. Look at Freddie.'

Joanna preferred, for the moment, not to look at Freda, whose career, since she descended on Hollywood over four years ago, had petered out in a number of a second-rate films. They made money and were good enough of their kind, but they certainly did not stretch Freda as an actress. Anyone with far less talent than she had could have made them, although perhaps with not quite so much success. The continuing saga of her marriage with Jeff Warwick, from lavish Hollywood wedding in the autumn of 1974, through its well-publicized decline – rows, separations, reconciliations, the birth of their daughter, Antigone, in 1976 – to their latest blazing row amidst all the splendour of a gala night at the Hollywood Bowl, was rarely out of the papers. She attracted attention as a flame attracts moths, and her infrequent letters home were full of bravado and an underlying unhappiness. Her younger sister, Joanna reflected, had never been able to make up her mind what

293

she really wanted out of acting: the glamour of Hollywood stardom or to prove herself on the legitimate stage.

She became aware that Davina was asking her a question and relegated Freda and her problems to the back of her mind.

'Sorry, love. What did you say?'

'I said what's Anthony doing nowadays? Is he still in practice in Bath?'

Joanna nodded and passed her cup for more tea.

'Yes. Samantha calls him an old stick-in-the-mud, but says he'll never change. Apparently he loves being a GP. His father died suddenly some years ago, but his mother's still alive. He and his family moved back to Lyncombe Manor to live with her. As you know, there's no shortage of money. I remember reading somewhere that Mr Douglas left over two million.'

Davina handed back the replenished cup. 'Cash was never Anthony's problem.' She had herself well in hand again, and the shock of hearing her daughter's name after all these years had been overcome. 'Well,' she added brightly, 'it's good to know that I did the right thing. Claire seems to have made a much more satisfactory mother.'

'You don't know that.'

Davina chose to ignore this remark. A little frown appeared between her brows.

'Anthony's right, though, to insist on Samantha going to university. If she's as intelligent as you say, it would be a pity to waste it on a notoriously dodgy profession like the theatre. Not everyone can be as lucky as Freda's been. In fact the vast majority never make it.'

'No. But Samantha has her heart set on the stage, and I think it will be very difficult to dissuade her.'

'Funny, isn't it,' Davina said, 'how the acting bug keeps cropping up in our family? Dora undoubtedly influenced Freddie when she was young, but the same can't be said for Samantha.'

'I think it was Gramps, more than Aunt Do, who influenced Freddie. He was always telling us about some actor

294

or play that he'd seen. Ivor Novello, Barry Sinclair; Sybil Thorndike in *Saint Joan*; George Devine and Peggy Ashcroft in *Hedda Gabler*; Paul Scofield and Claire Bloom in *Ring round the Moon*; John Gielgud and Diana Wynyard in *Much Ado about Nothing*.'

Davina smiled. 'You've a better memory than I have. But, then, I wasn't at home as much as the rest of you.' There was another silence while the logs crackled and flared in the hearth. Then Davina asked abruptly: 'Do you ever see Alex Ferrer nowadays? I guessed you'd met him again, that time you were staying with me in Exeter. You were suddenly so happy. There was a special look about you which only Alex could ever induce. And when you asked to come down again, so soon afterwards, I was sure I was right. But when he was had up on that drugs charge and it turned out he was gay I didn't know what to think. Had you ever suspected that he was a homosexual?'

Joanna shook her head. 'No. No, never. It came as a total shock. For a while I was devastated, but then . . . Larry died and it . . . well, it rather took my mind off it. But you're right in thinking that I was seeing Alex while I was in Exeter. We still keep in touch. We're friends, but it's very discreet. Now that I'm an MP, I can't afford to have – what shall I say? – suspect contacts.'

'You're still in love with him,' Davina hazarded, but once again Joanna shook her head.

'Not any longer. Not in the way you mean. But I am extremely fond of him and always shall be. We see each other now and then, but not when he's in London. He visits Bath occasionally, when I'm at home. He needs me, Davey. In some obscure way, he needs me. Sadly, I've outgrown my need for him.'

'No special man in your life, then, at the moment?'

'Not one. I've taken to the celibate life, like you. We'll have to leave all that sort of thing to Freddie.'

'I shall be seeing her in the summer,' Davina remarked, getting to her feet as the maid, in the pale green and cream uniform of the Forest Moor domestic staff, came in to clear

295

away the tea things. 'I've been invited on a lecture tour of the States by the Daughters of Magna Carta. The tour includes an address to the chapter in LA, so I'm hoping to call on Freda. Now, come and see your room. It's a quiet one, overlooking the old park, so you can mug up on your notes for tomorrow in peace, if you need to. Dinner's in the main hall at seven. A bit on the early side, I'm afraid, but we like the girls to be in bed by ten.'

Joanna stood on the little wrought-iron balcony of her room and looked out over what used to be the deer park when Forest Moor was a private home. There were no deer any more; just a wide grassy stretch set with clumps of trees, leafless now beneath a sky dark crimson, before the night clouds came. A stone urn, at the top of a broad flight of stone steps, leading down from the terrace, was white with snowdrops, their delicate green-veined heads nodding in a freshening breeze. The pupils were not allowed on this side of the house, and there was an unnatural quiet – an almost unhealthy quiet, Joanna thought – fragile and empty, like a hollow shell. Forest Moor girls were too well disciplined. Joanna preferred what she recalled as the more natural chaos of Haddington Grange, on the one occasion she had visited it in her sister's company.

It was nearly dark and very cold. She shivered and stepped back through the balcony doors into the centrally heated warmth of her room; a pleasant room with solid oak furniture and soft furnishings in varying shades of blue. Joanna unpacked her overnight bag, hung up her good black dress in the vast emptiness of the wardrobe and went into the adjacent bathroom to run her bath. Three fluffy blue towels were draped, ready for use, over the heated towel-rail. The whole place reeked of money, and she could understand better why Davina, living most of her life in such an atmosphere, had never really fitted into Nightingale Close when she came home for the holidays; why she had preferred to spend most of her time with

Anthea; why, in Exeter, she had moved from the convenient little semi, close to Haddington Grange, to the flat overlooking the Cathedral Close.

When she had finished her bath and was wrapped in the cotton kimono which served her as a dressing-gown, Joanna padded back into the bedroom, switched on the lights and pulled the curtains. She felt suddenly lonely and depressed. There was no one special person she belonged to; there was no one special person who belonged to her. She had told Davina that she no longer needed Alex, but it was not altogether true. There were occasions, like the present, when she needed him desperately, and the canker of resentment at what he had put her through ate into her very soul and made her bitter. He had no right to be as he was. Why couldn't he be sexually normal, like other men?

She pulled herself up short. She was beginning to fall into what her grandfather termed 'a state of exaggerated desperation'. She reminded herself sharply that Alex was not abnormal, and took from her handbag the note he had sent her a few days after Freda's ill-fated party, and which she had carried with her ever since. It was not really a note, just seven lines from Marlowe's *Edward II*, scribbled on a sheet of exercise paper.

The mightiest kings have had their minions;
Great Alexander loved Hephestion;
The conquering Hercules for Hylas wept
And for Patroclus stern Achilles drooped;
And not kings only, but the wisest men:
The Roman Tully loved Octavius;
Grave Socrates wild Alcibiades . . .

She reread the words yet again, then returned the paper to her bag, zipped it away in an inside pocket and resolutely turned to the file of notes which she had brought with her for tomorrow's lecture to the Forest Moor sixth form: 'My Life as a Backbencher'. Not a very original title but, then, that was what she had been asked to talk about, and that was what she would give them. The career, all four and a half years of it, of Joanna Walden, MP.

In a room a few yards further along the corridor, Davina was also looking out over the darkening park. She had been more deeply disturbed than she cared to admit, even to herself, that her child had been brought up unaware of her existence. Suddeny, it irked her unbearably that Claire Neville should take all the credit for Samantha. And yet why not? Claire deserved all the credit. Davina knew it, and tried desperately, with all the rational cold logic of her historian's mind, to make herself acknowledge the justice of the other woman's claim. She had not the merest pretence of a stake in her daughter's future. She had never before exhibited the smallest interest in whether Samantha were alive or dead; yet now, totally unexpectedly, after all these years, she was experiencing the stirrings of maternal instinct. It was ridiculous, irritating and completely incomprehensible. She had absolutely no right to demand that Samantha be told the truth; but, even as she tried to persuade herself, she was moving towards the telephone. She dialled the operator.

'I want the number, please, of Dr Anthony Douglas, Lyncombe Manor, near Bath.' And, even before the operator came back to her, she found she could remember it. It was still there, as it must always have been, filed away in her memory. Nevertheless, she wrote it down with shaking fingers before replacing the receiver. Then, carefully, deliberately, she lifted the receiver again and started to dial.

31

ANTHONY DOUGLAS put down the phone and found that he was trembling; not with rage or with indignation, as he had every right to be, but because, as soon as he had heard Davina's voice, it was as though the past sixteen years had never been. All the intervening time with Claire, the birth of their two children, might never have happened.

The room he used as a study was on the far side of the house, well away from the kitchen quarters, where the family always seemed to congregate; away from his mother's room; away, as far as possible, from the children's rooms and the blare of their respective record-players. Twelve-year-old Malcolm and ten-year-old Jacqueline inhabited a world of constant noise, even when doing their homework; a world dominated by such exotically named beings as Ian Dury and the Blockheads, Blondie, Village People and Boomtown Rats. Sometimes, in odd moments, Anthony wondered whatever had become of ordinary-sounding people like Ruby Murray, Frankie Laine and Johnnie Ray.

The study was an oasis of quiet, where he could go over the day's case-histories before joining the family for supper; and where, when he was on evening call, he could take the messages passed on from the surgery. This was in Bath, located in a small close of Georgian houses at the top end of the town; a lucrative practice which he shared with his three partners, two male and one female, all of whom had a far more astute financial sense than he did. Not one of them had given up private patients, as Anthony had done, in order to devote himself entirely to the National Health Service. It was a constant bone of contention between himself and Claire, who thought such a gesture unnecessarily altruistic; one of the many bones of contention which littered their married life like so many insurmountable hurdles.

When Anthony allowed himself time to think about it, he supposed that his and Claire's marriage had been overshadowed from the start by Samantha's presence, a perpetual reminder to Claire that she had only been second-best, and by the darker shadow of Theresa's suicide. What he had felt about that, no one knew except himself: both at the time and since, he had kept his emotions on a very tight rein. If he did not, he was in danger of sinking into a mire of guilt. Even now, after all these years, he felt that he was somehow to blame. He should have broken the news more gently to her that he was going to marry Claire, and he had asked himself a thousand times if he had not been responsible for the way she had misread his intentions. He thought she had realized that once Davina had rejected him he had to cut himself off completely from her and all her family, in order to preserve his sanity. It was the reason he had put off, time and time again, telling Samantha the truth about her parentage. Claire and his mother had kept on at him for years, warning him that his elder daughter would resent the secrecy.

'The older she is when she finds out,' Claire had said, 'the bigger will be her identity crisis. Besides, it's not fair on me.'

His mother had endorsed what he knew to be an eminently sensible point of view.

'For God's sake, tell her!' Cicely Douglas had exhorted him angrily, only last week. 'You daren't delay much longer, Tony, or Sam will find out for herself. Far better it should come from you.'

He knew it, of course, but had continued dithering. Now, abruptly, the matter had again been forced on his

300

attention, and from a totally unexpected quarter. His brain was still reeling from the shock it had received when, in answer to its summons, he had picked up the phone. He had been waiting for a call from Bath Royal United Hospital, where one of his patients was expecting her fourth child. Instead, it had been Davina's voice at the other end of the line.

He had realized from Samantha's recent conversation that she had met Joanna, without having the slightest idea who she was, apart from the exciting fact that she was Freda Marshall's sister.

'*The* Freda Marshall, Daddy! The film star!'

But he had not expected Joanna to do anything about it. Or perhaps, more accurately, he had not expected Davina, if told, to do anything about it. After all, why should she? She had evinced not the smallest interest in her daughter for the past sixteen years, and had forfeited all rights in the matter. Now, suddenly, here she was, ringing up out of the blue, demanding – yes, demanding, there was no other word for it – that Samantha be told the truth.

'And put your foot down on all this going-on-the-stage nonsense!' she had told him severely.

Anger began to seep back, drowning out other, more complex emotions. How dare she! *How dare she!* The sheer audacity of it was breathtaking!

'Of all the bloody nerve!' he said out loud.

He got up from his desk and started pacing up and down the book-lined room. At thirty-seven, Anthony had lost none of his aquiline good-looks, although he had thickened with the passing years. There was more flesh on his bones nowadays, and a few grey hairs showed among the blond; but his female patients found him, if anything, more attractive than when he was fairer and thinner and younger. They had no complaints, except the ones they brought with them to his surgery.

There was a rap on the study door, and when he called 'Come in!' Samantha's head appeared in the opening.

'Mum says supper's ready. Don't hang about, because it's cheese soufflé and it will spoil.'

'Sam,' he said hesitantly, 'come in and – er – sit down. I . . . I have to talk to you.'

'But Mum says—'

'Yes, I know. But the soufflé will just have to go flat for once. Now, do as I say!' He smiled, moderating his tone. 'Please, Sam. This is serious.'

'It was a splendid lecture,' Davina said, as she escorted her sister upstairs again to her private quarters. 'The girls were enthralled. It almost made me wish I'd become a politician instead of going in for education.'

'Rubbish!' Joanna laughed, pleased, none the less, by Davina's praise. 'You love teaching, although I suppose you don't get to do a lot of that nowadays.'

'Oh, I keep my hand in with the sixth form.' Davina led the way into her sitting-room, where lunch had been laid for two on a table in the big bay-window. 'Do you have to go back to London this afternoon? Couldn't you stay over for another night? I don't seem to have seen very much of you lately.'

Joanna was touched by this evidence of Davina's concern and reflected that time had mellowed her elder sister.

'I'd love to,' she said, taking her seat at the table and unfurling a white damask napkin. 'But I'm afraid I can't. There's too much doing just at present. Anti-Shah riots in Iran, a threatened strike by about three hundred thousand civil servants, the Incomes Policy in shreds and a general election in the offing. I suppose I'm luckier; I do see you more that you see me. On television whenever I can. That education programme has made you quite a celebrity. You're its only regular panellist.'

Davina grimaced. It was to her credit, Joanna thought, that she never made much of the instant fame which her television appearances had brought her. Davina infinitely preferred that people should know her for her books.

'Are you writing anything at the moment?' Joanna asked, as the maid brought in the soup.

Davina shook her head regretfully. 'I simply haven't had time since returning to Forest Moor. I don't think I ever appreciated how hard Aunt Thea worked. The administration load is fearsome.' She broke a bread roll in half between her long thin fingers. 'Jo, I telephoned Anthony last night. I told him it was time Samantha learned the truth. That I'm her mother.' She glanced at her sister's face, then away again. 'I can see what you're thinking. That it was a bloody cheek. And you're quite right. It was. I simply don't know what got into me.'

'Did . . . did he agree to do it?' Joanna asked, awed. 'I mean, to be honest, Davey, if I'd been him, I'd have told you to go straight to hell!'

'Well, he didn't,' her sister retorted with some asperity. 'He said he'd think about it. He thought I was right, and it was time Samantha knew. The trouble is now I wish I hadn't done it. What do you think Samantha's reaction will be?'

Joanna shrugged. 'Don't ask me. You know what my opinion has always been. That you should never have left her. That you let Aunt Thea influence you far too much.'

'I was – am – fond of Aunt Thea. She's interested in my welfare.'

'You were fond of Anthony. You agreed to marry him.'

'I was in love with Anthony,' Davina corrected her quietly. 'But I was too young. My whole life was ahead of me. And now I want to make sure that Samantha gets the same opportunities that I had. You tell me she's intelligent. Clever. A brilliant academic record at school. I told Anthony that he must nip all this theatrical nonsense in the bud. She has to go on to university.'

Joanna was momentarily bereft of speech. Eventually, she laid down her soup-spoon and said: 'I do not know how you had the gall!'

Davina had the grace to look ashamed before her

attitude changed to one of defiance. 'I am her mother, after all. Surely I'm entitled to some say in the matter. It's for Samantha's own good, Jo.'

'I wish now I hadn't said anything to you,' Joanna said crisply. 'It was a mistake. I just thought you'd like to know that Sam was well and reasonably happy. It did surprise me, it's true, that Anthony hadn't yet told her the truth, but I didn't expect you to go poking your nose in.'

'Thanks!' Davina snapped. Both sisters sensed that a quarrel was brewing and both simultaneously drew back from the brink. Neither was prepared to risk their deepening friendship.

Joanna murmured, 'Sorry,' at the same moment as Davina burst out with: 'Oh, no! You're right, Jo. I didn't mean to stir up a hornet's nest. Let's hope Anthony has the good sense to ignore my interference.'

The maid had removed the empty soup-plates and was just serving them with roast lamb and green peas when Davina's secretary appeared apologetically at the sitting-room door.

'I'm so sorry to bother you, Miss Marshall, but there's a young lady downstairs in the hall who insists on seeing you. Right away, she says. She refuses point-blank to take "no" for an answer.'

'That's right, I do.' Samantha, who had followed the secretary upstairs, pushed past her and came into the room. She was a little taken aback to see Joanna, but recovered her poise instantly. 'Hello, Mrs Walden. Or should I say "Aunt Joanna"? And this, I suppose' – she looked at Davina, who had risen to her feet – 'is my long-lost mother.'

Davina took charge with an aplomb which Joanna could only envy.

'Take off your coat, Samantha, and sit down,' she said, in the same tone of voice which she kept for recalcitrant pupils. 'Have some lunch. I'm sure you must be hungry. Mabel!' She addressed the maid, who was avidly watching the proceedings, storing up every word to regale her fellow-servants with in the kitchens. 'Set a third place, please, and inform Cook that I have another luncheon guest. Hurry, please. You know I hate to be kept waiting.' She turned back to her daughter, who, Joanna was amazed to note, had done precisely as she was bidden, although not without a certain resentment. It was plain that the meeting was not going as she had planned. Davina added: 'Do your parents know that you're here?'

Samantha shook her head. 'They think I'm at school,' she answered sullenly. She saw Davina glance at her red woollen dress and went on quickly: 'I changed in the train. My school uniform's in there.' She indicated the Union Jack carrier-bag she had been holding and which was now propped against the side of her chair.

'Then, you must telephone one or the other of them immediately after lunch and tell them where you are,' Davina said.

But she was less in command of herself than she sounded. Joanna noted the tell-tale trembling of her sister's hands as she resumed her place at the table.

'This is ridiculous!' Samantha exclaimed, as the maid reappeared and set a bowl of soup in front of her. 'I didn't come here to have lunch! I came to find out what sort of a mother you are to have abandoned me before I was two years old.'

'We'll talk about it later,' Davina said, 'when we've eaten. In this cold weather, you need food inside you, and I don't like having my meals disturbed. Afterwards, when you've telephoned home, we'll discuss things and you can make up your own mind what sort of a person I really am. Pass the mint sauce, please, Joanna.'

Anthony asked one of his partners to take his afternoon surgery and returned to Lyncombe Manor, in response to Claire's urgent telephone call. She was waiting for him, pacing up and down in fury in the long drawing-room. He was vaguely aware of his mother, hovering anxiously somewhere in the background.

'What's the matter?' he asked, bracing himself for his wife's reply.

'I'll tell you what's the matter!' Claire pivoted on her heel and stormed towards him. 'Samantha didn't go to school this morning. Instead, she went to Southampton to see Davina! She's just phoned. She borrowed the money for the train fare from your mother!'

'I didn't know what she wanted it for, Tony!' Cicely Douglas protested tearfully. 'If I had, I wouldn't have given it to her.'

'You might have used your common sense and guessed!' Claire rounded angrily on her mother-in-law. 'You couldn't have been unaware of the little drama that was being enacted here last night. All thanks to your precious son, who didn't even have the courtesy to consult me first before he finally decided to tell Sam the truth. You and I have been urging him to tell her for years, but our wishes were, as usual, ignored. But one call from *her*—! One call, after sixteen years! That's all it took, and Anthony was jumping to obey. Of course, I've always known I was second-best, but until yesterday evening I didn't realize quite how second-best I really am.'

Ignoring his wife, Anthony went across to his mother and put a comforting arm around her shoulders.

'It's all right, my dear,' he said quietly. 'Of course you didn't know why Sam wanted the money, so stop crying. No one's blaming you.'

'Oh, aren't they?' Claire snapped. 'Well, I am, for one. And I'll tell you something else. I'm sick of the way Cicely clings to you. I'm sick of living in her house. I want my own place, Anthony. *Our* place. Or, at least, I did once. Now I feel that perhaps it doesn't matter any more.'

'Shut up a minute, Claire!' Anthony demanded rudely. He released his mother and went across to his wife, taking her by the shoulders. The ormolu clock on the mantelpiece struck three, its delicate fluting note contrasting

306

oddly with their angry voices. 'Calm down, for God's sake! Sam had to be told some time or other, and once she'd got friendly with that Nugent boy and met Joanna Walden it seemed to be only a matter of time before she found out. It had been in my mind to tell her for several weeks. Davina's call merely decided me that the moment was ripe.' He saw Claire's mouth open in protest and forestalled her. 'OK! I realize I was wrong not to consult you, and I'm very sorry. It was a spur-of-the-moment decision, and if Sam hadn't put her head round the study door at that particular second I probably should have waited until I'd spoken to you. The shock of hearing from Davina after all these years tipped me a bit off balance. I repeat, I'm sorry.' He added sternly: 'And I think you owe my mother an apology. *I* decided to move back here, with your agreement. Mother didn't ask us to come and look after her. Anyway, I thought you liked it here, close to your own parents. Plenty of space and fresh air for the children.'

For a moment, Claire stared fiercely back at him, her dark eyes hugely dilated in the small pointed face. Then she relaxed, shrugging and twisting out of his grip. She had always been thin and waif-like. At thirty-six and after two pregnancies, she still hadn't put on any more weight, remaining at a constant seven and a half stone. The nearly black hair was untinged by grey and still cut in a Dutch-doll bob, the heavy fringe falling almost to her eyebrows. The little girl, her father's darling, Anthony thought meanly, who had never grown up.

'I'm sorry, Cicely,' she said carelessly, dropping into a deep armchair, covered in floral cretonne. 'I shouldn't have said what I did. Heaven knows why I'm letting myself get so upset. Samantha isn't my child.' She added vindictively, but not without cause: 'I've just had the bother of bringing her up. We've never really got on.'

And that, Anthony reflected, was true. There had never been any love lost between them, particularly when Samantha was younger. She had been too sharp-witted, too quick-thinking for Claire, who, in any case, had naturally preferred her own children once they were born. There had always been a coolness, a detachment, in her relationship with her step-daughter, which had made his revelation of last night easier for Samantha to bear. If there had been any deep-rooted affection, things could have been a great deal worse.

32

'YOU'RE TAKING THIS remarkably calmly,' Davina said. 'I'm proud of you.'

Joanna had gone, back to Southampton to catch the London train; back to the frenzied activity of Westminster; back to the empty, echoing, ugly little flat in Crozier Street. Davina had asked her sister why she didn't move away from the ghosts and the memories.

'Maybe I'm staying there as a kind of punishment,' Joanna had answered. 'Call it a form of masochism. Maybe I feel that I owe it to Larry to remember it was my selfishness that killed him.'

'What rubbish!' Davina had been angry. 'Stop wallowing in guilt, Jo. It's a luxury you can't afford.'

Nevertheless, she was herself experiencing something closely akin to guilt as she sat looking at her daughter. They had moved from the sitting-room into the study, where Davina could be on call, in case she was needed. But Wednesday afternoons at Forest Moor were devoted to games, and most of the girls, except the few excused on health grounds, were out on the hockey-field or the netball-pitch. The staff were either in attendance or thankfully taking a well-earned rest in their respective rooms.

At half-past three, Anthony had telephoned to say that he was driving down to Forest Moor and would be taking Samantha back with him.

'I'll be there about five-thirty. It shouldn't take longer, even in this weather.'

'You must stay to dinner,' Davina had said, matching his

coolness; although, to her annoyance, her heart was thumping.

Meantime, she had two hours in which to get to know something of her daughter. The log fire had been kindled on the hearth, adding to the background warmth of the central heating; an extravagance which seemed less of one in this bitter winter weather. In remoter parts of the country, isolated villages and houses were cut off by snow in what the television pundits were calling the Big Freeze of 1979. The west and south had escaped remarkably lightly, but the weather was still extremely cold.

Samantha's long legs, in their heavy ribbed tights and expensive black leather boots, were stretched towards the fire. She sat in the same chair which Joanna had occupied the previous day.

'I don't expect', she admitted candidly, 'that I'm as calm as I look. I don't suppose', she added shrewdly, 'that you are, either.'

Davina was betrayed into a laugh, but she did not want to make the mistake of getting drawn towards this daughter, who was going to be whisked away from her in just a few hours.

'No, probably not.' She took a deep breath. 'When you first arrived, you accused me of abandoning you. And, of course, you were right. So would you be willing to listen to my side of the story?'

Samantha hesitated before saying coolly: 'Yes. If there is one.'

'There are always two sides to everything. Trite, I'm afraid, but true.' Davina folded her hands in her lap. 'Judgement depends on how good you think the other side is. In this case, in retrospect, maybe a lot of my reasons don't hold water or, worse, seem entirely, even brutally, selfish. But I would ask you to try to remember that to me, at the time, they made a lot of sense. And also, as I'll explain, two other people were involved who conspired together to distort the truth. I realize I'm making excuses in advance, so here goes. From now on, I'll just stick to the facts.'

310

Thirty minutes later, Davina finished speaking and sat back, waiting for her daughter's verdict. Retelling the events and looking at them through Samantha's eyes, had been an unedifying experience. Actions she had never before questioned now seemed suspect. Everything she had done appeared to have been from purely selfish motives. She had accepted long ago that she was a selfish person, but there were degrees of selfishness, and it seemed to her, looking back clearly for the first time in sixteen years, that hers had been of a very high order. It was true that Anthea's influence and Anthea's lies, put into Theresa's mouth, had played their part, but they had been the more potent because they had bolstered her own inclinations. It was unnerving to discover, at thirty-six, that she did not like herself all that much.

Samantha leaned forward, elbows on knees, cupping her chin in her hands. She did not look directly at her mother, but stared instead into the heart of the fire, at the flickering blue and orange flames.

'You've done very well, haven't you?' she asked at last. 'You're very young to be the headmistress of a place like this. I suppose, if it comes to that, you were very young to be a mother.'

'Eighteen,' Davina answered. 'The same age as you are now. It was your birthday at the beginning of the month. The second.'

The blue eyes, so like Anthony's, glanced up mockingly.

'Is that meant to impress me? My mother remembers the date of my birth. Big deal.' Faintly, borne on the wind, penetrating the old-fashioned sash windows, came the sound of shouting, as someone on one of the hockey-fields scored a goal. Samantha grimaced. 'Sorry.'

'No, you've every right to be bitter.' Davina spoke quietly. 'It was wrong of me to leave you, but even worse to thrust myself back into your life.'

'Oh, I don't mind that.' Samantha sat up straighter. 'I've never really got on this well with Mum . . .' She broke off, looking confused, then amended the last word to 'Claire'. 'I

311

think I knew, in some obscure way, that we didn't belong. And she was always fonder of Malcolm and Jacqui. I can see now why she and Dad were always reticent about the date of their wedding, when they got engaged, where they were when I was born. Things like that. Because Claire must have been over twenty when she married Dad, whereas to be my mother she should have married him when she was only seventeen.' Samantha sank right back in her chair, suddenly relaxing. 'Now, at last, I feel I really know who I am. I can't think why I haven't found out before. I blame Dad. He should have told me earlier.'

'You mustn't blame your father for anything,' Davina told her sharply. 'Nor Claire. And don't you think you ought to go on calling her "Mother"? She has more right to that title than I have.'

'Oh, I've no intention of calling *you* "Mother".' The offensiveness, the hurt and bitterness were back once more in Samantha's voice. Then they were gone, replaced by excitement, showing her to be still adrift in a bewildering whirlpool of emotions. 'I shall call you "Davina", if that's all right with you.'

'Yes, of course. It's more than I deserve. I'm surprised you want to talk to me at all.'

'Oh, I don't know.' Samantha jerked forward again, linking her hands around one slim knee. 'It's rather fun to find that I'm part of a family of self-made women. Especially when one of them is a famous actress. And I've a great-aunt, too, according to Dad, who's quite well known in the profession.'

Davina frowned. 'Your father wants you to go to university, or so Joanna tells me. If that's so, he's right. Anyone with your academic record – and again I'm quoting Jo – owes it to herself. Get a good degree before deciding what to do with the rest of your life. The stage can be very problematical. You need an awful lot of luck.'

Samantha's lips set mulishly. Davina could see the resemblance to Freda.

'I've made up my mind. Nothing you or Dad can say

will make me alter it.'

Davina, thinking fast, had a sudden inspiration.

'I'll make a bargain with you,' she said. 'This summer, I'm going on a lecture tour of the States. One of those American women's organizations has asked me over to give a series of talks on fourteenth-century history. One of the stops on the itinerary is Los Angeles, so I'm taking the opportunity to stay with my sister Freda in Beverly Hills. If you promise to try for a place at university, I'll take you with me on the tour. Provided, of course, that Anthony agrees.'

She watched the warring emotions chase one another across her daughter's face. She could almost see the calculations going on in that beautiful head; the chance to be seen in Hollywood, to be snapped up by some talent scout who would immediately recognize screen potential when he saw it; the short cut to fame and fortune. Only, of course, it wouldn't be like that, but Samantha was too young and too impressionable to realize that the odds against anything of that sort happening were enormous.

Samantha's abstracted gaze suddenly narrowed, and, for a moment, Davina thought she had lost the argument. Then she said slowly: 'OK. Done. I'll try for a university place, provided my "A"s are sufficiently satisfactory and provided Dad agrees I can go with you to the States. But I warn you: getting a degree isn't going to make any difference in the long run. I'm still going to go on the stage.'

'I, the Returning Officer for the district of Avonvale, hereby declare the number of votes cast for each candidate to be as follows . . .'

The Returning Officer paused to clear his throat, and Joanna, standing behind him on the platform, in the main hall of Shipp's Causeway Comprehensive School, felt David Nugent squeeze her fingers reassuringly. It had been a long tough election campaign, aggravated by the feeling of being on the losing side. The 'winter of discontent', the prospect of the first woman Prime Minister, the

313

sense that a completely new era was beginning in British politics had all combined to strengthen the electorate's conviction that James Callaghan's Labour government was on its way out; a tired, dreary, unimaginative administration which had reached the end of its tether. During the past few weeks, Joanna had encountered more forthright animosity from Conservative voters, more apathy from the hard core of Labour, and more waverers, doubters and 'don't knows' than on any previous occasion since Lawrence had first contested the seat, fifteen years before.

The Liberal candidate, standing next to Joanna, shuffled his feet and muttered something to his wife. The Conservative stared straight ahead, his huge blue rosette half-masking his long pointed chin.

When, four weeks earlier, the Leader of the Opposition, Margaret Thatcher, had tabled a motion of 'no confidence' in the Government, it had been carried by 311 votes to 310, and a general election had immediately been called. Now, on this evening of 3 May 1979, the moment of truth was at last at hand. Joanna gripped David Nugent's hand even more convulsively as the Returning Officer, throat at last cleared of phlegm, continued with his announcement.

'Markham, Henry George: 19,421; Davidson, Peter Alan: 8,926; Walden, Joanna Mary: 20,452 . . .'

Her supporters, in the body of the hall, erupted in frenzy, and the Returning Officer's final statement, announcing her as the duly elected Member of Parliament for Avonvale, was all but drowned. She had done it! She had increased her majority by nearly seven hundred votes.

The other two candidates came across to congratulate her and shake her hand – the Liberal, who had never had any hope of winning, cheerfully, the Conservative, who had scented victory, looking tired and disappointed.

'Thank you,' she said to both of them, and turned to David Nugent, who was grinning broadly, unable to conceal his delight. 'And thank you. I know how many hours you've put in during the last four weeks, and what time you've been getting to bed, if at all. I just want you to know how very much I appreciate it.'

It was time for her to step up to the microphone and make a short speech. She looked out over the sea of faces, some delighted, some sullen, and said quickly and a little breathlessly: 'Thank you for your support and your confidence. I hope that, whatever your political persuasion, you won't hesitate to call on me if you have any problem with which you think I can help.'

Her supporters and party workers were waiting impatiently to sweep her off to the Labour committee rooms, where a celebration party was already in progress.

'Supposing I'd lost,' she said to David Nugent.

He grimaced. 'We'd have had the party anyway, but it would have been a wake. As it is, have some cider. I'm afraid we couldn't run to champagne.'

As the night wore on, however, and the television set in the corner kept spewing forth the bad news, it became clear that Labour had lost, and lost badly. By six o'clock the next morning, as they sat on, bleary-eyed, half-heartedly nibbling at the last of the sandwiches, now limp and curling at the edges, and munching cold and soggy sausage rolls, James Callaghan had already conceded defeat and Margaret Thatcher had made history by becoming Britain's first woman Prime Minister. Joanna, dazed from excitement and lack of sleep, could scarcely credit that she had hung on to her seat. But her victory had lost some of its gloss, and she did the obligatory 'thank-you' tour of the constituency in a very subdued frame of mind. Afterwards, she went back to the Nugents' house in Oxford Road, fell on the bed in the spare room, which was now regarded by both David and the children as hers, and was asleep before she had time to kick off her shoes.

When she eventually awoke it was mid-afternoon and David was standing beside the bed, holding a cup of tea.

'I've been up twice before,' he said, 'but you looked so peaceful it seemed a shame to disturb you. There have been masses of telephone calls. People ringing up to congratulate you, including your parents and your grandfather and both your sisters.'

Joanna sat up, conscious that she must look a mess, and took the cup of tea gratefully. It was warm and sweet and stimulating. After a few sips, she began to feel better.

'Both my sisters?'

'Yes, Freda called from California as soon as she heard. There was also a call from that girl Stuart knocks around with, Samantha Douglas. She wanted to add her congratulations to the rest, which surprised me somewhat. I had her and all her family down as dyed-in-the-wool Tories.'

'Oh, yes, they are,' Joanna said awkwardly. She had mentioned nothing to David, as yet, about her relationship to Samantha. Davina had given her a brief summary of what had transpired between her and her daughter after Joanna had left Forest Moor, and added that Anthony agreed to her proposal that she take Samantha with her to America in the summer. Meantime, Samantha had apparently returned to Lyncombe Manor and was carrying on as normal. No general announcement had been made, and Joanna felt that it was not up to her to leak the story. When her niece wanted Stuart Nugent to know the truth, she would presumably tell him herself. Joanna added: 'I suppose, having met me, she thought it was the polite thing to do. I hope you were suitably grateful.'

'You know me.' David sat down on the edge of the bed. 'A born diplomat. You look all in.'

'I feel it. And the confusion of my emotions doesn't help. Inwardly, I'm laughing and crying, glad and sad all at once. This suave sophisticated woman-of-the-world act is just a front.'

He laughed, showing even, very white teeth. David Nugent had given up smoking some years ago, and nowadays, instead of finding himself the odd man out at social gatherings and parties, he was becoming one of a growing band of people who were convinced that tobacco was bad for the health.

'I know what you mean. The Conservatives are in with an overall majority of forty-four and a majority over Labour of seventy-one.'

Joanna groaned. 'I suppose, after the chaos of the last six months, it was only to be expected. Oh, well, we'll just have to resign ourselves to a spell in Opposition. I must be thankful, at least, that I'm home and dry.'

'More than that, I think,' David said, looking suddenly smug. 'Fifteen minutes ago, someone called from James Callaghan's office. I lied and said you were out, but he wants you to ring back as soon as possible. Our leader would like a word with you, it seems. I think it may mean promotion to the front benches.'

Joanna choked, thrust her almost-empty cup and its saucer into his outstretched hand and struggled off the bed. As she ran out of the bedroom in her stockinged feet, David shouted after her: 'The number's on the pad by the phone.' Joanna nearly fell down the last three steps and grabbed the receiver.

Five minutes later, she hung up and turned to David, who had followed her downstairs.

'He's offered me the job of Shadow Spokeswoman on Education. I accepted.'

'No more than you deserve.' David led the way from the hall into the kitchen, where he started to prepare the evening meal. 'You've worked damned hard these past four years. You've hung on to your seat when all about you were losing theirs, and you've increased your majority against the national trend. That deserves some recognition.'

She watched him, busy peeling potatoes, and wondered how on earth he had coped for all this time without a wife, with two teenage children to bring up and a demanding job to hold down. Yet he had managed, only occasionally showing signs of stress.

'You know, I couldn't possibly have done it without you,' she said.

He glanced over his shoulder and grinned. 'Of course I

317

know that. I'm not this modest self-effacing chap you seem to think me. I'm very quietly very big-headed, or hadn't you noticed?'

Joanna did not answer. She was too busy struggling with the astonishing revelation that she was in love with David Nugent.

Just when she had fallen in love with him, Joanna found it impossible to say. She had always liked David, admired and respected him for the way in which he had held his family together in the nightmare days following his wife's death. He had always been a ready and sympathetic listener, and his rock-like strength had supported her through difficult and stressful times. She had grown to depend on him, she realized now, more than she knew. Solid, dependable, there whenever she needed him, he had been the background to her life for so many years that she had failed to see him clearly. It was only now, suddenly, for almost the first time, that she was conscious of him as a whole person.

And with that consciousness had come the knowledge that she loved him, deeply, passionately, with the sort of love which would endure. She wanted him, needed him, both as a lover and as a friend; someone with whom to share the rest of her life.

33

'DAVEY darling! How lovely to see you. And this, I suppose, is Sam. What a turn-up for the book, you playing mother!'

The house in Bel Air was a large, single-storey, Spanish-style building, with all the trappings of Hollywood stardom; guard dogs; electrically operated, high-security gates; a kidney-shaped swimming-pool; a Rolls-Royce and a Chevrolet in the garage; its own screening and projection rooms; and several acres of carefully stocked and watered gardens.

Samantha, still reeling from the pace and sheer hard work of the trip with Davina, which, so far, had covered twenty-two states, was less enamoured of Hollywood and its sights than she might otherwise have been. Until now, she and her mother had stayed in the homes of local chapter officials of the Daughters of Magna Carta, and the very charming lady who had met them this morning at Los Angeles airport had expressed disappointment that, on this occasion, they had made other arrangements.

She didn't even seem impressed when we told her who we were visiting, Samantha thought, covertly taking stock of this second, and so far unknown, aunt.

She was a little disappointed. She had seen several of Freda's films, including the British-made *Watershed*, and had not made sufficient allowance for the effects of soft lighting and concealing make-up. Her first impression was of a very ordinary woman, not so pretty as Davina, in navy slacks and white silk blouse and a great deal of heavy, chunky gold jewellery. Freda's face, though bronzed by the Californian sun, was devoid of make-up except for a smear of blue eye-shadow.

'We're having tea by the pool,' she said, leading the way. 'Carmelita and her husband will see to your luggage.'

Samantha and Davina followed obediently, leaving the Mexican servants to dispose of their cases, across a room where nearly everything, from carpet to ceiling, was in a soft, rather sickly shade of pink, out on to a sun-drenched patio. Two men, sitting in pool-side loungers, were maintaining a hostile silence.

Freda said carelessly: 'This is my husband, Jeff. Jeff Warwick. And that idle young puppy over there' – her voice, until now high and brittle, dropped to a low, suddenly tender note – 'is Steve Jordan. You may have seen him in a television series called "The Man from Venus". It was a science-fiction thing, but I don't know if it was ever shown in England.'

'It was a floperoo,' Jeff Warwick remarked acidly, making no attempt to get up to greet the new arrivals. 'A real no-goer.'

Davina was instantly conscious of the tension in the air. After only ten minutes, she was beginning to wish that she and Samantha had stayed in Los Angeles. The cause of dissension was not far to seek. Steve Jordan, young, handsome, strong, blond and blue-eyed, looked to be in his early twenties. Not a day over twenty-three, if that, Davina decided. What the Americans called a hunk of beefcake.

Jeff Warwick, on the other hand, was, like Freda, in his mid-thirties, but ageing badly. The mixture of Chinese and Italian blood which had given his face a distinctive piquancy when he was younger threatened to degenerate into something much odder and uglier with the advancing years. Davina had never met him in the flesh before, but she had seen *Watershed* when it was first released, and recognized that the thickening waistline and bags beneath the eyes were not part of the original image. It was obvious, too, after an hour in his company, that he still adored Freda, who, in her turn, was head over heels in love with

Steve Jordan. This was not going to be an easy visit. Thank God it would be mercifully brief.

It had not been the easiest of trips altogether, and Samantha had soon regretted her bargain with Davina. The lecture tour had demanded a stamina that had taxed the strength of both women, but Davina at least had the compensation of being the centre of attention and of flowing adrenalin before addressing each meeting. Samantha, on the contrary, rapidly became bored with her subordinate role. The stopovers in each city were too short to permit her seeing much of anything: her impressions of Detroit, Maine, Michigan, Seattle and the rest were mainly from plane and car windows; a quick bird's-eye view or ribbons of urban development which flashed past her before she had time to assimilate them. She was, on the other hand, thoroughly conversant with American open-plan living and the warmth of American hospitality, but they were poor substitutes for what she had hoped to gain from the visit.

She had, moreover, begun to suspect quite early on that her mother had conned her. She had passed her A levels with grades sufficiently high to win a place at Bristol University, so she had kept her side of the bargain. But long before they reached Los Angeles she had realized that their visit would only be of sufficient duration for Davina to deliver her lecture, before they would be off again on the final leg of their journey to New York, and then back home to England. There would be no Hollywood parties, no thunderstruck talent scouts, no tours of the studios. She would be able to say that she had spent two nights and one whole day at the home of her aunt, Freda Marshall, and that was as far as it went. Samantha felt cheated and bitterly disappointed.

When they had drunk their iced tea beside the pool, Freda said: 'You must come and see Antigone. She's a darling.'

'Why on earth did you call the poor child that?' asked Davina critically, wishing it was not so hot. She had never

321

liked heat; it made her wilt. Samantha appeared to thrive on it.

Freda's eyes followed Steve Jordan's bronzed young body as he rose leisurely from his chair, shed his towelling robe and dived into the pool.

'I played the part once, and the name must have stuck.' She added with a shrug: 'In any case, it's already shortened to Ann or Annie, so what does it matter? At least I've broken with the family tradition of giving the girls names which can be shortened to boys'. Even you fell into that trap. Anyway, come and see her. Samantha, do you want to say hello to your cousin?'

Samantha shook her head. 'I think I'd rather unpack and have a swim, if you don't mind. I'm terribly hot.'

'You don't look it.' Freda's tone was acid. 'Cool as a cucumber, if I may say so.' Her eyes were once again on Steve Jordan, who had swum back to the side of the pool and was treading water, shaking the drops from his face and hair in a bright iridescent fountain.

'Let the kid come on in, Freddie. She can see Annie any time.'

Davina noted the angry flush on Jeff Warwick's face. It was plain that he resented Steve Jordan's assumption of authority.

'Is Steve a frequent visitor?' she asked her sister, when the Mexican maid had been summoned to show Samantha to her room and help her unpack, and Freda had led the way to the nursery. 'He seems very much at home.'

'He doesn't live here – yet!' Freda pushed open the door of the high white room where the two-year-old Antigone, practically dressed in pale yellow shorts and T-shirt, was having tea, assisted by her English nanny. The elfin face beneath the straight black hair was suddenly wreathed in smiles at the sight of her mother. Freda walked forward, lifted the child out of her chair and smothered her with kisses, oblivious of the honey and peanut butter which were being smeared on her white silk blouse.

'OK, Mabel,' she said, nodding towards the nurse. 'I'll

322

finish giving Antigone her tea. Take a break. You've earned it. This, by the way, is my sister, Davina Marshall. Davey, meet Mabel Patterson. She's from Keswick, in Cumbria.'

'A very beautiful part of the world,' Davina murmured politely as the two women shook hands. 'Where did you find her?' she asked Freda, as the nursery door closed behind the nanny.

'Oh, there are loads of English nurses and domestics in the States,' Freda answered carelessly as she settled into an armchair, her daughter on her lap. 'The pay's so much better than at home. Well, what do you think of her? Annie, I mean, not Mabel Patterson.'

Davina sat down in another armchair and regarded her niece thoughtfully. 'She's very like Jeff,' she said at last.

Freda nodded in agreement. 'She is, isn't she? All the more strange that I should love her so much, when I can't stand the sight of her father.'

Davina's gaze strayed to the frieze of nursery-rhyme characters marching round the dazzling white walls. All this clear white light was hurting her eyes. She could only presume that the child was used to it.

'As bad as that, is it? Jo did once give me a hint that you weren't madly in love with Jeff Warwick.'

'And that's the understatement of the century. I've stuck it for five years because I felt I owed him that much, and, after Annie was born, I felt, too, that I owed it to her. But these last twelve months, since Jeff's career really hit rock bottom, he's become absolutely impossible to live with. He's on the booze and pills from morning to night. Tranquillizers, pep-ups, soothers, goers; he takes them all, just like a child eating sweets. It's not altogether his fault; that's why I've tried to stand by him. That bitch Gabriella's never ceased hounding him from the day of the divorce, and the public and press have been right behind her. She's bankrupted him, and what money there is is mine. And that's because I've never refused anything that was offered me. Those two shitty films, commercials, a crap television

323

series that was never, thank God, screened at home, chat shows, you name it, I've done it and I've kept our heads above water. But Jeff – the great Jeff Warwick – he could never get used to the idea of not being a hot box-office property, able to choose his own parts. He wouldn't lower himself to do the things I've done.' Antigone, who had been eating chocolate-chip ice cream, now scrambled off her mother's lap and toddled over to an elaborate four-foot doll's house, where she began pulling all the contents out on to the floor. Freda ignored her and continued: 'So I've had enough. As far as I'm concerned, it's over. It was over long before I met Steve' – her voice grew soft as she mentioned the name, and her eyes were misty – 'but I can't deny that knowing him has finally made up my mind for me. Especially now that I'm going to have his baby.'

Davina looked startled, and her wandering attention was caught once more. Unlike Joanna, she had never been a good listener to other people's problems.

'You're pregnant?'

'Yup. Two months. And it's definitely Steve's. Jeff and I haven't made love in over a year. The child's due next March some time, which will give me just long enough to complete the load of garbage I'm working on at present. A television movie, loosely based on an Agatha Christie story, set in a version of rural England which doesn't exist outside the American imagination. You know the sort of thing.'

'Does Jeff know yet?'

'No. I thought it wouldn't be fair on you and Samantha to tell him before your visit. And talking of Samantha – I'm agog. How come, after all these years, you've finally heard the call of motherhood? Tell me all about it.'

Samantha returned to the pool-side, thanking her lucky stars that she had, after all, packed the one-piece black bathing suit which she had bought in Bath just before leaving on the trip. To call it a one-piece was true, but misleading, the costume being cut to conceal the minimum

324

and reveal the maximum amount of flesh. She had seen it in the window of Jolly's in Milsom Street and, in spite of the price, had known she must have it. It was very expensive, but Anthony had been generous in his appreciation of her passing her A levels.

When she had tried it on at home, however, Samantha had experienced some qualms. The bathing suit was extremely revealing, and she had entertained some doubts about Davina's reactions. So she had packed her old school swimming costume instead, but at the very last moment had decided to take the black one, just in case; although in case of what she wouldn't have liked to hazard a guess.

Now, though, she knew. She had never in her life seen a man she thought as handsome as Steve Jordan. She guessed him to be a few years older than herself, twenty-two or twenty-three. Just the right age. Far too young for Freda.

Jeff Warwick's chair was empty, and he was nowhere to be seen. Steve Jordan was lying on a scarlet air-bed in the middle of the pool, watching for her. When she reappeared, he yelled: 'Come on in!'

At school, Samantha had been good at all sports, but particularly at swimming. She went to the far end and climbed to the top platform of the diving-board, executing a near-perfect forward somersault as she dived in. Surfacing again, she found herself within a few strokes of the air-bed.

'Hey! That was some dive!' Steve Jordan grinned appreciatively and moved over, stretching out a lean brown hand to help her climb aboard. 'Yes, ma'am. That was pretty impressive.'

'Thanks.' Samantha rolled on to her back, suddenly and uncomfortably aware of the amount of herself that she was showing. Steve, however, appeared to find nothing amiss and gave her an admiring glance. No doubt he was used to such scanty costumes.

'So you're Freddie's niece,' he said. 'How come she

325

never mentioned you until last week? And I sure as heck haven't seen a photograph of you anywhere. I should have remembered.'

'It's a long story.' Samantha closed her eyes. The sunlight was as warm and as comforting across her wet body as a fur coat. 'My parents were divorced when I was two. My mother and I have only recently met up again, after sixteen years.'

She was acutely conscious of his proximity; of the long brown legs with their faint fuzzing of little blond hairs; of the brief blue swimming trunks; of the muscular chest with its mat of fair hair.

'Divorce!' he exclaimed. 'Don't talk to me about divorce. I had five step-mothers before I was ten years old. I guess that must be some sort of record, huh?'

Samantha giggled. 'I guess so.' It was all too easy to slip into the vernacular. She sighed contentedly. 'Mmm. This is lovely. I wish I could stay.'

'No problem. I'll fix it with Freddie.'

Samantha sighed again, this time regretfully. 'My father wouldn't let me, and Davina would create hell. I'm going up to university in October.'

His fingers clasped hers firmly. They felt hard and muscular. He had the strong square hands of the practical man. The air-bed shifted slightly beneath the weight of their bodies, and the sunlight rippled across the surface of the pool. The distant mountains shimmered in the heat. A rose bush shed its crimson petals on the water.

Freda, emerging from the house with her sister, took in the whole picture at a glance. No one knew better than she did the value of a romantic atmosphere, or its dangers. Davina saw her features set and harden.

'Enjoying yourself, you two?' she called. Her voice, even to her own ears, was harsh and grating.

Samantha jumped, nearly overturning the air-bed, but Steve Jordan grabbed her just in time. He shouted guiltily: 'You should get two air-beds, Freddie. It would save your guests having to share one.'

326

Freda ignored this. 'Time you started getting ready for dinner,' she said. 'We're eating early tonight.'

'Sure. We're coming.' Steve rolled off the air-bed and swam leisurely in her direction, cleaving the water with firm easy strokes. Samantha followed, climbing out of the pool to stand beside him. She had temporarily forgotten the brevity of her swimming costume and only recollected it when she noticed Freda and Davina's eyes riveted to her body. Now that it was wet, what there was of the suit fitted her like a second skin. Steve, too, was taking another look.

'That's some outfit,' he observed, his blue eyes sparkling with renewed enthusiasm. 'Davey, your daughter sure has a swell figure. What do you say, Freddie? Isn't this niece of yours a sight for sore eyes?'

'What I say', Freda responded icily, 'is that you'd do well to keep your eyes to yourself, Steve. Especially now that you're about to become a father.'

34

'DID YOU enjoy it?' David Nugent asked, as they left the theatre. He took Joanna's elbow and guided her through the crush.

He had come up to London for the weekend on party business, and had arrived unexpectedly on the Friday morning. He contacted Joanna at the House of Commons. She had been collecting her mail from the Member's Post Office, just off the Central Lobby, when an attendant had told her that she was wanted on the telephone.

'Hi, Jo!' At the sound of his voice, her heart began to pound. 'I'm a day early. A friend's given me two tickets for the National tonight. He and his wife were going, but now one of their children has been taken ill. It's the Olivier Theatre. Opening night of something called *Amadeus*, and I thought you might like to go. Know anything about it?'

'I know Peter Shaffer's the author. He wrote *Royal Hunt of the Sun*. That was brilliant. This play's about Mozart and Salieri. I'd love to go.'

'Good.' He sounded genuinely pleased. 'I'll pick you up in Crozier Street at seven. Give us time for a drink first and we'll go somewhere for supper afterwards. I'm staying at the usual place, by the way.'

That meant the Cumberland. He liked big impersonal hotels of the kind that Joanna thought of as all chrome and plastic. He hated small intimate places and being overwhelmed by personal service.

'You're mad,' Joanna would say, and he would laugh.

'You'll never change me.'

She did not want to. She loved him just as he was. She could feel the pressure of his fingers now, like a small electric shock, through the material of her dress. She wondered if he had any idea at all how she felt about him.

'The play was wonderful,' she said. 'Thank you.'

'Good. Splendid. I thought it sounded like your sort of thing.' He turned his head and smiled at her. 'I'm glad you enjoyed it.'

They paused in the foyer to put their coats on. It was a cold night. With 5 November only three days away, there was already a smell of fireworks in the air.

'Come on,' he said, 'we'll get a taxi. I've asked them to reserve a table at the hotel.'

In the back of the taxi, they sat distanced from one another, just as they had sat formally side by side in the theatre all evening, touching only by accident, each confined to his and her own space. Joanna had to keep reminding herself that they were only friends. There were still moments when she wondered if he even really liked her.

She remembered their first meeting, all those years ago, when Lawrence had been standing as Avonvale's no-hope Labour candidate, just to gain experience. She had gone along to lend her support, but had deserted Lawrence as soon as Alex had crooked his little finger. And five years ago it had been Alex again, and her involvement with him, which had led indirectly to her husband's death. David had always liked and respected Lawrence; considered that, in one way and another, life had dealt him an imperfect hand. He probably thought of her as the joker in the pack. But, then, again, maybe he didn't. She never really knew what David Nugent was thinking.

The taxi dropped them outside the Cumberland, and they went inside to the restaurant. Watching David, as he ordered the food and the wine, Joanna wondered how she could ever have supposed herself in love with Alex. She loved Alex, which was different, but there had always been something wrong with their relationship, a fact

329

which she had resolutely ignored. It had been her inability – or refusal – she wasn't quite sure which – to distinguish between loving and being in love which had been at the root of the problem.

She heard from Alex from time to time and wrote to him in return. He was living quietly with Derek Conway on an allowance made to him by his mother, after his father had thrown him out of the house and out of the firm. Olwen, to do her justice, had refused to add to the scandal by suing for divorce, and still lived at King's Acre Court with her parents-in-law. Alex had imputed other, less worthy motives to his wife's decision, but Joanna had replied that he should be more charitable and give Olwen the benefit of the doubt. He had promptly telephoned her and begged her not to be so self-righteous. It didn't suit her, he had said, and they had both dissolved into laughter.

They had become like brother and sister. No, perhaps not quite that, she thought, forking up a mouthful of smoked salmon and scrambled eggs; more like very close friends; the sort of friendship more usually found between two women. Which figured, she supposed. Their meetings were rare, Alex being conscious of the damage that being seen in his company might do to her career. Tom Birkenshaw was still the MP for West Yorkshire Moors and still inimical in his attitude towards Joanna. So she and Alex kept in touch by letter and telephone.

David Nugent remarked: 'You're very quiet. Is it anything I've said?'

'Of course not. I was just thinking about the play,' she lied.

'Is there any truth in it?' he asked. 'Did Salieri murder Mozart?'

Before she could reply, a voice behind her exclaimed: 'Jo! Fancy meeting you here.'

She glanced round to see Davina advancing towards them.

Joanna's first instinct was to reply in kind. The

330

Cumberland Hotel was not one of her sister's haunts, but out of deference to David's feelings she merely replied: 'I had no idea you were in town. Why aren't you staying at your club?'

'I am. But I was passing in a taxi when I saw you come in, and as we haven't seen one another lately I thought it was too good an opportunity to miss. So I got the taxi-driver to drop me in Bryanston Street and walked back. I'm sorry. I didn't realize you had someone with you.' She smiled at David.

Reluctantly, Joanna made the introductions, noting crossly that David was looking rather overawed.

'We haven't actually met before,' he said, 'but of course I've seen you often on the box, most recently in that new BBC programme, "Question Time". And I watched the series on education. You were the only one who consistently talked sense.'

Davina flushed with pleasure. 'How kind of you to say so. As a matter of fact, the reason I'm in London is because I was doing another "Question Time" last night. So I'm staying on for a couple of days to do some shopping.' She glanced over her shoulder at a waiter who was anxious to show her to a seat. 'Would it be all right if I joined you? I'm not butting in?'

'Of course not! We'd be delighted, wouldn't we, Jo?'

'Delighted,' Joanna echoed hollowly. She said nothing more until the waiter had taken Davina's order. Then she asked: 'How's Samantha?'

It was some months now since Samantha's relationship with Davina had become common knowledge. Samantha had made no secret of it, telling Stuart Nugent, who had passed on the information to his father, who, in his turn, had made it plain to Joanna that he knew. So she had put him in possession of all the facts. What he made of them she wasn't sure. As ever, he kept his opinions to himself.

If she had thought to disconcert her sister, her luck was out. Davina replied without a trace of embarrassment: 'She's playing the dutiful daughter with Claire at the moment. I've ceased to be flavour of the month. She felt she was tricked into going to university, although heaven knows why! I kept my side of the bargain. And Anthony says she's beginning to enjoy it. Being Bristol, she can live at home as long as she wants to, and she switched at the last moment to doing a four-year course in drama and English. That's mollified her somewhat. Of course, what she really wanted was to stay on in Hollywood with Freda and be "discovered"!' Davina flashed a smile at David Nugent. 'Do you know about me and my daughter? Has Jo put you in the picture?'

He smiled back. 'Yes, she has. Has she told you all about me?'

Jo exclaimed angrily: 'Shut up, the pair of you! You're making me sound like some horrible gossipy old woman.'

Two pairs of eyes, one grey and one hazel, were turned towards her in astonishment. Both David and her sister seemed taken aback by her annoyance. Davina reached out a hand and laid it on Joanna's arm.

'Jo love, don't be like that. Nothing was further from my mind, and I'm sure it never crossed David's.' How easily she had slipped into first-name terms. 'It's perfectly natural that you should have told us about one another. He knows that I've been a rotten mother – no mother at all, in fact – while he's been a marvellous father.'

'I wouldn't say that,' David disclaimed with unbecoming modesty. At least, Joanna thought it unbecoming. 'As Davina says, it's natural that we should be acquainted with each other's background. And all my information doesn't come from you. Samantha hasn't been exactly discreet in what she says to Stuart.'

'Good heavens! I was forgetting you've met Samantha.' Davina turned back to him, her concern for her sister instantly forgotten. 'How stupid of me, when it was her friendship with your son which . . . how shall I put it?'

'Sparked off your latent maternalism,' Joanna suggested drily.

Davina finally blushed and gave a half-laugh which ended with a shrug.

'And a fat lot of good it's done anyone. I've probably caused more harm than good. Although', she added, brightening a little 'Anthony doesn't seem to think so. He's coming down to Forest Moor next week to see me. He feels now that Sam knows all about me I might as well be kept in the picture.'

'And what does Claire feel?' Joanna couldn't help asking.

The waiter returned with her and David's main course and Davina's smoked salmon.

'Anthony doesn't say much about her at all,' Davina admitted, picking up a fork. 'I don't think they get on . . .' Her voice tailed off, as though she were anxious to change the subject.

Joanna, however, was in no mood to let her sister off the hook so easily, and ready to pursue the subject, when David gallantly stepped in and forestalled her.

'We've been to the opening night of the new Peter Shaffer play,' he said. '*Amadeus*. About Mozart and Salieri. Before you arrived, I was asking Jo if there was any truth in the story that Salieri was responsible for Mozart's death.' He tilted his head to one side and smiled at Davina. 'Do you know?'

Joanna wanted to shout: 'I was the one you asked that question. Why don't you wait for me to tell you?' But she knew how childish it would sound. So she maintained a morose silence, hoping against hope that her sister would not know the answer.

But of course she knew. Smiling graciously, Davina was already murmuring something about Ignaz Moscheles's autobiography and his account of a visit to his teacher, Salieri, when the latter was a very old man.

'Salieri assured Moscheles that there was no truth whatsoever in the rumour that he poisoned Mozart. "Tell the world, dear Moscheles, that old Salieri, who is on his death-bed, has told you so." '

Trust her elder sister, Joanna thought bitterly, not just to know the answer, but to be able to quote chapter and verse. Sourly, she noted David's attitude of rapt attention.

Joanna passed a bad night, unable to rid herself of the notion that David Nugent had been smitten with Davina, both by her looks and by her erudition.

The Crozier Street flat had never felt emptier. Joanna had never felt more alone. At one in the morning, she conceded defeat and switched on her bedside lamp. She tried reading for a while, but even her favourite Barbara Pym novel failed to soothe her. She needed company, someone to talk to. At last, in desperation, she rang Alex.

It was Derek Conway who answered. He sounded cross, as well he might, at being roused at such an unearthly hour of the morning. There was a lot of bad-tempered muttering until, finally, Alex's voice sounded at the other end of the line.

'Jo, what's the matter?'

'Nothing really. Can't sleep. Just feeling down.'

'OK,' he said. They were long past the stage of demanding explanations of one another. Whenever one was in distress of any sort, the other was always there to offer comfort. 'What do you want to talk about?'

'I don't know.' Then, after a pause, she added: 'How about sisters?'

He chuckled. 'Don't have any, but I get the picture. Which sister in particular? The schoolmarm or the film star?'

'Davey'll do for a start. She's always been the disruptive force in our family, snatching at other people's happiness. The trouble is, she doesn't mean to be disruptive. She just is.'

'You don't have to let her be. You're too negative where Davey's concerned.'

'I'm a negative person.' Joanna heard the note of self-pity and was horrified by it. 'Sorry, Alex. That's not true. But I'm not as positive as she is. Put it that way.'

'Again, not true. Jo love, you're a woman of definite personality. You wouldn't have got where you are today, on the Labour front benches, if you hadn't been. Fight for what you want, whatever it is, and even if you eventually lose you'll have the satisfaction of having put up a struggle. I thought it was probably Freddie you wanted to talk about. She's been hitting the headlines again with her divorce from Jeff Warwick and all those messy child-custody proceedings.'

Joanna sighed. 'She's hopeless. Whatever does she see in Steve Jordan? Apart from his looks, that is. Did you ever see any of that ghastly series he made, "The man from Venus"?'

'I caught the odd episode. And *odd* is the operative word. Didn't the ITV people cancel it after just one series? Mind you, I thought he was rather splendid. All flashing teeth and gleaming biceps.' The throaty chuckle sounded again, this time in self-mockery. 'Pity he has to sit on his brains, though. Must be very uncomfortable for him. Must be a peculiarity of Venusians.'

'Perhaps he really is one,' Joanna suggested, her mood lifting to match Alex's. 'Davey tells me Freddie's pregnant by him. Perhaps my future niece or nephew will be born complete with antennae.'

'Bitchy, darling. Bitchy. Feeling better?'

'Yes, heaps.' It was on the tip of her tongue to add, 'I bet Derek must be fuming,' but somehow she couldn't. The thought of them in bed together disturbed her, and she preferred not to acknowledge the fact, however obliquely. Instead she said: 'Thanks, Alex.'

'For what?'

'For just being there.'

'I'll always be here.' He added quickly: 'No, no! That's tempting fate. As long as I can be, I'll be here whenever you want me. And Jo!'

'Yes?'

'If you have to go down, go down fighting.'

When Anthony was ushered in, Davina was seated behind her desk. She rose and very formally held out her hand.

'Tony. How kind of you to come.'

335

She had deliberately arranged to receive him in her study. Ever since that day, almost six months ago now, when she had contacted him about Samantha, she had been disturbingly conscious of her steadily increasing affection for him. For years, her emotions had been ruthlessly suppressed; stoppered down like a genie in a bottle. Then, briefly, she had allowed herself to remove the cork and the damage had been done. However hard she tried to put the genie back into its prison, it eluded her. And, strangely, its years in the dark had only made it grow stronger.

Anthony took her hand and pressed it, refusing to play her game.

'You've done well for yourself, Davey,' he said. 'Maybe that aunt of yours was right after all. Have you been happy?'

'Yes, in my fashion. My lifestyle wouldn't suit everyone.' She tried to keep her voice as formal as her handshake. She needed to get the meeting back on a more correct footing. 'Won't you sit down?' She indicated the chair facing her on the other side of the desk.

He did not seem to hear her, but instead moved restlessly around the room, plainly in the grip of some powerful emotion. Davina was at a loss. The interview was not going the way she had planned.

'Please,' she said again, 'won't you sit down?' and was annoyed at the uncertainty in her voice.

He stood in the middle of the room, blinking at her, obviously not seeing her, his thoughts turned inward. Then, as though his vision had suddenly cleared, he moved abruptly towards the desk, leaning on it, braced by his arms and hands.

'I still love you, you know.' His voice was hoarse, and he spoke jerkily, as though it took an enormous effort to say the words. There was a pause before he forced himself to go on: 'There's never been anyone else. Not from the time we first met. Sam's my favourite child because she's yours. I've tried not to show it. I've fought against it desperately. I

336

suppose it's why I put off telling her the truth for all those years. I didn't want to talk about you. I tried to forget you.' There was an even longer pause. Davina did not know what to say. She could see by his face what it was costing him to make these admissions. Finally, he asked: 'How about you? How do you feel about me? Have your feelings changed towards me?'

'I . . . really, I . . .' Davina swallowed and said frantically: 'I thought you'd come here to discuss Samantha. Surely that was the purpose of this meeting?'

He sat down and buried his face in his hands. When he eventually looked up, she noticed that his eyes were red-rimmed and heavy, like those of someone who had been sleeping badly.

'Yes. Yes, it was,' he answered unsteadily. 'But ever since you asked me to come I haven't been able to think of anyone or anything but you. Your invitation made me realize how badly I wanted to see you.' He took a deep breath. 'Sam's OK. For the time being, at least. But I think she'll always be something of a problem. She's strong-willed, like you. Davey!' He leaned forward again, hands clasped so tightly between his knees that she could see the white gleam of his knuckles. 'Davey, I'm . . . I'm going to ask Claire for a divorce. Wait a minute! Don't say anything just yet! Hear me out. We haven't been happy for a long time. Perhaps we never were. I've thought and thought about it, and I just don't know any more. She can have custody of Malcolm and Jacqueline, provided I can see them sometimes.' He lifted a ravaged face and stared at the ceiling, as though hoping for some sort of answer to be written there in letters of fire. 'Oh, dear God! I know it's a rotten thing to ask of her, but I swear I wouldn't even have contemplated it if I wasn't certain that she's as indifferent to me as I am to her.'

Davina still said nothing, but her heart was beating in quick suffocating strokes. Anthony still loved her, had always loved her, she thought exultantly. She barely registered what he was saying about Claire. Claire and her feelings were unimportant.

337

He got up and came round the desk, perching on the edge and taking both her hands in his. 'Davey, I'm going to ask you a question.' Again, his voice shook with emotion. 'I don't want an answer straightaway. Give yourself time to think. But if Claire does agree to a divorce do you see any prospect, however remote, that one day you might agree to marry me?'

35

THE PARTY MEETING broke up at four o'clock, and Joanna left the committee room, on the ground floor of the House of Commons, a few minutes later. In these early months of 1980, inflation, under the Tories, was heading for 20 per cent and unemployment for over 2 million, and the Opposition Shadow Cabinet had been planning its strategy.

She checked the message-board in the Members' Lobby to see if there was a light beneath her name, but when she found the bulb unlit headed for her tiny office on the second floor. As she pushed open the door, she recollected that her secretary had left the day before, to go to Australia, and until this moment Joanna had had no time to speculate on her replacement. A familiar figure rose from behind the ancient typewriter.

Joanna exclaimed joyfully: 'Selina! Selina Driver!'

'The very same.' Selina, as blonde and as bubbly as ever, if a little older and heavier, beamed happily in return. She was wearing a very smart grey suit, dark red blouse and a pair of black-rimmed spectacles, pushed high on her forehead. 'I've been appointed as your new secretary. And, yes, the name is still Driver. I've thought about getting married once or twice, but never quite made it. I got fed up with my promotion prospects at the MOD, so I took a secretarial course to augment my ability to speak three languages. A sad comment on our times, I felt, but there you are. Possession of a degree doesn't necessarily mean good job prospects nowadays.'

'Vote Labour, that's the answer,' Joanna said with a grin.

'Whatever happened to our old friend Sweeting?'

'God knows. And only He cares,' Selina answered tartly. 'Sweeting got promotion eventually and passed out of my life.' She turned back to her desk. 'There's a pile of mail here, awaiting your attention. Mostly, I'm afraid, from disgruntled constituents. There's a request for you to open the Avonvale Summer Fayre, some time in August, and there was a telephone call from your sister Davina, asking that you contact her as soon as possible at Forest Moor school. I've written the number on your message-pad, in case you've forgotten it.'

Joanna sat down at her desk and stared thoughtfully at the Forest Moor number. She had seen very little of her elder sister in recent months, but had heard plenty about her from David Nugent. He seemed to have contrived a number of meetings with Davina since their introduction last November, and it was plain from what he said that they enjoyed one another's company. It was equally apparent that he was in love with her, but what Joanna could not discover was how Davina felt about him.

She had seen her sister briefly at New Year, before Davina and Anthea left Bath for their annual winter holiday abroad. Davina had spoken of David Nugent warmly, but only as a friend. As far as Joanna could make out – and her jealousy made her sensitive to every inflection of her sister's voice – Davina felt no more for him than she would for any other personable, intelligent, well-informed man. She had given no impression of wanting to give up the headship of Forest Moor, either for marriage or to pursue her writing and television career full-time; but with Davina Joanna could never be sure. Her elder sister had always been the most secretive of the four of them.

It was unprecedented for Davina to telephone her at the House, or indeed at all during the day. Her calls, which were few and far between, were usually made late at night to Crozier Street, or, during parliamentary recesses, to their parents' home in Nightingale Close. Joanna, her heart beating uncomfortably fast, decided to postpone the dubious pleasure of speaking to her sister for as long as she could.

'I'll deal with the mail first,' she said, smiling at Selina with false brightness. 'Let me have the letters in order of priority, and if there's one from a Mrs Moxton, who reckons her house is being bugged by little green men, for God's sake leave it until last.'

Selina laughed. 'I don't think we have one of those, but I'll remember for the future. Oh, I almost forgot.' She picked up a blue airmail envelope, set aside from the pile. 'This letter is personal, so I didn't open it. It's from California. Address on the back says "Freda Marshall, Bel Air".'

Joanna's eyebrows shot up. She hadn't heard from Freda, who had obviously lost her Crozier Street address, in months, and now, by coincidence, she had written a letter which had reached Joanna on the very day that Davina was trying to contact her by phone. It was often that way with a family. There seemed to be some strange telepathy between its members. She tore open the airmail envelope.

'Don't let on,' Freda wrote in her almost illegible scrawl, 'because I want it to be a surprise, but Steve and Annie and I are flying over for Gramps's eightieth birthday. I don't want Mum and Dad told, either, until nearer the time, but I feel somebody ought to know of our intentions, in case of accidents. I've already made reservations with the Royal Crescent Hotel. We shall have Nanny and a couple of body-guards with us, far too many for Mum to put up. Besides, I guess you and Davey will be staying in Nightingale Close.'

Joanna breathed a sigh of relief. Davina was, in all probability, trying to get in touch with her about their grandfather's birthday celebrations as well. It had nothing to do with David Nugent. She said to Selina: 'Get me the Forest Moor number, will you, please? I've decided to speak to my sister right away.'

There was some delay at the other end of the line while Davina was located, but eventually her clipped professional tones sounded in Joanna's ear.

341

'Jo? I've been trying to get hold of you all morning.'

The note of reproof almost had Joanna apologizing, but she checked herself just in time, recollecting Alex's advice. Her time was just as precious as Davina's.

'I've been in committee since ten o'clock and I have to be in the Chamber for a debate on education by two. Surprising as you may find it, MPs do work for their living. I presume you're contacting me about Gramps's eightieth birthday. I've had a letter from Freddie to say she's coming, but she wants it kept secret for the present. A vain hope, I fear. Her arrival in Bath will make all the local papers, if not the nationals. A pity really. I don't want her stealing Gramps's thunder.'

'I don't suppose he'll mind about that. He's terribly proud of her, even though you've always been his favourite. I shall be there of course, but that isn't what I'm ringing about. Well, yes, it is, in a way.' Davina paused, while Joanna waited, once again tense with anxiety, wondering what her sister was going to say. After what seemed an eternity, Davina went on: 'The thing is, I shan't be coming alone.' Joanna's heart was racing faster now, her knuckles white as she gripped the edge of the desk with her free hand. 'What I mean is,' Davina continued, 'that I shan't be alone on the Sunday. On the actual birthday.' Joanna heard her draw in her breath sharply. 'Anthony and Samantha will be there as well. Jo! Claire has agreed to a divorce, and Anthony has asked me to marry him again. I think I'm probably going to say "yes"!'

'But what made you decide to give it a second go?' Joanna asked, sitting on the edge of her sister's bed in Davina's old room at Nightingale Close.

It was late on the Saturday afternoon, and Davina had only just arrived from Southampton to find Joanna and her aunt Dora already installed, having travelled down from London together. Even with a very pregnant Freda and her entourage stopping in Royal Crescent – and immediately besieged by the press – the house seemed

342

uncomfortably full. Nevertheless, Davina felt that this was one occasion when she could not stay with Anthea; and in, any case, the sense of being overcrowded was, she soon realized, largely due to her mother's untidiness and general mismanagement. Jean's panic at providing Sunday lunch for six and tea for the entire family lay over the house like a pall. And the additional information that not only Steve Jordan, but also her former son-in-law and unknown grand-daughter would be present as well had brought her to the brink of hysteria. It had been bad enough when Freda's arrival had been revealed to her, without all the rest. Only Dora's assurances that she would superintend every stage of the cooking had managed to calm her down.

'Why on earth she didn't get caterers in to do the evening meal, I do not know,' Dora had remarked earlier to Joanna; and her niece had tried to explain that such beings as caterers had never been a part of her mother's existence; they were an unknown quantity; beyond her ken. But Dora had drifted too far from the working-class, Nonconformist world in which she had been raised – the world of hard work, self-reliance and, above all, thrift – to appreciate the working of her sister's mind or the economics of her household budget. Dora would have hired the services of a catering firm and worried about how to pay for them afterwards.

At Joanna's question, Davina looked up from the task of unpacking her overnight case and stared thoughtfully at her sister.

'I suppose', she said, after a pause, 'that I've always loved Anthony. Deep down, I've never stopped loving him. And I'm ready for marriage now. I was thirty-seven last month and I've done all the things I set out to do; all the things which twenty years ago seemed so important.' She sat down on the opposite edge of the bed. 'I suppose, if I'm honest, being one of the youngest-ever heads of Forest Moor was, for me, an end in itself, not a way of life as it was for Aunt Thea. My writing and television work, they're

343

different. At least, my writing is. But, you see, I can go on doing that after I'm married. In short, and before you say it first, I want to have my cake and eat it, too. What's more, I'm going to.'

Joanna laughed. 'You always did. Life's always worked out for you, Davey, because you've had the luck and the ruthlessness to make it.'

Her sister grimaced. 'Oh dear! But, yes, I suppose you're right. I learned that ruthlessness, as you call it, from Anthea.'

There was a moment's silence, while Joanna stared at the well-remembered picture over the head of the bed; one of those depressing nondescript prints turned out in their hundreds at the beginning of the century. This one depicted some sort of country scene, with two swans gliding in ghostly fashion across the dark surface of a glassy stream, and, in the background, the churning yellowish waters of a weir.

'I had a "surgery" this morning, in Avonvale,' she said at last. 'I saw David Nugent, so I told him you were thinking of getting married again. He was ... rather upset.'

'Upset?' Davina frowned. 'Why should he be?'

'Oh, Davey! He's in love with you. Surely it can't have escaped your notice.'

Her sister's frown deepened. 'It never occurred to me,' she said. 'We've seen each other a few times since last November, but I've never thought of him as anything but a friend. Not even that, really. More as a friend of yours. I was civil to him for your sake.' She considered this last remark for a moment, then added: 'No, that's not strictly true. He's a very nice man. I like him for his own sake.' She paused again, mentally reviewing this new and hitherto unsuspected fact presented to her by Joanna. She half-smiled, plainly titillated by the idea of David Nugent's affection, without having any notion of returning it. To do her justice, she had no inkling of Joanna's feelings for him. 'Well!' she exclaimed softly, getting off the bed and

344

preparing to finish her unpacking, 'I'm really rather flattered.'

Reginald Harding cut the cake which bore the simple message '80' in blue icing on white, blew out the eight candles and sank back in his chair to a chorus of 'Happy Birthday', sung mainly by Freda and Dora, while the rest joined in half-heartedly, looking suitably embarrassed.

The dining-room at Nightingale Close was crowded. As well as the immediate family, Anthony and Samantha had driven over from Lyncombe Manor and Steve Jordan had insisted on bringing two of his bodyguards with him, a pair of huge bronzed Californians, looking, like their employer, ill at ease and out of place in the midst of this extremely English domestic scene.

Strangely enough, Freda in spite of her jewellery and designer-label maternity clothes, blended in immediately with her surroundings. It was something to do with attitude of mind, Joanna decided. The moment Freda had walked through the front door of Nightingale Close, she had been at home. The film star, with the notorious lifestyle and the seven-figure annual salary, reverted without effort to being the spoiled younger sister, daughter, granddaughter of her youth. Perhaps, Joanna reflected cynically, there wasn't much difference between the two.

Steve Jordan, on the other hand, made no effort to conceal his boredom with his wife's family until the arrival of Samantha. He recalled her from her visit to Hollywood the previous year, when he had thought her attractive enough to flirt with, although then it had been mainly to annoy Freda and make her jealous; a warning to her to get rid of Jeff Warwick as soon as possible and marry him; a threat that his attention might otherwise stray.

Now, however, now that he had her prestige and money legally behind him, he was already tiring of being Mr Freda Marshall, and finding the ten-year age-gap between him and his wife wider than he had expected. And he had not been pleased about the baby: in the early months, Freda had had a difficult pregnancy. He thought her mad, coming all this way with the child due to be born, just for her old grandfather's birthday.

Samantha, five years his junior, was a pretty girl with good legs and a good figure, just the way he liked his women. She wanted to be an actress, and had a flattering way of deferring to him as someone who knew all about the business. Not once did she mention that disastrous series 'The Man from Venus'. He sensed, too, that she was as uneasy in this gathering of the Marshall clan as he was. Freda had told him the story of her niece's background; daughter and grand-daughter in name, but in fact only recently catapulted back into a family whose members had, for so long, evinced no interest in her; reunited with a mother who had rejected her in favour of a brilliant academic career.

The presents had been given, and Dora was demanding that her father make a birthday speech, but Reginald Harding remained adamant.

'I told you this morning, Do, no speeches. I meant it. I'm too old to make a fool of myself and I haven't your training. I should only forget my words halfway through and embarrass you all.' His grey eyes glanced round at his family, as bright and as shrewd as ever. 'But I do just want to say how very pleased I am, how very happy, to see my two great-grand-daughters here today.' He smiled fondly at Freda. 'Antigone's a lovely child and does you credit, my dear. As for Samantha, it's been too long, and I'm delighted to hear that her mother and father are thinking of getting back together again. I don't really approve of divorce, but ... well ...' His voice tailed off, and there was a moment's uncomfortable silence.

Freda, as ever, stepped gracefully into the breach.

'I'm sure that everyone here will agree that that non-speech by Gramps was a pretty good one.' She clapped her hands, and everyone else laughed and joined in. 'And now', Freda went on, 'I've an announcement to make of my own. Even Steve doesn't know what I'm going to say, because I haven't told him. I've decided to come back to this country for good. To live, Steve, my wonderful darling.' She blew him a kiss, certain that whatever she wanted he would want, too, and oblivious to the look of shocked horror on his handsome face. 'I'm fed up with the crap I'm being offered in the States. I've a yen to be a legitimate actress again, and now I can afford to be without worrying about the money – or lack of it. Thanks to my ex-husband – honour where it's due – I've made some very sound investments over the years. So there you are, everybody! What do you think of that? In the future, you'll be seeing a lot more of me.'

'Now, see here, Freddie . . .!' Steve Jordan began hotly, just as the telephone rang in the hall. Joanna slipped out to answer it.

It was Cicely Douglas, calling from Lyncombe Manor and sounding frantic.

'Tell Anthony to get back here at once! It's Claire! Oh, my God, Joanna, she's tried to cut her wrists!'

PART SIX

1982–5

36

THE LATE-SEPTEMBER EVENING had developed a chill. When they left the theatre, there was a wind blowing off the river, and Joanna was glad she had brought a coat. Selina Driver, on the other hand, was shivering in her thin silk dress.

'I told you', Joanna admonished her, 'that you should at least have worn a cardigan. Nights can be very treacherous this time of year.' She glanced up and down the road. 'And never a taxi in sight when you want one.'

Selina laughed good-naturedly. 'It's that wretched play that's making me shiver. Why were the Elizabethans so obsessed with murder and revenge?'

They had been to the National, to the Cottesloe Theatre, for the opening night of *The Spanish Tragedy* by Thomas Kyd. Neither woman had known anything previously about the play, and both had been a little overpowered by its intensely gloomy atmosphere. Joanna remembered some words she had read somewhere, 'images of death', and thought that they summed up the evening's entertainment very well.

They managed to get a taxi at last and arrived back in Crozier Street, which Selina now shared with Joanna, just after eleven-fifteen. Selina went into the kitchen to make some tea, while Joanna sank wearily into a chair and closed her eyes. It had been a strenuous day at the House, even though she was once again a mere backbencher.

James Callaghan's resignation as party leader in the October of 1980 had been a blow to her and his other protégés, but as he was well into his sixties Joanna had seen it coming, and she had always got on with Denis Healey, whom she assumed would be elected in Callaghan's place. When, however, the veteran left-winger Michael Foot had beaten his chief rival by a clear majority of ten, she had been extremely disappointed, and, foolishly, had not hesitated to express an opinion. As a person, she admired Michael Foot very much and shared a lot of his views, but at sixty-seven he was even older than James Callaghan had been when he succeeded Harold Wilson. Moreover, although a good orator and debater, he did not, in Joanna's view, have the necessary incisive edge to combat Margaret Thatcher. The party, she said openly, needed someone younger and more dynamic. As a result, when the new leader came to pick his Shadow team, Joanna had once again been relegated to the back benches.

'Don't despair,' David Nugent had told her. 'I doubt if Michael will carry us to election victory next time, so wait and see what happens after that. My guess is that before very long we shall have another leader. For what it's worth, take my advice and cultivate Neil Kinnock.'

Throughout the following year, which had seen the engagement and marriage of Prince Charles and Lady Diana Spencer, race riots in Toxteth and Brixton and the Penlee lifeboat disaster, the popularity of the Conservative government had gradually waned. The terrible blizzards during the first few weeks of 1982 had done nothing to make the public any less discontented, and Joanna had been considering the possibility of a Labour election victory with strangely mixed feelings.

But two things happened in quick succession to dash Opposition hopes. In February the founding of the Social Democratic Party had robbed Labour of some of its most eminent party members and MPs, who felt that it had swung too far to the left for their comfort. And the following month Argentina had invaded the Falklands.

The subsequent brief war in which Britain had emerged

victorious had aroused a chauvinistic fervour unequalled since the patriotic displays of August 1914. What the press was now dubbing 'the Falklands factor' had lifted the Government in general, and the Prime Minister in particular, high on a wave of popularity which would have seemed impossible at the beginning of the year. Whenever Margaret Thatcher chose to go to the country, it seemed likely that she would be returned with a massive majority. Joanna didn't know whether to laugh or cry.

Selina returned with two mugs of tea which she had made with tea-bags. She handed the rose-patterned mug to Joanna and sat down in the other armchair, kicking off her shoes with a sigh of relief.

It was over a year since she had come to live in Crozier Street. She had been given notice to quit her bed-sitter in Earls Court and had been lamenting the difficulty of finding alternative accommodation.

'You must share the flat,' Joanna had said. 'It's the obvious answer.'

They got on well together. Apart from the fact that it was virtually impossible to quarrel with Selina, they had mutual interests; their work, the theatre, their years at Oxford and in the MOD. They were, too, both in their thirties, with a shared apprehension about the onset of middle age.

'I shall live and die a spinster,' Selina had once declared. 'I've decided that being single is what I'm best at.'

And it was true that, although she had a constant stream of men friends, she seemed disinclined to settle down with any of them.

She said now, looking up from the evening's programme notes, which she had been studying in more detail: 'Do you know that Thomas Kyd was only thirty-six when he died? He'd been accused of "vile heresies and conceits" and tortured. Put on the rack. No wonder the poor man was obsessed by thoughts of vengeance. He fell under suspicion because he'd been a friend of Christopher

Marlowe. Does that mean, I wonder, that he was homosexual?'

'Why?' Joanna demanded, putting her mug down with an angry clatter. 'It's not a disease. You can't catch it.'

'Sorry.' Selina glanced up contritely. 'The remark wasn't meant in any derogatory sense. Have you . . . er . . . seen Alex lately? You haven't mentioned him for a while.'

'I'm sorry.' Joanna leaned back and closed her eyes. 'I shouldn't have bitten your head off like that. Alex and Derek Conway have gone abroad for a while, to Derek's villa in the south of France. I gather they've been getting a bit of hassle recently. Unpleasant telephone calls, anonymous notes pushed through the letter-box, vague threats. Things like that. I suppose it was only to be expected. Toleration's becoming a bit of a dirty word again, especially after the Falklands.'

Selina nodded. 'I know what you mean. Macho men are definitely in. By the way.' She leaned forward, searched through a pile of magazines on a nearby table and pulled out the following week's *Radio Times*. 'I noticed, when I was looking through this at breakfast this morning, that Freda's in a BBC play next week. One of those big prestigious productions, full of famous names. There's an article about her, too, at the front, with photographs of that dirty great place she's bought near Bath. Yes, here it is.' Selina folded back the page and passed the magazine to Joanna. 'There's a picture of her and the two children playing on one of the lawns.'

Joanna took it and stared down at the black and white photograph, which showed Freda, in trousers and anorak, playing ball with Antigone, now five, and Steve's son, the two-year-old Adrian. In the background was the façade of Kelmscott House, the eighteenth-century mansion which she had bought shortly after her decision to stay in Britain. Also in the picture were two large Labrador dogs and the nanny, Mabel Patterson. There was no sign of Steve and very little mention of him in the accompanying article, apart from two or three lines. 'Miss Marshall's second husband, former Hollywood actor Steve Jordan, gave up his own film and television career to become her manager when she decided to come back to live in England.' This was followed by the obligatory snide reference to 'The Man from Venus', but that was all. There wasn't, as Joanna well knew, much more to say. The marriage was falling apart at the seams. Freda, when she had the time and energy, was frantically trying to cobble it together again, but her visits to Kelmscott House were limited. Her portrayal of Hedda Gabler had been attracting capacity audiences at the Royalty Theatre in London for over a year, and seemed set for at least another six months' run. In between performances, she fitted in television and radio work. She was much in demand since her talents as a serious actress had been rediscovered. Steve's position as her manager was purely nominal. The real work devolved on her agent, Maurice Benson, who had welcomed her back with open arms.

Joanna knew that Steve drank a lot. On at least three occasions when she had gone to visit the children during Freda's absence, she had found him in various states of inebriety. The last time, he was almost senseless. Mabel Patterson had told Joanna that it was becoming increasingly difficult to keep staff because of his behaviour. She was herself, she confided, thinking of handing in her notice. Joanna had managed to dissuade her with a promise to speak to Freda about the problem.

But when approached Freda had merely shrugged. 'What can I do about it, Jo? I've tried to find him work, but nobody wants to know. It's no good blinking the fact that the poor love isn't the world's best actor.'

Joanna considered this to be an understatement and said so, bluntly. Freda had immediately fired up in Steve's defence.

'He's not that bad. He just hasn't found his feet over here, that's all. There aren't that many parts going for Americans. But I've got Maurice keeping his ear to the ground. Something's bound to turn up eventually.'

So far, however, nothing had.

Joanna returned the *Radio Times* to Selina, yawning and stretching.

'God, I'm tired. I don't know if it was the debate this afternoon or the play this evening. I really could have done with something to cheer me up.'

Selina finished her tea and glanced shrewdly at Joanna.

'I don't think it was either,' she said. 'It was that phone call from David Nugent, asking if you'd pass on a message to your sister.'

Joanna felt her colour rise. Just before they had gone out this evening, David had telephoned on various constituency matters and, when he had finished, had asked Joanna to give his regards to Davina.

'Remind her that I'm still alive, will you?' he had asked with a shaky laugh. 'I haven't heard from her for at least four weeks.'

Joanna said now: 'What nonsense! Why should that make me tired?'

'Suppressed emotion,' Selina retorted. 'Churning it over in the back of your mind all night.'

Joanna knew that her friend was right, but did not want to admit it.

'They've been friends for quite a while now,' she answered tartly. 'It's only natural that they should pass messages to one another through me.'

Selina said nothing for a moment or two. Then she asked with apparent irrelevance: 'Is Anthony Douglas still with his wife?'

'I don't see ...' Joanna was beginning stiffly, but she was suddenly too tired for any more verbal fencing. 'Yes.' Her voice was weary. 'He won't leave her, ever. And I think Davey's beginning to accept that at last.' She bent down and switched on a bar of the electric fire. It was nearly midnight, and the room had grown very cold. 'I realized it from the start. How could he, after her suicide attempt? He couldn't possibly go through all that trauma again. He's still carrying the guilt for Terry's death. He

356

couldn't burden himself with Claire's as well.'

'Was it a real suicide attempt, do you think? Or just a cry for help? Or even moral blackmail?'

Joanna shrugged. 'I don't know. I doubt if anyone does, not even Claire. The real point was – and is – that just as Anthony had misjudged the strength of my sister's feelings for him all those years ago, so now he'd misjudged Claire's. He thought she wanted a divorce, that she was happy about the idea. But she wasn't.'

'I thought you said they fought a lot.'

'So I understood. And, given the circumstances of their lives, who could doubt it? Claire must have known from the first that she was only second-best.' Memories of Lawrence intruded uncomfortably, and Joanna hurried on: 'Be that as it may, she apparently had no wish to divorce Anthony, and either by luck or by judgement picked the one sure way to make him stay.'

'And you think that Davina's come to terms at last with the fact that Anthony won't leave her?'

Joanna bit her lip, staring at the red-hot filament of the electric fire. Then she blinked rapidly and looked away, reaching for her half-empty mug of cooling tea. She took a sip, grimaced and replaced the mug on the table.

'Ironic, isn't it, that this time *he's* deserted *her*, although not for the same sort of reason? Davina wouldn't accept it at first. Until recently, she's been convinced that he'd either manage, eventually, to persuade Claire to give him a divorce or he'd leave her. She's the only one who really can't understand his reasons for not doing so. After all these years she's decided that she wants to marry him again and that nothing must be allowed to prevent her.'

Selina said astringently: 'I've always thought she was a thoroughly selfish person. Why's she trying to filch David Nugent from you?'

'No, no! It's not like that at all!' Joanna was distressed. 'You're one of the few people who knows how I feel about David. So there's no question that Davey's filching him from me, as you put it. But she's unhappy and she could

357

well turn to him for solace. She likes him. Likes his company. Of course, he's head over heels in love with her.'

'Does she realize that?'

'Yes. Unfortunately, I told her at the time of my grandfather's eightieth birthday.'

'Why "unfortunately"?' Selina groped round on the carpet for her discarded shoes. It was high time they were both in bed.

'Because I think she might use him. Use his affection for her. Davey's pride has been hurt by what she sees as Anthony's defection. She is, as you say, a selfish person. It's not her fault. Aunt Thea taught her to be that way. She's the sun and the rest of us are merely planets circling around her.'

'You mean she's always got her own way.' Selina rose and, picking up the empty mugs, carried them through to the kitchen. 'Supposing David asks her to marry him?' she called over her shoulder.

Joanna sat very still, staring down at her clenched fists. Slowly, she unclenched them and got to her feet, taking her handbag and coat from the table, where she had dropped them.

'Not a clue,' she answered lightly. 'I've no idea what goes on in Davey's mind where men are concerned. I'm just afraid that she'll be thoughtless and hurt David.'

'In that case, you can be on hand to pick up the pieces.' Selina emerged from the little kitchen where she had washed up the mugs and left them to drain.

Joanna laughed. 'You're as bad as Alex. That's what he said, or something similar, in his last letter.'

'There you are, you see. Great minds, et cetera.'

'I don't think I want a man on those terms,' Joanna answered abrasively. 'And now I must get to bed. Thanks for the talk. See you in the morning.'

She went into her bedroom, where the curtains were already drawn and the bedclothes turned down. Always neat and methodical, she had seen to everything before she went out. She put on the bedside lamp, which cast a suffused pink glow over its corner of the room, and sat down on the edge of the bed, making no attempt for the moment to get undressed. She felt too tired to move. She even toyed with the idea of lying down as she was and drifting off to sleep.

Then the effects of the tea began to make themselves felt and she was suddenly awake again. She glanced disparagingly around the little room. She was thirty-eight years old, no children, no husband, no lover, living in a rented flat. Even her career was moving backwards. She had nothing whatsoever going for her at all . . .

Then, it was time she had. It was time she took life by the scruff of the neck and shook it. She recalled Alex's words to her a few years ago. 'Jo love, you're a woman of definite personality . . . If you have to go down, go down fighting.' She slipped off the bed and began to undress. She would telephone David first thing tomorrow and ask him to arrange a 'surgery' for her for Saturday morning. She would, as always, have lunch with him and Stuart before she went on to Bath to see her parents. Perhaps she could find out exactly what his intentions were towards her sister, and how matters stood between them.

Since Laura Nugent had gone up to university, Joanna no longer spent nights in the house in Oxford Road, but travelled down to Avonvale by the early Saturday-morning train. She was not prepared to give anyone, especially not Tom Birkenshaw, the slightest excuse for gossip. She had learned that lesson thoroughly with Alex. She climbed into bed, switched off the light and snuggled down under the bedclothes.

She drifted towards sleep, scenes from the day's events and the evening's play all jumbled up together in her head. But as she reached the point of oblivion she was once more jerked awake by the ringing of the telephone bell.

37

REGINALD HARDING had died peacefully in his sleep that same evening. Five days later, he was buried on a hillside overlooking Bath, following a simple ceremony at the local Methodist chapel. The family returned to Nightingale Close after the interment.

Joanna and Dora, as on the occasion of Reginald's eightieth birthday, had travelled down from London together, the previous Friday, and spent the weekend at Nightingale Close. Joanna had been forced to abandon her plan of visiting Avonvale; and Dora, for the moment, was 'resting'. Both were too upset to talk much during the journey from Paddington, and when Bernard met them both at Bath station Dora had burst into tears. Awkwardly, he had put his arm around her shoulders.

'It's all right, Do. It's all right,' he kept muttering. 'He didn't suffer. He was as happy as a sandboy when he went to bed last Wednesday evening. He'd been reading about that television play of Freddie's in next week's *Radio Times* and making plans to watch it.' Dora's sobs became louder and Bernard more flustered. 'He was eighty-two, after all,' he offered desperately. 'He'd had a good innings.'

Joanna, taking pity on her father, had guided her aunt to a taxi and got in the back with her, leaving Bernard free to sit beside the driver. She remembered Davina telling her that her father and Dora had once been lovers, and reflected that they were always uncomfortable in one another's company. Still holding her aunt's hand, Joanna stared thoughtfully out of the taxi window.

Freda arrived at Kelmscott House on the Sunday, having completed a week's performances as Hedda Gabler.

'But I'm not going back until tomorrow,' she said now, perching on the arm of Reginald Harding's empty chair and unconsciously smoothing the material with a restless hand. 'They can damn well use my understudy for just one evening.'

Her eyes were bright with unshed tears, and she was dressed in unrelieved black. She wore no jewellery at all, except for the broad gold band of her wedding ring. Before leaving home for the funeral, Steve had exclaimed angrily: 'For God's sake put some colour somewhere! You look dreadful!'

'I feel dreadful!' she had flared back at him. 'I loved Gramps very much. OK, latterly I didn't see him all that often, but I knew he was there. Now he's gone, and a whole chunk of my life's gone with him. I feel like I look. Dreary.'

But in fact black suited her very well, unlike Davina who had never looked good in it. She had travelled up from Southampton late the previous evening, having had what she called 'a typical school crisis' to deal with before leaving.

'Two sixth-formers breaking bounds to meet boy-friends. It happens with every generation. I did it myself, once. Aunt Thea was furious.'

Anthea herself had not bothered to put on mourning, but was looking majestic in a pale grey suit with a frilled white blouse and a small toque made of purple velvet. Her suede handbag, gloves and shoes were of the same rich colour, and Jean remarked acidly to Joanna that Anthea's outfit would have been more fitting for a wedding.

To Joanna's surprise, her mother was less affected by grief than any of them. Indeed, relief seemed to be Jean's paramount emotion, and she was already making plans for her father's room now that it was once again empty. Joanna had at first been shocked by her mother's attitude, but on reflection she supposed that if *she* had been totally

361

responsible for her grandfather, running his errands, subservient to his whims, she, too, might be feeling relieved. Old people, as she knew from dealing with some of her constituents, could be very trying and more than a little demanding. Sorrow would probably come later for her mother, when Jean had recovered from her sense of release.

The surprise visitor to the funeral was Samantha, who arrived just before the cortège set out from Nightingale Close.

'I hope you don't mind my coming,' she had said, a trifle defensively, as Jean ushered her into the crowded drawing-room. 'Although we didn't know each other very well, Mr Harding was still my great-grandfather.'

'No, of course we don't mind. How could you even think such a thing?' Dora had sniffed, going forward and tearfully embracing Samantha. 'How sweet of you to take the trouble.'

Davina smiled approvingly now at her daughter. Samantha had just started her third year at Bristol University, and had grown even more attractive since she had last seen her. They met from time to time, but their relationship had never ripened as Davina had once hoped that it might. For this, she blamed Anthony, whose decision to remain with Claire had deeply upset her. If he had kept his promise, she and Samantha would now be living together as mother and daughter.

Not for a single moment did Davina believe that Claire had meant to kill herself. She had simply decided, at the last minute, that her rival shouldn't have him and had picked on the most effective way of keeping him. And Anthony had fallen for it. Couldn't he see how scheming Claire really was? It wasn't as though he were happy. He spoke to her, very occasionally, over the phone about Samantha, and had once admitted that he and Claire quarrelled as much as ever.

Ever since they had returned from the cemetery to Nightingale Close, Davina had been hoping for a private word with her daughter to discover how matters really stood at Lyncombe Manor, but Samantha had proved elusive. At the moment, she was deep in conversation with Steve Jordan, and even as Davina eased her way across the room towards them they made their escape through the french doors and into the garden.

'Hey!' Steve exclaimed, following Samantha around the corner of the house. 'That's better. The atmosphere's really oppressive in there. And the booze isn't exactly flowing.'

Samantha giggled. She suspected, from his slightly slurred speech, that he had been drinking pretty heavily before he left home that morning. She noticed, too, that his features were beginning to thicken and coarsen, the sign of an incipient drunkard. But she still thought him one of the handsomest men she had ever seen. He made all the boys she knew at university seem like children.

There had been a wet start to the morning, but now the day had brightened a little. A few sodden chrysanthemums and dahlias drooped in the flower-beds, and a chill wind was ruffling the silver-edged grasses, but the garden was preferable to the gloom indoors. Had it not been for Steve Jordan's presence, Samantha would have made her excuses and left as soon as the funeral was over.

Standing with him now, in the lee of a chimney buttress on the south side of the house, Samantha decided that Steve could still prove to be the short cut to a Hollywood career that might otherwise take years of struggle to achieve. He was plainly dissatisfied at living in Freda's shadow, and made no secret of the fact that he hated living in England and yearned for the fleshpots and sunshine of California. She edged closer to him, pretending to shiver, and snuggled against his side.

'I hate this weather,' she said. 'In fact it's not been a very good summer altogether.'

Steve grunted and shifted so that he could get an arm around her.

'Don't you Brits ever talk about anything but the goddam weather?'

She gave him a slant-eyed look. 'What would you like me to talk about?' she asked him softly.

'How about yourself? Hey!' He squeezed her shoulders. 'I've got a better idea. Why don't we just sneak away? I bet they won't even miss us. We'll go in my car.'

'Where?' Samantha was curious.

'Anywhere . . . Got it! We'll go back to my place.' Not by so much as the flicker of an eyelid did Samantha suggest that she knew Kelmscott House had been bought with Freda's money. Steve continued: 'Why not, for Pete's sake! You're my niece, God damn it!'

Samantha giggled again. 'So I am. By marriage, at any rate. But won't there be people there? What about the servants and the children and that nanny, Mabel Patterson?'

Steve smiled. 'Honey, that house is so big, and there are so many different doors and staircases, that you can get in and out without anyone even knowing you've been there.' He glanced at his watch, a present from Freda, gold with a broad linked band. 'It's just after two now. The kids'll be having their siesta, and Mabel Patterson will be in her sitting-room, next to the nursery. The domestic staff will be taking advantage of our absence to play a hand of poker or pontoon in the kitchen. They're a lazy lot. And only two of them live in. The others will probably have gone home early. So what do you say? I can get you in and out of the house without anyone being any the wiser.'

Samantha considered the proposition. She had no illusions as to the outcome if she went with Steve. Did she really want him to make love to her? The answer to that was probably 'yes'. She had slept with a few men, the first of whom had been Stuart Nugent. They had both been virgins, and the result of their inexpert fumblings had been more hilarious than romantic. There had since been a couple of fellow-undergraduates, neither of whom had made her feel that there was anything special in the sexual act. But Steve Jordan was different. There was a sexuality about him, an aura of having been there many times

364

before, that made her want him, and want him badly. And then there was the other consideration, that he was her link to that world of glitter and glamour that was Hollywood and the American film world.

It did cross Samantha's mind, standing there shivering in her thin black coat and skirt – the only black garments she had been able to find – that Freda might be a better link, but she knew intuitively that her aunt would do nothing for her. For one thing, she suspected that Freda saw her as a rival, and a younger rival at that. For another, Freda had once talked virtuously to her about achieving success the hard way. The occasion had been Freda's first return to the London stage after settling in England. It had been a production of Oscar Wilde's *A Woman of No Importance*, in which she had played Mrs Allonby. Samantha had gone up to London to see it, and afterwards she had visited her aunt backstage. Freda had received her with a certain amount of reserve, and when Samantha had suggested, not very subtly, that she might arrange introductions for her to some of her Hollywood friends Freda had replied shortly: 'I don't believe in cutting corners.' After a pause, she had added: 'It's only merit that gets you good parts in the end. Otherwise you end up with crap.'

But Samantha was in a hurry. She wanted fame and fortune and the big break before she was twenty. She came to a decision.

'OK.' She linked her arm through Steve's and smiled at him. 'Let's go to your place. But I'm not taking any risks, you understand me?'

'Oh, sure,' he grinned. 'You can trust me.'

'Where the hell did you get to, you and that niece of mine?' Freda pitched her hat and gloves on to a chair. 'What have you and that little slag been up to, Steve?'

Steve, who for once was reasonably sober, put on his most innocent expression.

'I took her home, for God's sake, that was all. The poor kid was going out of her skull with boredom, and I offered

365

her a lift. I was bored, too. Afterwards, I came back here. I knew you'd get a taxi. I mean, let's face it – if you'd really been worried what I was up to, you'd have phoned or come home sooner.'

'It was my grandfather's funeral! I couldn't up and leave, just like that.'

'You mean you didn't want to.' Steve got up and lounged over to the sideboard, helping himself to a whisky and soda. 'You could've gotten away from that party of dowdies any time you had a mind to.'

'That's my family you're talking about,' Freda said, suddenly and dangerously quiet. Then her anger flared once more. 'And, anyway, I don't believe a word about you taking Samantha straight home. You brought her back here and fucked her.'

Steve winced. He had been raised in the Bible Belt of America's Midwest and there were certain things which could still shock him.

'Don't say things like that!' he shouted at her.

'You mean it's OK to do it, even with my own niece, but not OK to talk about it. You're a hypocrite, Steve. You make me sick, do you know that?'

He had swallowed his whisky in three quick gulps and was now pouring himself another. Added to the quantity he had previously drunk that day, it was making him feel pleasantly hazy. But at Freda's words an alarm-bell was triggered inside his head. He wasn't ready for divorce, not just yet. Until he could see his way clear, he needed her and the lifestyle that her money brought him. He put down the second glass without touching its contents.

'Nothing happened,' he lied, turning on the charm for all it was worth. 'I keep telling you, I just took the kid home. If you don't believe me, ring her mother – or her step-mother, or whoever she is. Ask her what time Samantha got back.' It was a gamble, but one he had to take in order to sound convincing. He didn't think Freda would bother to check if he could make the story sound believable. 'Ask Mabel Patterson what time I arrived here. I went up to the nursery and spoke to her.'

Freda hesitated. She was perfectly well aware that there were half a dozen ways he could have smuggled Samantha into Kelmscott House without bringing her through the front door. And what better alibi could he have than by going at once to speak to Mabel Patterson? She could find out if Steve were speaking the truth by telephoning Lyncombe Manor.

But she wanted to believe him. She wanted their marriage to work because she was still in love with him. She dithered, undecided, and in that moment was lost. Scenting victory, Steve went over and put his arms around her, a voluntary gesture of affection which he had not made for some time. Freda's anger evaporated. She returned his embrace hungrily, raising her face for his kiss.

'Steve, Steve,' she murmured desperately, 'I do love you. And you love me, too, don't you, darling?'

'Of course,' he answered glibly, eyeing his abandoned whisky and soda on the sideboard. God, how he could do with it just at this moment!

But Freda was mumuring in his ear: 'Come on, let's go to bed. Right this minute. I want you, Steve. I want you so badly.'

There was no way he could get out of it. If he refused, all her suspicions about his afternoon with Samantha would be rekindled. Hell! He wasn't sure if he could manage to make love again, particularly when he remembered Samantha's smooth young body and contrasted it with Freda's. It was true that his wife was only thirty-six and, according to most people, still an attractive woman, but he had discovered a taste for young girls with their firm taut flesh.

Half an hour later, exhausted, lying by Freda's side, he asked: 'How come that ex-brother-in-law of yours lives in a place like Lyncombe Manor? I thought you said he was just a country doctor.'

Freda, satisfied and sleepy, murmured: 'He has a practice in Bath. That's hardly the country.'

'Oh, sure. But English docs don't get paid anything like they do in the States, and even there not many live like he does.'

Freda rolled on to her back and stretched luxuriously. 'That's true. But Anthony's father made a fortune out of pickles and sauces. He left millions when he died.'

Steve, who had hoisted himself on to one elbow, preparatory to getting up and dressing, paused, an arrested expression on his face.

'You mean . . . the family's rich?'

'Stinking rich,' Freda muttered, too relaxed to be on her guard, too contented to resurrect her suspicions.

Steve enquired cautiously: 'How did . . . how did the old man leave the money? To the son? I mean . . . anything to the grandchildren?'

'I've no idea,' Freda said sleepily. 'I think his widow's still alive.' Her voice now was merely a whisper. She would doze for an hour before getting up and dressing for dinner. 'But I don't know any details.'

Sleep drifted nearer. Tomorrow, she would have to go back to London and *Hedda Gabler*, but for tonight she was free. She and Steve would dine alone. She would make him see that she was still a desirable woman. Later, they would make love again. She smiled. What had begun as a day with few expectations of happiness had turned out to be one of the best that she could remember in a long time.

38

JOANNA had hung on as MP for Avonvale by the skin of her teeth, with a greatly reduced majority; but, as David Nugent pointed out, she had done better than many others. Tony Benn had lost his Bristol seat after more than thirty years.

The general election of 9 June 1983 had been even more disastrous for the Labour Party than the last one. This was partly due to the continuing sense of national euphoria, nearly a year after the end of the Falklands war, and partly because of the redrawing of constituency boundaries. Some MPs had lost their constituencies altogether; but Joanna, fortunately, had not been one of them. Nevertheless, part of the Shipp's Causeway district of Avonvale had gone; a locality from which she had derived much of her support. Another reason for her reduced majority had been the success of the SDP candidate, who had polled a substantial number of votes, largely at the expense of the socialists. She had won, however, by a margin of fifty votes, and was determined to work even harder in the future to regain her constituents' confidence.

The night of the election, she stayed, as she had always stayed, at the Nugents'.

'Damn what people might think for once,' David said. 'You're too exhausted to drive all the way to Bath at this hour of the morning. Stuart's home. He can act as chaperon.'

So, once again, Joanna slept in the familiar bed at the back of the house and was lulled to sleep by the trickle of the little rill which formed the boundary at the bottom of the garden. But she was overtired and dreamed heavily, with the result that she got up in the morning with a headache and feeling stale. She went to stand by the open window, taking in great gulps of air in an effort to wake herself up. The early sun was sucking up mist from the little stream, and a mass of purple foxgloves thrust tall stems through a neighbour's hedge. Beyond, rising towards the open ground of the green belt, was a high overgrown embankment, starred with the pink and white of bindweed flowers.

When she eventually made her way downstairs, David was cooking breakfast, his glasses propped on his forehead, useless in the kitchen's steamy heat.

'I've done you bacon and eggs,' he called from the kitchen. 'And don't say you can't eat it. You've the thank-you round of the constituency to do yet and you need something inside you. Toast and cornflakes aren't enough.'

Joanna laughed and sat down at the table. After a few minutes, he came in with a plate of bacon, eggs, tomatoes and fried bread.

'I can't eat all this,' Joanna protested, horrified.

'Yes, you can,' he answered, pouring coffee with a practised hand. 'So stop arguing and get on with it. Stuart had his and went off to work an hour ago. I thought you could do with the lie-in. Besides, it means I've got you to myself and I want to talk to you.'

Joanna's heart missed a beat. Her fingers suddenly seemed to have become all thumbs.

'What about?' she mumbled.

He did not reply at once, but attacked his own breakfast with every appearance of enjoyment. Then he asked: 'What's the current situation between your ex-brother-in-law and his wife? Is there any more talk of a divorce?'

'Don't you know?' Joanna chased a piece of bacon round her plate. 'Samantha's a friend of Stuart's.'

'Not any more. Oh, I don't mean they've quarrelled or

anything like that, but they don't go out together these days. There was never anything serious in it anyway, and Stu gathers that Samantha has other fish to fry. She's been heavily involved with someone since last autumn. That was more or less when he got the elbow. I don't think he was very upset. Half-expecting it ever since she went to university.'

'Who is this man?' Joanna asked curiously.

David shrugged. 'No idea. One of her fellow-undergraduates, Stu thinks. It would be natural.'

'Yes, I suppose so.' Joanna forced down a morsel of fried bread. 'Why do want to know about Anthony and Claire?'

David cleared his plate, neatly laying his knife and fork side by side, fiddling and fussing with them without looking up. He said abruptly: 'I'm going to ask Davey to marry me.'

Joanna felt sick, but she managed to keep her voice steady as she asked: 'You'd be content to be second-best?'

He smiled ruefully, continuing to stare down at his empty plate.

'Life's full of people who've settled for being second-best. There would be a lot less married couples if there weren't. Yes, I'm happy to be that if Davey will have me. Of course, I'm not counting on the fact that she will. After the sort of life she's led, I'm hardly a star attraction. All the same, I intend to ask her. I just want to be sure that Anthony Douglas is out of the picture.'

Joanna pushed her plate aside, three-quarters of the food untouched. 'I don't think you need worry about that. He won't leave Claire as long as she wants him, and there doesn't seem to be any doubt on that score.'

'So I'd be safe in asking Davey?'

'Quite safe, I imagine.' Joanna saw his mouth open and added roughly: 'But don't ask me how she feels about you, because I don't know.'

David smiled. 'I wasn't going to. I was merely going to remark that you haven't eaten your breakfast. All my effort wasted.'

'A lot of effort is wasted,' Joanna replied cryptically and swallowed the dregs of her coffee. 'And now, if you'll excuse me, I must finish getting dressed. I promised to be at the Committee Rooms before ten o'clock.'

Joanna reached Paddington late Friday evening and telephoned Selina from the station to say that she would not be going straight home.

'I want to see Freddie. Don't wait up for me. I don't know how long I shall be.' She cut short her friend's congratulations on retaining her Avonvale seat and hung up.

Hedda Gabler was in the final days of its almost two-year run at the Royalty; a run which had been sustained, latterly, solely by Freda's brilliant portrayal of the title role. When the taxi dropped Joanna at the stage door, she noted that there was already an end-of-term atmosphere about the place. Only the doorman, reading the *Evening Standard* in his cubby-hole, seemed unaffected by it. The notices on the notice-board were curling and faded; rehearsal calls and requests for actors to see the producer were a month or six weeks old. There were carrier-bags of personal belongings stacked outside dressing-room doors. The actors, coming off stage after their final curtain call, looked jaded and more than a little weary.

Joanna waited for her sister in the star's dressing-room. Freda's face lit up with pleasure when she saw her.

'Jo darling! What a lovely surprise! And many, many congratulations on hanging on to your seat when all about you were losing theirs. Let me get out of these things and we'll go and have a quiet supper somewhere.'

She sat down at the brightly lit dressing-table and with a sigh of relief removed her elaborate wig. Her dresser undid the back of the frilled and bustled watered-silk dress.

'I'm sorry,' Joanna said, 'I'd love to, but I'm bushed. It's been a very hectic twenty-four hours.'

She watched her sister stand up and step out of the costume, letting it fall round her feet on the floor. Corsets and other items of nineteenth-century underwear followed, and Freda slipped on a pink silk wrap. She sat down again and started to take off her make-up, glancing at Joanna in the mirror.

'So why did you come?' she enquired, generously plastering her face with cold cream.

'I don't know really.' Joanna, seated in the room's one armchair, shifted uncomfortably. Why on earth had she come? But ever since David had mentioned Samantha's new boyfriend that morning she had felt uneasy. However much she told herself not to jump to conclusions, she could not help remembering her grandfather's funeral and the way in which her niece and Steve Jordan had mysteriously disappeared. Freda had told her later that Samantha had been bored and that Steve had gallantly escorted her home, an explanation which Freda herself seemed to have accepted. Joanna had remained unconvinced. She had no doubt that Steve had driven Samantha home eventually, but after how long an interval? And what happened between them in that intervening time? She suspected that her brother-in-law never did anything from altruistic motives; and it fitted, too, with David's definition of 'last autumn'. Joanna told herself that she was making bricks without straw, but felt that with even such nebulous suspicions she should warn her sister.

Her eyes met Freda's again in the mirror. Freda paused in the act of wiping her face with a clean pad of cotton waste and asked: 'Well? There must be some reason.'

Joanna said hesitantly: 'David told me today that Samantha has a new boyfriend. Since last autumn, when she broke up with Stuart.'

'So?' Freda resumed her task. 'What's it got to do with me?'

Joanna felt more uncomfortable than ever. 'I . . . Look, Freddie, please don't take this the wrong way, but . . . well, I did just wonder about her and Steve.' She went on hurriedly, as Freda swivelled angrily to face her: 'They did go off together the afternoon of Gramps's funeral.'

Freda's eyes glared, basilisk-like, through the

373

surrounding mask of cream. 'Are you daring to suggest', she demanded furiously, 'that my husband and Davey's little bastard are having an affair?'

Joanna regarded her sister shrewdly. She had evidently touched a raw nerve there.

'Sam may have been conceived outside wedlock,' she reminded Freda gently, 'but she was born inside it. My guess is that you do – or did – suspect something.'

'At the time,' Freda admitted reluctantly, after a momentary hesitation. 'But I was upset by Gramps's death and the way Steve had gone off without letting me know what he was doing. But he explained it. I told you so at the time.' Her voice had risen, and she was conscious of being on the defensive. She turned back to the mirror and finished cleaning her face. Deliberately she forced herself to be calm. 'As a matter of fact, Steve and I are getting on very well at present. We've never been happier. Our sex life, when we're together, is extremely good. I should know if there was another woman.' She forced a smile. 'I appreciate your motives, Jo, because I know you've never been one to make mischief, but as far as I'm concerned the idea's absurd, so let's forget it, shall we?'

'OK.' Joanna was relieved that the purpose of her visit was accomplished without any open breach between them. 'If you say so, of course I accept your word. As you pointed out, you'd be bound to know.' She shouldered her handbag and got up, retrieving her case from the corner where she had left it. 'I must go. I'm sorry, Freddie, if I've upset you. I'll be seeing you. What are you doing after the show closes?'

'I'm having a good long rest at Kelmscott with Steve and the children. I've promised myself that. Mind you,' Freda added, tossing the cotton waste on to the floor, 'I've a couple of television projects lined up, and Maurice called yesterday about a part in a new British film . . .' Her voice tailed away, and she grimaced at her reflection. She was thirty-seven, and her face, denuded of make-up, clearly showed a few lines and wrinkles. 'I know what you're thinking. I'm a workaholic. But we all are, all three of us. Look at you and Davey.'

Joanna laughed and went out. Freda waved gaily at the closing door but, once left alone with her dresser, her smile and general air of confidence faded. She sat staring at herself in the mirror, thinking about Steve and her niece. And the longer she thought, the more uneasy she became. Damn Joanna!

Morning prayers at Forest Moor were over, and Davina had returned to her study. Without stopping to remove her gown, she walked over to the window and stared out, remaining motionless for quite some time. She saw, without seeing it, the avenue of lime trees, the leaves bright and inviting in the sunshine. The previous evening, she had received an unexpected telephone call from David Nugent. He had asked her to marry him.

'Don't decide right now,' he had said. 'Take time to think it over.'

In spite of her conversation with Joanna, three years earlier, his proposal had still come as a shock. On recent occasions when they had met, sometimes in London, but mostly in Bath, she had come to the conclusion that if he had ever felt any more for her than ordinary friendship those days were over. They still enjoyed one another's company, laughed a great deal, went to the cinema or the theatre, but his attitude towards her had contained no hint of the lover-like, and he had never even tried to kiss her. He treated her with respect and deference, listened to her plans for a new book on the subject of Richard II, sympathized with her moans that it would probably never be written – as head-mistress of Forest Moor, she told him, she simply did not have the time – and generally acted the part of a friend. She had grown used to their sporadic relationship and relied on him in much the same way that Joanna relied on Alex: someone who was always willing to listen and advise. Now, suddenly, David wanted to change all that. The strange thing was that she had not immediately refused him.

Davina went back to her desk and sat down. There was a pile of school reports awaiting her signature and the morning's mail, already opened by her secretary and laid ready for her attention on the big leather-bound blotter. She had never felt less inclined to start work in her life. The real trouble was that she did not know what she wanted.

Oh, but she did! She wanted Anthony. She would have had him, too, if Claire hadn't played her tricks . . . Davina got up again, pacing restlessly about the room. Why, after all these years, was the life she had made for herself no longer sufficient? She had achieved everything she had set out to do and she was only just forty. She ought to be one of the happiest women alive.

She paused in front of 'Les Laveuses', looking at the four women, standing and kneeling on the bank of a river, beating their linen and floating it in the swiftly running water. The picture hung where Anthea's copy of 'The Road to Sydenham' had been, and Davina recalled earlier times, earlier days in this same study . . .

She had achieved what Anthea had wanted her to achieve; perhaps that was why she wasn't happy. Perhaps what she had really wanted was to marry Anthony and be his wife . . .

But she had married him. She had been his wife and it had not been enough. She felt confused; everything was blurred round the edges. The only fact which stood out with any clarity was that what had once satisfied her, and had most certainly satisfied Anthea, no longer seemed to.

Davina returned once more to her desk. Her head was aching, and she rummaged in one of the drawers for some aspirin. She thought again of David Nugent's proposal, wondering what she was going to do about it, and then the idea came to her. If she became engaged to David, if Anthony thought she was going to marry someone else, might he not call Claire's bluff? Might he not feel that he had to do something drastic before it was too late?

Davina knew at once that what she was proposing to do was wrong. She felt ashamed of herself for even contem-

376

plating the idea, but her resolve was unshaken. She wanted Anthony and she had always got what she wanted. Anthea had taught her that lesson when she was still very young: know what you want, go after it and get it, no matter what the cost.

Davina's secretary knocked and put her head around the study door.

'Don't forget you have a staff meeting in the Mistresses' Common Room at nine-thirty.'

Davina glanced at her watch. It was almost that now. She nodded.

'I haven't forgotten, but I'll be a few minutes late. Would you be kind enough to tell them? There's an important telephone call I have to make.'

39

ANTHONY WAITED until Mrs Hemmings had closed the back door of the surgery carefully behind her, then pressed the bell on his desk. As Mrs Hemmings's footsteps receded down the path at the side of the house, his receptionist ushered in the next patient, a tall, fair-haired, good-looking man whose name Anthony could not recall, but whose face, he felt sure, he had seen somewhere before. He glanced down at the pile of folders laid ready on his desk.

'Mr Jordan is a new patient,' the receptionist informed him. 'This is his first visit.'

'Hi, Doc!' Steve Jordan eased himself into the chair on the other side of the desk and beamed. 'We've met, but you probably don't remember. It was at old man Marshall's eightieth birthday.'

Anthony frowned. 'Do you mean Reginald Harding?'

'Was that his name? My mistake. I just assumed his name was the same as Freddie's.'

The pieces fell into place. Anthony recognized the young American as Freda Marshall's second husband and recalled the painful circumstances of their first meeting. It had been the day when Claire had tried to cut her wrists; the day when he had accepted that his hopes for a divorce would come to nothing; that his remarriage to Davina was just a dream. The birthday party had been spoiled as he and Samantha had dashed from the house in Nightingale Close. He had known that everyone there must be thinking of Theresa. Small wonder that he had forgotten the

378

lesser details, like the presence of this blond Adonis.

'Mr ... er ...,' he began. What had the receptionist called him? Anthony glanced down at the pristine file-cover alongside the bulging and well-worn one of Mrs Hemmings.

'Jordan. Steve Jordan. Freddie and I have got that big place, Kelmscott House, a mile or so outside the city.'

'Ah, yes.' Anthony vaguely recollected reading an article about it. There had been a photograph of Freda playing with two children and a couple of dogs on one of the lawns. 'So what can I do for you, Mr Jordan? You do realize', he added, 'that I don't take private patients?'

'Sure. Freddie explained it to me. Hell of a fine thing, if I may say so.'

Anthony raised his eyebrows and commented drily: 'It's nice to find an American who approves of the National Health system.'

'Oh, I'm a very public-spirited guy.' Steve smiled winningly.

Anthony said: 'You must have been living over here for several years now. Haven't you ever needed a doctor before?'

'Nope. I'm a healthy man.' Anthony doubted this, noting the slightly bloodshot eyes and the coarsening nose, both signs of a heavy drinker. Reading his thoughts, Steve grinned disarmingly. 'OK. So I like a drink now and then. Does no harm. As I say, I'm pretty fit. I've only come to you now because of this pain in my shoulder. Freddie and the kids go to some old fogey she's known ever since she was in diapers. Me, I gotta have someone younger. Someone with more up-to-date ideas.'

'I'm flattered.' Anthony stood up and came round the desk. 'Which shoulder is giving you trouble?'

Five minutes later, he resumed his seat. 'There's nothing much the matter that I can see. It's probably just a touch of rheumatism. The joint's mobility is in no way impaired. I could prescribe pain-killers, but in my experience aspirin, provided it doesn't upset your stomach, is as effective as anything, and you can buy that as cheaply as you can get it on prescription. But I will make you out a prescription, if you wish.'

'Hell, no.' Steve Jordan slipped on his jacket and came to the real reason for his visit. If only Samantha would be a little more open with him, there would be no need for this elaborate charade. But in all their numerous clandestine meetings he had never been able to discover anything about her financial situation. Under that pretty exterior, she was a hard-nosed little bastard, but he wasn't prepared to leave Freda for her unless he knew that he was financially secure. 'Hey!' he went on, as though suddenly struck by the thought. 'How's that lovely daughter of yours? Samantha, isn't it?'

'Do you know Sam?' Anthony looked up, surprised. He had no knowledge of her visiting her Aunt Freda.

'I took her home from the old man's funeral, last fall. Seemed a nice kid.'

'Hardly that. She's twenty-two now and in her last year at university.'

'Is that a fact? I guess she just seemed young to me.' Steve shrugged. 'I prefer mature women, like Freddie. That's some place you've got there. What's it called? Lyncombe Manor?'

'That's right. It belongs to my mother.'

'Yeah. Freddie was telling me. It must be nice having a father who was a multi-millionaire.'

'Oh, I don't know. The money's all tied up in different trusts and things.'

'You mean for your kids? Stuff like that.' Steve rose, straightening his jacket, trying to sound casual, as though he were making polite conversation on his way out.

'Something of the sort.'

'It must be a great relief to know they're provided for.'

'I suppose so.' Anthony was already glancing through the next file, his mind on other things. Steve cursed to himself. It wasn't going to work. Then, as he moved reluctantly to what was obviously the surgery exit, Anthony looked up and said thoughtfully: 'I'm not really sure that I approve of inherited wealth. In the wrong hands, it can inhibit initiative. Not that I think that applies to Samantha. She's absolutely determined to become an actress.'

'She has money of her own?'

No alarm-bells rang in Anthony's head. He was, after all, talking to the husband of Freda Marshall.

'A very great deal. Half a million or thereabouts. It's been hers since her twenty-first birthday.'

Steve whistled appreciatively. 'Gee, I wish my grandfather had left me that sort of dough. Anyway, I musn't take up any more of your time. Thanks, Doc. I'll give your regards to Freddie.' Steve paused, his hand on the handle of the door leading into the garden. 'Did you hear about her sister, Davey, getting married? Sure thing! She's just got herself engaged to some guy called David Nugent. He's a friend of Jo's.'

'No,' Anthony answered tonelessly. 'I hadn't heard. Was it . . . was it recent?'

'Coupla days ago. She telephoned Freddie from Southampton.'

Anthony said nothing, but after Steve's departure it was a few minutes before he again pressed the bell for the next patient.

'So Neil and Roy have done it,' Selina observed with quiet satisfaction, as she and Joanna strolled along the sea-front at Brighton, where the Labour Party Conference was being held that year.

A few days after the general election, Michael Foot had announced that he would not be standing for the position of party leader at the annual conference in October. The vote for the new leadership had taken place on the Sunday before the conference began, with Neil Kinnock, as expected, an easy winner. Roy Hattersley, his closest rival, had been elected deputy.

381

Selina went on: 'You ought to get offered something, Jo. It's high time you were back where you belong, on the front benches. Neil Kinnock likes you.'

Joanna said nothing, staring out to sea. It was warm for October, and there was a faint heat-haze, merging water into sky. Tresses of dark seaweed floated lazily on the surface of a small rock-pool. She knew Selina was right. She had always got on well with the fiery-haired Welshman who was now the Labour leader, and at one time she would have been excited at the prospect of a resurgence in her career. But somehow, nowadays, she could no longer whip up enthusiasm. It was David who had told her to cultivate Neil Kinnock, and, as always, his advice had been sound.

The news of his engagement to Davina had come as a terrible blow to her. She had never really believed that her sister would accept him. It didn't make sense. Joanna was convinced that Davina was still in love with Anthony, so why would she consent to marry David Nugent? Surely she wasn't desperate to be married at any price? Not the headmistress of Forest Moor! Author! Broadcaster! There would be no point in marriage for its own sake.

Joanna had seen David and Davina together once, shortly after the engagement had been announced. Freda had insisted on holding a family party for them at Kelmscott House, but it had not been a great success. Anthea had been present, registering strong disapproval; Stuart and Laura Nugent had made it abundantly plain that they would much have preferred Joanna as a step-mother; Joanna herself had found it a strain to conceal her true feelings; while Davina had seemed quiet and abstracted. Steve Jordan had been drinking heavily, and halfway through the evening he and Samantha had disappeared for over an hour, to Freda's fury. Only David had been contented.

'I can't believe my luck,' he had said to Jean and Bernard in Joanna's hearing. 'I can't believe that a wonderful woman like Davey would wish to marry me.'

Joanna had wanted to say: 'She doesn't. She wants to

marry Anthony Douglas. She's only using you to make him jealous.'

Was that the truth? she wondered now. Was that really what Davina was doing? Trying to force Anthony's hand. Make him leave Claire. But she would not succeed. Davina simply would not admit that Anthony dared not risk taking the responsibility for a second woman's death.

'Penny for them,' Selina teased. 'You're miles away.'

'Sorry.' Joanna turned her head and smiled at her friend. 'Just thinking over what you said. Neil won't say anything until the conference is over of course, but I think I'd better stay in London this coming weekend in case the phone rings.'

She and Selina had become very close since those heady days when Joanna had merited a House of Commons secretary. Apart from sharing a flat, they had a lot in common; they were both of the same social and political background, they both loved the theatre. And wasn't it a truism that every woman needed another woman to confide in? Yet that was what Joanna could never do; she could never talk with complete frankness to Selina. Selina knew of her feelings for David Nugent, but it was knowledge she had culled more from observation than from anything she had been specifically told. Occasionally, as on the evening they had been to see *The Spanish Tragedy*, the evening of her grandfather's death, Joanna would open up, but such moments were rare.

There was only one person in whom Joanna confided without restraint, and that was Alex. She had not seen him since just before he went abroad the previous year, but he wrote regularly, long amusing letters, from Derek Conway's villa near Cannes, and telephoned her at least once a month, listening calmly and patiently to all her problems, proffering what was usually sound and sensible advice. But the last time he had spoken to her, two weeks ago, Joanna had been left with the impression that all was not well with him. It was not that Alex had been any less understanding, any less courteous, but she had felt that his

383

heart had not been in it. 'Going through the motions' was a phrase which had sprung to her mind. She had also been struck, on reflection, by how little of himself and his own affairs he had lately revealed. It was as though he were deliberately avoiding the subject . . .

'Come on,' said Selina's voice, breaking into her uneasy thoughts, 'it's time we were getting back.' As they turned once more in the direction of the conference centre, she eyed Joanna curiously. 'Is anything wrong?' she asked. 'You're shivering, and it's not even cold.'

'Am I? I wasn't aware of it.' Joanna shrugged. 'Someone must have walked over my grave.'

Samantha stretched out on the bed and ran her fingers down the length of Steve Jordan's spine. He was lying prone beside her, his handsome face half-buried amongst the pillows. The half which she could see wore a sullen expression. Samantha eased one of her legs over his and began to rub it up and down.

'Are you sure Freda's out all day? I mean, she isn't suddenly going to burst in on us, is she?'

Steve muttered crossly: 'I've told you. She's at the HTV West studios in Bristol, working on this mini-series about Dr Crippen.' He sniggered. 'She's playing the wife who gets done in. They don't want her for the junior leads any more.'

'Belle Elmore's a much more interesting part than Ethel Le Neve,' Samantha retorted. 'I wish I could land parts like that. Aunt Freda's never out of work. That's more than you can say for me.'

She had graduated from Bristol University in the summer, since when she had been haunting theatrical agencies and auditioning for every part, however minor, advertised in the *Stage*. She sometimes felt as though she must have applied for every assistant stage manager's job in the country, but so far without success. She was spending a small fortune in train fares.

Steve propped himself on his elbows. 'I keep telling you,'

he said angrily, 'come to the States with me. I'm going soon anyway. I can't stand this house or this miserable country much longer. I've got contacts in Hollywood and LA. Not everyone's written me off, though you'd think so, to hear Freddie talking. We'd make a great team. We'd get married once my divorce had gone through. No one can stop you. You're free, blonde and over twenty-one.'

Samantha hesitated, looking down admiringly at the naked contours of her body, at the long legs, the firm young breasts and the flat stomach. This proposal of Steve's was what she had once wanted; it had been the object of this whole, rather sordid affair. But now she was not so sure. A certain native caution held her back. She wanted to be an actress, didn't she? If she wanted, one day, to rival Freda's reputation, she would first have to learn her craft.

And there was something else. A chance remark dropped by her father a few months back had revealed that Steve Jordan had consulted him as a patient. This alone Samantha had thought a suspicious circumstance, because Steve was never ill; but when Anthony also revealed that they had discussed her financial situation and the amount of money left to her by her grandfather Douglas's will she had wisely decided that she needed to be very careful indeed. It was one thing for her to use Steve, quite another for him to use her, and for the moment she could not see her way clear. The affair drifted on, with Steve becoming ever more importunate, while she grew more indifferent and less sure of what she wanted from life. Her earlier dreams of Hollywood and fame now seemed a trifle childish.

She sat up, linking her arms around her knees. The bedroom was old-fashioned, full of antiques which Freda had bought with the house. The previous owner's death had left his heirs with heavy death duties and they had been glad to sell off as much of the estate as possible. Samantha thought it gloomy and forbidding. She preferred Derek Conway Interiors.

Now it was Steve who ran his fingers down her back, rolling on to his side and letting his hand caress her spine as far as the gently swelling buttocks. He wriggled forward, lowering his head to kiss each one in turn.

Samantha giggled, but said: 'Stop it, Steve. I'm trying to think.'

'What's to think about?' he asked. 'Come to America with me. It's where you belong.'

'Why don't you do what you said? Simply leave Freda and go. I can always follow on later.'

He pouted. 'I wasn't serious. I shan't leave Freddie unless you come with me. What would be the point?'

What, indeed? she wondered. What would be the point of abandoning one fortune until he had made certain of another?

There were voices outside the bedroom door; Mabel Patterson's followed by Freda's.

'Don't fuss,' Freda was saying. 'It's only a migraine. I've had them before, and they're not serious. But I was useless on the set. I had to come home. But I'll be fine by tomorrow. I'll lie down for an hour or two with the curtains drawn.'

The door opened, and Freda came in.

40

THE WEEKEND FOLLOWING the Labour Party Conference, Joanna and Selina returned to Crozier Street, making sure, throughout Saturday and Sunday, that one or the other of them was always in the flat.

'Someone's got to be here in case Neil rings.'

'Suppose he doesn't,' Joanna said despondently. 'There's no guarantee he's going to offer me anything. I think we're wasting our time.'

'Wait and see, as Mr Asquith was so fond of remarking.' Selina settled down in her favourite chair and switched on the television. Joanna picked up a book and retired to her bedroom. There were times when she found Selina's unremitting optimism hard to take. She sat down at the desk in front of the window and began a long-delayed letter to Alex.

By lunch-time on Sunday, her own expectations were in tatters, but Selina said briskly: 'Give the man a chance. He hasn't been back from Brighton forty-eight hours, and there are all the major posts to fill. I still think you'll be back on the front benches at the start of the next parliamentary session.'

The afternoon wore on, and the silence of the telephone bell began to get oppressive. Joanna wanted to go for a walk, but Selina was adamant.

'We're staying in at least until midday tomorrow.'

'I ought to have gone down to Avonvale yesterday,' Joanna protested fretfully. 'I haven't held a "surgery" in over a month.'

'David would have told you if anything urgent had needed your attention. As a matter of fact, I talked to him about it on Friday, at the conference, and he agreed that for a day or two you ought to stay put.'

Joanna shrugged and said nothing. She had spent the whole of the past week at Brighton avoiding David Nugent as much as possible, politely refusing his request for a dance at the party on the final evening, and leaving him confused and bewildered.

'He doesn't understand your attitude,' Selina was saying now. 'He can't make out why you've changed towards him.'

'I hope you didn't do anything silly, like trying to hint at the truth,' Joanna upbraided her sharply.

Selina looked hurt. 'As if I would! What sort of a fool do you take me for?'

'Sorry. I'm not thinking straight.' Joanna rose from her chair and wandered around the room, fiddling with the ornaments, picking them up and putting them down again until Selina could bear it no longer.

'Didn't you ought to be getting on with that article you're writing for the *Guardian*? I thought you said the deadline was Tuesday.'

'It is. I finished it last night, after I'd written to Alex.'

Not for the first time, Selina found herself envying her friend's powers of concentration. However many distractions were occupying her mind, if a thing had to be done, Joanna could always manage to do it. She went back now to her seat, sighing with frustration, and took up her book again.

The telephone bell sounded loudly in the silence. Both women jumped, their eyes meeting in a look of startled interrogation. Then Selina got up and went across to the table by the window, lifting the receiver with a hand that was not quite steady.

'Hello,' she said. 'Selina Driver speaking.' Joanna sat like a statue, her book gripped between her hands. She could hear a man's voice, faintly, at the other end of the line.

Then she saw her friend's face crumple with disappointment. 'Hold on a minute,' Selina said. 'I'll get her.' She held the receiver towards Joanna. 'It's that man, Conway.' Her tone was edged with disapproval. 'He's calling from France. He wants to speak to you urgently.' As Joanna took the phone from her, she whispered: 'Don't let him keep you. We want that line kept clear.'

'Derek?' Joanna spoke tentatively. She had never known Derek Conway well, and it was many years since they had had any direct communication.

Five minutes later, she hung up, her face white and drawn. Then she picked up the receiver again, dialled Enquiries at Heathrow airport and enquired the time of the next flight to Cannes.

'What do you think you're doing?' Selina demanded as Joanna hung up once more. 'Jo! What's this all about?'

'Alex is very ill. In fact he's dying. Derek says if I don't get there tonight I shan't see him alive again. Fortunately, there's a flight to Paris just after five and I can get an internal flight to Cannes fifty minutes later. Don't get in my way, Selina. I'm going to pack. If you want to be useful, call me a taxi, there's a dear.'

'Joanna!' Selina almost screamed. 'Supposing Neil phones?' She followed her friend into the bedroom.

Joanna wasn't listening. She was hastily packing a few necessities into an overnight bag and rummaging in a drawer for her passport. She checked her money. 'I'll have to go to the *bureau de change* at Orly.' She glanced at the other woman and managed a smile. 'It's no good looking at me like that. Even if I knew for a fact that Neil Kinnock was going to phone me this very afternoon, offering me the post of Shadow Chancellor, I'd still have to go. Alex is my best friend. He's been a part of my life for more years than I care to remember, and now he's dying.' Her voice broke, and she blinked back the tears.

'What's wrong with him?' Selina asked, subdued. 'I mean, this Conway man might be wrong. Alex may not be as bad as he thinks.'

Joanna did not bother to reply. 'Just phone for a cab, please, Selina,' was all she said.

Twenty minutes later, she waved goodbye to Selina as the taxi pulled away from the kerb. When it had vanished round the street-corner, Selina turned and went back upstairs. As she opened the front door of the flat, the telephone started ringing.

The taxi sped out of Cannes on the Nice road, then turned off towards the picture-book town of Mougins. It was dark; too dark for Joanna to receive anything but the vaguest impression of the countryside; of the tree-clad slopes of the Tanneron Massif which lay south of Grasse. Not that she would have noticed much had it been daylight. Her thoughts were centred entirely on Alex and the fear that she would not be in time.

Just beyond Mougins, the taxi swerved sharply to the right, along a narrow dirt road, pulling up with screeching brakes before a two-storey building. Derek Conway must have been on the watch for her arrival because he came out on to the porch almost immediately, switching on an overhead light as he did so. The front steps became visible amid the surrounding darkness.

'Go in,' he said brusquely to Joanna. 'I'll pay the driver.'

The inside of the house was softly illuminated by concealed wall-lighting, and through various open doors she glimpsed rooms beautifully decorated in the Derek Conway style. The hall floor was covered in a thick pale-green carpet, and the walls were a delicate shade of pink, a background to two David Hockney paintings which Joanna knew without the shadow of a doubt were genuine. She followed Derek up a pitch-pine staircase, across a landing decorated like the hall, but boasting a Chagall and a Klee, and into a bedroom where a struggling fire was burning on an open hearth. A nurse, who had been sitting by the bed, rose at their entrance, said something in rapid French to Derek Conway, then moved away to the far side of the room. Joanna was hardly conscious of her. She had eyes for no one but Alex.

He was propped up in bed, but she would not have recognized him until he smiled. His face and body were skeletal, the bones sticking up through the parchment-coloured skin. His eyes were sunk deep into their sockets, and his lips were bloodless. Only the self-mocking, faintly ironic look he gave her revealed that the old Alex, the Alex she knew and loved, was still there, inside this emaciated wreck of a man.

She said in an undertone to Derek Conway: 'What's wrong with him? Can't anything be done?'

Derek shook his head. He looked frightened. 'The doctor says no. I don't think he even knows what it is. He's tried everything. Every antibiotic he can lay his hands on. But none of them seems to do any good. Alex just gets weaker and weaker.' Derek turned away and began to cry.

There was a movement from the bed. Horrified by what she had just been told, Joanna knelt down beside Alex and took one of his hands in hers. It was icy cold. She had to lean close to him to hear what he was saying.

'Punishment for a misspent life.' Again there was a gleam of sardonic humour.

'What nonsense!' she protested vehemently.

Derek Conway said, his voice taut with fear: 'Perhaps he's right! Christ! What are we going to do?'

'God's caught up with us at last.' Alex's voice was fainter still, and the clutch of his fingers very feeble. 'He's on the side of the righteous after all. Sinners will get their comeuppance.' This time the smile only lit his eyes. It was too much effort to move his lips. 'Very tired,' he managed after another few minutes, making an enormous effort. 'Stay with me . . . until morning.'

Derek found Joanna a chair and settled her into it, next to the bed. He brought her food, but she was unable to eat it, drinking instead innumerable cups of coffee. She held one of Alex's hands, and Derek, on the opposite side of the bed, the other. Now and then, one of them was forced to go to the bathroom. Whenever that happened, Alex's eyes would flutter open and he would be restless until the three of them were together again. Occasionally, the nurse would come to the bedside to take Alex's pulse or to give him a sip of water.

About four in the morning, there was a sudden change in his breathing. The rhythm of death had started, alternating between deep and shallow. Joanna began to shiver uncontrollably. Suddenly, Alex's eyes, which had been closed for the past half-hour, opened wide, staring blankly at her.

'Alex!' she cried. 'Alex!'

Slowly the blank look faded. As the nurse rustled towards the bed, the intelligence returned and he gave a wide cynical grin. It was so like the Alex Joanna had always known that she was momentarily convinced that he had turned the corner and would recover. She gave an answering grin and laughed out loud. As she did so, the scandalized nurse leaned over and closed his eyes.

'He is dead, madame,' she said in English.

Joanna stayed for the funeral, three days later, in spite of frantic telephone calls from Selina to say that Neil Kinnock wanted her to contact him urgently. Nothing, for the moment, seemed of any importance beside the fact that Alex was dead. She had lost both the men she loved: David belonged to her sister, and Alex was no longer with her. And in Alex she had lost, as she had told Selina, her best friend.

Derek Conway had contacted Alex's family, but no one was prepared to come to the funeral. Sir Herbert said that as far as he was concerned his son was dead already and had been for many years. Olwen declined politely but firmly, and Lady Pamela was now confined to a wheel-chair with rheumatoid arthritis. Claire and her parents, the only other of Alex's relatives known to Joanna, were as hostile as Sir Herbert had been when approached.

'So that just leaves us,' Joanna said gently to her host. 'But we both loved him, and that makes up for a lot.'

Joanna had expected a very quiet funeral, just herself

and Derek at the Protestant church in Cannes. What she had not foreseen was the bevy of English photographers and reporters waiting for them at the graveside and around the cemetery gates. The fact that the two men had been lovers was quite sufficient to attract the attention of a certain section of the press, and Alex Ferrer had been headline news once already. The two facts in conjunction made a sufficiently interesting story to warrant attention from the tabloids, and the presence of a well-known woman Labour MP among the mourners was a bonus. When Joanna flew into Heathrow the following morning, it was her own face which greeted her from the news-stands.

She went straight from the airport to Westminster, where Selina, who had returned to the House of Commons secretarial pool since Joanna's relegation to the back benches, sought her out.

'What on earth do you think you've been playing at?' she demanded, bursting into the tiny ground-floor office which Joanna shared with two other Labour MPs. 'Why didn't you come straight home when I telephoned you? And now this!' she went on without waiting for an answer. She slapped two of the morning papers down on Joanna's desk. Both displayed front-page photographs of her standing beside Alex's grave.

Joanna glanced at them indifferently, then up at her friend. Selina was shocked to note her haggard appearance.

'I really don't care,' Joanna said contemptuously. 'Alex meant a great deal to me. Did you really think I'd desert him? What a low opinion you must really have of me.'

'Oh, Jo my dear, I didn't mean it like that.' Selina was distressed. 'But not everyone thinks like you do. A lot of people look on homosexuality as a sin or a crime. There hasn't been a call from Neil Kinnock's office today, and I have it on very good authority that Tom Birkenshaw was seen in earnest conversation with Neil earlier this morning. And he had copies of both these papers under his arm.'

Joanna shrugged, but felt the familiar sinking sensation in the pit of her stomach which Tom Birkenshaw's name always aroused. As the numbness she had experienced following Alex's death began to wear off, she realized how much she had wanted this promotion to the front benches. And now her old enemy, armed with fresh ammunition, was once again doing his best to block her chances.

'Has David been in touch?' she asked abruptly.

'Three times. He phoned the flat Sunday evening, Monday and again last night. I had to tell him what was going on.'

'What did he say?'

'Nothing much. And it's difficult to guess what he's thinking. He never gives much away. Oh, and your sister, Freda, keeps ringing you. She wants you to contact her urgently. During the day, you can get her at the HTV West studios in Bristol.'

Joanna nodded. As Selina prepared to leave, she said: 'Thanks.'

Her friend looked surprised. 'What for?'

'For being concerned enough to care what happens to me.'

'Don't be such an idiot!' Selina exclaimed roughly, but she was smiling as she went out and shut the door.

Joanna looked at her watch. She had an hour and a half before she need be in the Chamber for a debate on education which she very much wanted to hear. She supposed she ought to get some lunch, but she wasn't hungry. She might as well telephone Freda while she had the office to herself. She dialled the Bristol code, followed by the HTV studio number.

But Freda wasn't available: she was on set and could not possibly be disturbed. If the caller could possibly phone again later . . .

When Joanna entered the Chamber at two-thirty, Neil Kinnock was sitting in his place on the Opposition front benches. Tom Birkenshaw, the new Shadow spokesman on farming, sat a few feet away from him. The Labour leader glanced round and met Joanna's eyes. He smiled and gave a little nod, but that was all. He seemed to have changed his mind about wanting to speak to her.

Damn! thought Joanna. I've blown it, and Tom Birkenshaw has put the boot in. I wish to God I knew what that man has against me.

She got back to Crozier Street halfway through the evening to find Selina already home, with a meal prepared and in the oven. She smiled her gratitude and went into her bedroom to unpack her overnight bag. It felt like an age since she had left Cannes that morning, and Alex already seemed very far away.

And then she knew that he would never be far away again. He would be with her all the time. The idea was oddly comforting, and she felt the wretched tiredness, which had dogged her since his death, slowly drain away. As she opened her bedroom door and emerged into the sitting-room, the smell of Selina's chicken casserole wafted in from the kitchen. Joanna realized that she was ravenously hungry.

The telephone rang. Selina, who was laying the table, said: 'OK. I'll get it.' She tried to keep the excitement out of her voice. But once again she was disappointed. As she held the receiver out to Joanna, she said flatly: 'It's for you. It's Freda.'

41

'SO I'VE sent him packing. I've told him to get out,' Freda stormed. 'Having it off, Jo, in *my* bed, in *my* house, as bold as brass. And the bedroom door wasn't even locked! Either of the children, or Mabel Patterson, could have walked in on them.'

'And has he gone?' Joanna wanted to know.

'Oh, he's gone all right.' Freda's voice was full of venom. 'To a hotel for the time being. What he does after that is his business.'

'You don't sound very upset,' her sister mused. 'Or are you just putting on a brave face for my benefit?'

There was silence at the other end of the line, then Freda gave a short laugh.

'Strangely enough, I'm not in the least upset. Not in the way you mean. I'm furiously, blazingly mad at having my trust betrayed, but that's different. Odd, isn't it? A few months ago I should have been devastated at the prospect of losing Steve. But now it's actually happened I couldn't care less. I can't understand it.'

'Perhaps you've accepted that he isn't worth bothering about. That he was just after your money. But I'm delighted you've come to your senses. By the way, what do Davina and Anthony Douglas have to say about the affair?'

'As far as Anthony's concerned, I've no idea. I haven't contacted him. Davina's livid. She blames me.'

'That's ridiculous. Take no notice. She's upset and feels she has to blame someone, but guilt prevents her blaming Samantha.' Selina was signalling that the chicken casserole was getting cold. 'Freddie love, I have to go, but I shall be in Bath this weekend. I'm holding a "surgery" at Avonvale first thing on Saturday morning, but I'll be in Nightingale Close by lunch-time. I'll phone you from there. Perhaps we can arrange to meet.'

She hung up and met Selina's eyes, which were full of suppressed amusement.

'I could hear most of that from here,' she said. 'What a rotten thing to have happened.'

'No, it's not.' Joanna sat down at the table, while Selina spooned chicken and vegetables on to her plate. 'It's the very *best* thing which could have happened. Steve Jordan was no good for Freddie. That man's a born sponger, and she was too soft with him. Mmm. Your cooking gets better and better. This is absolutely delicious.'

When she telephoned David Nugent and said she wanted her 'surgery' arranged as early as possible on the Saturday morning, he suggested that she drive down to Avonvale on the Friday evening and stay the night.

Somewhat to her own surprise, as well as to his, she agreed. She supposed she had to get back on a normal footing with him some time and it might be better if she did not postpone it any longer. But when, mid-evening, she finally got to Oxford Road, weary after a long day at the House, she found that she had to park her car in the road because Davina's smart new Renault was already blocking the driveway.

'Shit!' Joanna said out loud in the darkness. The last thing she had wanted was to intrude on a *tête-à-tête*. But when Stuart let her in a few minutes later the first sound she heard was her sister's voice raised in anger.

'Bloody great row,' Stuart whispered. 'I'm keeping well out of it. So's Laura.' And he disappeared upstairs.

Joanna, unannounced, walked into the sitting-room, where she found David, seated in one of the armchairs, an expression of mule-like obstinacy on his face, and Davina, standing in the middle of the floor, hands on hips, the classic picture of outraged femininity.

'How can you possibly imply that it's not my business?' she was demanding furiously. 'Samantha's my daughter, for God's sake! I have every right to drive down to Lyncombe Manor tomorrow and talk over this whole bloody mess with Anthony, if I want to.'

'Samantha is twenty-two years old,' David said, pushing his glasses further up his nose and glaring through them. 'Neither you nor that ex-husband of yours can stop her doing anything she wants to, particularly as, as I understand it, she's financially independent. This visit you're proposing to make can serve no useful purpose. It could, on the other hand, do a great deal of harm. It could upset Claire Douglas, a woman who has tried to commit suicide once already on your account.'

'Crap!' Davina's jaw set in hard rigid lines. 'If you believe that woman meant to kill herself, you'll believe anything.'

David got out of his chair and seized her by the shoulders, giving her a little shake.

'Shut up, Davey! Shut up! I hate hearing you talk like that. It's not like you.'

She twisted free of him. 'On the contrary, it's very like me, and if we're going to be married you'll have to get used to it. I'm not a nice person. I never have been. So the sooner you take me down off this pedestal you've put me on, the better. I'm going to Lyncombe Manor tomorrow, to see Anthony.' She added viciously: 'And nothing you can say will stop me.'

Joanna decided it was time to intervene and draw a little of her sister's fire.

'David's right, Davey. Unless Anthony has invited you to go, do you think it's wise?'

They both jumped at the sound of her voice and turned towards her.

'How long have you been there, eavesdropping?' Davina demanded rudely.

'Long enough to hear more than I should, I dare say.'

Joanna dropped wearily into David's vacated chair. 'You mustn't go, Davey. Samantha's Anthony's responsibility.'

'She's mine as well, or had you forgotten? Good heavens!' Davina exclaimed scornfully. 'If anyone's had experience in dealing with members of my own sex, I have. I've spent most of my adult life sorting out their problems. I was the one who persuaded Sam to go to university, wasn't I? Left to Anthony and Claire, she'd have opted out.'

Joanna replied quietly: 'She was younger then. Samantha's too independent not to make her own decisions. She won't let you influence her as you let Aunt Thea influence you. Besides, you're not a free agent any more, Davey. You're engaged to David. His wishes have to be considered. The fact that he doesn't want you to go to Lyncombe should surely carry some weight.'

'Jo, I can fight my own battles.' David smiled gently to soften the reproof.

Nevertheless, she found herself blushing. 'Sorry,' she murmured awkwardly, feeling near to tears.

But Davina was staring at her sister as though mesmerized. After a moment, she turned away, still abstracted, twiddling her diamond engagement ring round and round on her finger. Then she took a deep breath and smiled bleakly at David.

'Look,' she said, 'we're both tired. Can we sleep on it? I'll telephone you first thing in the morning.' She explained to Joanna: 'I'm staying with Aunt Thea for the weekend, in Royal Crescent.' She gave David a swift kiss, skilfully eluding his attempt to prolong it. 'I must go. I shan't be in Bath until nearly eleven, as it is.'

'Davey,' David began, but she had already vanished. They heard the front door bang, then the car engine revving into life. David, who had started to follow her, paused and shrugged. Slowly he came back and sat down in a chair by the table.

'I probably am being unreasonable,' he said. 'Samantha is her daughter.' Joanna began to reply, but he flung out a hand. 'Sorry, Jo. I don't mean to be rude, but I don't want to discuss it any more. Not with you. Not with anyone. It's between Davey and me.' He forced a smile. 'Let's talk about you instead.' He clapped a hand to his forehead. 'My God! I'm losing my manners. You've driven all the way from London and I haven't even asked you to have a cup of tea. Have you eaten?'

'Yes, thank you. I stopped at a motorway café. But I'd love a cup of tea.'

'So would I.' He got up and went into the kitchen, calling over his shoulder: 'So what's happened since you got back from France? Has Neil telephoned you again?'

'No.' She tried to speak cheerfully, going to stand in the kitchen doorway, watching him fuss with teapot and caddy. 'I'm afraid I've really blown it this time. After all those pictures of me at Alex's funeral appeared in the papers, Neil apparently received a deputation headed by Tom Birkenshaw. I can only guess what was said.'

'That man!' David rattled the cups and saucers angrily. 'I wish to God we knew what he's got against you.' He smiled encouragingly at her. 'But Neil's his own man. He won't be influenced by other people's opinions. He'll take time to consider them, but he won't let them sway him if he thinks they're not right. And he knows you deserve that place on the front benches, Jo.' David poured boiling water into the pot. 'We're a right couple, aren't we?' he asked, after a moment's silence. 'We both have a knack of scoring own goals.'

It was so many years since she had been in Lyncombe Manor that Davina had forgotten what it looked like. Now, as she stood in the large oak-panelled hallway, everything came back with a rush, and she knew that she had made the correct decision. She had tossed and turned for half the night in Anthea's spare bed and, at one point, had contemplated getting up to make herself a hot drink in the gleaming, handsomely appointed kitchen. But her aunt was a very light sleeper, and Davina had not wanted to disturb her. There would have been questions and explanations, and this was one decision that Davina wanted to be quite sure was hers, and hers alone. She had finally fallen asleep about four o'clock, and had been surprised, when she woke that morning, how refreshed she felt. It was as though the weight of years had been lifted from her mind; a cliché, perhaps, but none the less true for that. After breakfast, she had simply informed Anthea that she was going to Lyncombe Manor.

'If David telephones, you can tell him where I've gone, and that I'll be in touch as soon as I can.' She had kissed her aunt's wrinkled cheek, a gesture she had not made for many years now, and added: 'You've always known me best. Better than I've known myself, very often.'

Anthea had looked both touched and gratified, and also as though she might burst into tears.

The young home-help, who admitted Davina to the Manor, wore jeans and a check shirt, very different from the neatly dressed maids Davina remembered from former days. She asked to see Doctor and Mrs Douglas and was requested to wait, so she sat down on a long tapestry couch standing against one wall. It had always been there: very little had changed, she reflected.

Claire arrived first. She came through the door which led to the back of the house and the gardens. Her dark hair, which showed premature streaks of grey, was windswept, and there were hectic spots of colour in either cheek, which had nothing to do with the fact that she had been gardening. She wore Wellington boots, caked with mud, an old grey jumper of Anthony's, which stretched down to her knees, and a black skirt, short enough to reveal an inch of petticoat. She was still carrying an earth-caked trowel in her right hand.

'What do you want?' she demanded belligerently. 'You don't belong here. You never did. Get out!'

'Claire!' Anthony spoke sharply from the study doorway. He came across and put an arm protectively about his

401

wife's shoulders. 'It's all right,' he said soothingly. 'Davey's only come to talk to me about Sam.'

'No, I haven't.' Davina had risen and now faced them both, forcing herself to remain calm. 'Samantha's your daughter. She belongs to both of you. You brought her up, Claire. You gave her the love and affection that I should have done, but didn't. I had no right whatsoever to interfere or to intrude on your lives the way I did. I've caused nothing but harm, to you, to Sam, to Freddie. Without that first meeting in America, I doubt very much if Sam and Steve Jordan would have become . . . lovers. But, as usual, I thought of no one but myself and, what's more, I'm afraid I'm never going to change.' She smiled wistfully at Anthony. 'You and Claire belong together. I'm not the marrying kind. Something Joanna said to me last night made me see that very clearly. She was talking about David, my fiancé. She said his wishes had to be considered. She said I wasn't a free agent any more. It made me stop and think.'

Sunlight was streaming through the stained-glass window to the left of the front door, making a pattern of jewel-rich colours across their faces. Anthony asked quietly: 'What exactly are you saying, Davina?'

She moved a little to one side, out of the patch of sapphire-blue light which was hurting her eyes. She looked at him directly, and for a moment Claire was excluded. There was a streak of carmine down one side of Anthony's face, like a great red birthmark. Then he, too, moved, and the illusion was broken.

'I'm saying that I like my life the way it is. Headmistress of Forest Moor. My writing, my broadcasting. I'm too selfish ever to be part of a couple, and too set in my ways to want to consider the wishes of other people. I'm going back to my ivory tower, this time for good. It's what I want. It's where I belong. I should never have left it.' She turned and addressed Claire. 'I don't want your husband, and I doubt very much if he ever really wanted me.'

402

Anthony said: 'What about this fellow you're engaged to? This David Nugent.'

Davina hesitated. 'That's going to be the hardest part. Telling him it's over. That will be my punishment, knowing how I've hurt him. Fortunately, my sister will be around to pick up the pieces.'

'Joanna?'

'Yes. I realized something else for the first time yesterday. She's in love with him. Probably has been for quite a while; but, as usual, I was too wrapped up in myself to notice. Well!' Davina hitched the strap of her leather handbag more securely over her shoulder. 'I'll say goodbye to you both. I don't think, somehow, we'll be running into each other very often in the future. Don't worry about Sam. She'll be all right. She's too much like me not to land on her feet, know which side her bread is buttered or how many beans make five.' She held out her hand. 'Goodbye, Tony. Look after Claire. She deserves it. That's more than can be said about me.'

She turned away hurriedly, letting herself out of the front door, her fingers fumbling with the catch. The Renault was parked on the gravel sweep at the side of the house. She climbed in and started the engine.

When Joanna arrived at Nightingale Close, just in time for Saturday lunch, she found Freda and her two children there ahead of her. Her niece and nephew were chasing up and down the stairs, pursued by Bernard, who, given the chance, was proving to be a doting grandfather. Jean was complaining of a headache, but only in a mild half-laughing sort of way.

Joanna was amazed how well her sister was looking. In spite of Freda's insouciant attitude over the phone, she had expected to see some signs of wear and tear; some symptom of the wronged and grieving wife. But Freda looked blooming, better than she had done for months.

'Darling!' she exclaimed buoyantly, as they all took their places round the dining-room table. 'I've come to my

403

senses at last, and it's been like waking up from a nightmare. How I could ever have imagined myself in love with that man, I do not know. Apart from his looks, he has nothing at all to recommend him. His brains are in the seat of his pants.' She saw her mother's expression and laughed. 'Oh, good,' she said, adroitly turning the subject, 'Mum's shepherd's pie. My favourite.'

'The potato's burned,' objected Antigone.

'And it's all runny underneath,' added her brother, not to be outdone.

'Out of the mouth of babes and sucklings . . .' Bernard was beginning, when the telephone rang in the hall. 'Blasted invention,' he muttered, getting to his feet. 'Invariably goes at meal-times, or when I'm in the bath.' He went out.

'Jo!' exclaimed her mother. 'Take this plate before I drop it. You're wool-gathering as usual.'

'Sorry.' She could barely stop shaking. Neil Kinnock. Could it be? On Saturday?

Her father returned. 'It's for you, Jo,' he said. 'It's David Nugent.'

42

'I CAN'T THINK WHY you're so cheerful,' Jean said plaintively. 'Your sister's just jilted a very fine man, your own friend, and you're behaving as though it's your birthday.'

Lunch was over. Adrian and Antigone had been forced upstairs by their mother – loudly lamenting that she had not brought Mabel Patterson with her – for a nap, while Bernard had retired circumspectly to his study. He could see that his womenfolk were preparing to hold an inquest on Davina's broken engagement, and he had no wish to be part of it. Nothing anyone could say or do would change Davina's mind, and he had no doubt that it was due to Anthea's influence. His sister was a strong-willed woman, and his eldest daughter had always been her favourite. Davina was the substitute child Anthea had never had. Sometimes, on rare occasions, he could see the funny side of it.

'Davey wasn't in love with David Nugent,' Joanna told her mother quietly. 'She's done the right thing. The decent thing. She's in love with Anthony. She always has been.'

'But,' Freda objected, 'according to David, Davey's given Anthony the old heave-ho as well. She's going to become a dedicated careerist. As if she hasn't always been! She and that daughter of hers are both tarred with the same brush. Single-minded dedication to self.'

The three women were gathered round the big electric fire in the drawing-room. The October afternoon was cold, and Jean had lit all its three bars. Freda had offered, more than once, to have central heating installed in the old

405

Victorian house, but Jean and Bernard had refused. Jean was convinced that it was bad for the health, and Bernard could not stand the thought of all the upheaval. Outside, a Saturday-afternoon calm pervaded the little close, and the only sound was the rise and fall of their own three voices.

'What's happened to Samantha?' enquired Joanna.

Freda shrugged. 'I don't know and I don't care. But, as far as I have any information at all, she's still living at Lyncombe Manor, presumably while she thinks things over.'

'Will she go to America, do you think?' Jean asked, after a moment's silence.

'I've no idea. My guess would be not. My guess is that she's already rumbled my soon-to-be-ex-husband. By the way,' she added with a self-conscious smile, 'have I mentioned that Jeff – Jeff Warwick – may be coming to stay with me soon? He's been offered a part in a film to be made over here, and some of the location work is being done around Bath. It would be silly, I thought, for him to stay in a hotel, when I've all those acres of empty rooms at Kelmscott. And he naturally wants to see Antigone.'

Joanna and her mother exchanged significant glances, but judged it wiser to make no comment. Instead, Jean, with unusual tact, changed the subject.

'No word from Neil Kinnock yet, then, Jo, about promotion to the front benches?'

Joanna shook her head. 'No. I think I've blown my chances. All that furore in the press about Alex's funeral didn't do me any good in some quarters, and I understand from Selina that Tom Birkenshaw's been lobbying Neil about something. Probably me and my general unfitness for office. I wish I knew why that man doesn't like me.'

Freda glanced up.

'Is that the man you knew in Yorkshire?' Joanna nodded, and her sister gave a bark of laughter. 'I shouldn't worry about anything he does or says. In fact I'd take it as a positive compliment that he doesn't like you.'

'Why?' Joanna asked curiously. 'What do you know about him?'

Freda proceeded to give a graphic and pithy account of her one encounter with Tom Birkenshaw, while Joanna's eyes grew slowly wider.

'Well, well!' she exclaimed softly when Freda had finished. 'So that's been the trouble all these years. A bruised male ego. And he had no means of taking his spite out on you, so he revenged himself on me instead. I wish I'd known before. It makes me feel a whole lot better.' She squeezed her sister's hand. 'Thanks, Freddie, for resolving the mystery at last. Do you know, I think I might just pass on the story, in the strictest confidence of course, to one or two of my fellow-MPs who can be trusted one hundred per cent' – she paused, then added with a wicked grin – 'never to keep a secret.'

Freda laughed, and even Jean smiled her approval. But the smile quickly faded to be replaced by a frown. The turn the conversation had taken reminded her once more of Davina and David Nugent.

'Is David very upset?' she asked her elder daughter.

'Yes, at the moment. But that's only to be expected.' Joanna looked and sounded so tranquil that her sister gave her a sudden sharp look, alive with suspicion. 'But he'll get over it, once he fully accepts that Davey means what she says; that there's no possible chance of her changing her mind. Besides,' Joanna looked straight at her mother, 'I shall be around to help him. I intend to make him realize that it was all for the best.'

Freda asked straitly: 'Do you think that you can?'

Joanna smiled. 'I'm going to have a damn good try.'

'That's the spirit! Jo . . .' Freda hesitated for a moment, before going on: 'I haven't told you yet how deeply sorry I am about Alex. I think I know what he meant to you.'

'Thanks.' Joanna hoped that her sister would say no more. Alex's death was too recent and too raw a wound to bear probing. Some day, when she was less vulnerable to grief than she was at present, she would discuss Alex with Freda, the only member of her family who had really known and understood him.

She recognized how a lot of people viewed her relationship with him in the disapproving set of her mother's lips and the tightening of her facial muscles. Before Freda could say anything more on the subject, Jean cut in with: 'If you mean what I think you mean, Jo, about David Nugent, I should be more than delighted to see you take Davey's place. So would your father. We haven't seen a lot of David over the years, but what we have has convinced us both that he's a splendid man. It's high time you got married again. Your father was saying so, only the other night.' Joanna and Freda grinned at one another: it was an old trick of their mother's to attribute to Bernard opinions that she had either voiced, or would like to voice, herself. Jean went on: 'I can't think what Davina was thinking of, getting engaged to him in the first place, if she had no intention of seeing it through.'

Freda hazarded: 'I suspect she was trying to make Anthony jealous.' Joanna nodded in agreement, and Freda continued: 'Now, suddenly, for some reason of her own, she's decided that she doesn't want Anthony, after all, and so made up her mind to end the charade.'

Jean, who was staring into the flickering fake coals of the electric fire, remarked angrily: 'She's completely selfish, just like her mother.'

There was dead silence. Freda was frowning. Then Joanna said quietly: 'Do you mean Aunt Dora?'

'What?' Jean turned her head sharply. She looked confused and gave her head a little shake, blinking at Joanna. 'How do you know? Who told you?'

'No one,' Joanna reassured her gently. 'At least, not in so many words. Davey told me that Aunt Do and Dad had once had an affair. It was a long time ago. She overheard you quarrelling.'

'And she guessed?' Jean was looking guilty, Freda horrified.

'No, of course not. It never crossed Davey's mind.' Joanna got up out of her armchair and went to kneel beside her mother. 'For one thing, Davey doesn't much

408

care for Aunt Do. She rather despises her.'

'But . . . how did you know, then?'

'I didn't know for sure, but I guessed. It was Gramps, really, who told me.'

'It couldn't have been. He had no idea. No one knew, apart from your father and Dora.'

'No, no. But I asked him one day why you didn't seem to like Davey as much as the rest of us. He said he didn't know, but went on to tell me about the circumstances of her birth. How he and Grandma didn't even suspect you were having a baby until it was all over. How you went up to London to stay with Aunt Do during the war, and when you came back you had Davina. It just . . . started me thinking, that's all,' Joanna finished lamely.

'Mamma!' Freda leaned forward, her hands tightly clasped together. 'It's not true, is it?'

Jean was silent for a while. 'Yes,' she said at last, 'it is. But the information isn't to go beyond this room, and you're never to let on to your father that you know. It's my name that's on Davina's birth certificate, and to all intents and purposes I'm her mother. The strange thing is', Jean continued, relieved to be able to speak openly after all these years, 'that I could forgive your father and I could forgive Dora, but I couldn't forgive Davina. All her life, I've resented her, just for being who she is; for being a constant reminder of that affair.' She gave a wintry smile. 'Perhaps now that you two share the secret it will make a difference. Maybe I can begin to feel more charitable towards Davey. She must have sensed my hostility, even when she was little. That was why she turned to Anthea, who made a fuss of her.'

'You mustn't reproach yourself,' Joanna said gently. 'You've no reason to. And don't worry about anyone else finding out. We're not going to breathe a word, are we, Freddie?'

Freda shook her head. 'Absolutely not. That's a promise. Good God! What you must have gone through, keeping it to yourself for all this time. Do you and Aunt Do ever . . . well, mention the subject?'

'No. We made a pact, after Davey was born, that if I took the child she was to be mine and Dora would never interfere. It wasn't difficult for her to agree. She didn't want children. They would only have interfered with her career.'

Joanna laughed. 'And we always thought it was Aunt Thea's influence that made Davey the way she is. Instead, it was inherited.'

'And Dad?' Freda pressed. 'Don't you discuss it with him, either?'

Again Jean shook her head. 'Oh, I've thrown his affair with Dora in his teeth once or twice when I've been angry. But, fortunately as it transpires, never the fact that Davina isn't my child.'

'Would Davey have been that upset, do you think, if she'd found out?' Freda asked.

Jean considered the question. 'I don't know,' she admitted at last.

'Well, I do,' Joanna said firmly. 'We must make sure that Davey never discovers the truth. Whatever she says or however she acts, she couldn't bear the thought that she is just Dad and Aunt Dora's illegitimate child. And, anyway, as far as I'm concerned, she isn't. She is, always has been, always will be, the eldest sister of the four of us.'

The drawing-room door opened and Bernard put his head round, making them jump.

'What's the matter with you lot?' he demanded irritably. 'The telephone's been ringing for the past five minutes. It's for you, Jo. Again.' Bernard's manner underwent a change, and he added reverently: 'It's someone from Neil Kinnock's office.'

Joanna Walden, MP and Shadow Secretary of State for Social Services, and her political agent, David Nugent, were married two years later, in June 1985, at St Margaret's, Westminster.

The press was out in force. It was not often they were able to photograph the three famous sisters together. And on this occasion there was the added piquancy of Davina having once been engaged to the bridegroom. As far as the newspapers were concerned, a certain amount of scandal had always attended the doings of the Marshall women. It was one of the things which made them interesting.

Certainly, looking at the faces of the newly married couple, as they emerged into the rain of a very bad summer, no one, not even the most hardened and cynical of reporters, could doubt their happiness. Nor was there any suggestion of coolness between Davina Marshall, author of the recent bestselling biography of Richard II, and her former fiancé. They appeared to be on excellent terms. Her face, familiar from so many television appearances, was wreathed in smiles as she kissed her sister and wished her well.

It had, in fact, taken David Nugent over a year to realize that he and Davina would not have suited one another, and a further six months to accept that she had not only never loved him, but had also been using the engagement for her own ends. Once those two facts had become clear to him, however, his recovery was rapid, and it was his daughter Laura's casual remark that he 'really ought to marry Joanna' which had finally opened his eyes to the truth. He loved Joanna and had done so for quite some time. He soon found that he could meet Davina without a tinge of regret and they had once more become good friends.

But it was not principally Davina nor even the bride and groom whom the assembled pressmen had come to see. It was Freda, magnificent in a Zandra Rhodes pale blue and white dress, who was the true focus of attention as she emerged from the church of Jeff Warwick's arm. The rumours that they were about to marry again were rife, ever since he had moved permanently into Kelmscott House with her and announced his intention of settling in England. Since then, they had appeared in several television productions together, and Jeff had directed Freda in a revival of Priestley's *The Linden Tree* on the London stage.

Amongst the cast had been Samantha Douglas, playing the part of Dinah Linden; another little sensation for those gossip columnists who knew that she was Freda's niece and had been responsible for the break-up of her aunt's second marriage to Steve Jordan. Steve had now returned to America and relative obscurity, and aunt and niece were, if not the best of friends, at least on speaking terms.

Again, it was a process which had taken some time, but Freda's realization that Samantha had in fact done her a good turn hastened their reconciliation.

Samantha, too, was at the wedding, very smart in a beige suit and red hat. As they assembled for photographs outside the church, Joanna noticed that she was again charming the susceptible Stuart, giving him the full benefit of her most radiant smile and gazing raptly into his eyes. Poor Stuart, Joanna thought with a shrug and a sigh, but he would have to work things out for himself. She had made up her mind before marrying David that she was not going to be an interfering step-mother.

The rain had almost stopped, and the sun was struggling feebly through the clouds above Parliament Square. The official was asking for one final group before he packed up his camera and called it a day. At last he had finished, and Joanna and David were preparing to walk across the green to their car, anxious now to get to the reception, when one of the press photographers called out: 'Mrs Nugent! Can we just have a picture of the three of you together? You and your two sisters.'

Joanna hesitated, glancing round for Davina and Freda, seeking their approval.

'What do you think?' she asked them.

'Why not?' said Freda, grabbing Davina's arm. 'Come on, Davey, you stand next to me. Jo! You come on my other side.'

Joanna's eyes briefly met those of her elder sister. Davina winked. It was typical of Freda to place herself in the middle, even today.

'I believe it's known as taking centre stage,' Joanna hissed in Davina's ear as she passed her.

She linked one arm through Freda's as another photographer called out: 'Can you move closer together? We want to make sure we get all three of you.'

'Four of us, actually,' Freda murmured, so low that none of the crowding pressmen was able to hear. 'Move up, Jo love, and make room for Theresa.'

Joanna gave an uncertain laugh and said in a choked voice: 'You know, Freddie, even after all this time, you can still surprise me.'

'Ah,' Freda replied, a trifle obscurely, but knowing what she meant, and, more important, knowing that the other two knew what she meant, 'that's what it's all about. Being sisters.'

THE END

AN EQUAL CHANCE
by Brenda Clarke

She was married at eighteen to an American G.I. and, when she finally arrived in America she found her new husband had vanished – decamped ahead of her, not wanting the responsibility of a wife. She was stranded in New York and couldn't afford her passage home again. The only job she could get was as a waitress in the Last Chance Saloon, a rough diner with an even rougher clientele. Desperate, she took it.

It was the beginning of Harriet Chance-Canossa-Contarini-Cavendish-Georgiadis-Wingfield, one of the richest women in the world.

But as her great empire grew, as her wealth increased, as other men took the place of the husband who had abandoned her, she never forgot the secret so carefully concealed from those about her – the identity of the child she had left behind her in England so many years before.

0 552 132306

THE SISTERS O'DONNELL
by Lyn Andrews

They were called The Sisters O'Donnell in County Tipperary. They resembled each other a lot – both in temper and looks. They all had the flaming red hair of the O'Donnell clan and tempers to match.

When they came to seek their fortunes in the Liverpool of the 20's, they were full of ambition, hope, and a lust for life. Gina planned to be a star of the theatre, Mary Kate wanted to find a husband. And Bridget – gentle, timid Bridget – just wanted to get away from the fighting all around her and have a calm, peaceful life.

But Liverpool wasn't what they thought it would be, and neither was their Aunt Maura, who was supposed to set them on their paths to fortune. Maura turned out to be a miserable slattern, living in the poorest part of Liverpool, and Uncle Bart was a scrounging and lascivious old man. Work was impossible to find and their money was running out.

The O'Donnell girls had a long way to go before they could realise some of their dreams.

Also by Lyn Andrews
THE WHITE EMPRESS
and published by Corgi

0 552 13600 X

A SELECTED LIST OF FINE NOVELS
AVAILABLE FROM CORGI BOOKS

THE PRICES SHOWN BELOW WERE CORRECT AT THE TIME OF GOING TO PRESS. HOW-
EVER TRANSWORLD PUBLISHERS RESERVE THE RIGHT TO SHOW NEW RETAIL PRICES
ON COVERS WHICH MAY DIFFER FROM THOSE PREVIOUSLY ADVERTISED IN THE TEXT
OR ELSEWHERE.

☐	13482 1	THE WHITE EMPRESS	Lyn Andrews	£3.99
☐	13289 6	MOVING AWAY	Louise Brindley	£2.99
☐	13230 6	AN EQUAL CHANCE	Brenda Clarke	£3.99
☐	12887 2	SHAKE DOWN THE STARS	Frances Donnelly	£3.99
☐	12387 0	COPPER KINGDOM	Iris Gower	£3.50
☐	13631 X	THE LOVES OF CATRIN	Iris Gower	£3.99
☐	12637 3	PROUD MARY	Iris Gower	£3.99
☐	12638 1	SPINNERS WHARF	Iris Gower	£3.99
☐	13138 5	MORGAN'S WOMAN	Iris Gower	£3.99
☐	13315 9	FIDDLER'S FERRY	Iris Gower	£3.50
☐	13316 7	BLACK GOLD	Iris Gower	£3.99
☐	13384 1	A WHISPER TO THE LIVING	Ruth Hamilton	£3.50
☐	13616 6	WITH LOVE FROM MA MAGUIRE	Ruth Hamilton	£3.99
☐	10249 0	BRIDE OF TANCRED	Diane Pearson	£2.99
☐	10375 6	CSARDAS	Diane Pearson	£3.95
☐	10271 7	THE MARIGOLD FIELD	Diane Pearson	£2.99
☐	09140 5	SARAH WHITMAN	Diane Pearson	£3.50
☐	12641 1	THE SUMMER OF THE BARSHINSKEYS	Diane Pearson	£3.99
☐	12375 7	A SCATTERING OF DAISIES	Susan Sallis	£2.99
☐	12579 2	THE DAFFODILS OF NEWENT	Susan Sallis	£2.99
☐	12880 5	BLUEBELL WINDOWS	Susan Sallis	£3.50
☐	13136 9	ROSEMARY FOR REMEMBRANCE	Susan Sallis	£3.99
☐	13346 9	SUMMER VISITORS	Susan Sallis	£2.95
☐	13545 3	BY SUN AND CANDLELIGHT	Susan Sallis	£3.99

*All Corgi/Bantam Books are available at your bookshop or newsagent, or can be ordered from the
following address:*

Corgi/Bantam Books,
Cash Sales Department,
P.O. Box 11, Falmouth, Cornwall TR10 9EN

Please send a cheque or postal order (no currency) and allow 80p for postage and packing for the
first book plus 20p for each additional book ordered up to a maximum charge of £2.00 in UK.

B.F.P.O. customers please allow 80p for the first book and 20p for each additional book.

Overseas customers, including Eire, please allow £1.50 for postage and packing for the first book,
£1.00 for the second book, and 30p for each subsequent title ordered.

NAME (Block Letters) ....

ADDRESS ....

....